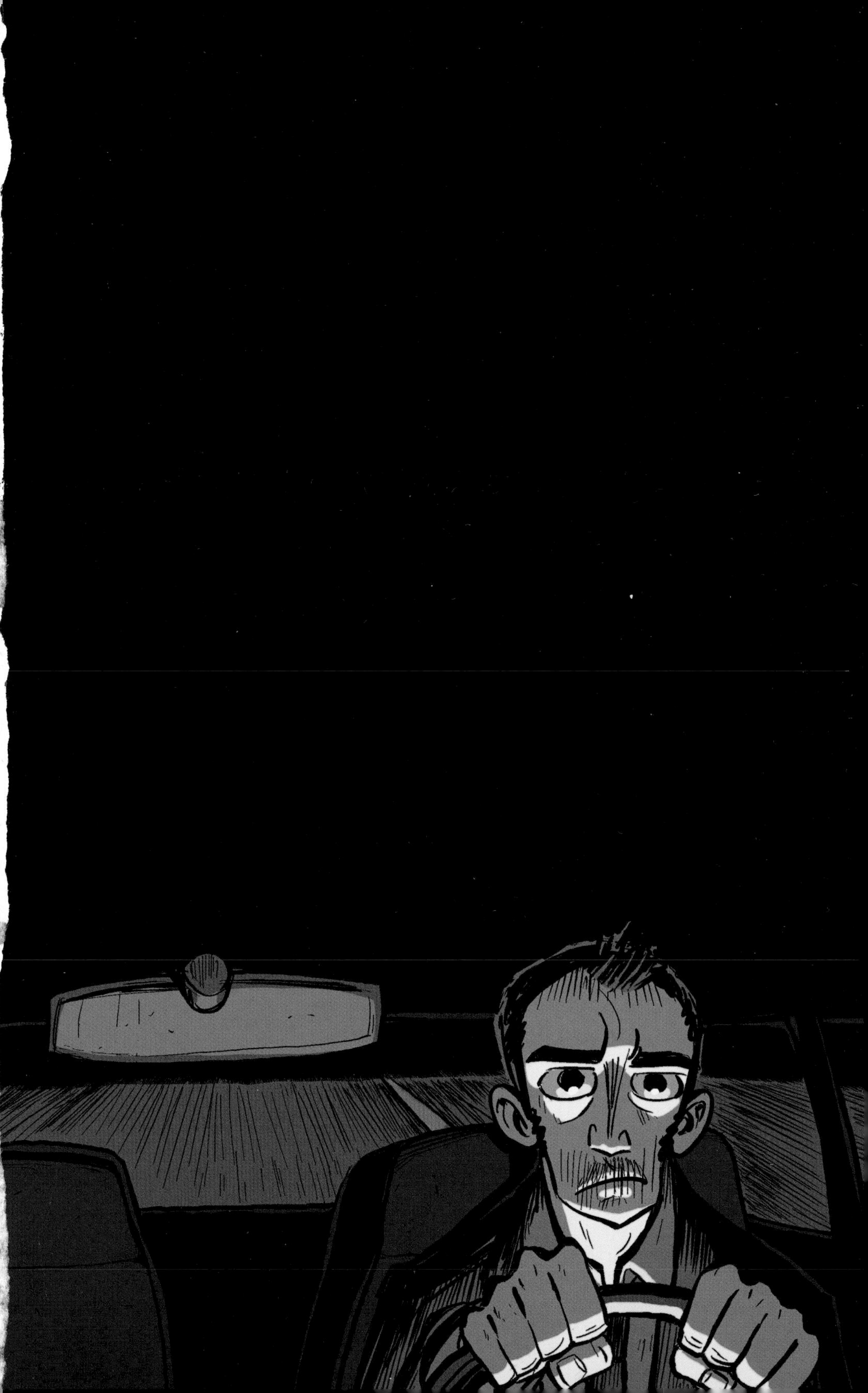

CREATED, WRITTEN, AND DRAWN BY
DOUG TENNAPEL

LEAD COLORISTS
KATHERINE GARNER
TOM RHODES

ASSISTANT COLORISTS
MATT LASKODI, AARON CRAYNE, WES SCOG, RICK RANDOLPH,
KENNY HITT, ETHAN NICOLLE, ERIC BRANSCUME, DIRK ERIK
SCHULZ, SEAN MCGOWAN, AND DAVID KOWALYK

BOOK DESIGN BY
PHIL FALCO

EDITED BY
ADAM RAU AND DAVID SAYLOR

CREATIVE DIRECTOR
DAVID SAYLOR

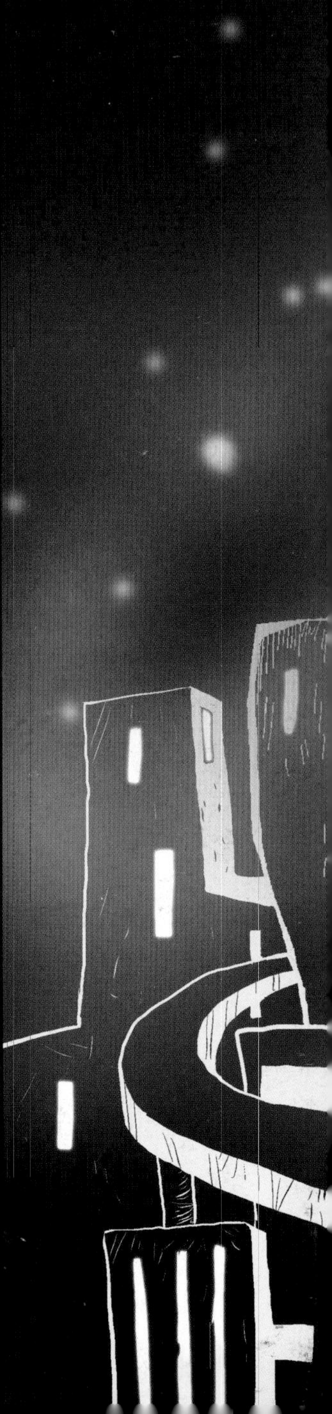

graphix

An Imprint of

SCHOLASTIC

New York Toronto London Auckland Sydney
Mexico City New Delhi Hong Kong

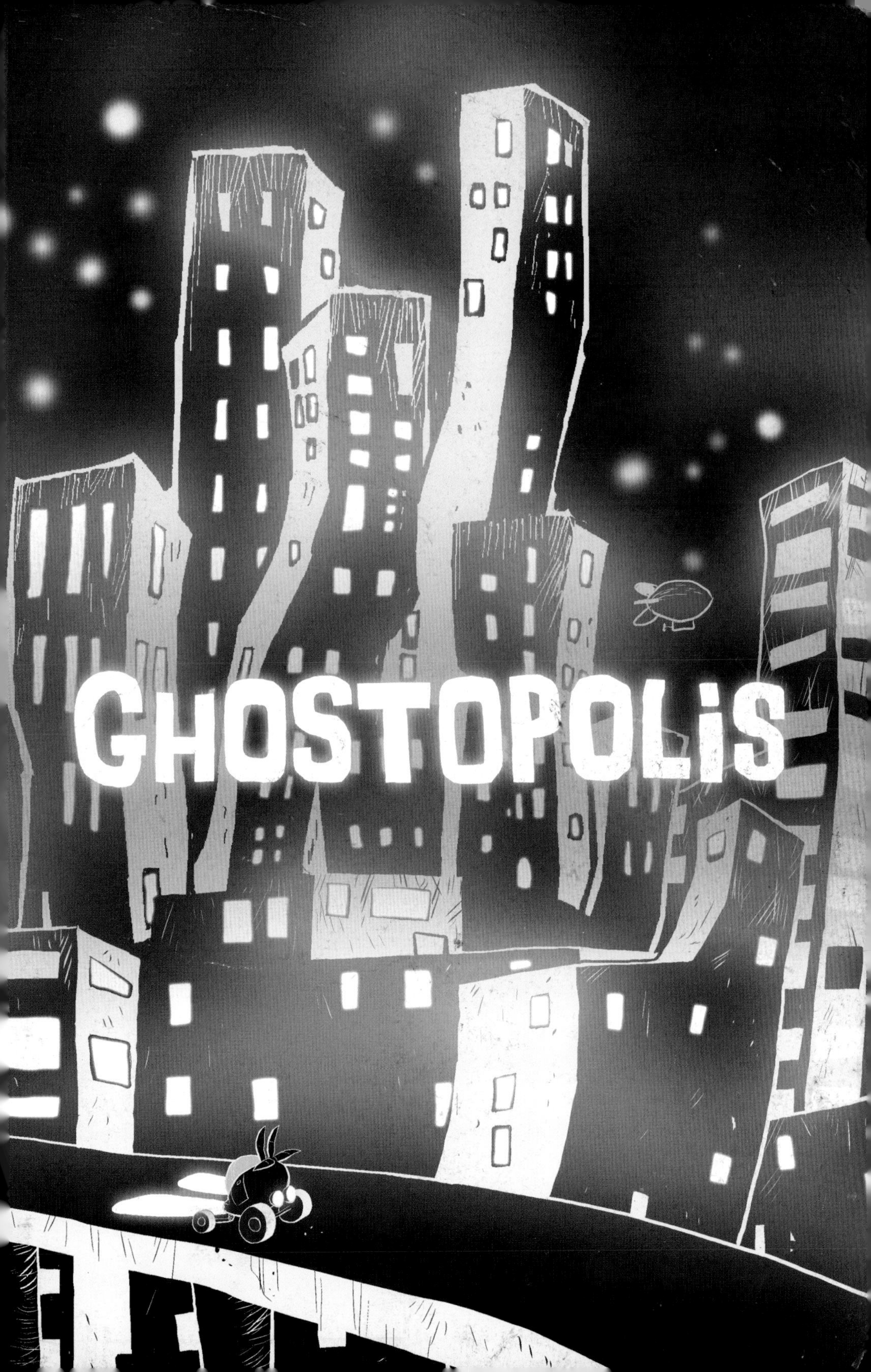
GHOSTOPOLIS

FOR DR. MICHAEL WARD

Copyright © 2010 by Doug TenNapel

All rights reserved. Published by Graphix, a division of Scholastic Inc., *Publishers since 1920*. SCHOLASTIC and associated logos are trademarks and/or registered trademarks of Scholastic Inc. No part of this publication may be reproduced, stored in a retrieval system, or transmitted in any form or by any means, electronic, mechanical, photocopying, recording, or otherwise, without written permission of the publisher. For information regarding permission, write to Scholastic Inc., Attention: Permissions Department, 557 Broadway, New York, NY 10012.

Library of Congress Cataloging-in-Publication Data Available

ISBN 978-0-545-21027-0 (hardcover)
ISBN 978-0-545-21028-7 (paperback)

10 9 8 7 6 5 4 3 2 1   10 11 12 13 14
Printed in Singapore   46

First edition, July 2010

This book was drawn digitally using Manga Studio EX 4.

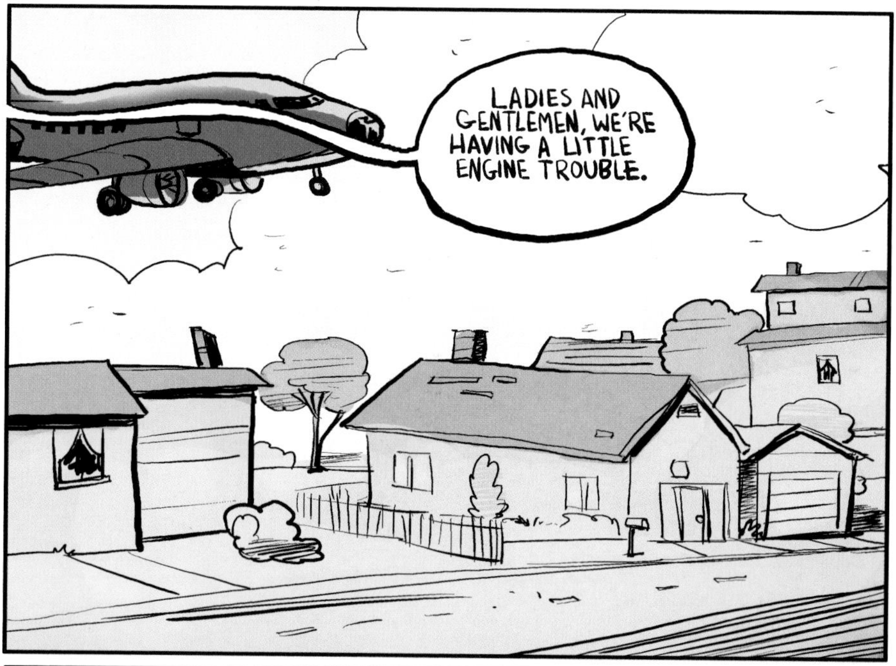
LADIES AND GENTLEMEN, WE'RE HAVING A LITTLE ENGINE TROUBLE.

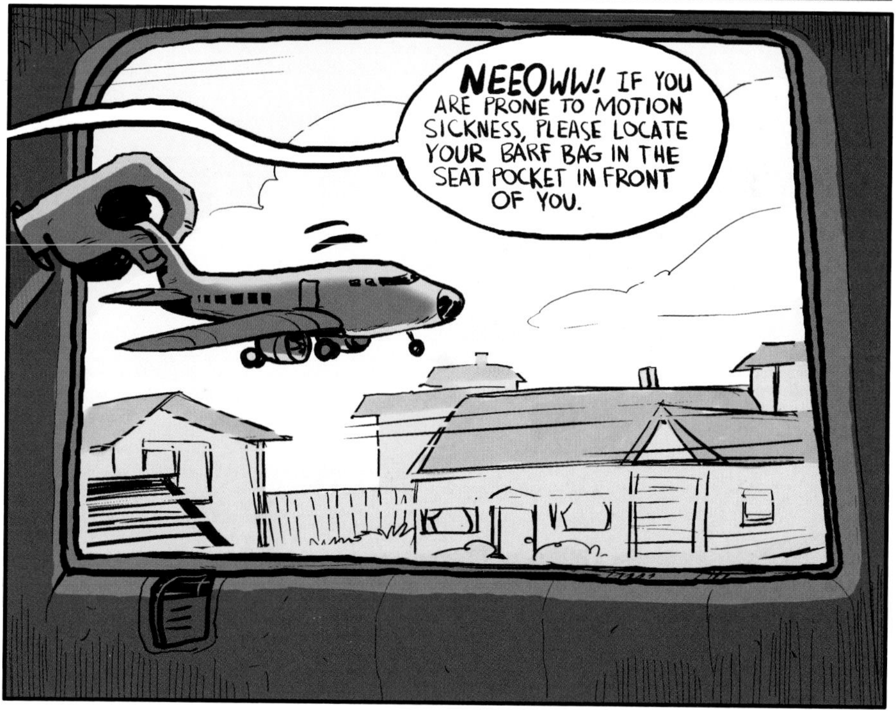
NEEOWW! IF YOU ARE PRONE TO MOTION SICKNESS, PLEASE LOCATE YOUR BARF BAG IN THE SEAT POCKET IN FRONT OF YOU.

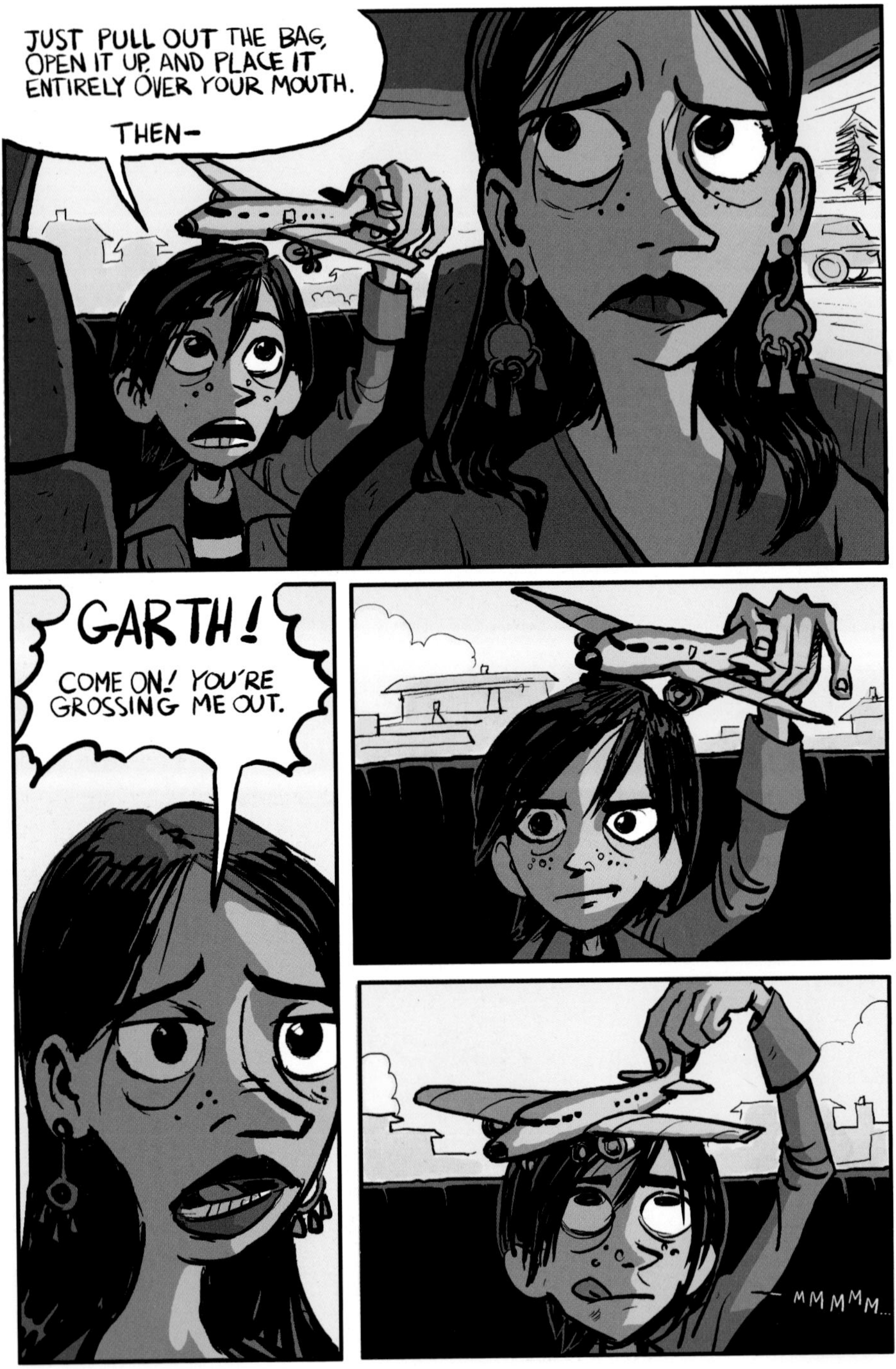
JUST PULL OUT THE BAG, OPEN IT UP, AND PLACE IT ENTIRELY OVER YOUR MOUTH.
THEN-
GARTH!
COME ON! YOU'RE GROSSING ME OUT.
MMMMM...

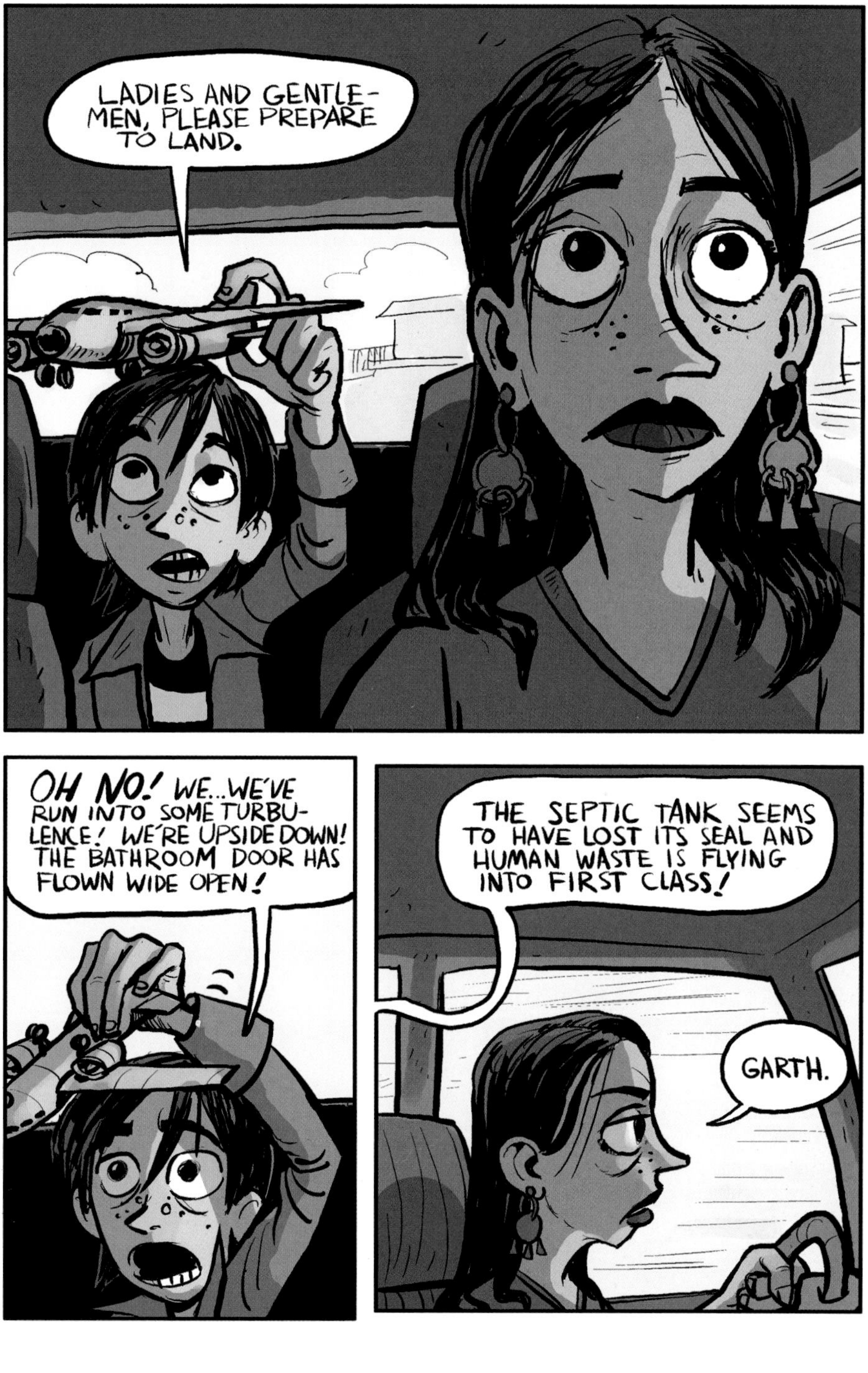
LADIES AND GENTLE-MEN, PLEASE PREPARE TO LAND.
OH NO! WE...WE'VE RUN INTO SOME TURBU-LENCE! WE'RE UPSIDE DOWN! THE BATHROOM DOOR HAS FLOWN WIDE OPEN!
THE SEPTIC TANK SEEMS TO HAVE LOST ITS SEAL AND HUMAN WASTE IS FLYING INTO FIRST CLASS!
GARTH.

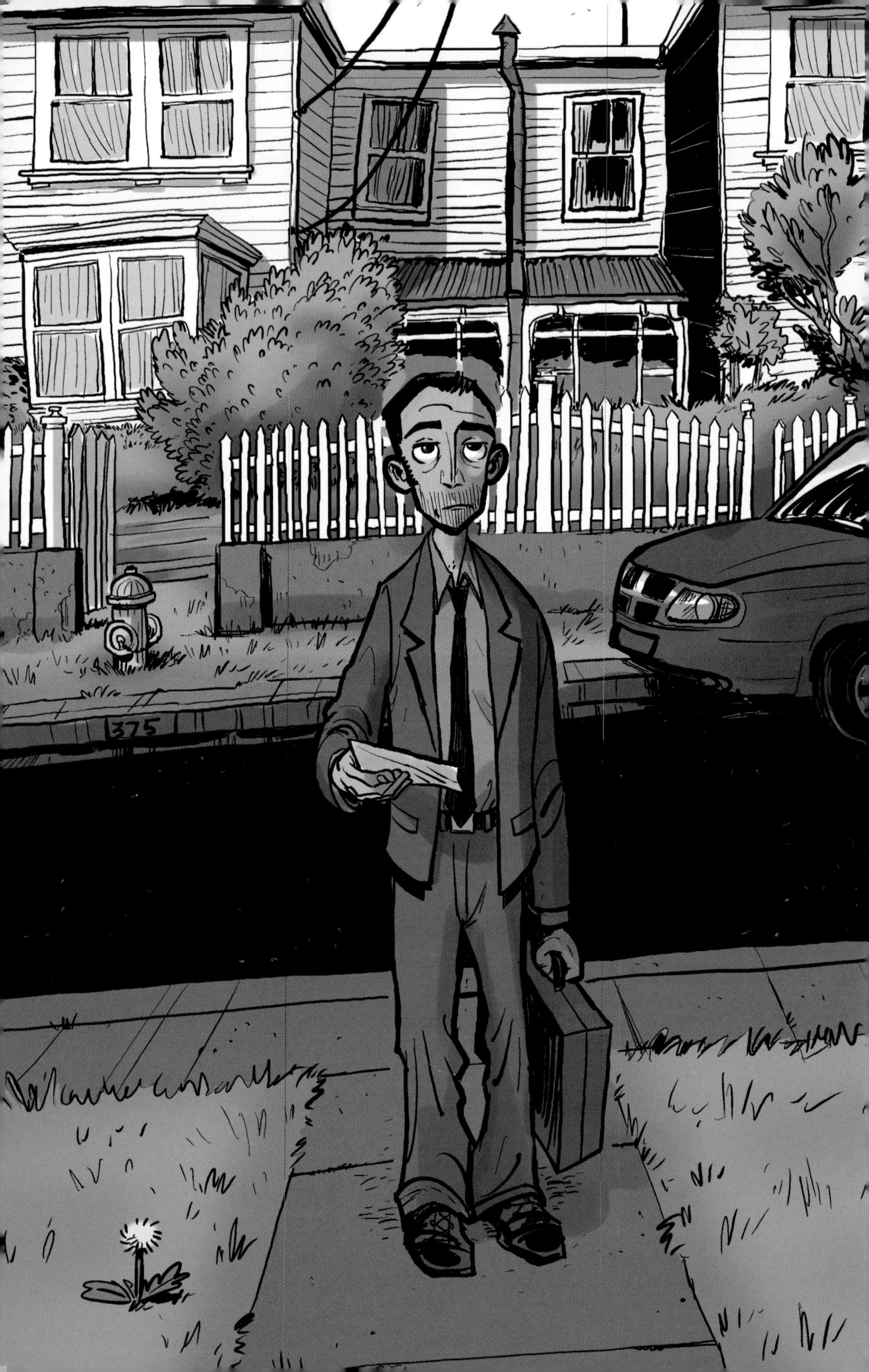
375

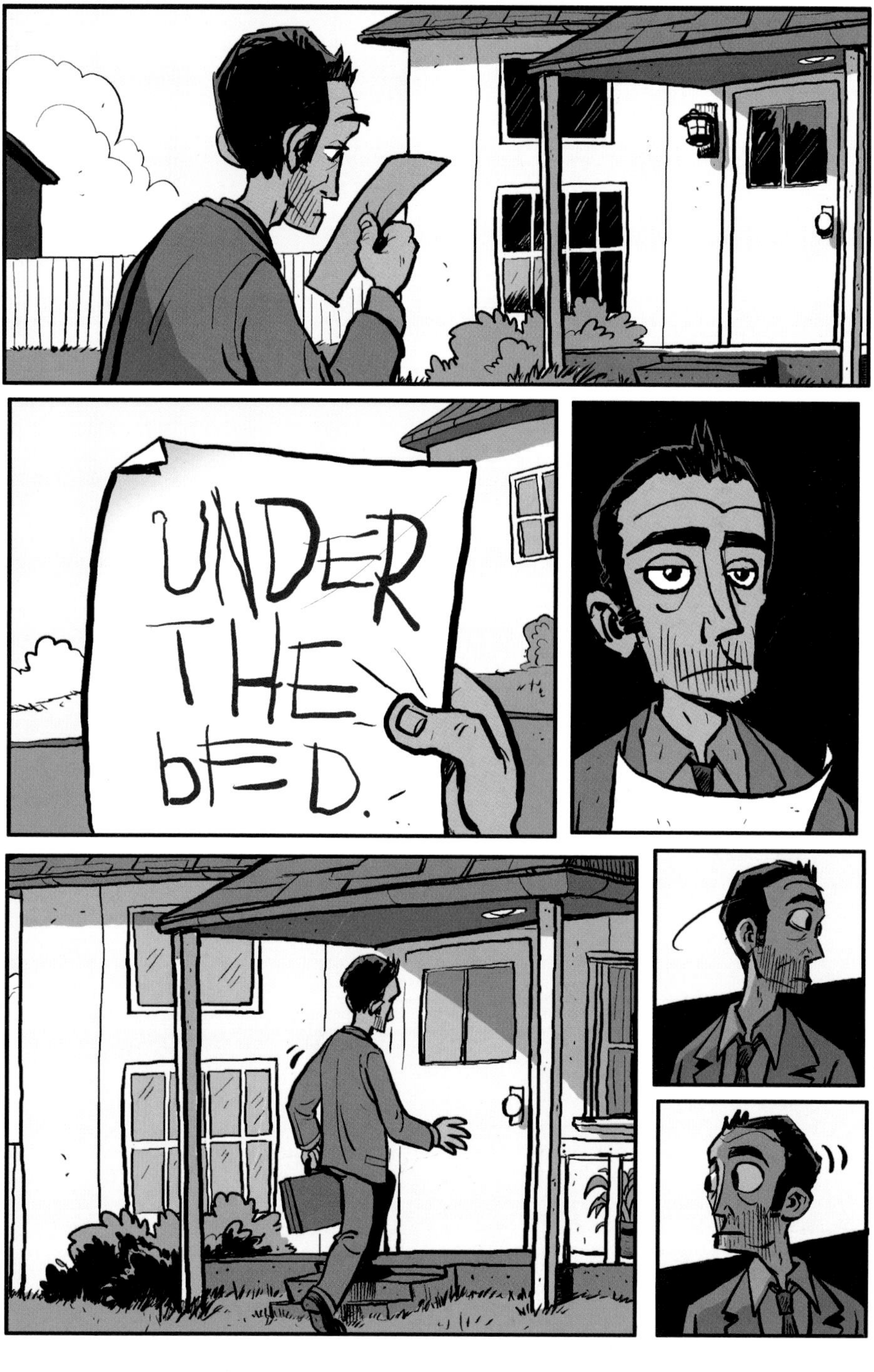
UNDER THE bED.

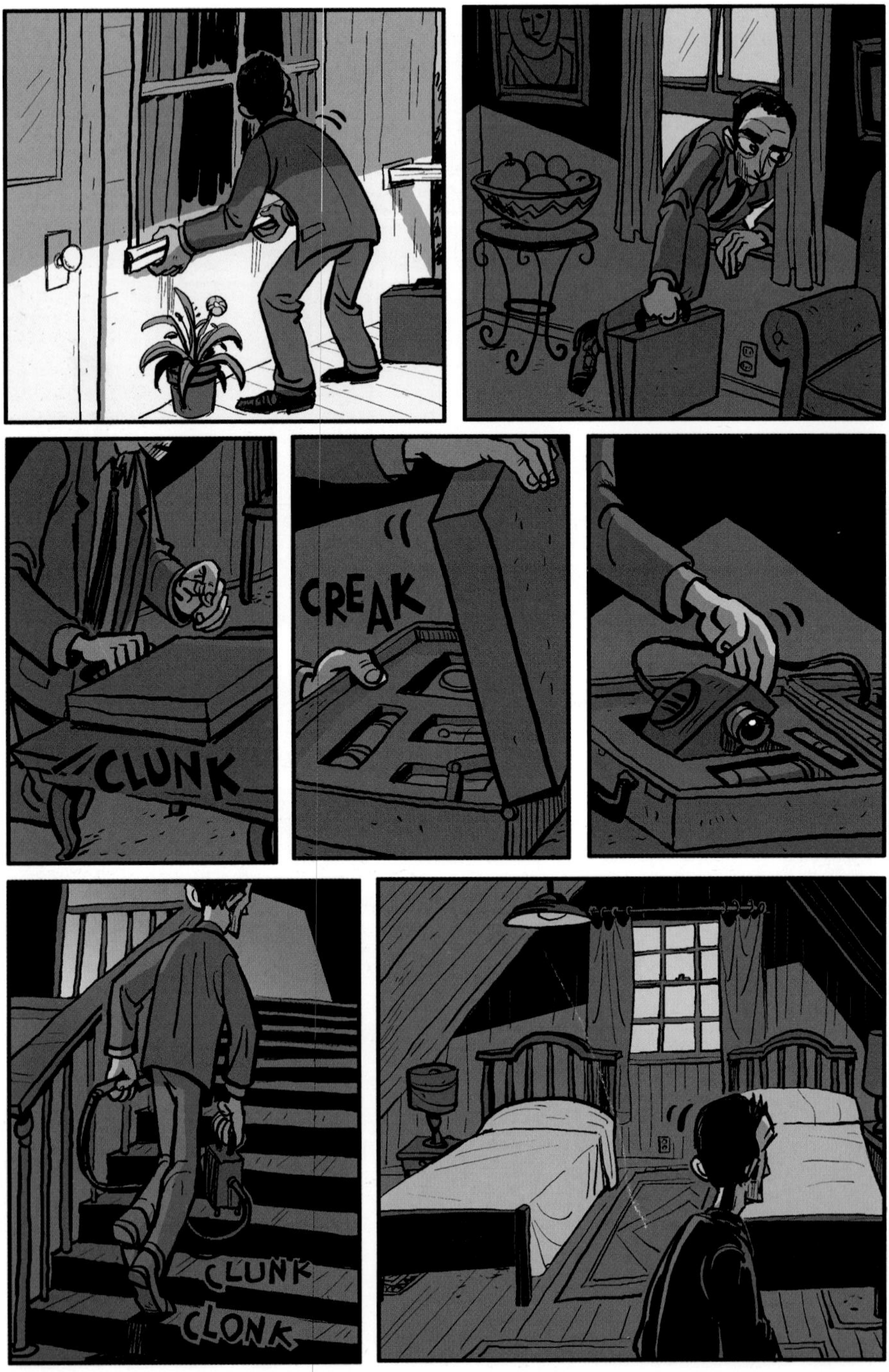
CLUNK
CREAK
CLUNK
CLONK

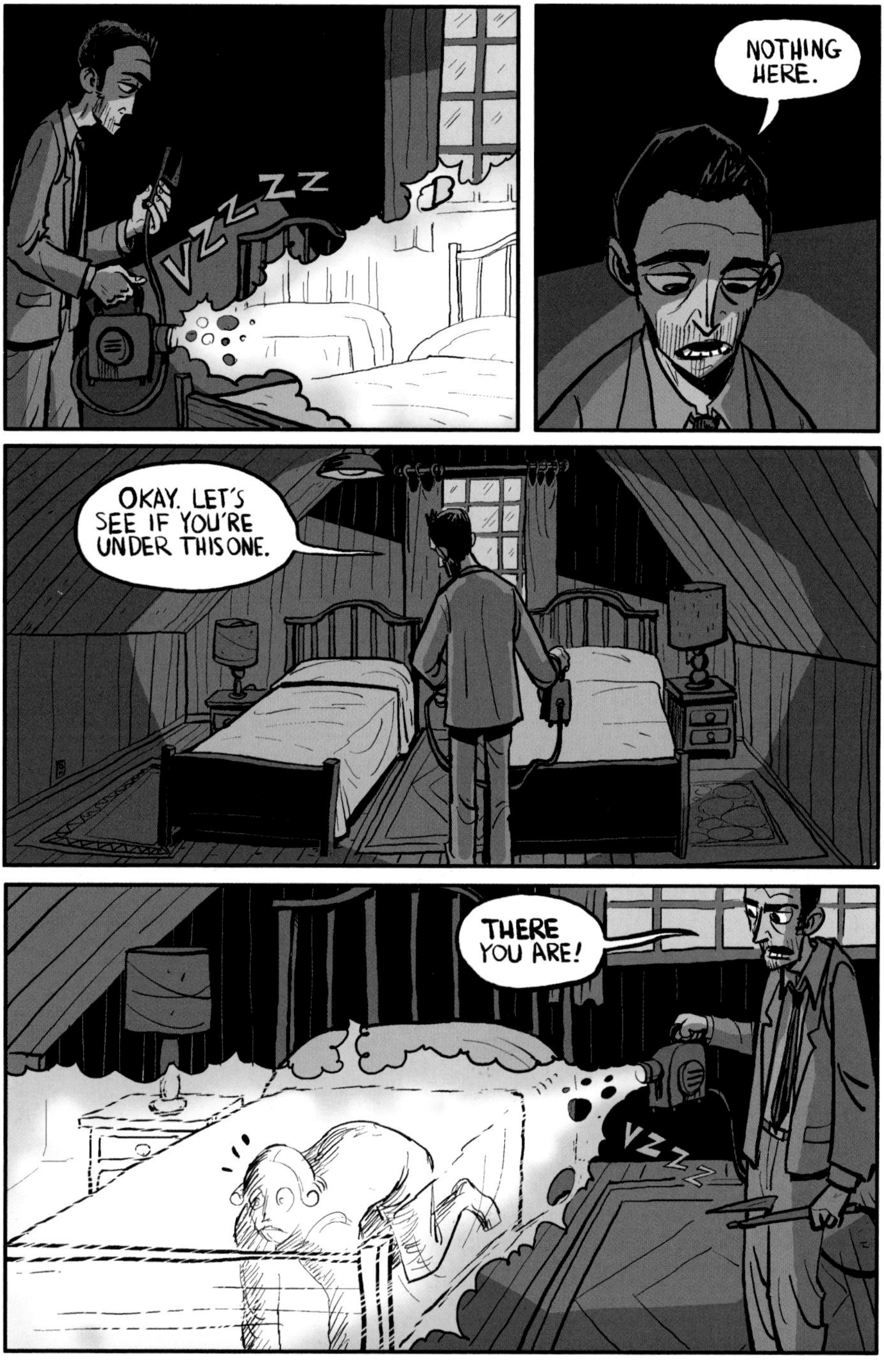
VZZZZZ
NOTHING HERE.
OKAY. LET'S SEE IF YOU'RE UNDER THIS ONE.
THERE YOU ARE!
VZZZZ

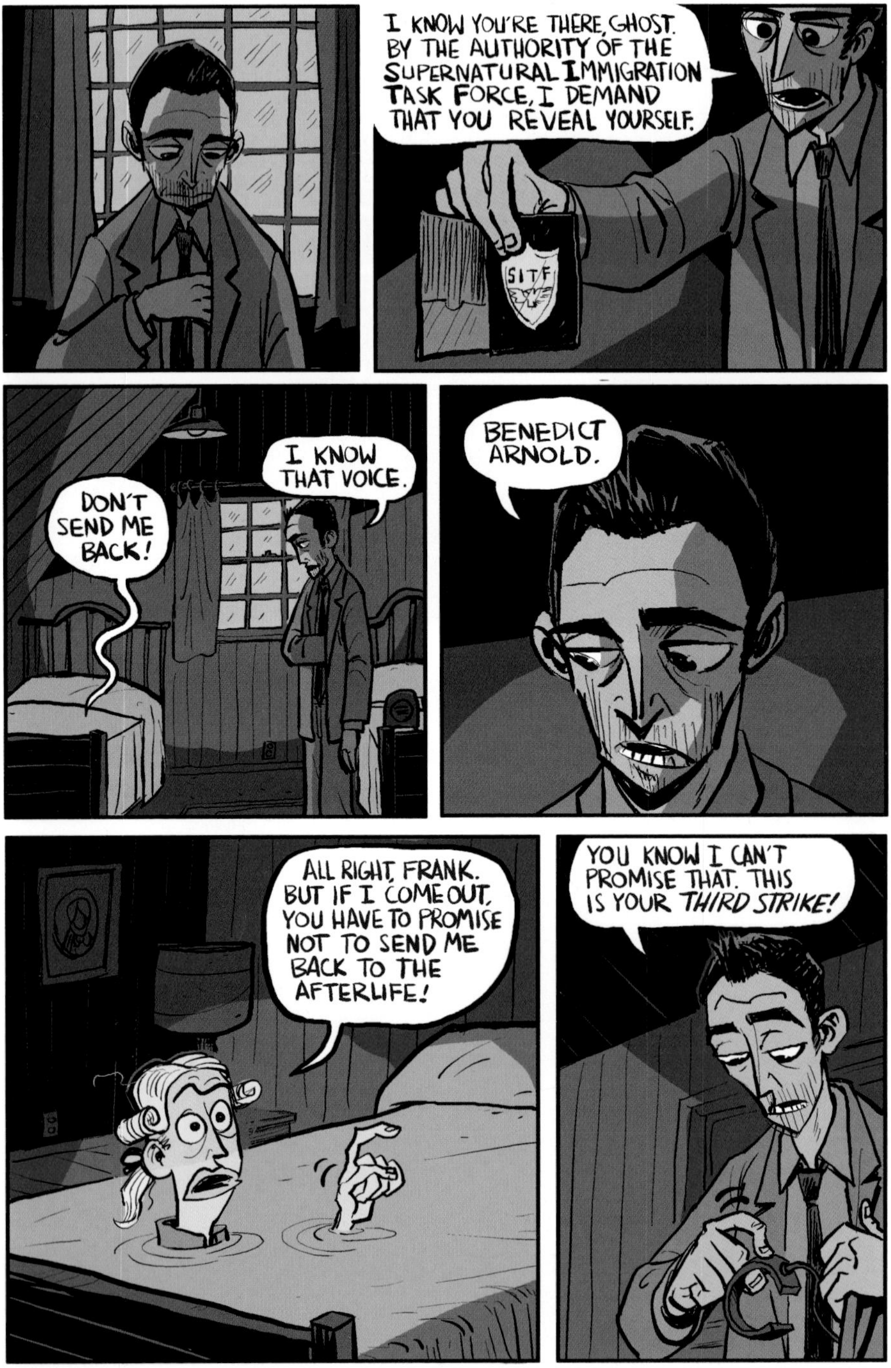
I KNOW YOU'RE THERE, GHOST. BY THE AUTHORITY OF THE SUPERNATURAL IMMIGRATION TASK FORCE, I DEMAND THAT YOU REVEAL YOURSELF.
SITF
DON'T SEND ME BACK!
I KNOW THAT VOICE.
BENEDICT ARNOLD.
ALL RIGHT, FRANK. BUT IF I COME OUT, YOU HAVE TO PROMISE NOT TO SEND ME BACK TO THE AFTERLIFE!
YOU KNOW I CAN'T PROMISE THAT. THIS IS YOUR *THIRD STRIKE!*

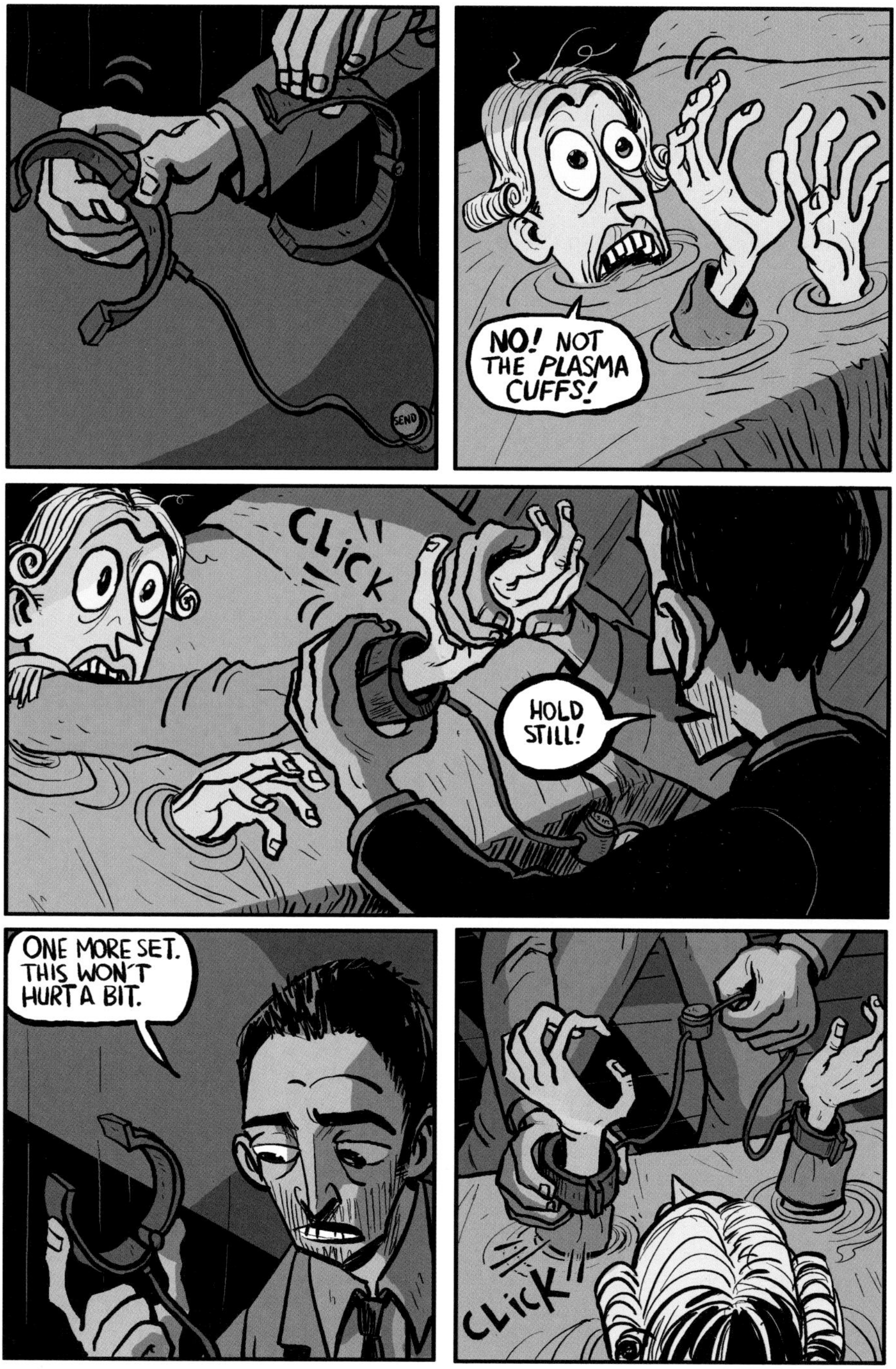
SEND
NO! NOT THE PLASMA CUFFS!
CLICK
HOLD STILL!
ONE MORE SET. THIS WON'T HURT A BIT.
CLICK

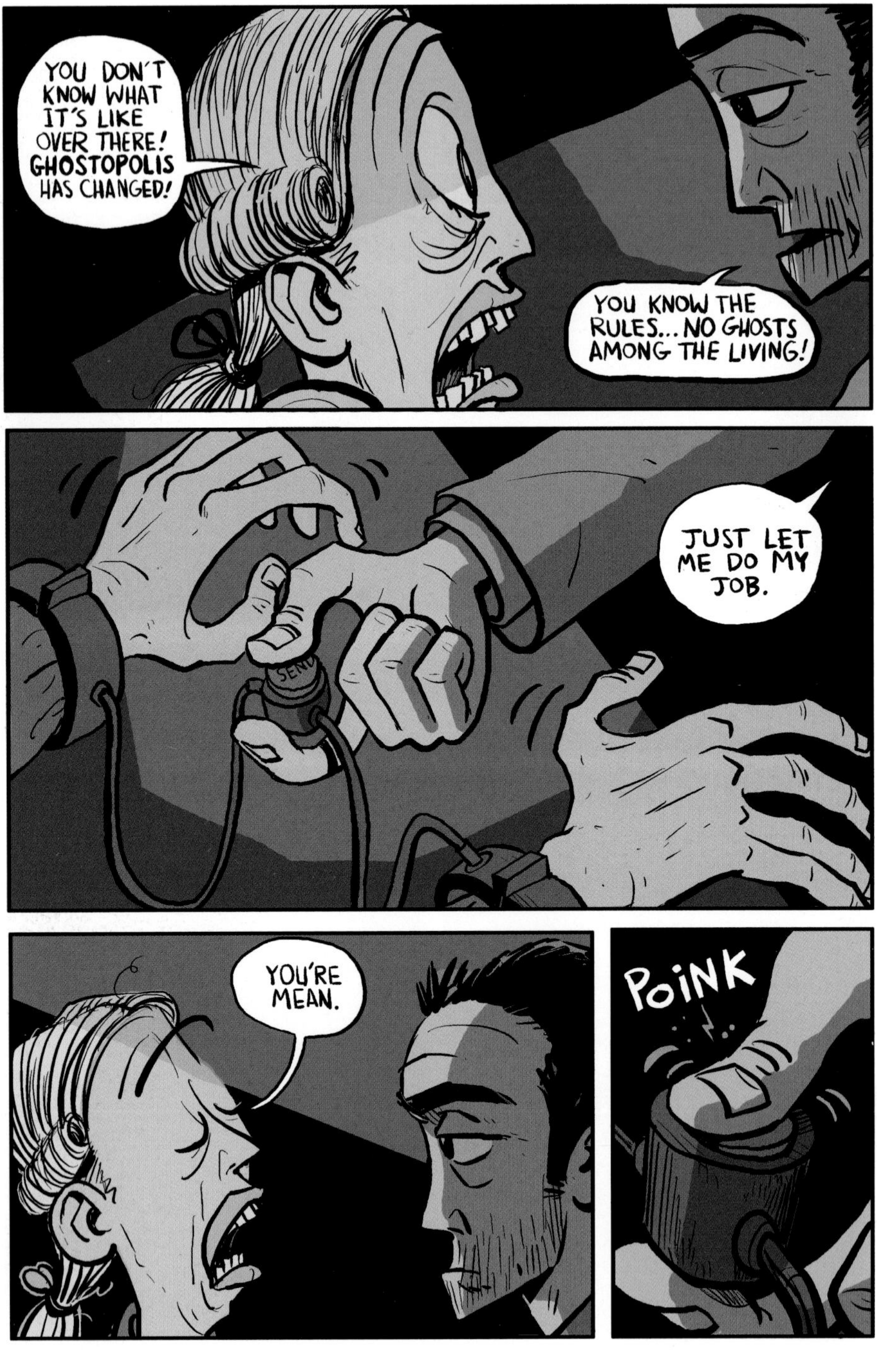
YOU DON'T KNOW WHAT IT'S LIKE OVER THERE! GHOSTOPOLIS HAS CHANGED!
YOU KNOW THE RULES... NO GHOSTS AMONG THE LIVING!
JUST LET ME DO MY JOB.
YOU'RE MEAN.
POINK

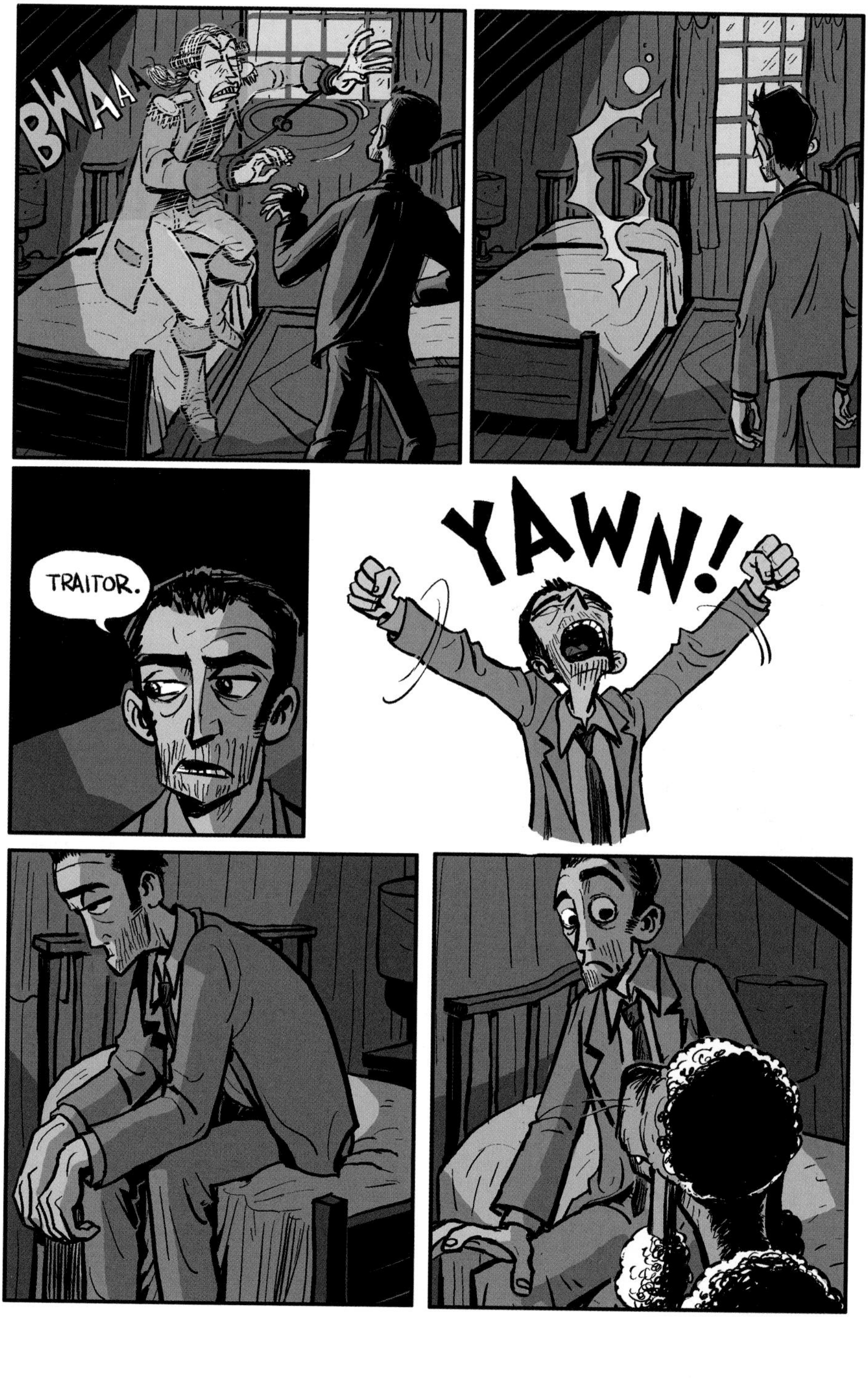
BWAAAA
TRAITOR.
YAWN!

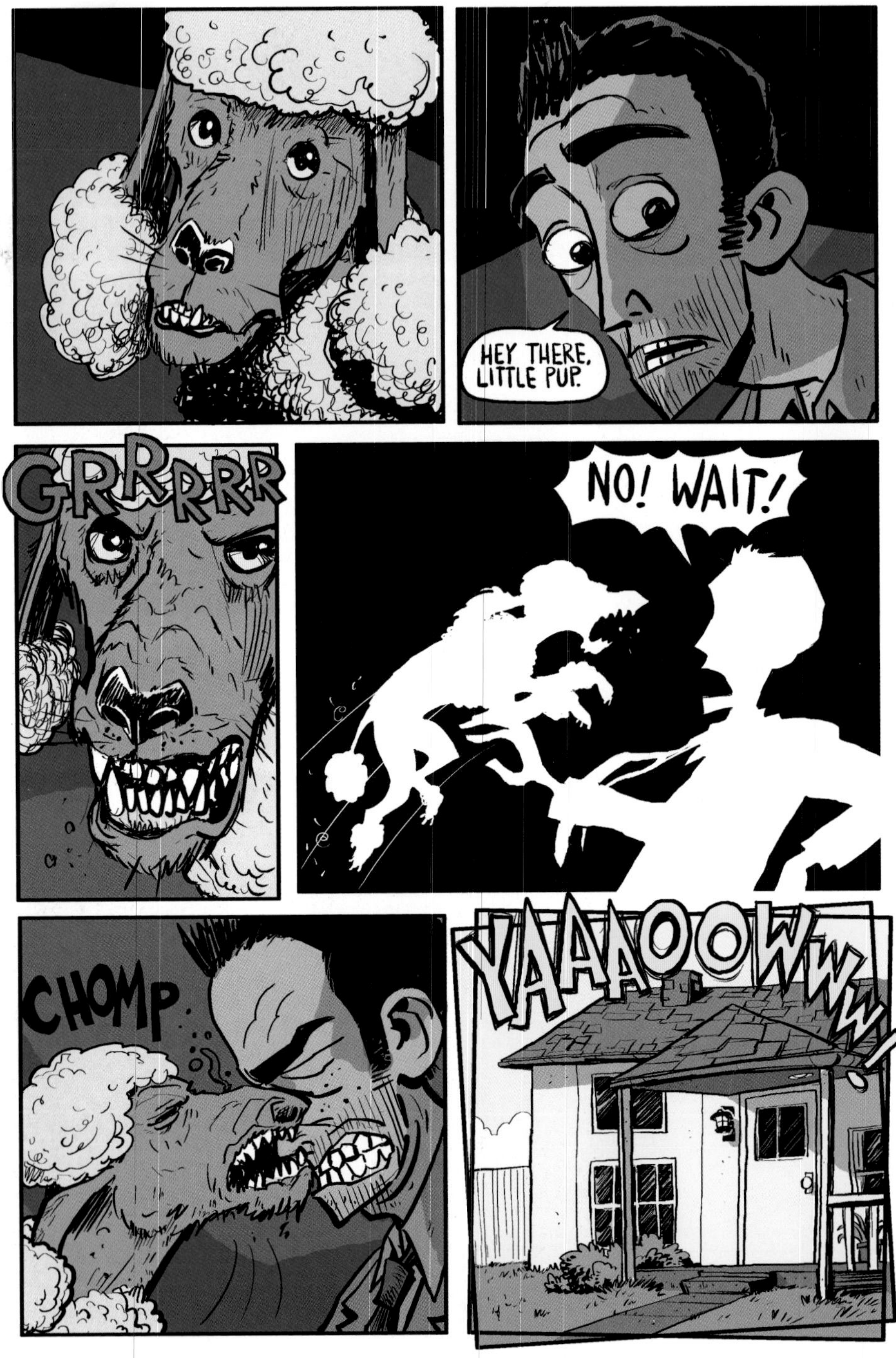
HEY THERE, LITTLE PUP.
GRRRRRR
NO! WAIT!
CHOMP
YAAAOOWWW!

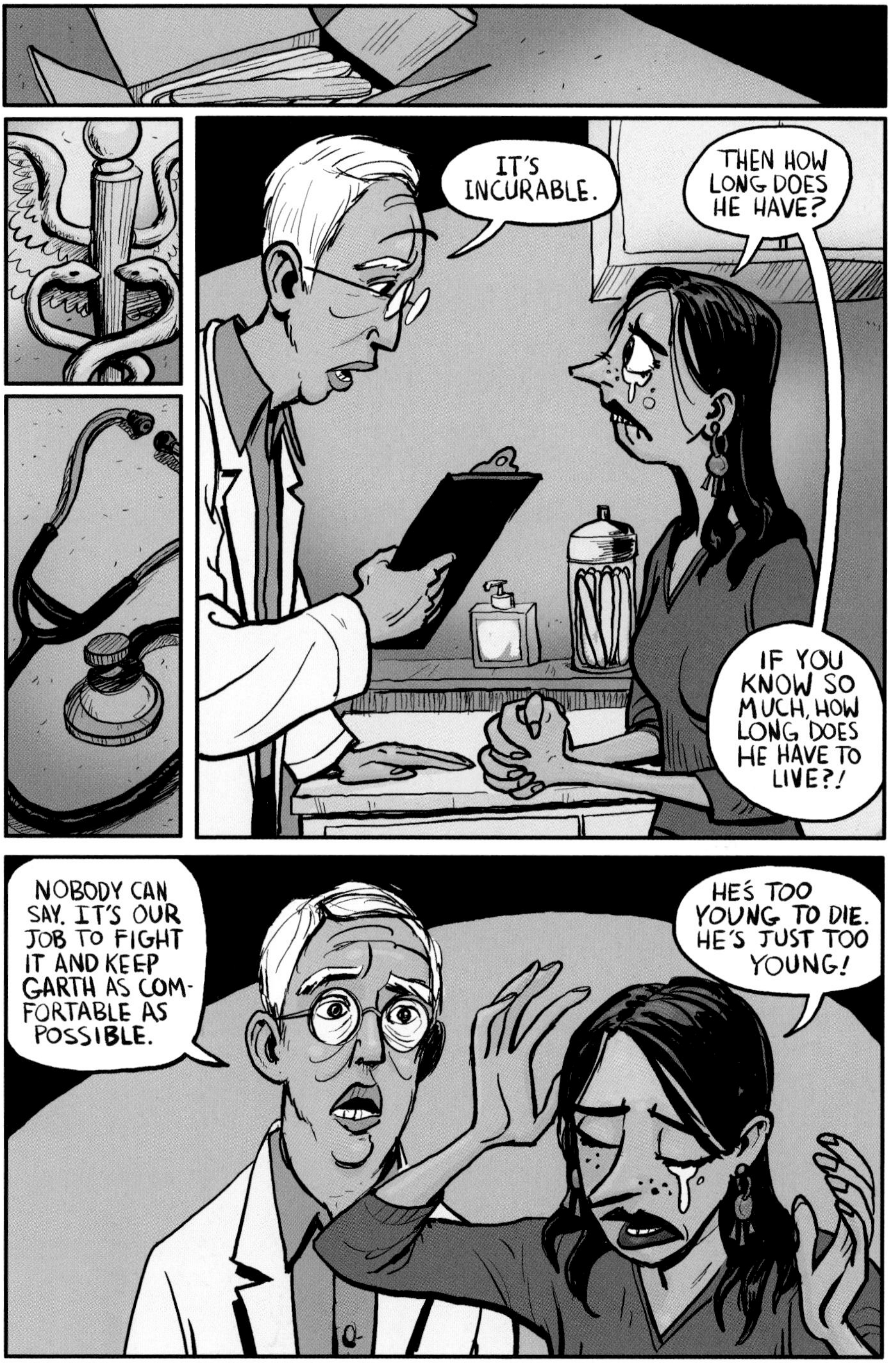
IT'S INCURABLE.
THEN HOW LONG DOES HE HAVE?
IF YOU KNOW SO MUCH, HOW LONG DOES HE HAVE TO LIVE?!
NOBODY CAN SAY. IT'S OUR JOB TO FIGHT IT AND KEEP GARTH AS COM-FORTABLE AS POSSIBLE.
HE'S TOO YOUNG TO DIE. HE'S JUST TOO YOUNG!

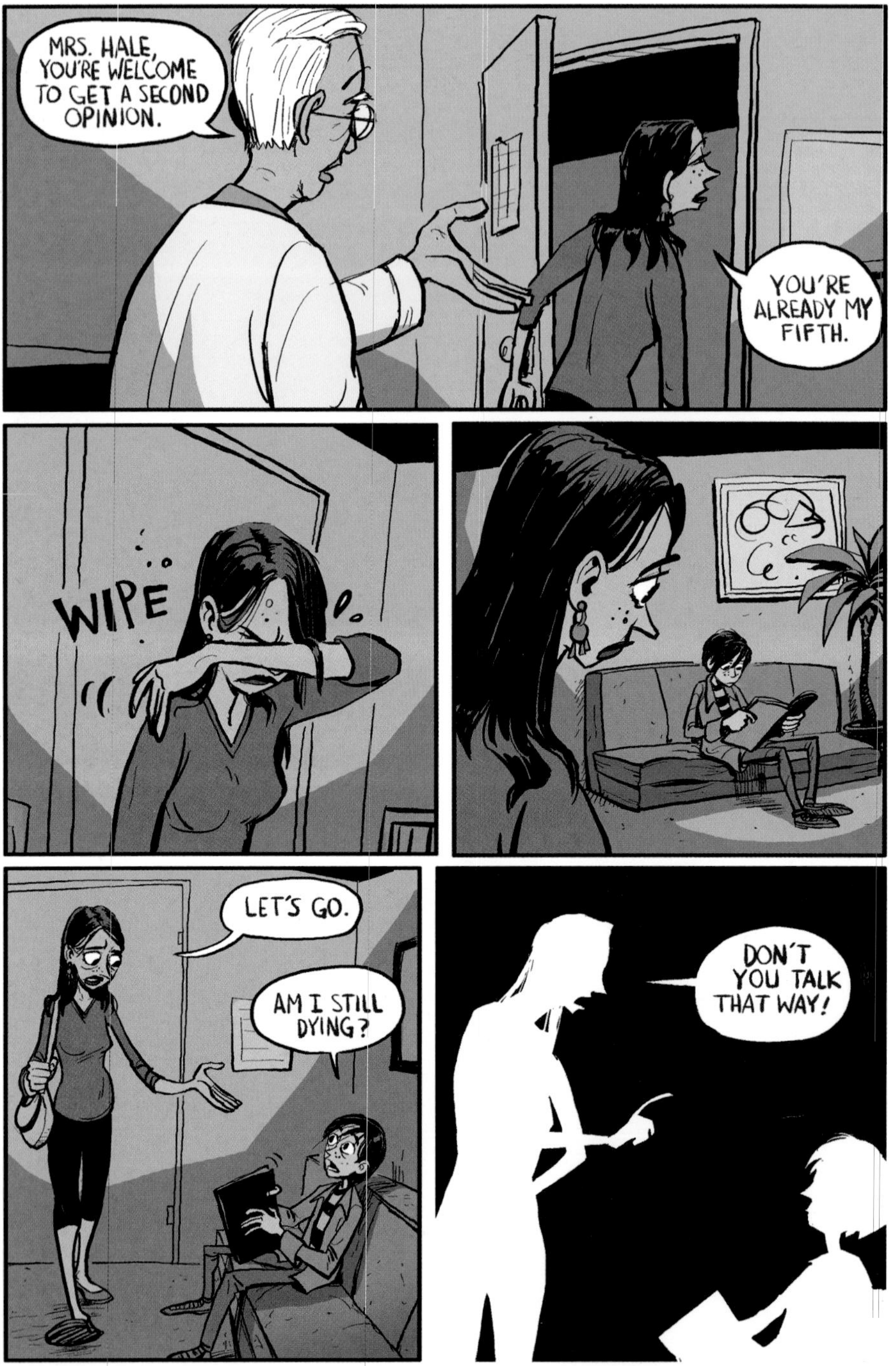
MRS. HALE, YOU'RE WELCOME TO GET A SECOND OPINION.
YOU'RE ALREADY MY FIFTH.
WIPE
LET'S GO.
AM I STILL DYING?
DON'T YOU TALK THAT WAY!

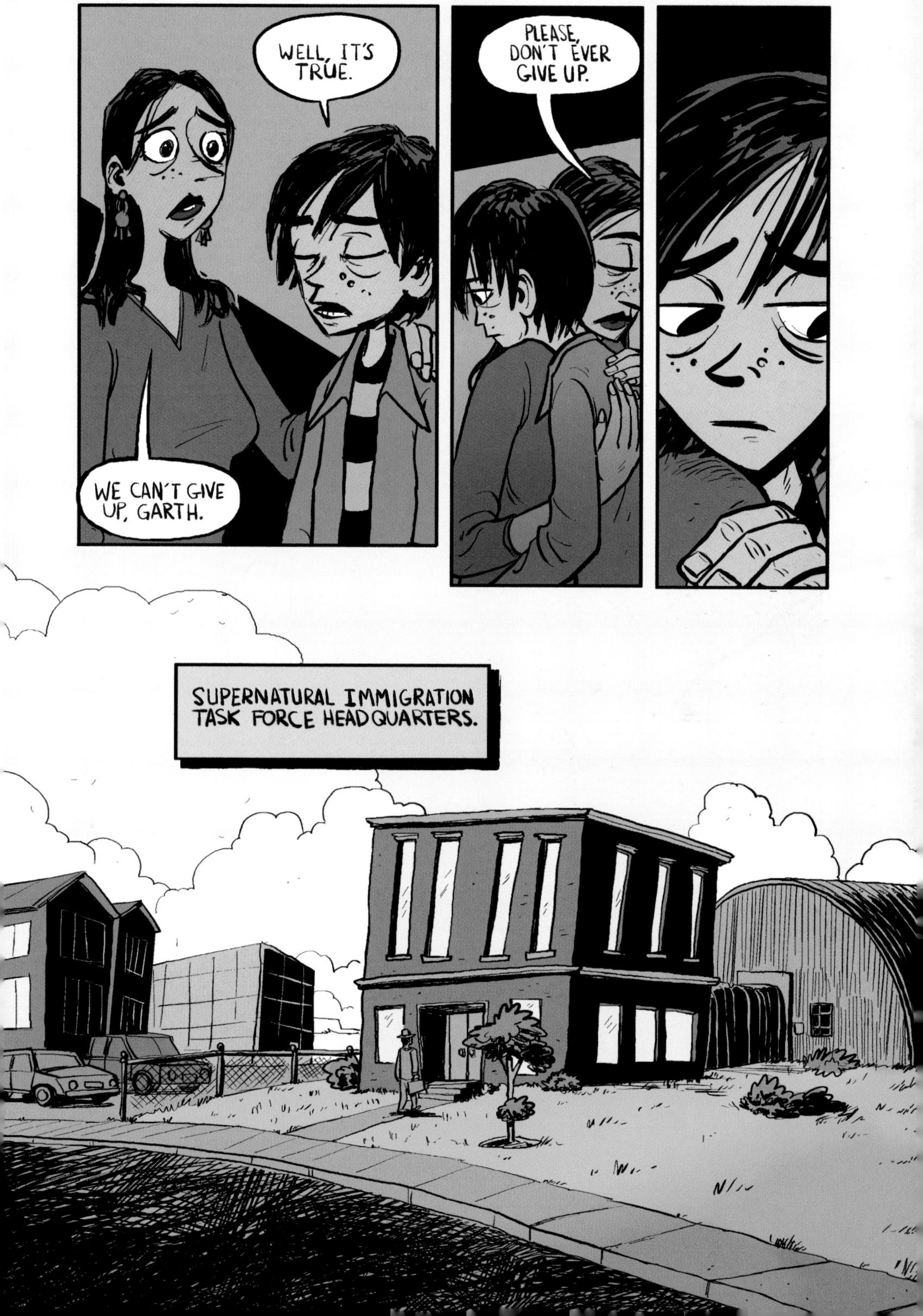
WELL, IT'S TRUE.
WE CAN'T GIVE UP, GARTH.
PLEASE, DON'T EVER GIVE UP.
SUPERNATURAL IMMIGRATION TASK FORCE HEADQUARTERS.

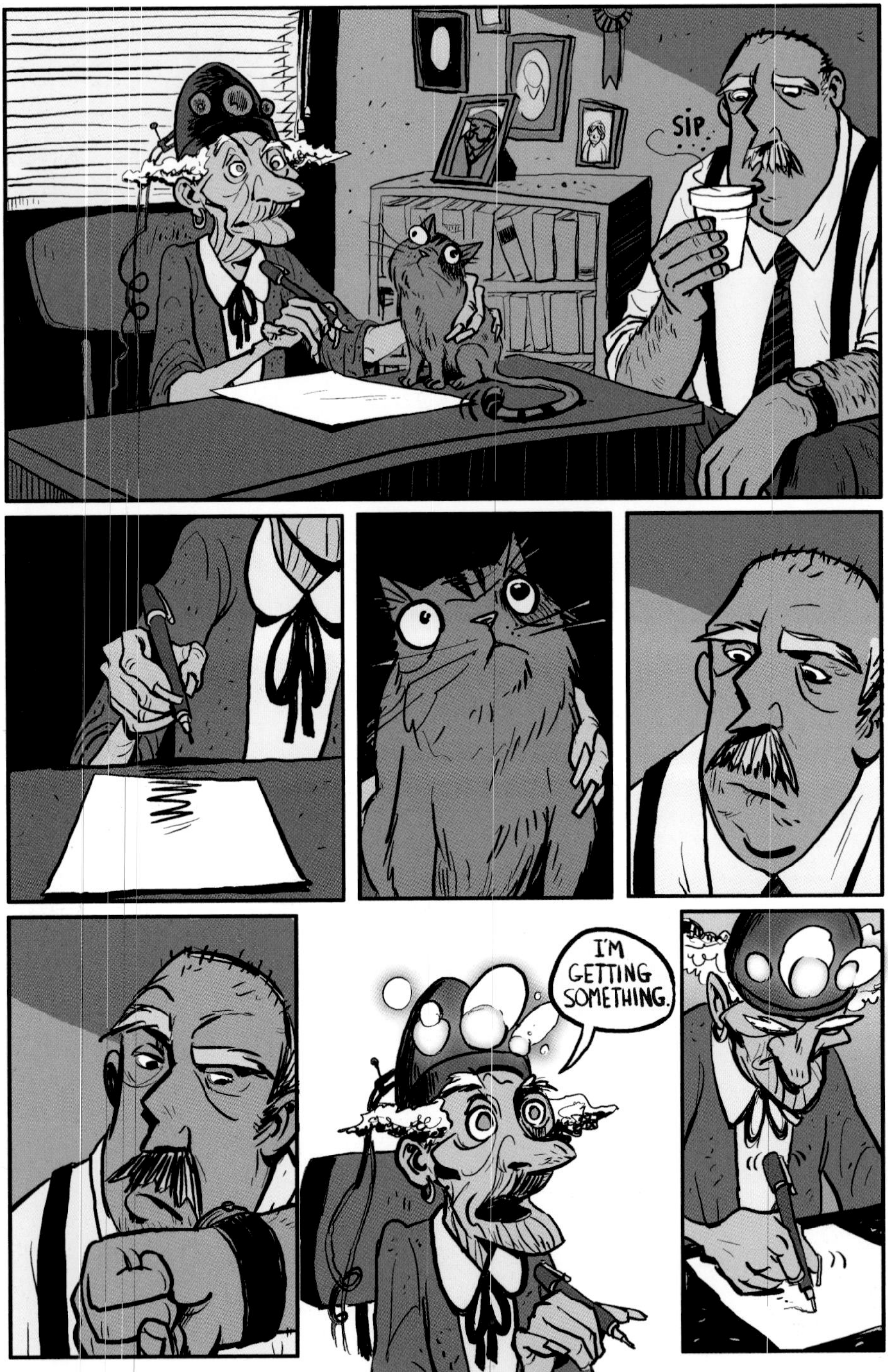
SIP
I'M GETTING SOMETHING.

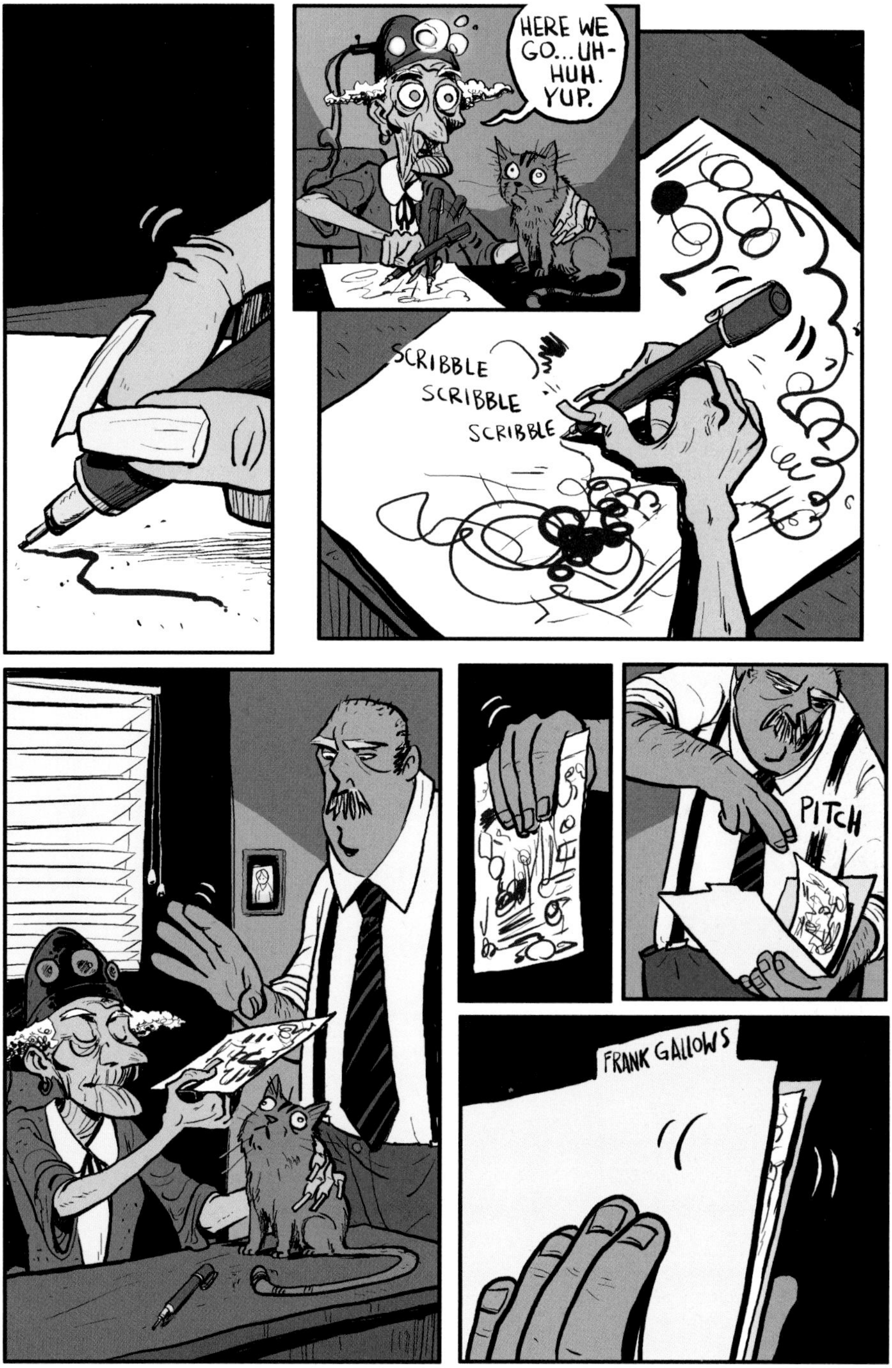
HERE WE GO...UH-HUH. YUP.
SCRIBBLE
SCRIBBLE
SCRIBBLE
PITCH
FRANK GALLOWS

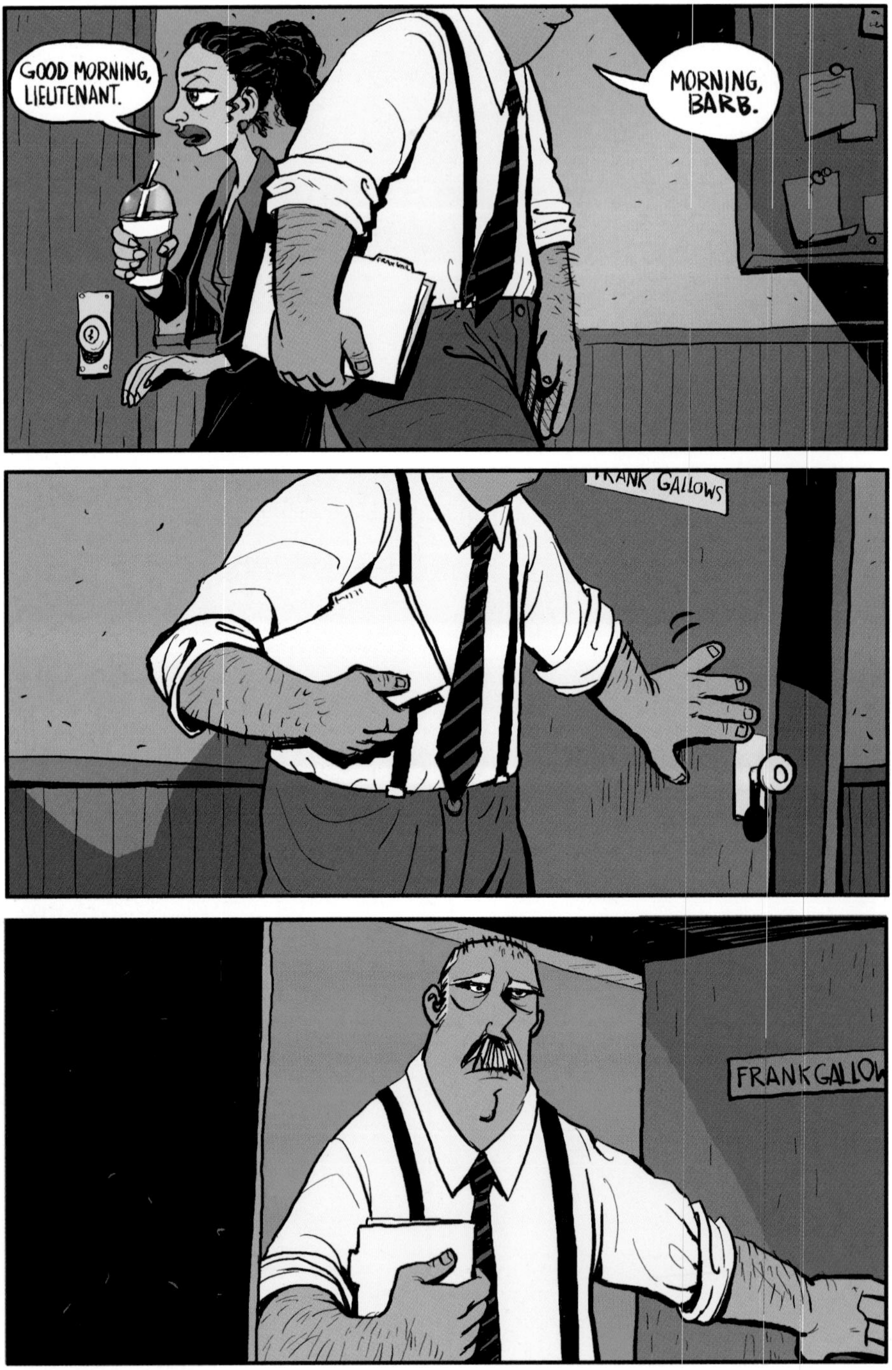
GOOD MORNING, LIEUTENANT.
MORNING, BARB.
FRANK GALLOWS
FRANK GALLOW

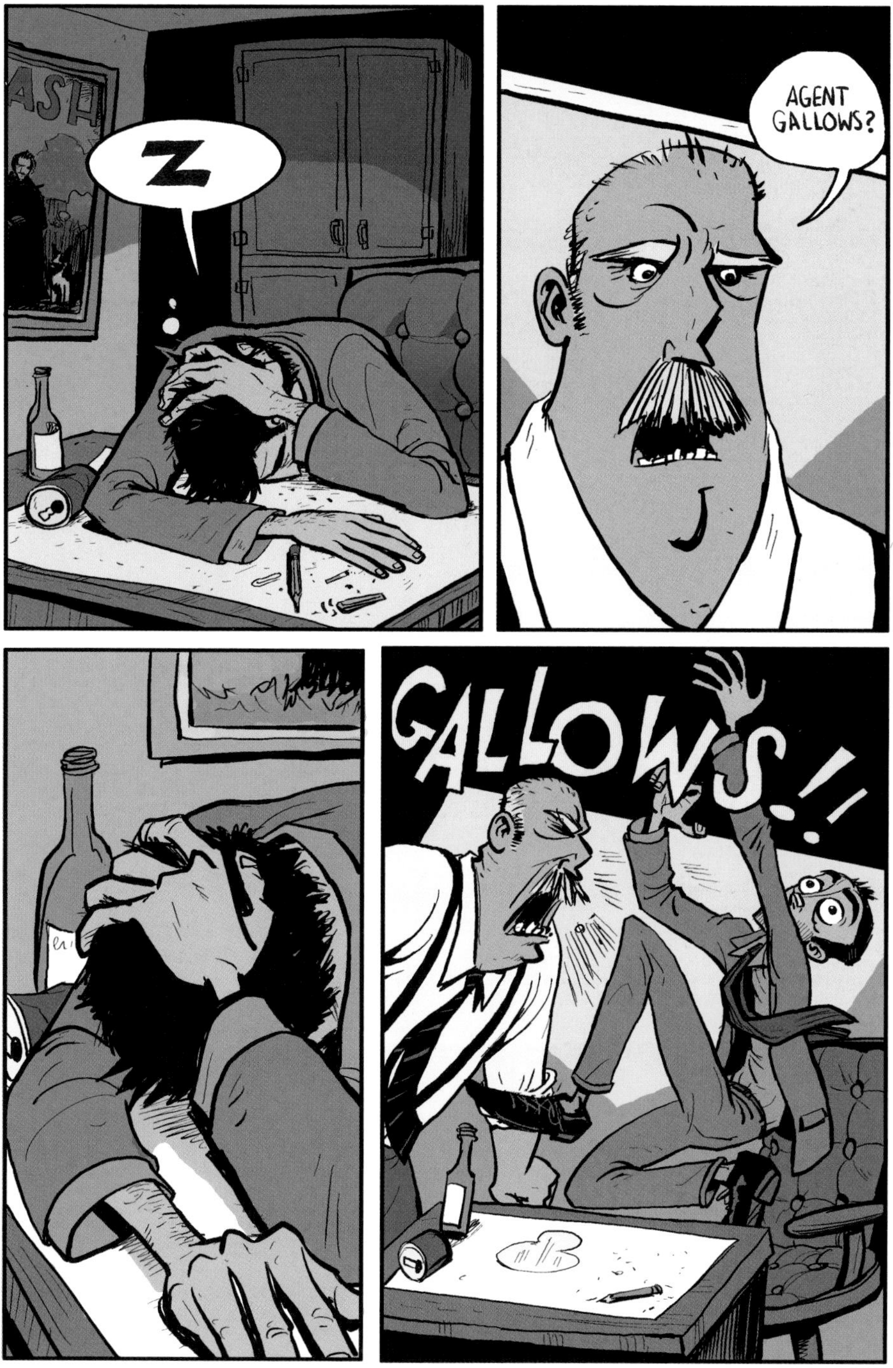
Z
AGENT GALLOWS?
GALLOWS!!

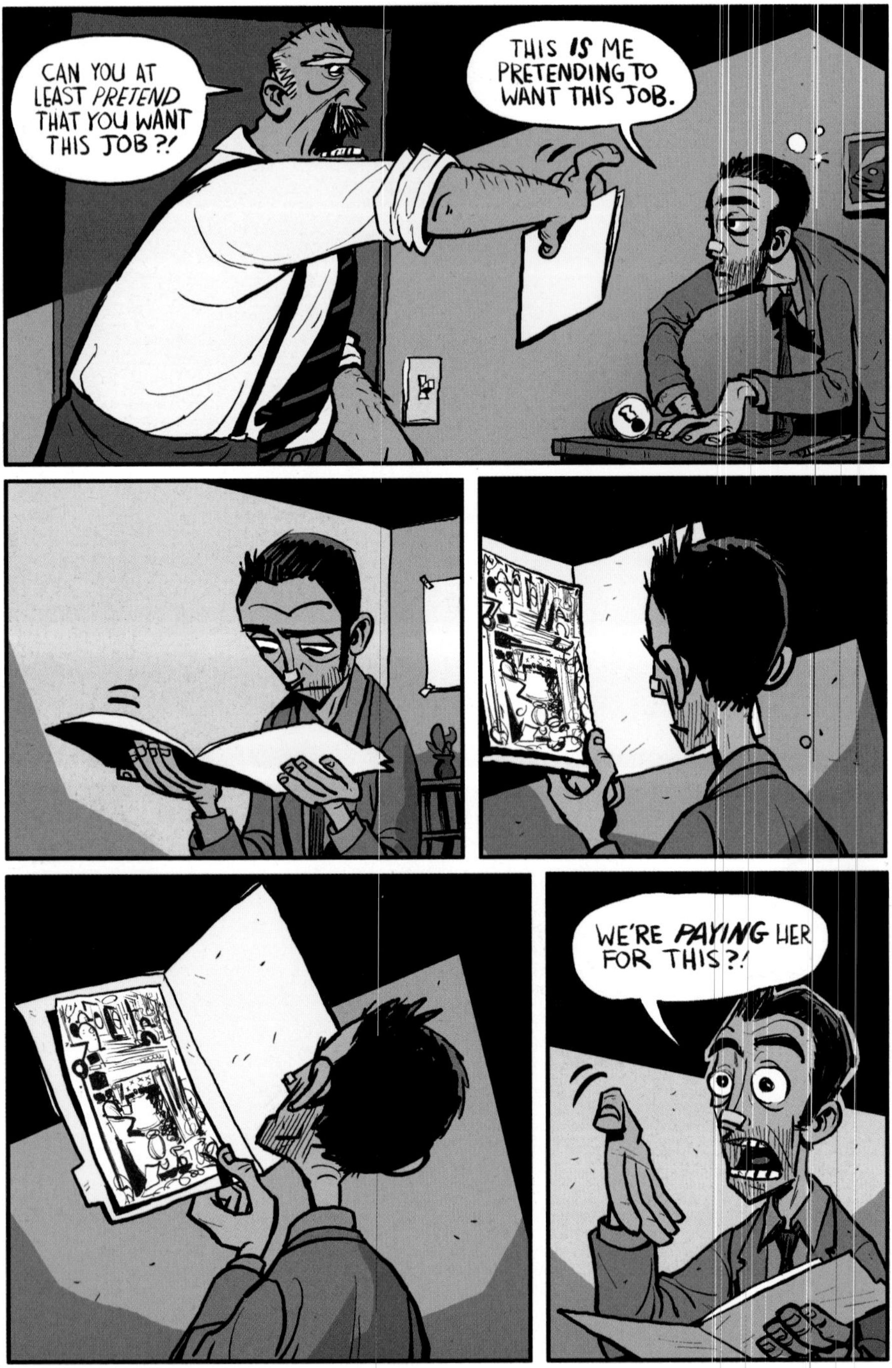
CAN YOU AT LEAST PRETEND THAT YOU WANT THIS JOB?!
THIS IS ME PRETENDING TO WANT THIS JOB.
WE'RE PAYING HER FOR THIS?!

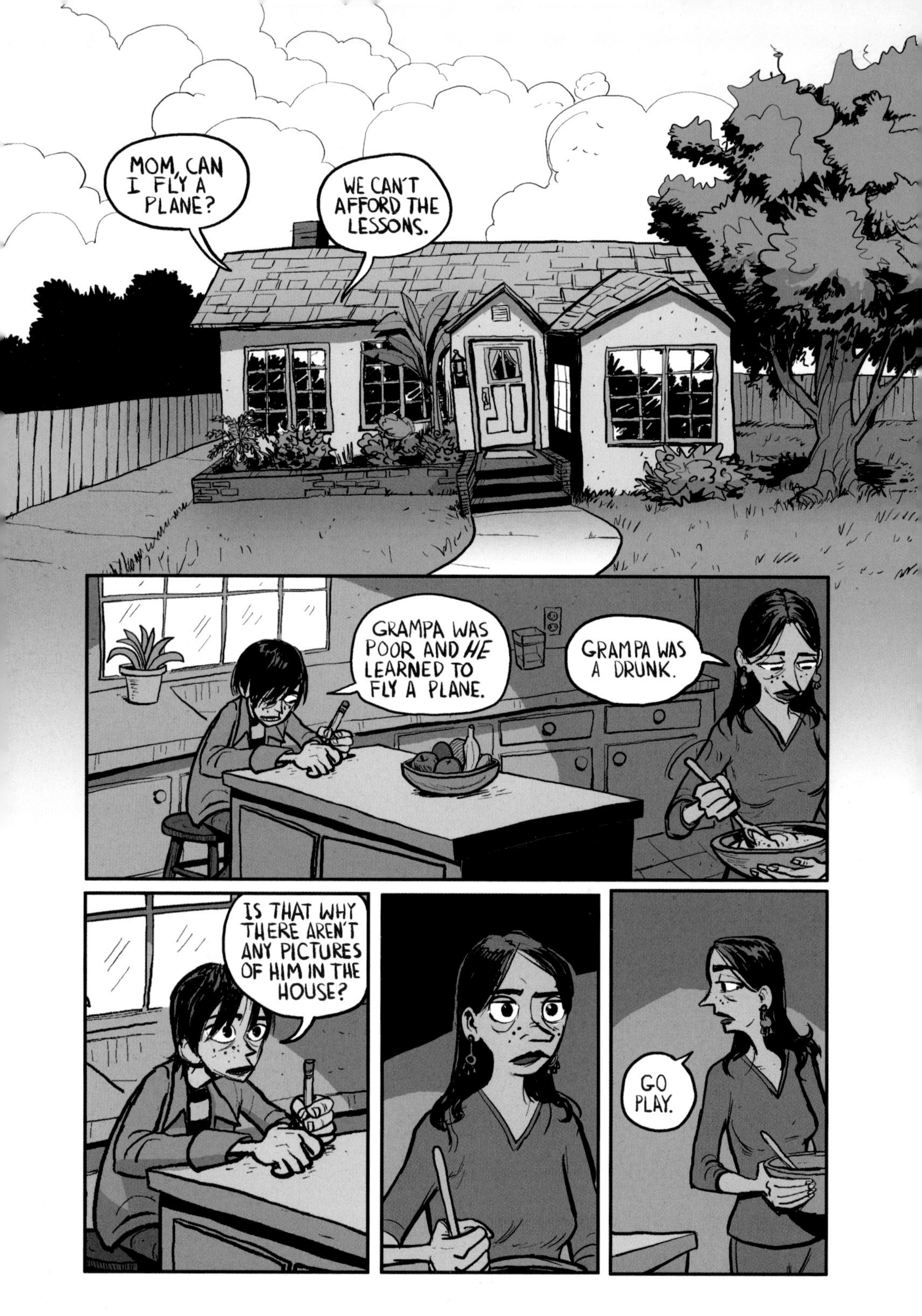
MOM, CAN I FLY A PLANE?
WE CAN'T AFFORD THE LESSONS.
GRAMPA WAS POOR AND HE LEARNED TO FLY A PLANE.
GRAMPA WAS A DRUNK.
IS THAT WHY THERE AREN'T ANY PICTURES OF HIM IN THE HOUSE?
GO PLAY.

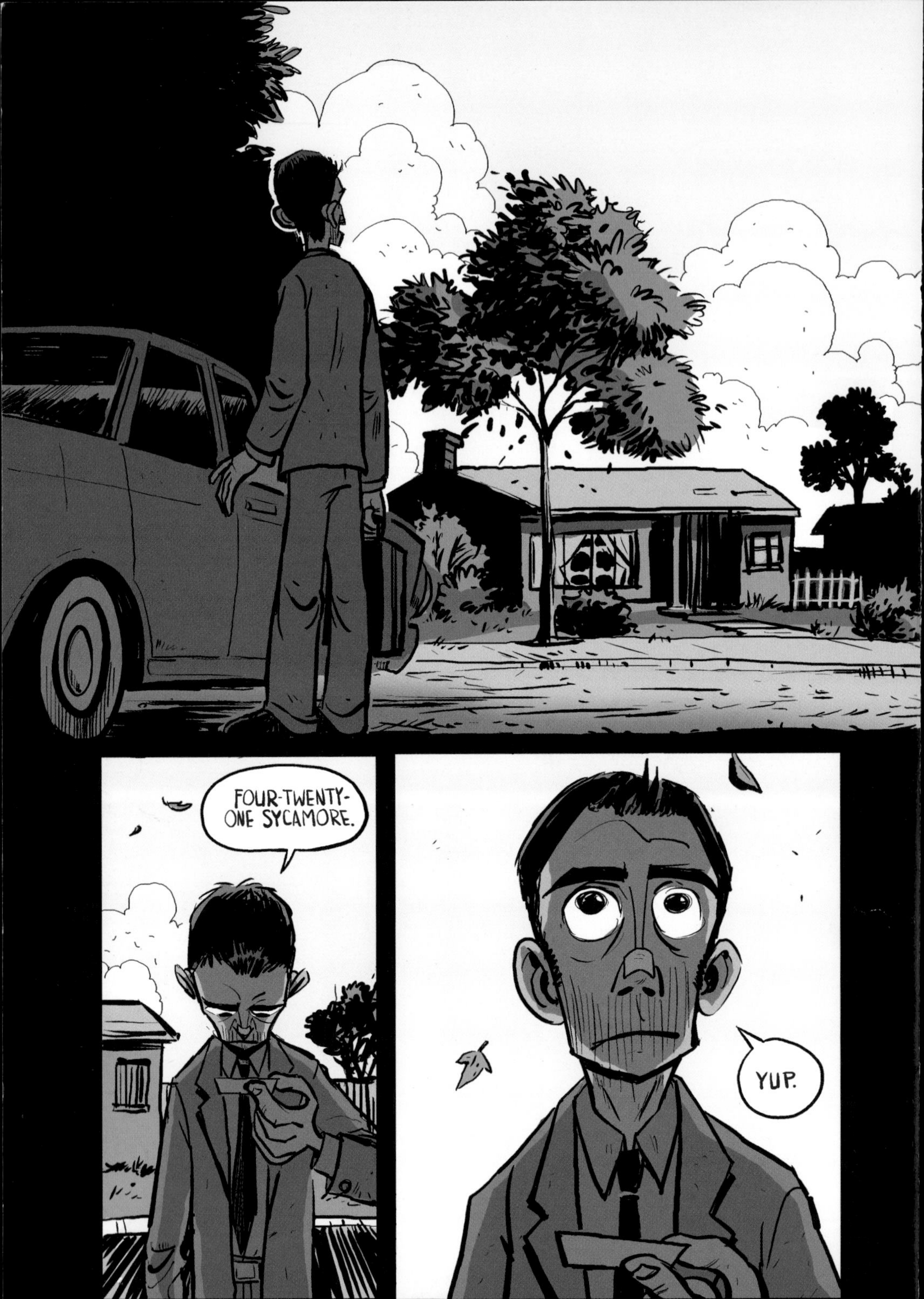
FOUR-TWENTY-ONE SYCAMORE.
YUP.

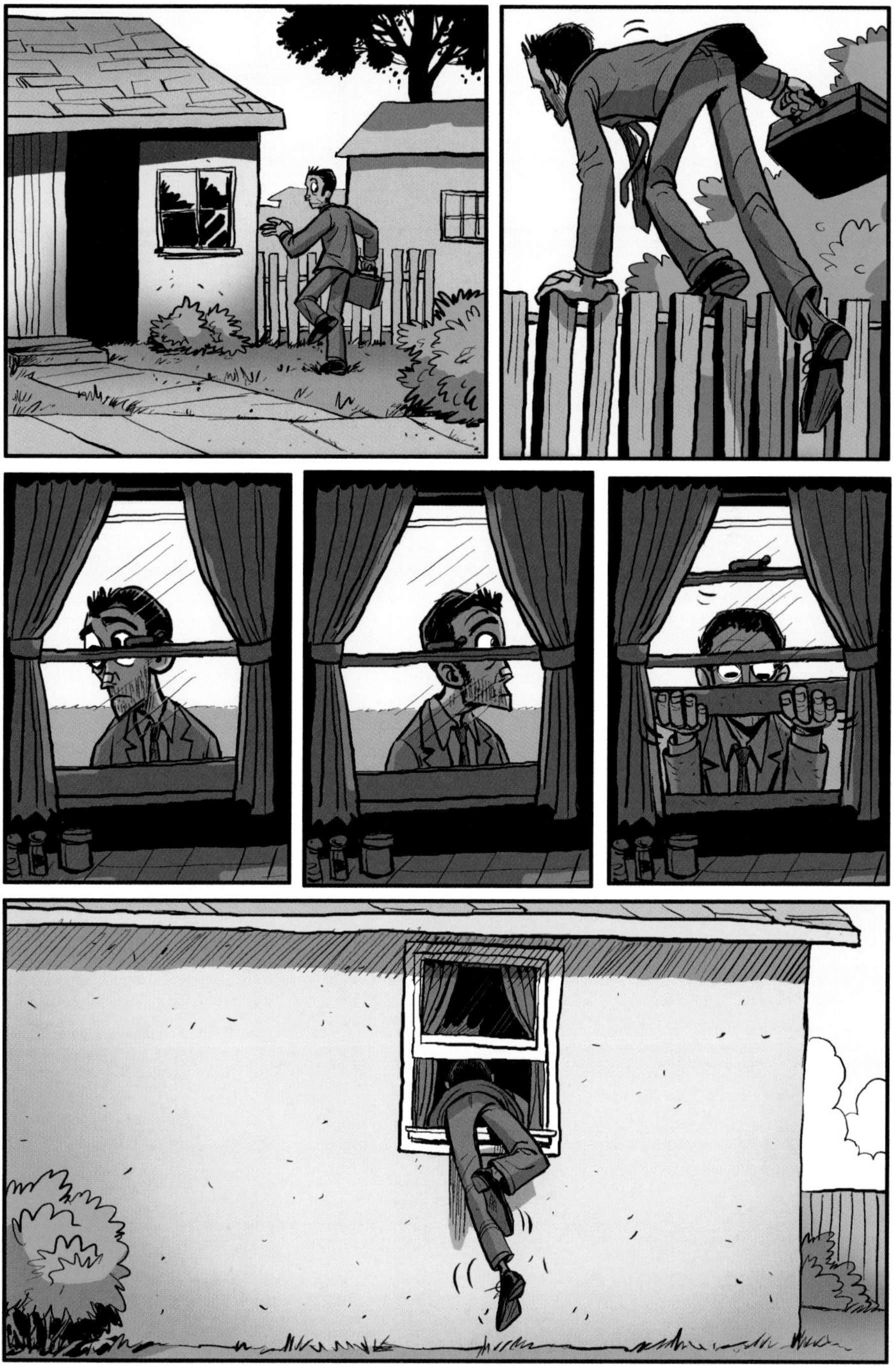

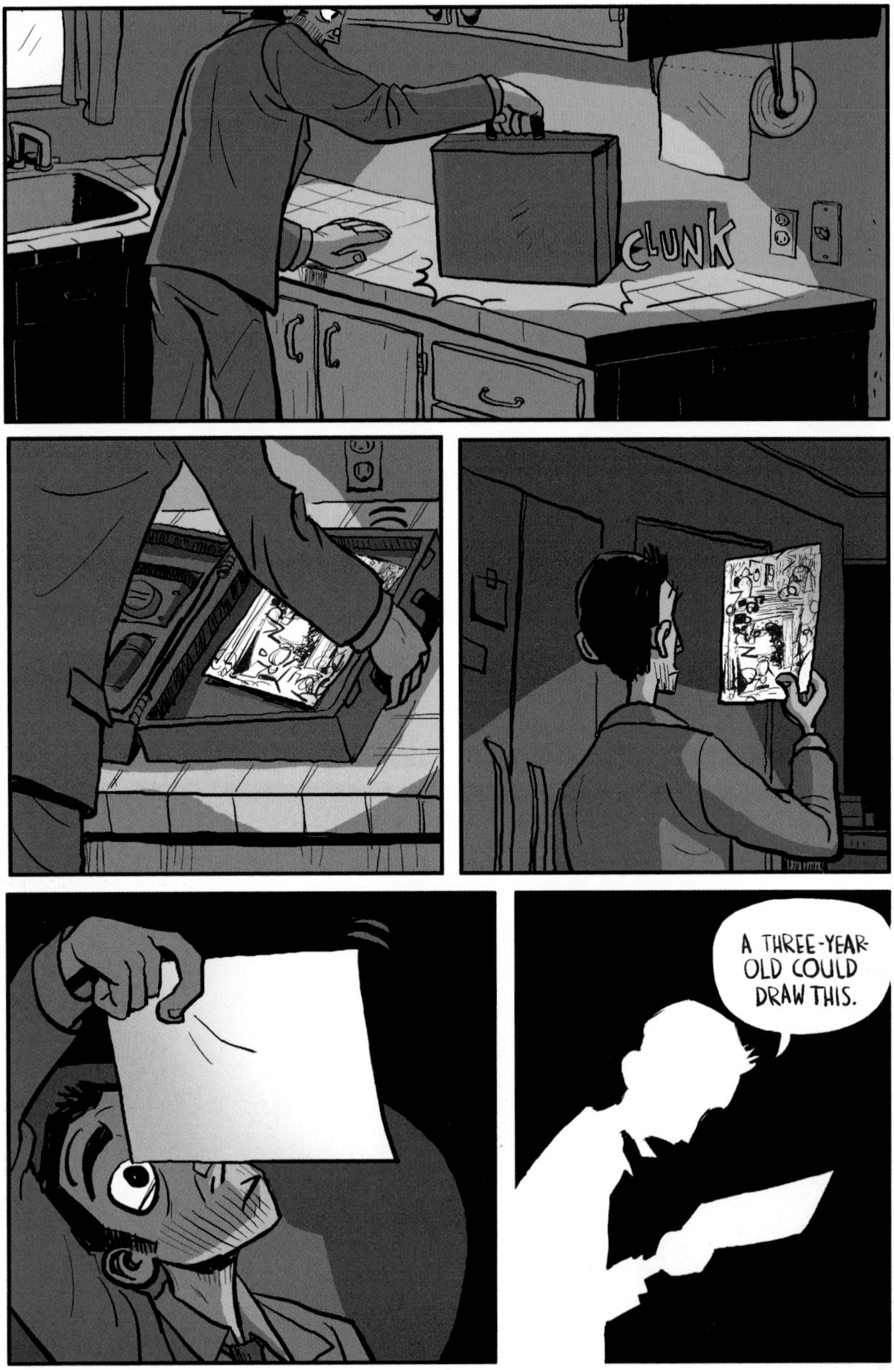
CLUNK
A THREE-YEAR-OLD COULD DRAW THIS.

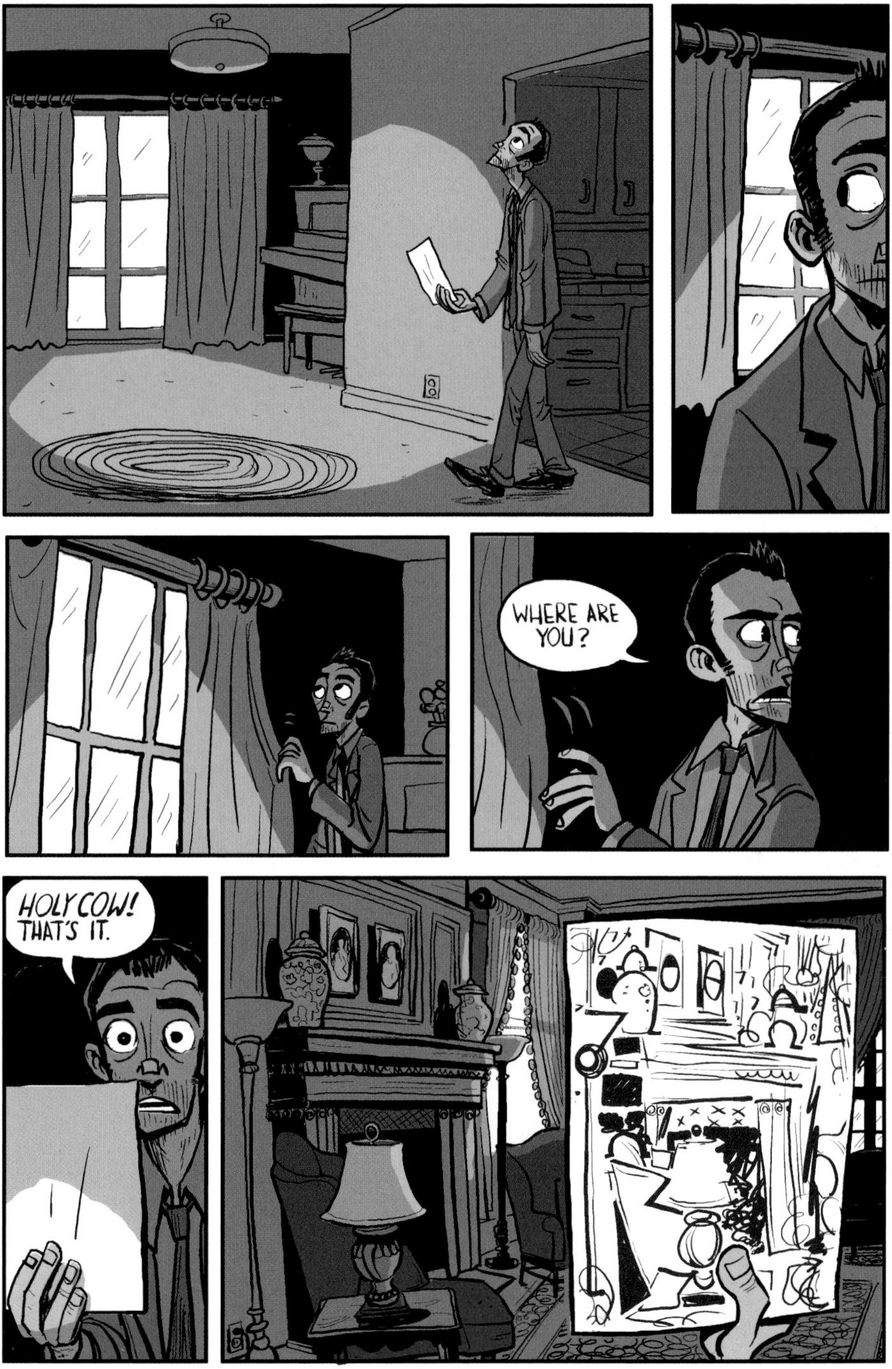
WHERE ARE YOU?
HOLY COW! THAT'S IT.

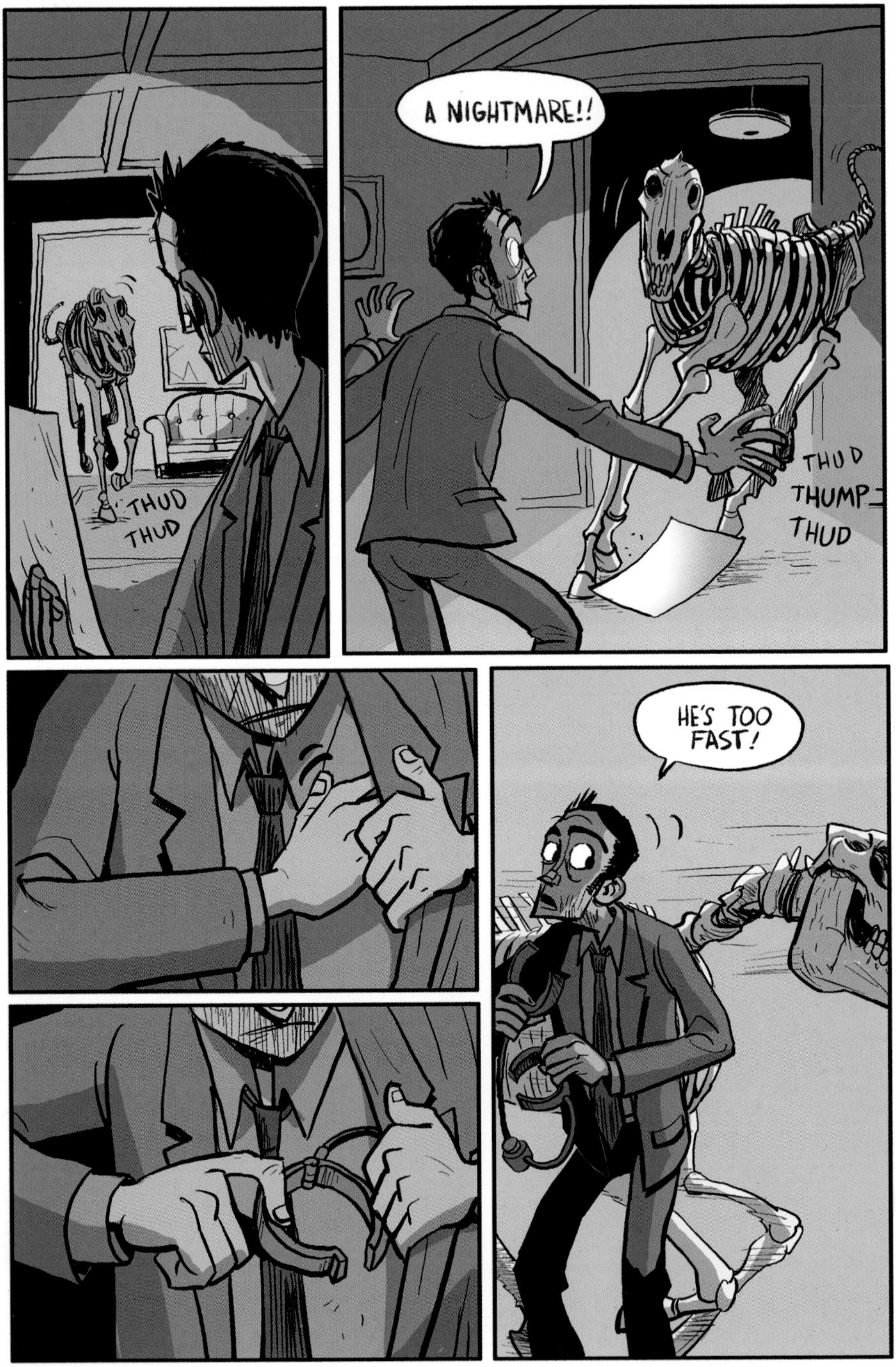
THUD
THUD
A NIGHTMARE!!
THUD
THUMP
THUD
HE'S TOO FAST!

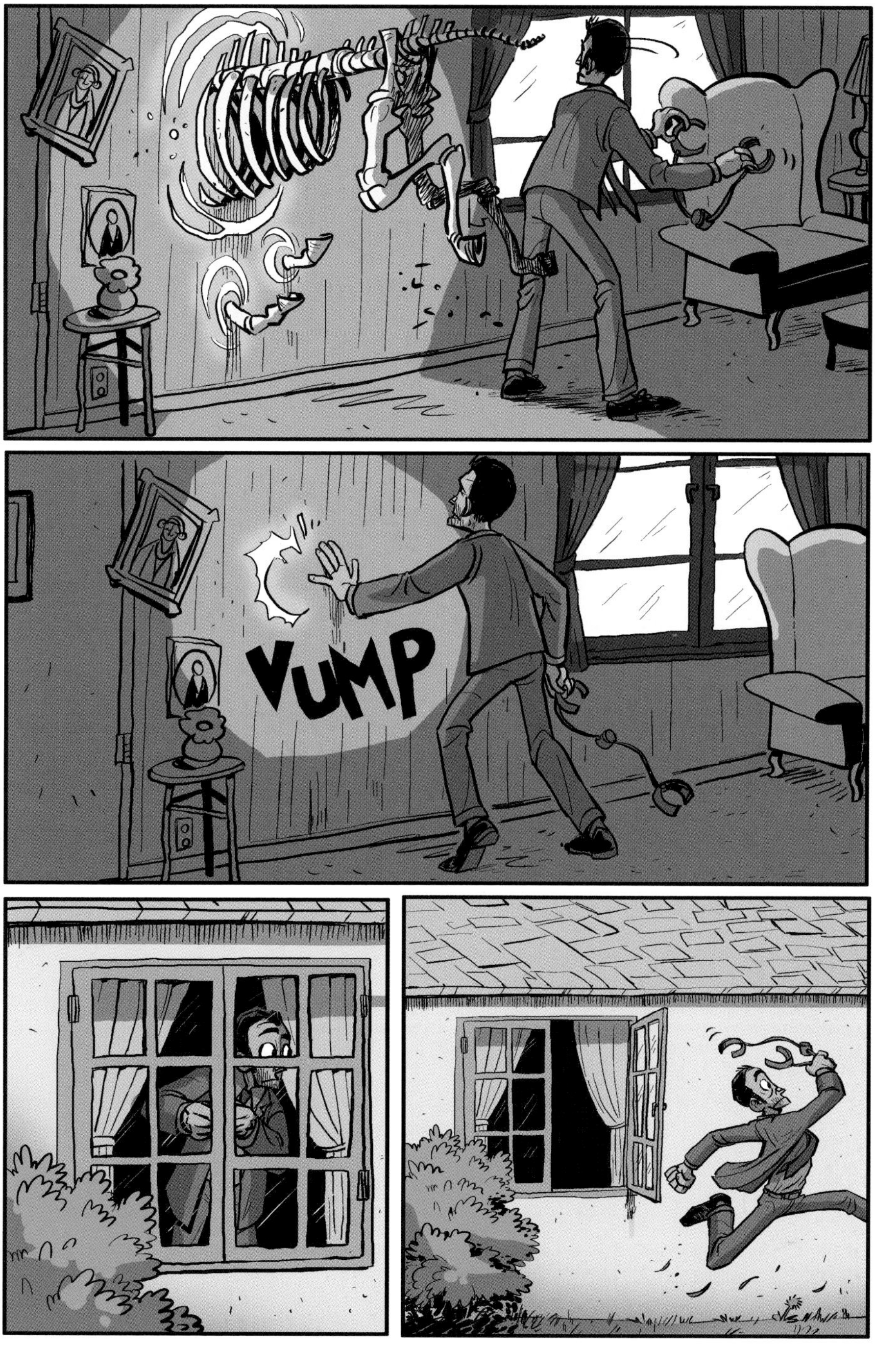
VUMP

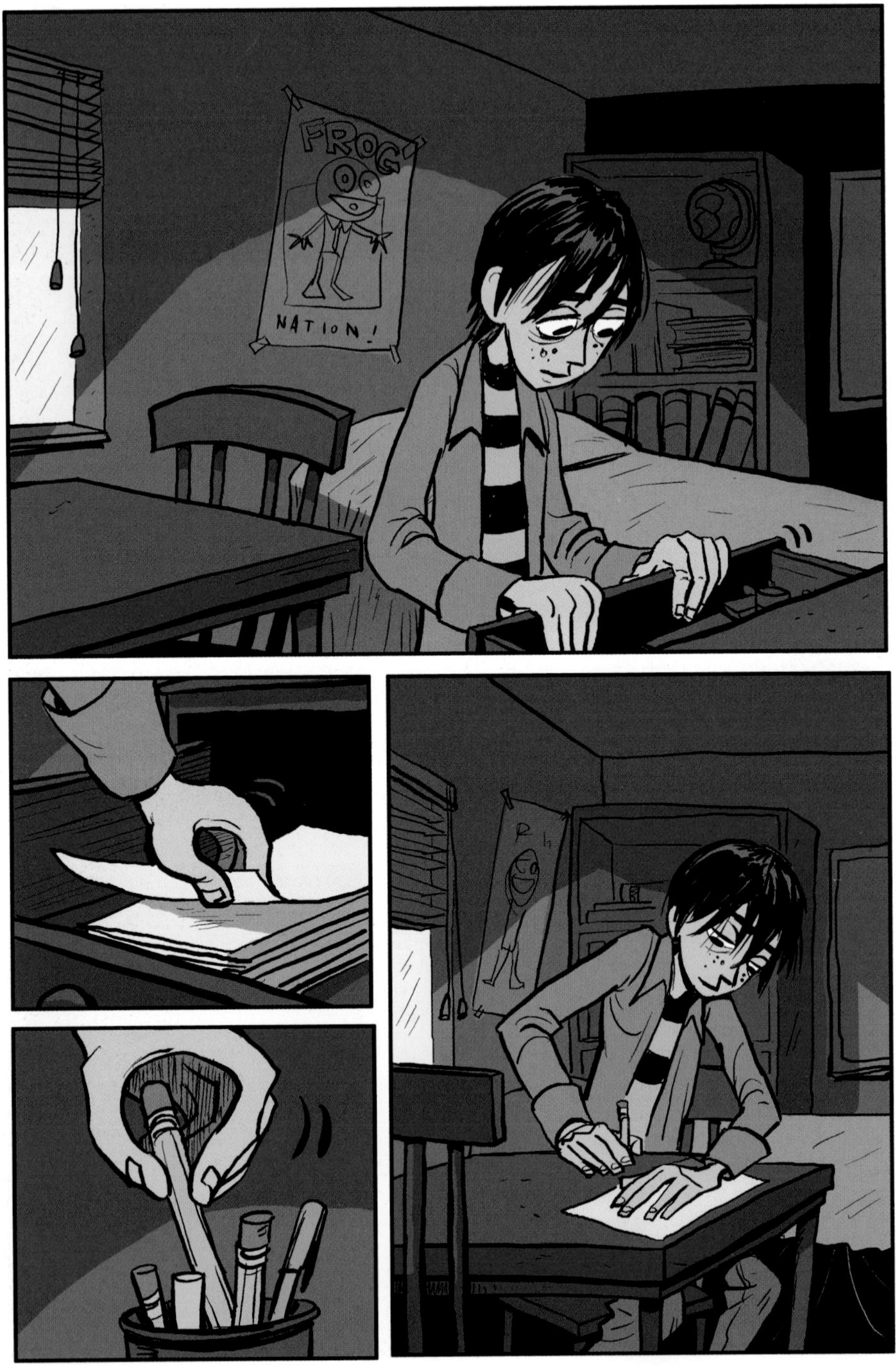
FROG
NATION!

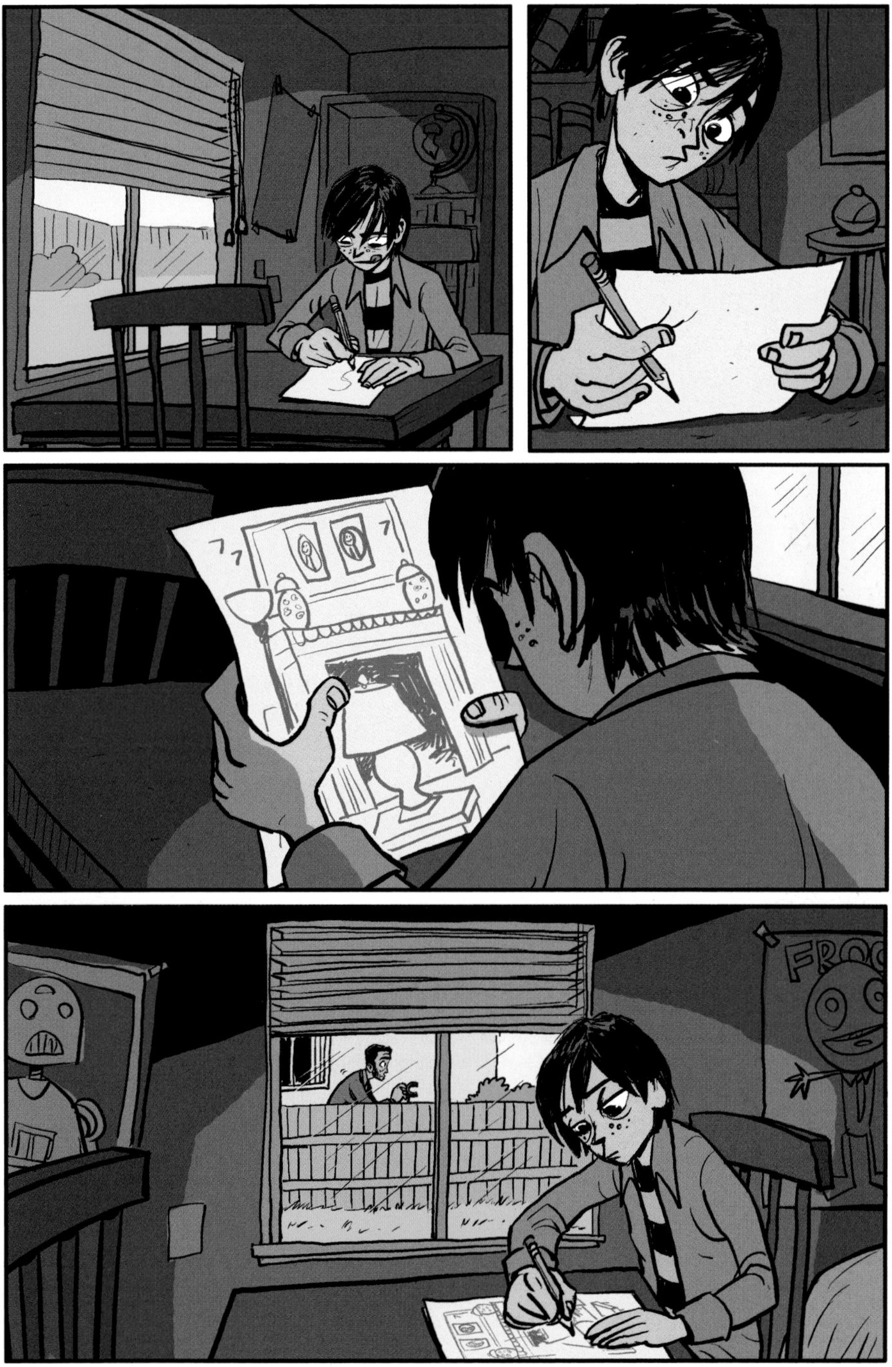

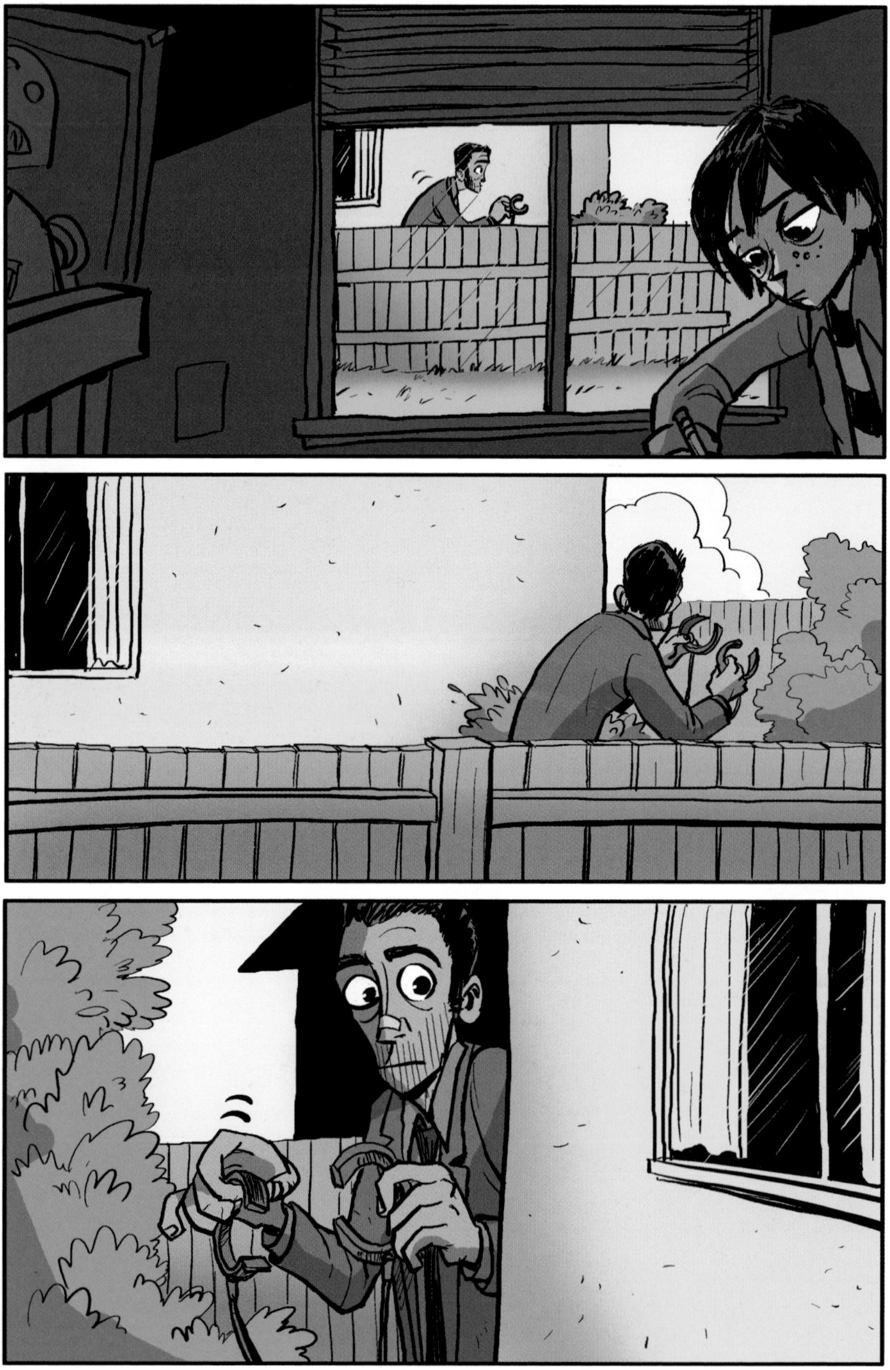

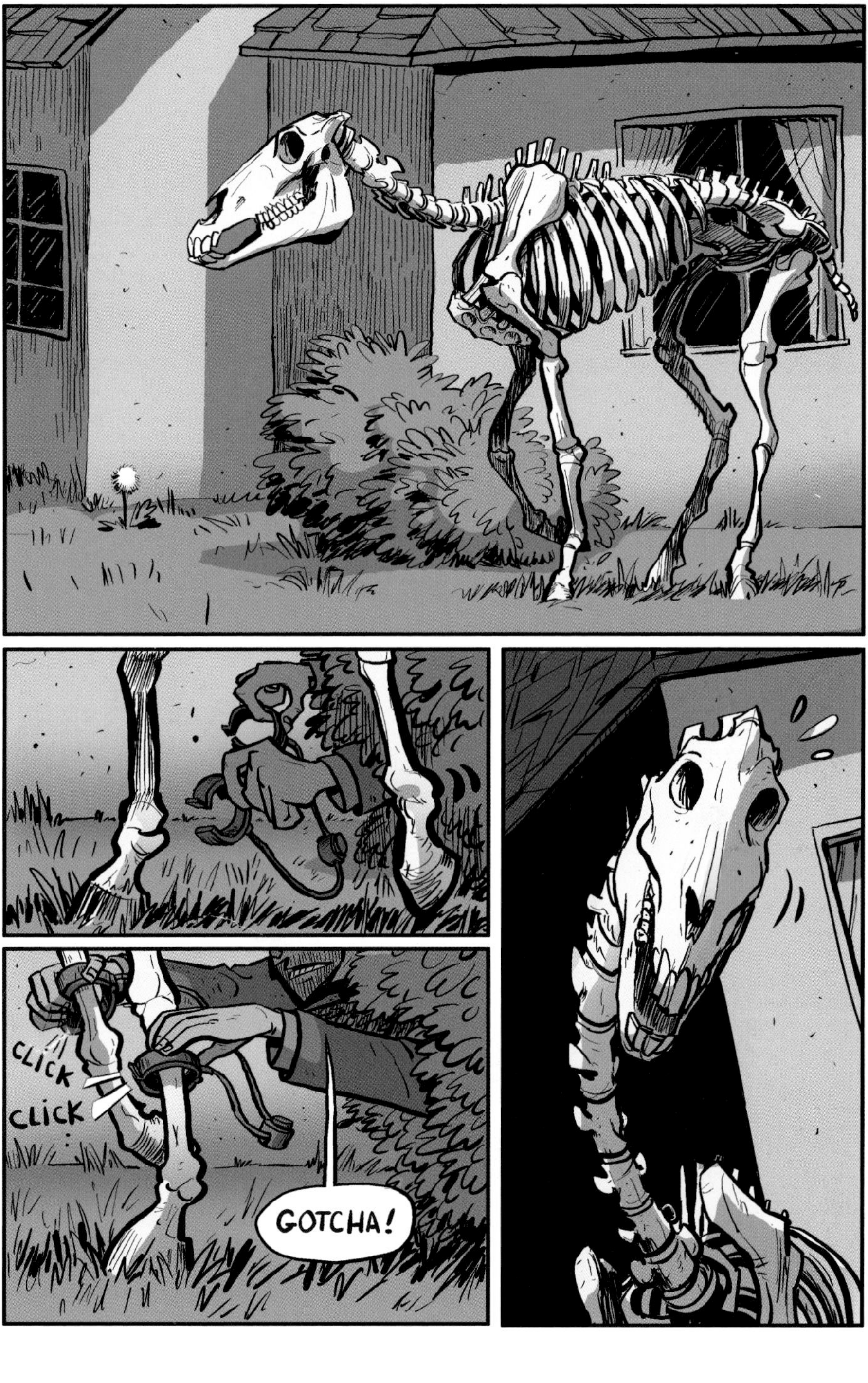
CLICK
CLICK
GOTCHA!

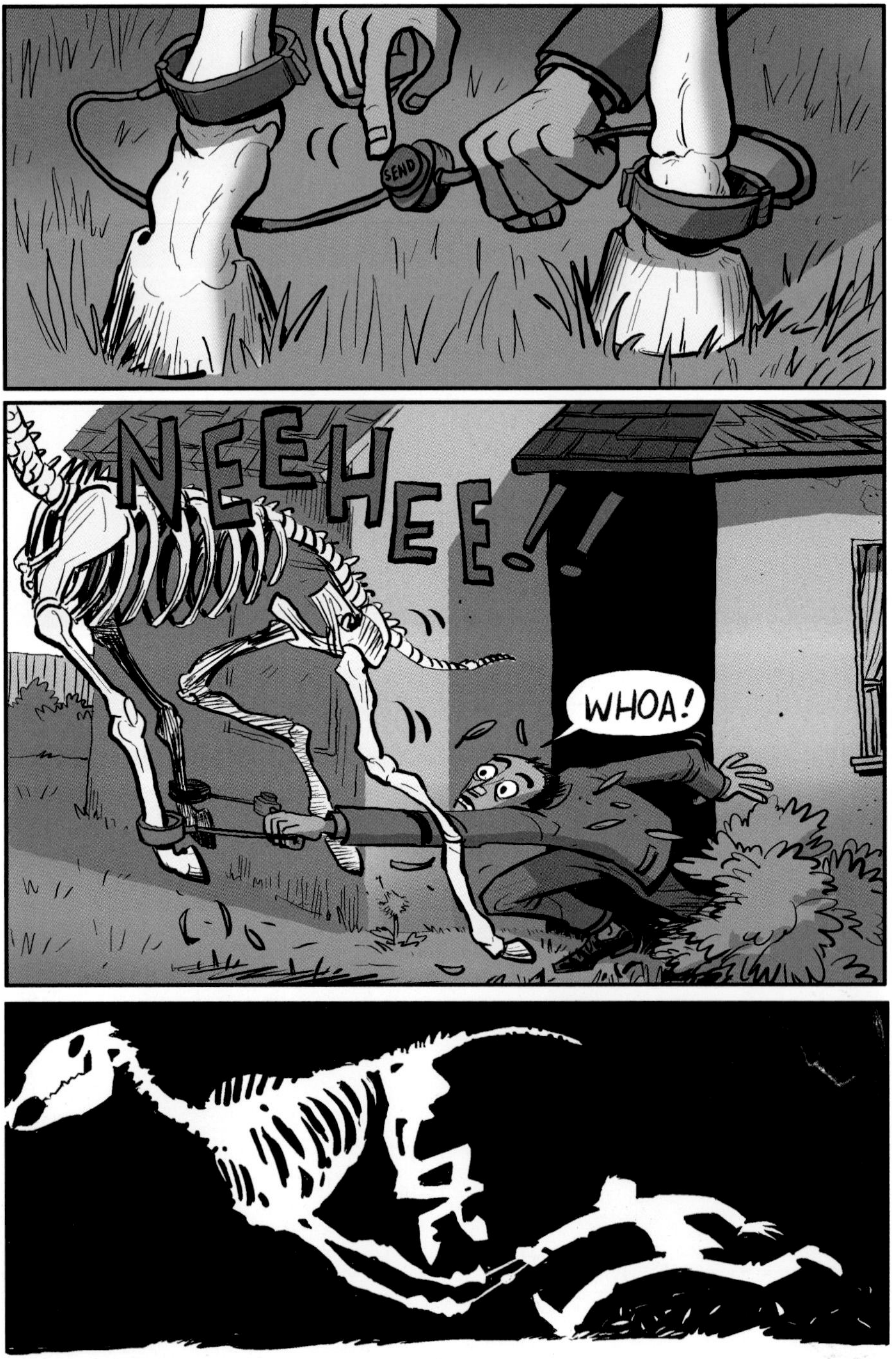
SEND
NEEHEE!!
WHOA!

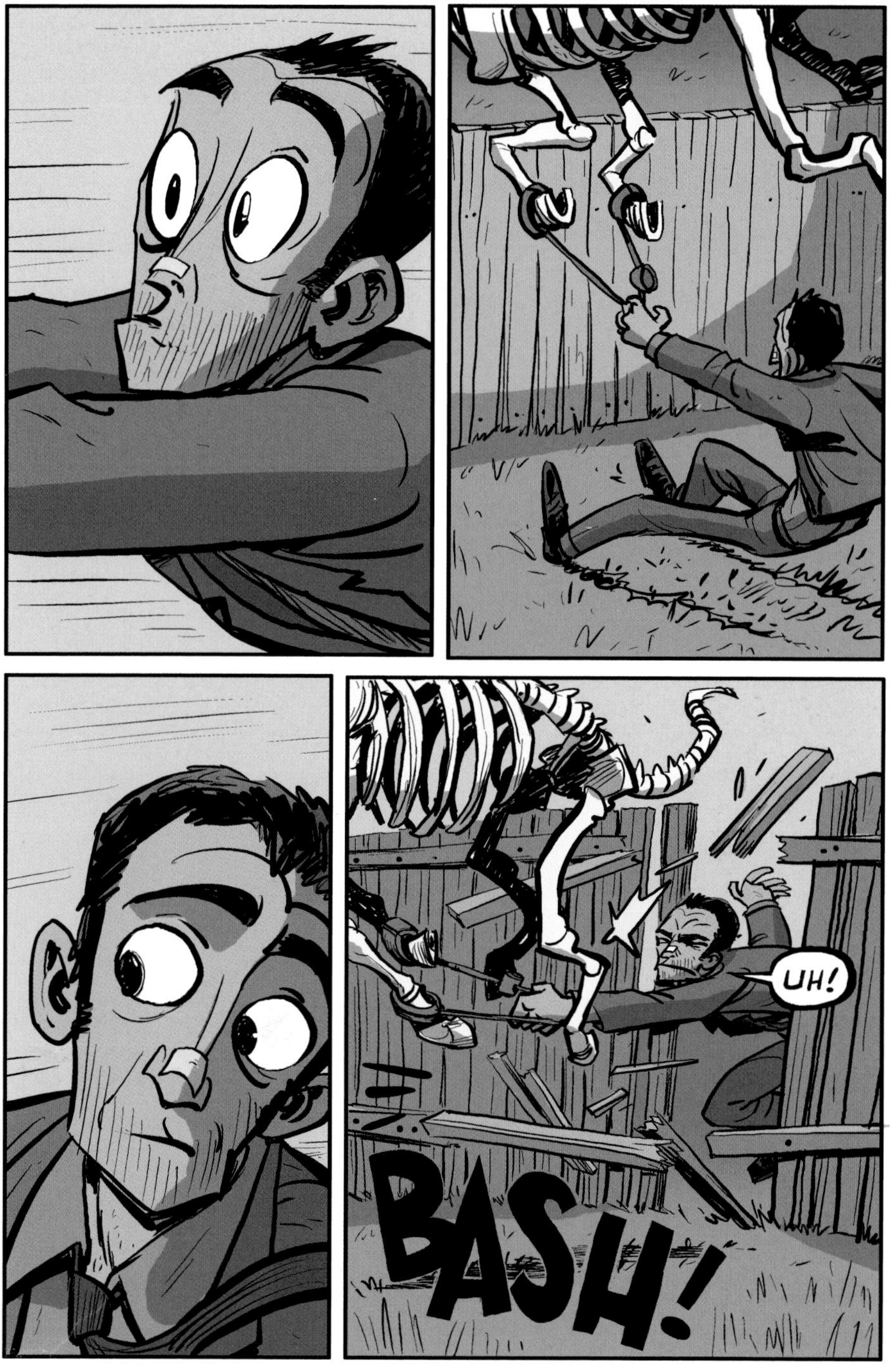
UH!
BASH!

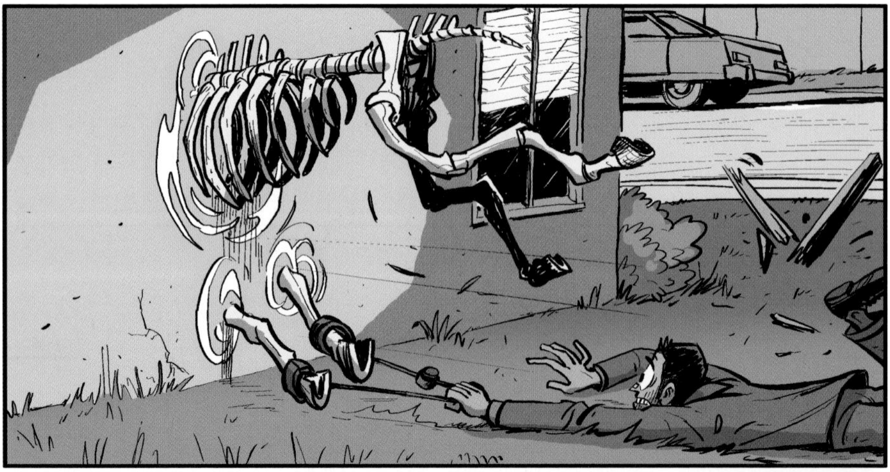

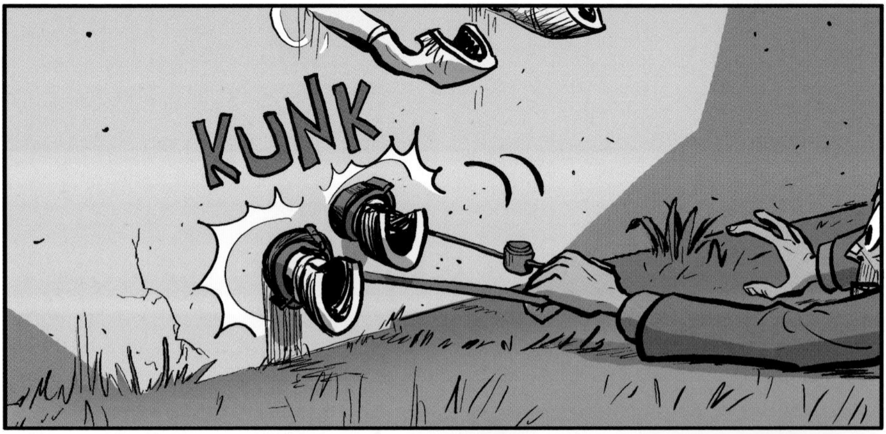
KUNK

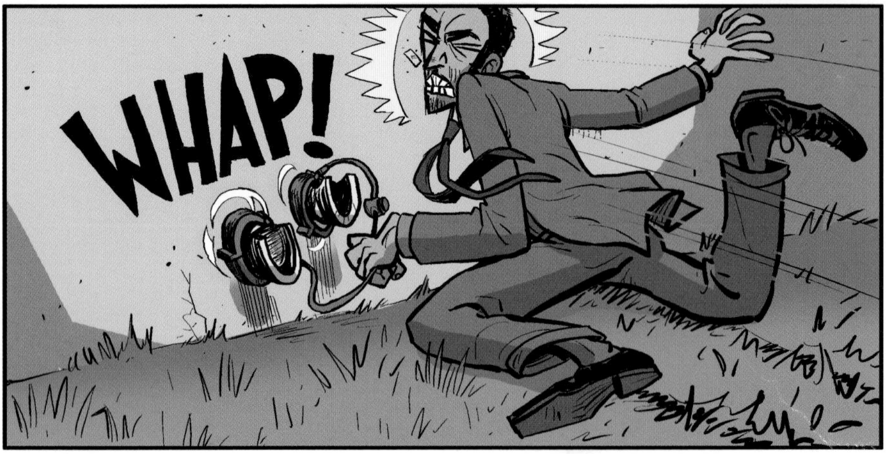
WHAP!

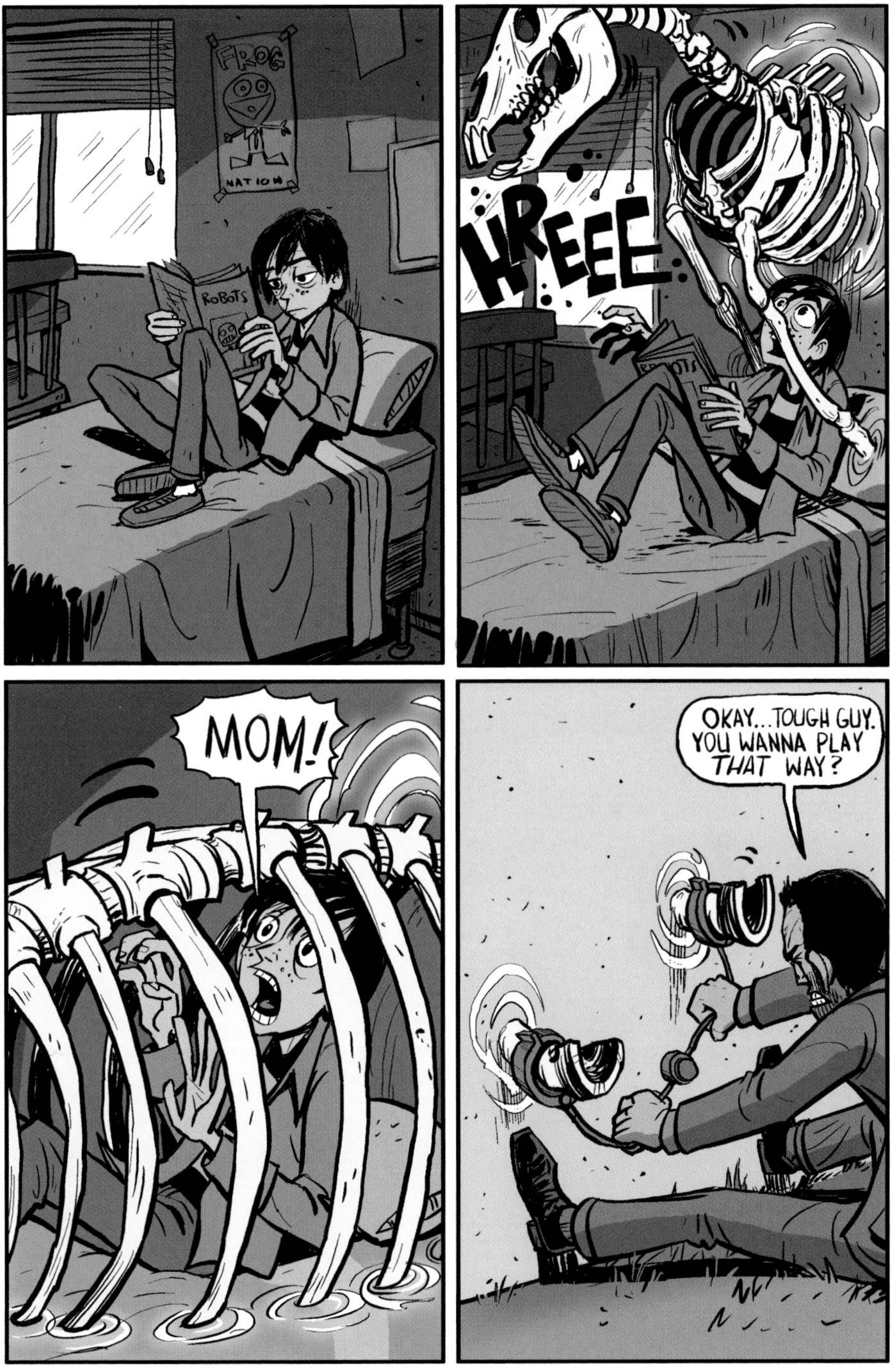
FROG
NATION
ROBOTS
HREEE
MOM!
OKAY...TOUGH GUY. YOU WANNA PLAY *THAT* WAY?

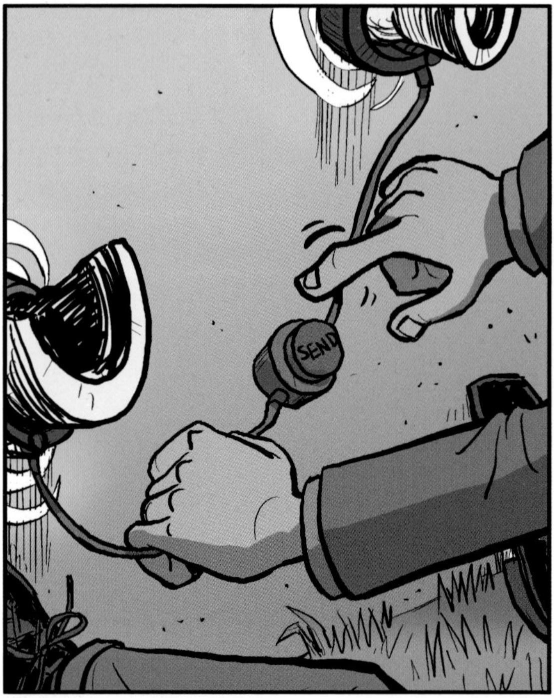
SEND

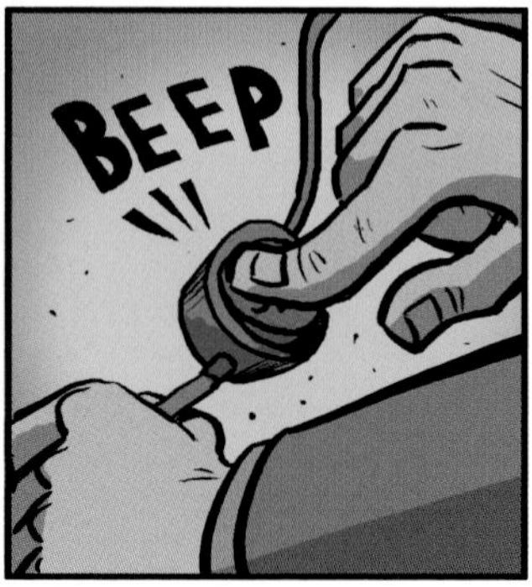
BEEP

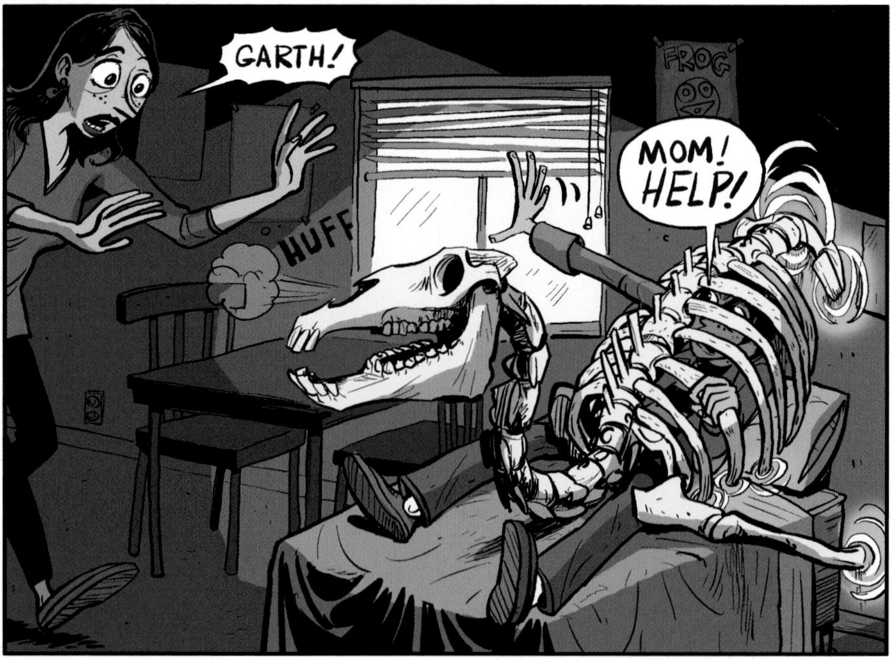
GARTH!
MOM! HELP!
HUFF
FROG

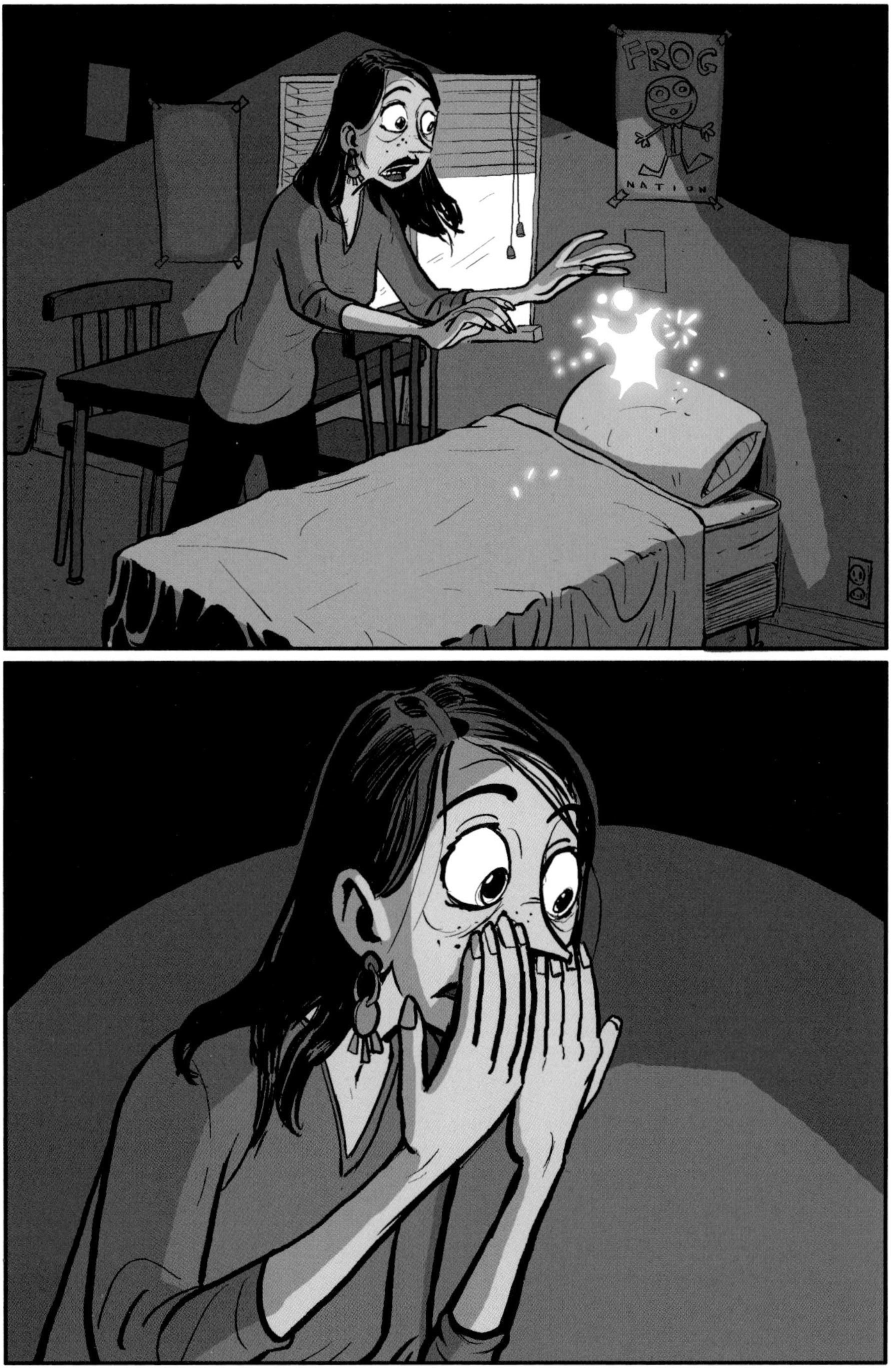
FROG
NATION

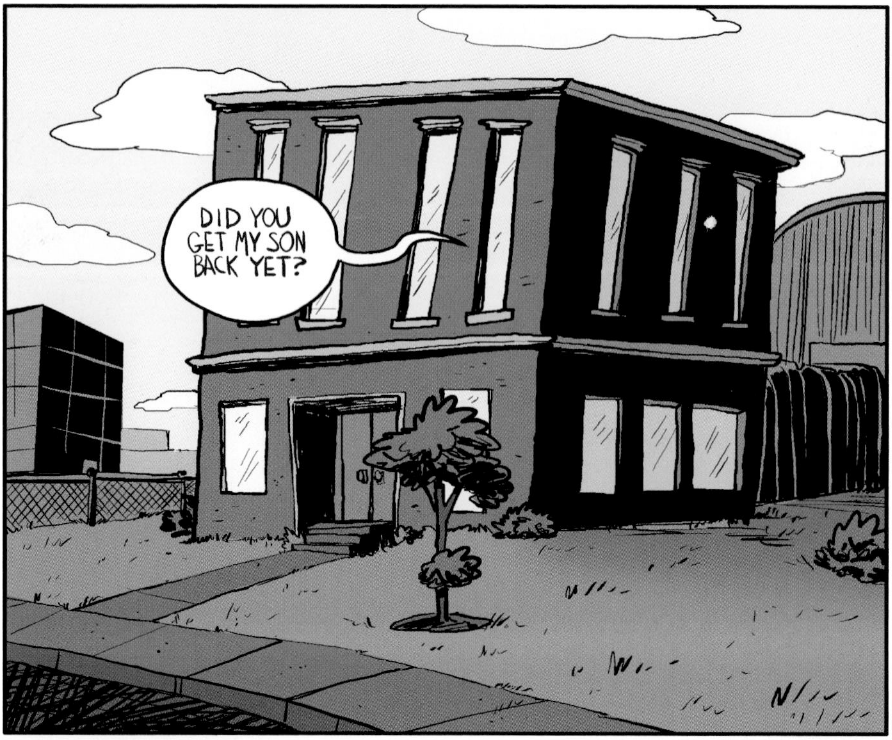
DID YOU GET MY SON BACK YET?

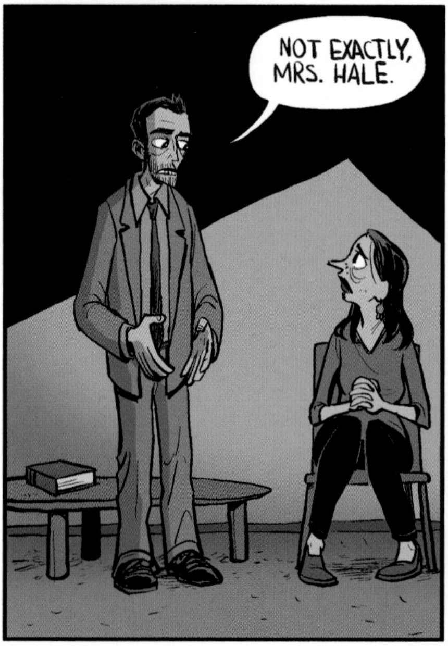
NOT EXACTLY, MRS. HALE.

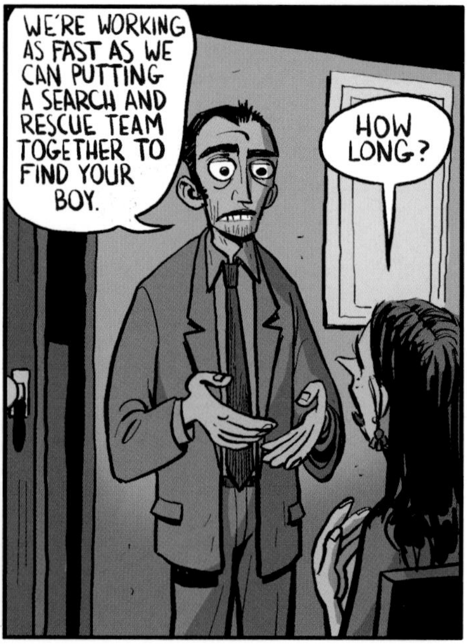
WE'RE WORKING AS FAST AS WE CAN PUTTING A SEARCH AND RESCUE TEAM TOGETHER TO FIND YOUR BOY.
HOW LONG?

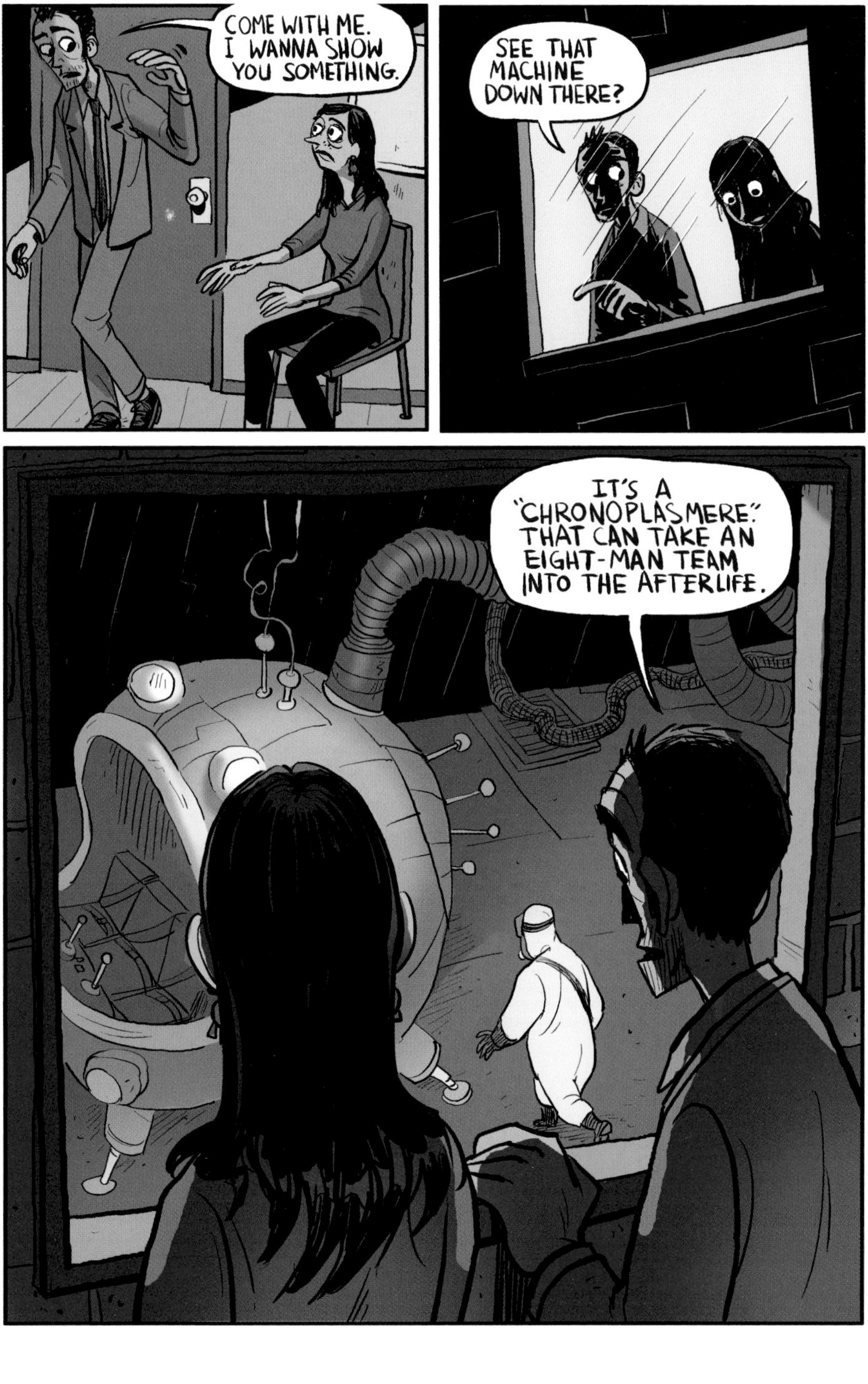
COME WITH ME. I WANNA SHOW YOU SOMETHING.
SEE THAT MACHINE DOWN THERE?
IT'S A "CHRONOPLASMERE." THAT CAN TAKE AN EIGHT-MAN TEAM INTO THE AFTERLIFE.

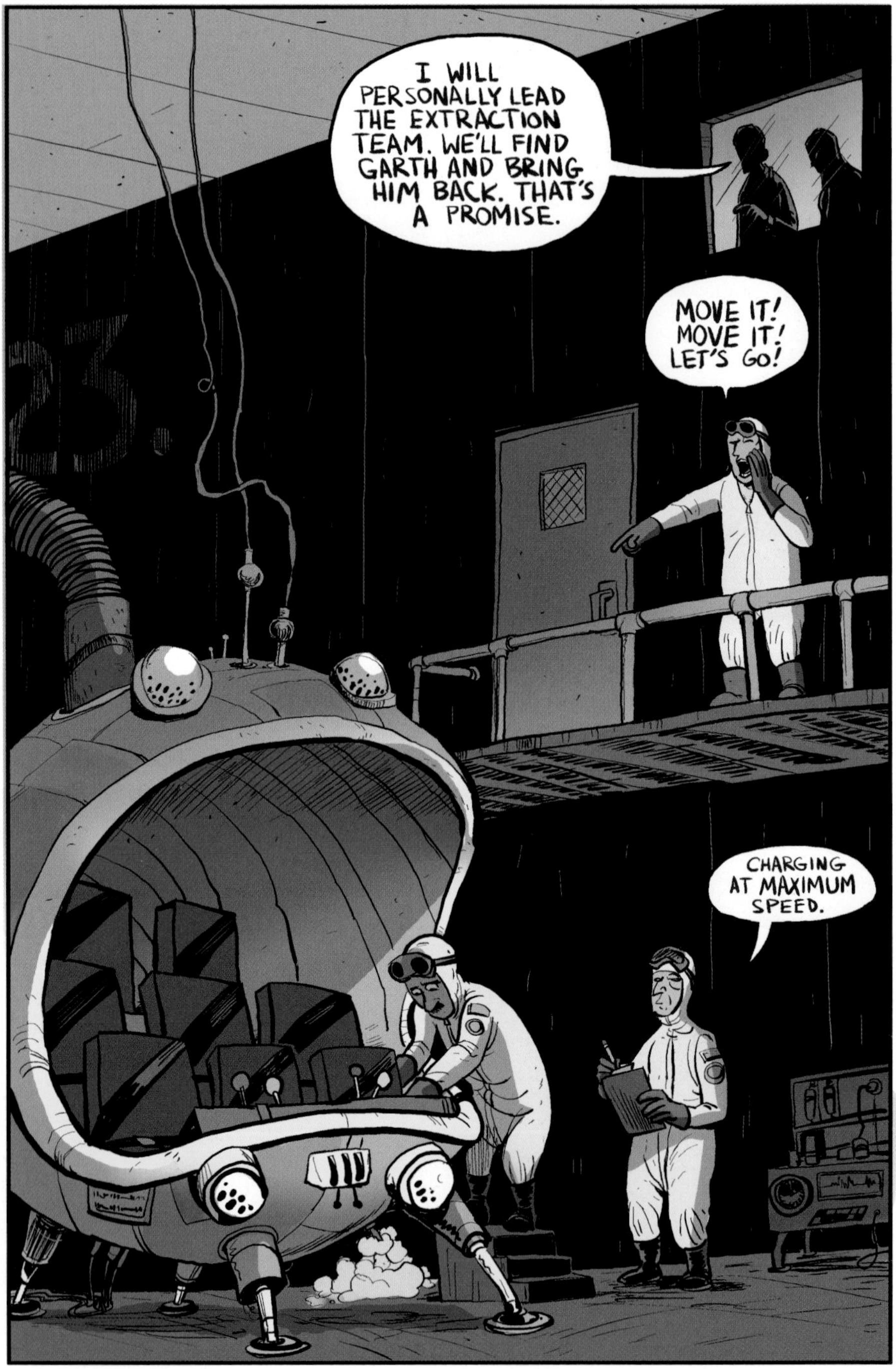
I WILL PERSONALLY LEAD THE EXTRACTION TEAM. WE'LL FIND GARTH AND BRING HIM BACK. THAT'S A PROMISE.
MOVE IT! MOVE IT! LET'S GO!
CHARGING AT MAXIMUM SPEED.

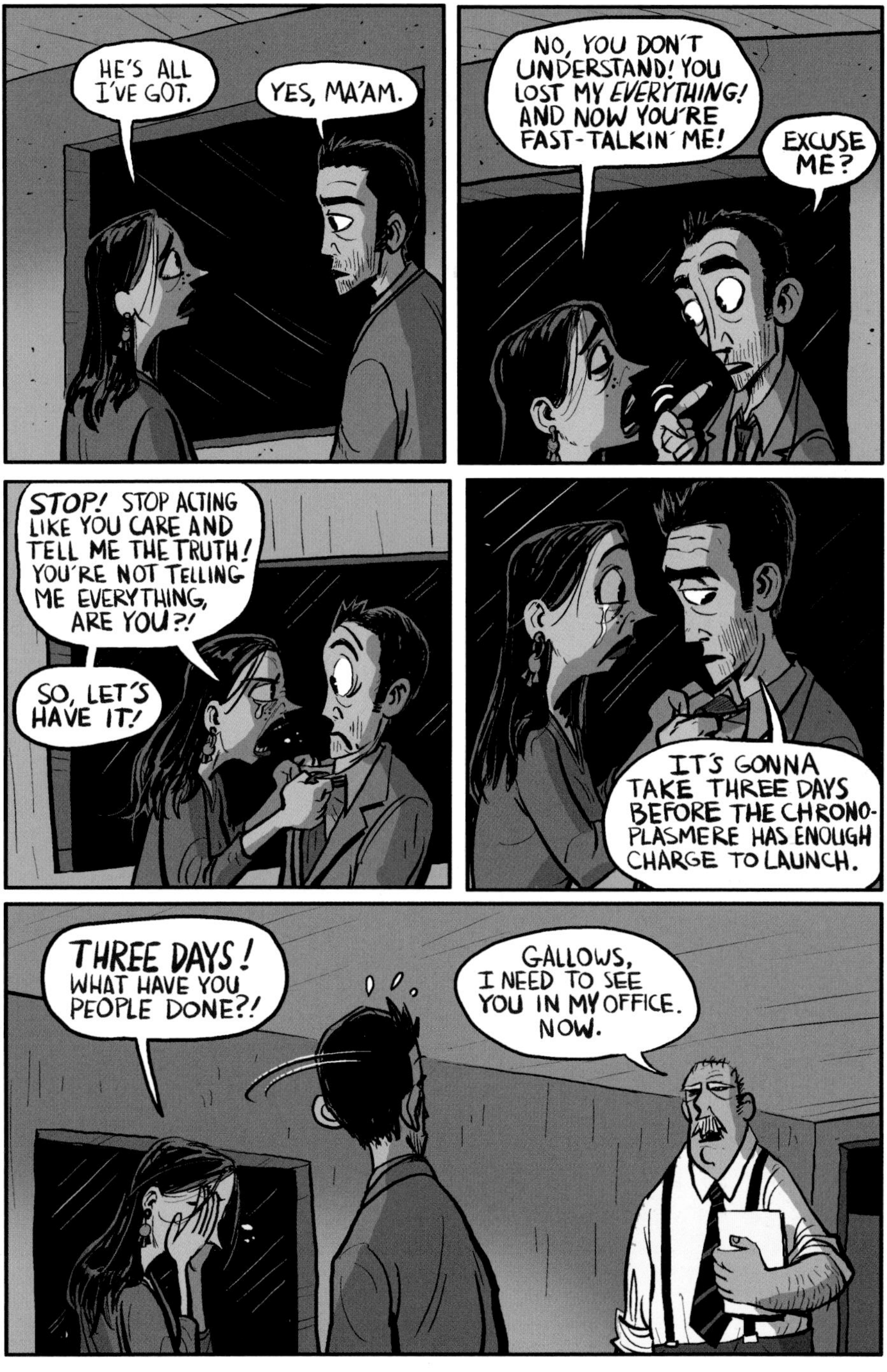
HE'S ALL I'VE GOT.
YES, MA'AM.
NO, YOU DON'T UNDERSTAND! YOU LOST MY EVERYTHING! AND NOW YOU'RE FAST-TALKIN' ME!
EXCUSE ME?
STOP! STOP ACTING LIKE YOU CARE AND TELL ME THE TRUTH! YOU'RE NOT TELLING ME EVERYTHING, ARE YOU?!
SO, LET'S HAVE IT!
IT'S GONNA TAKE THREE DAYS BEFORE THE CHRONO-PLASMERE HAS ENOUGH CHARGE TO LAUNCH.
THREE DAYS! WHAT HAVE YOU PEOPLE DONE?!
GALLOWS, I NEED TO SEE YOU IN MY OFFICE. NOW.

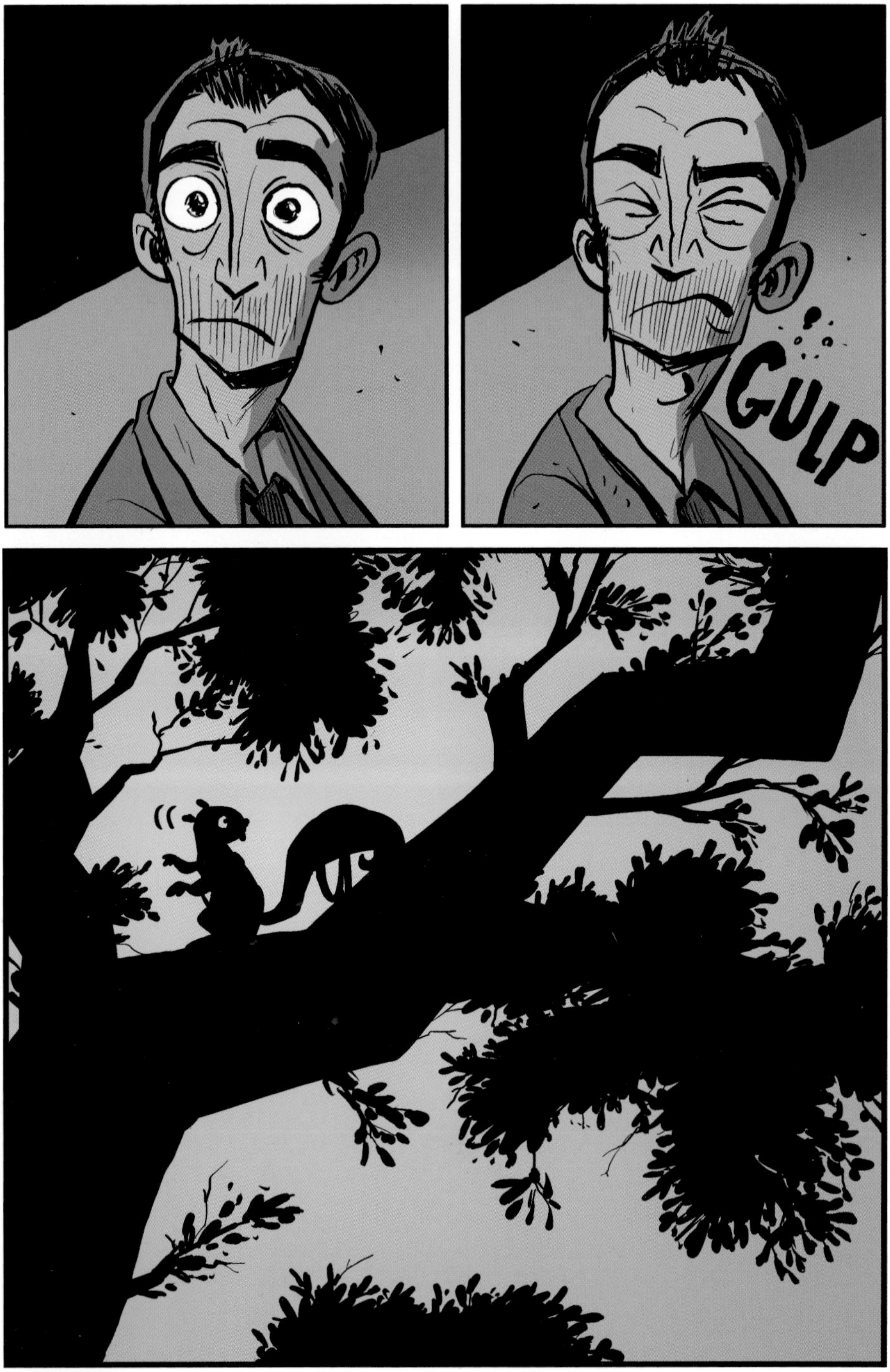
GULP

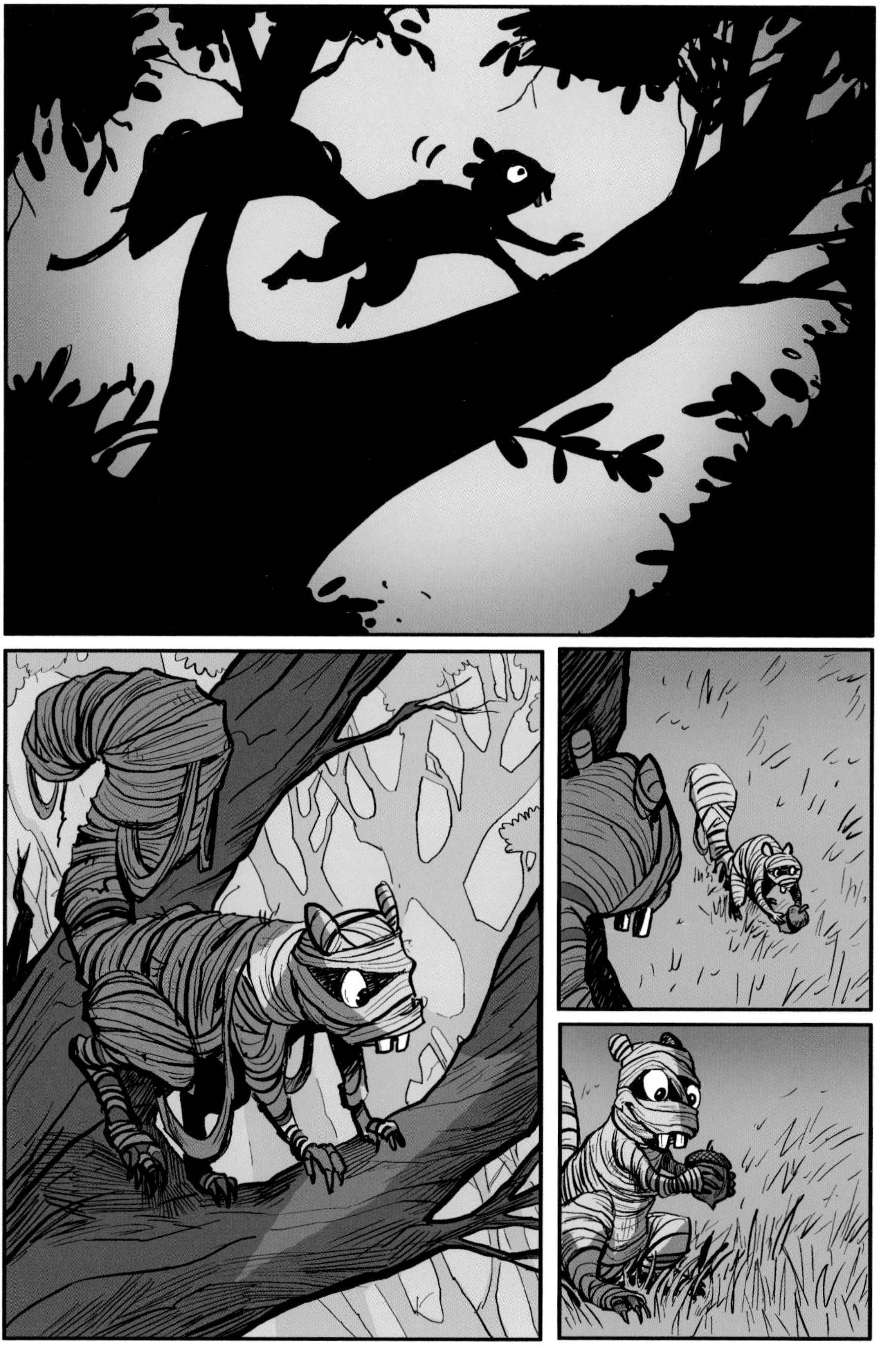

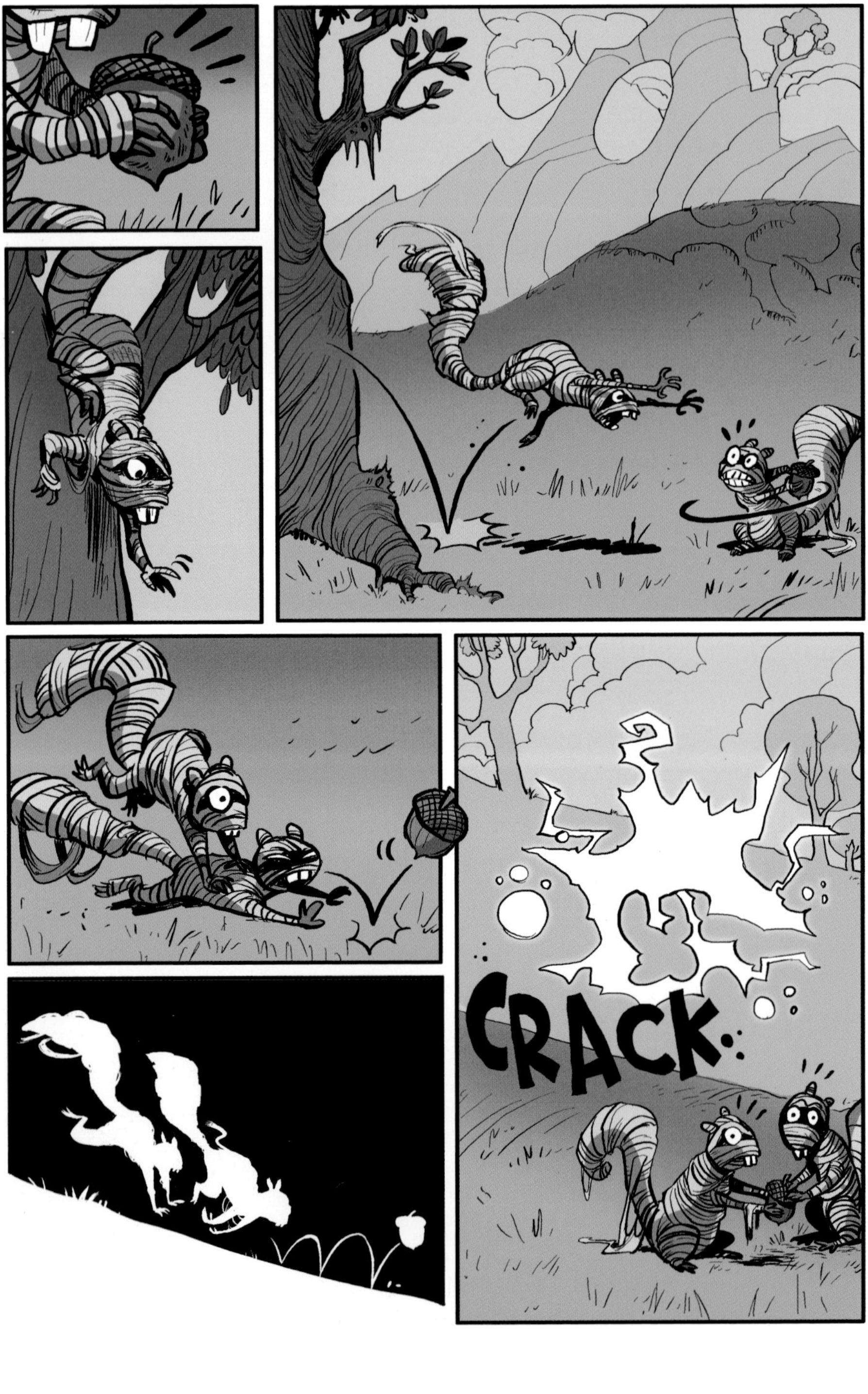
CRACK

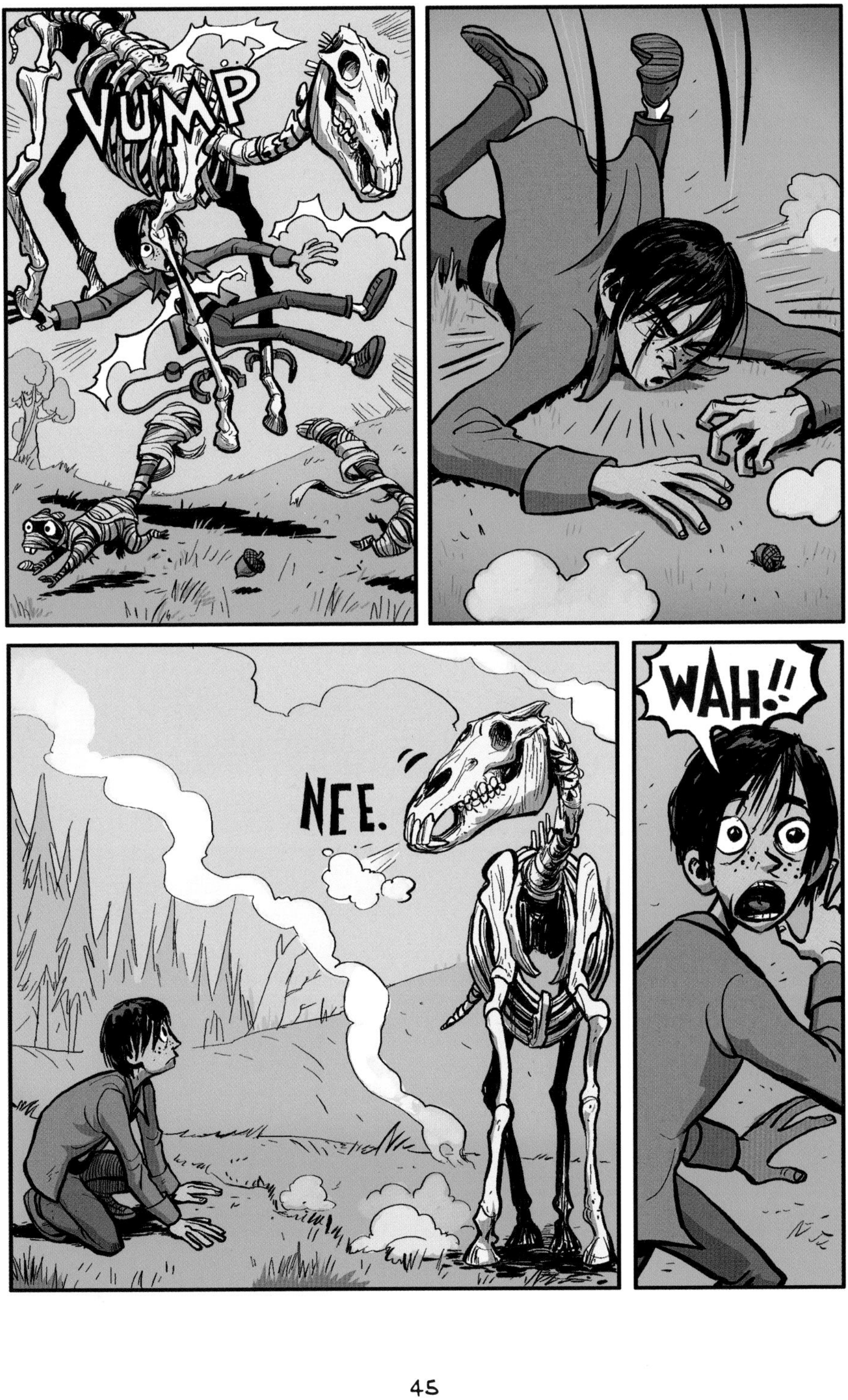
VUMP
NEE.
WAH!!

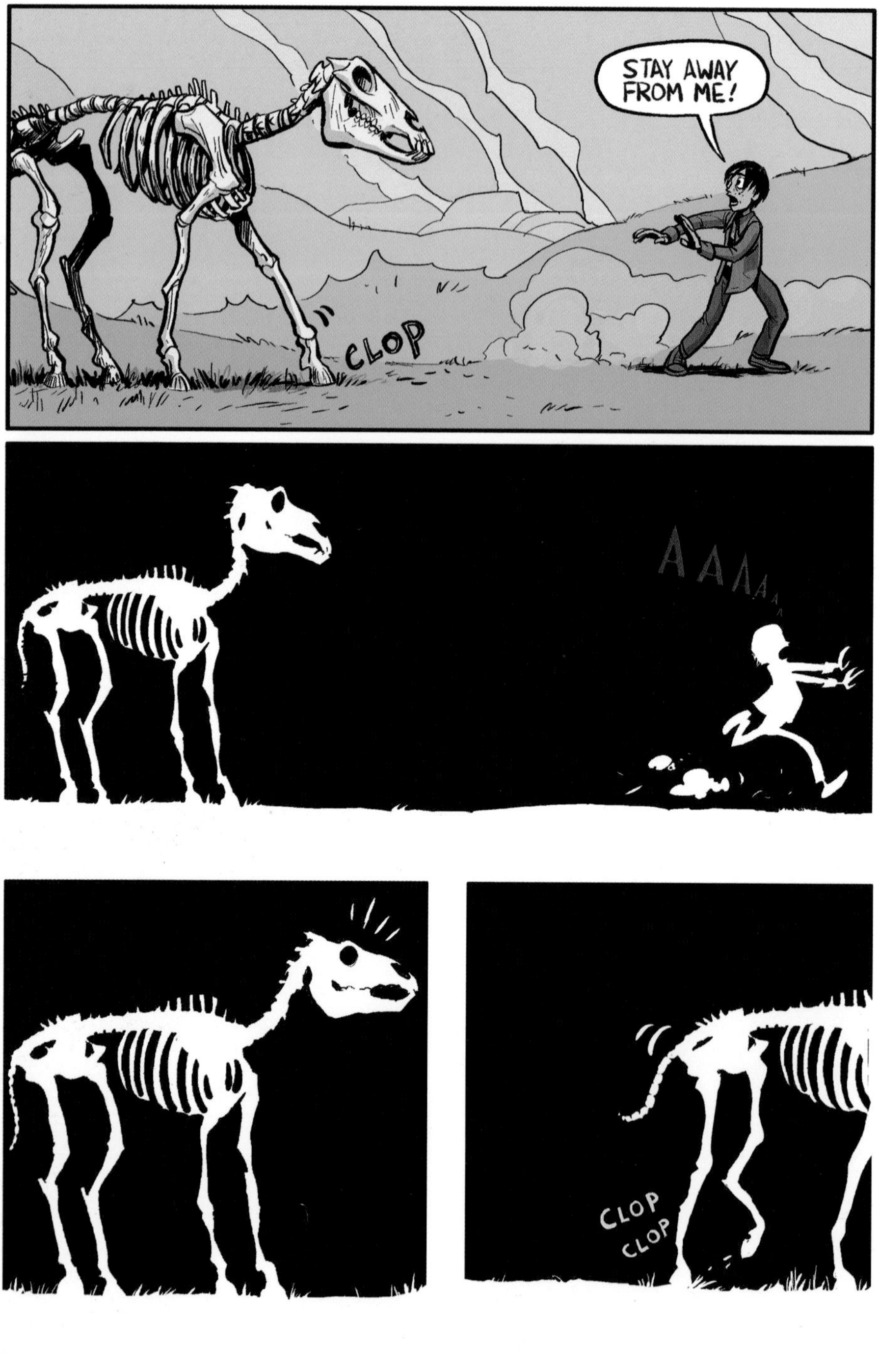
STAY AWAY FROM ME!
CLOP
AAAAAA
CLOP
CLOP

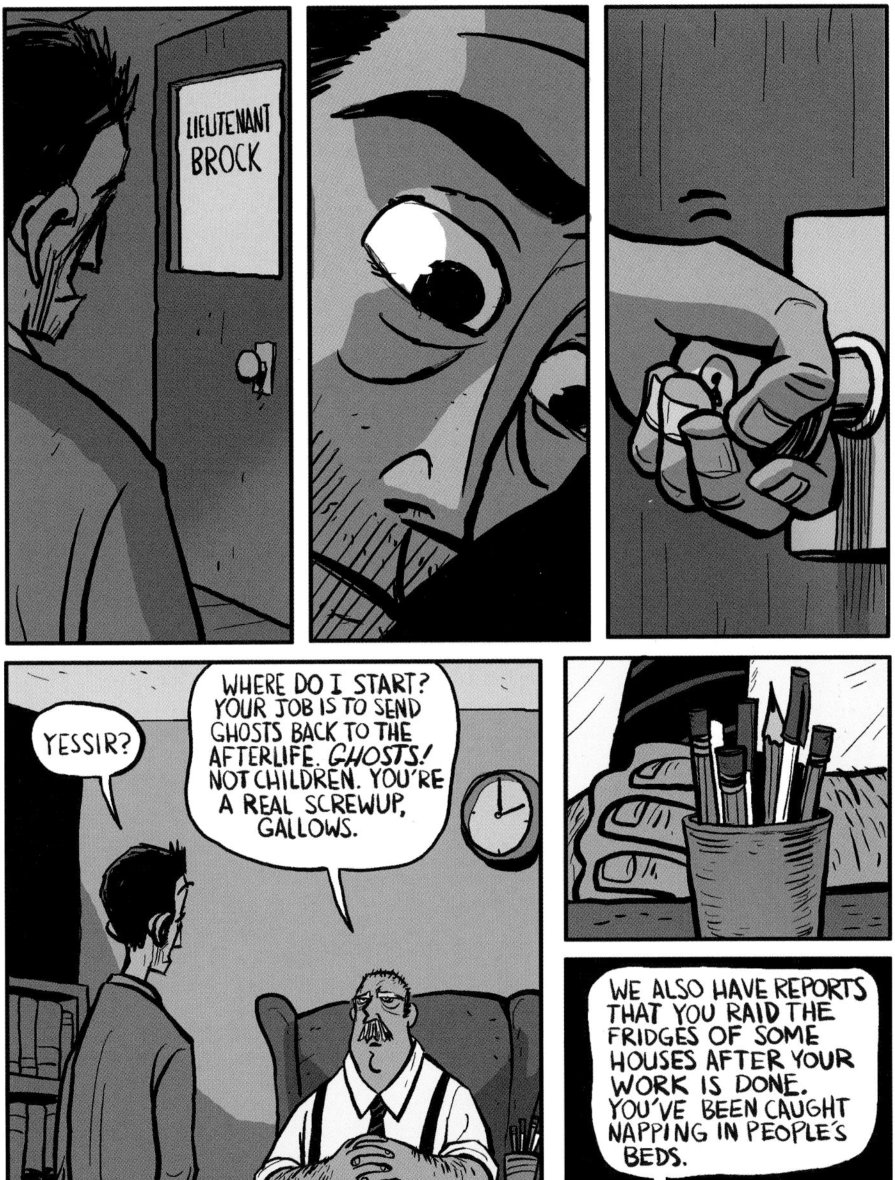
LIEUTENANT BROCK
YESSIR?
WHERE DO I START? YOUR JOB IS TO SEND GHOSTS BACK TO THE AFTERLIFE. *GHOSTS!* NOT CHILDREN. YOU'RE A REAL SCREWUP, GALLOWS.
WE ALSO HAVE REPORTS THAT YOU RAID THE FRIDGES OF SOME HOUSES AFTER YOUR WORK IS DONE. YOU'VE BEEN CAUGHT NAPPING IN PEOPLE'S BEDS.

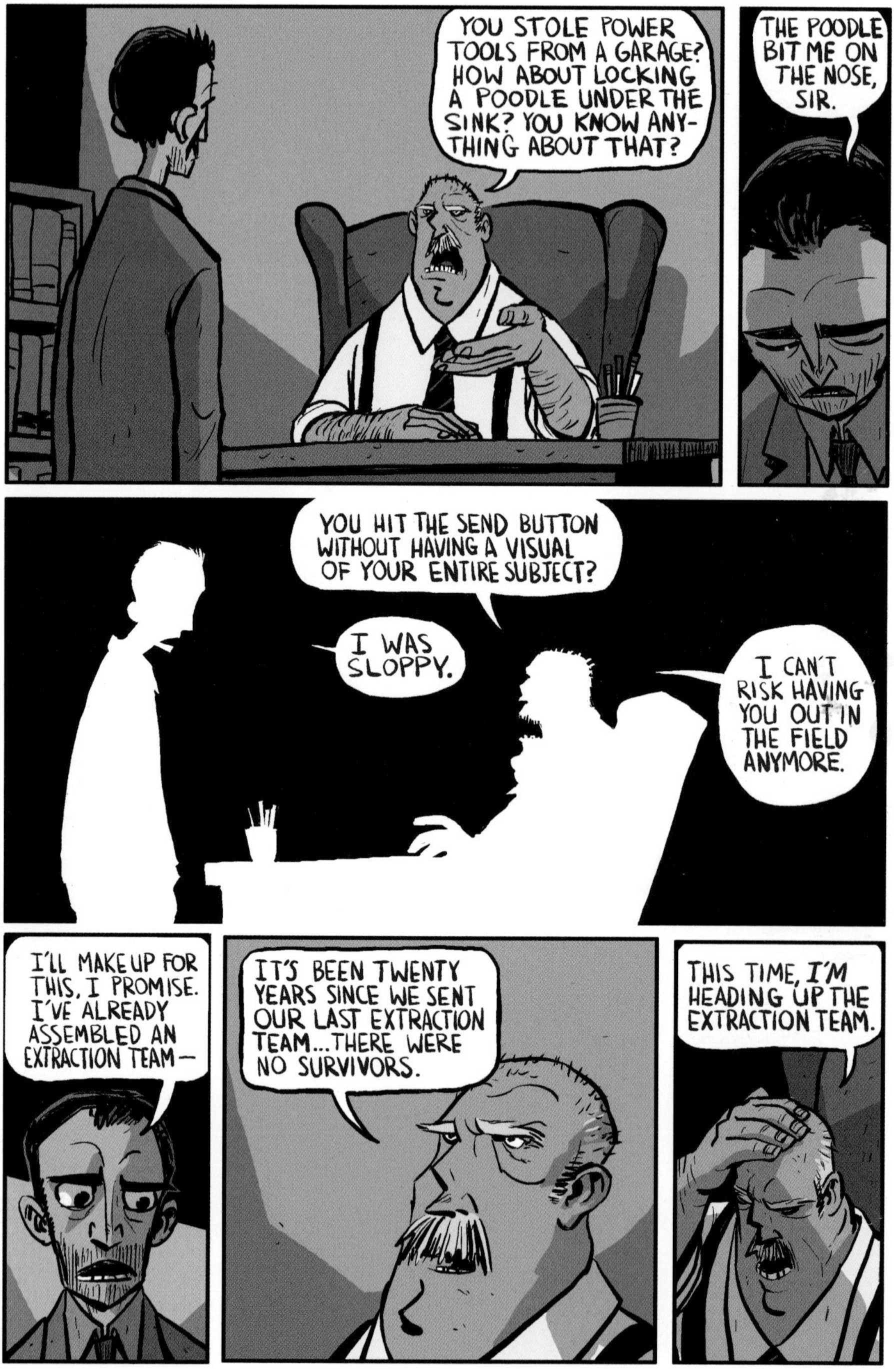
YOU STOLE POWER TOOLS FROM A GARAGE? HOW ABOUT LOCKING A POODLE UNDER THE SINK? YOU KNOW ANYTHING ABOUT THAT?
THE POODLE BIT ME ON THE NOSE, SIR.
YOU HIT THE SEND BUTTON WITHOUT HAVING A VISUAL OF YOUR ENTIRE SUBJECT?
I WAS SLOPPY.
I CAN'T RISK HAVING YOU OUT IN THE FIELD ANYMORE.
I'LL MAKE UP FOR THIS, I PROMISE. I'VE ALREADY ASSEMBLED AN EXTRACTION TEAM—
IT'S BEEN TWENTY YEARS SINCE WE SENT OUR LAST EXTRACTION TEAM...THERE WERE NO SURVIVORS.
THIS TIME, *I'M* HEADING UP THE EXTRACTION TEAM.

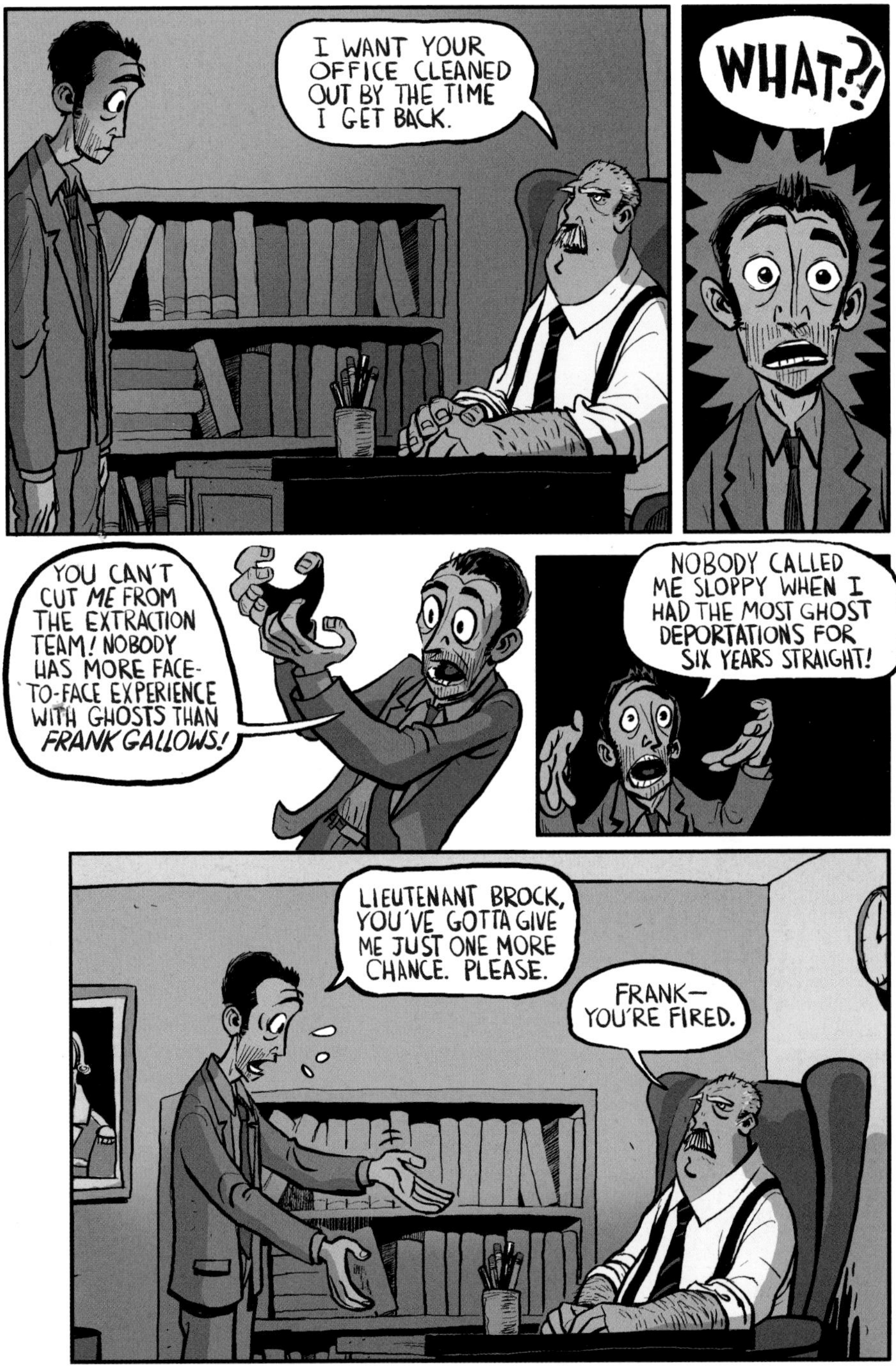
I WANT YOUR OFFICE CLEANED OUT BY THE TIME I GET BACK.
WHAT?!
YOU CAN'T CUT *ME* FROM THE EXTRACTION TEAM! NOBODY HAS MORE FACE-TO-FACE EXPERIENCE WITH GHOSTS THAN *FRANK GALLOWS!*
NOBODY CALLED ME SLOPPY WHEN I HAD THE MOST GHOST DEPORTATIONS FOR SIX YEARS STRAIGHT!
LIEUTENANT BROCK, YOU'VE GOTTA GIVE ME JUST ONE MORE CHANCE. PLEASE.
FRANK— YOU'RE FIRED.

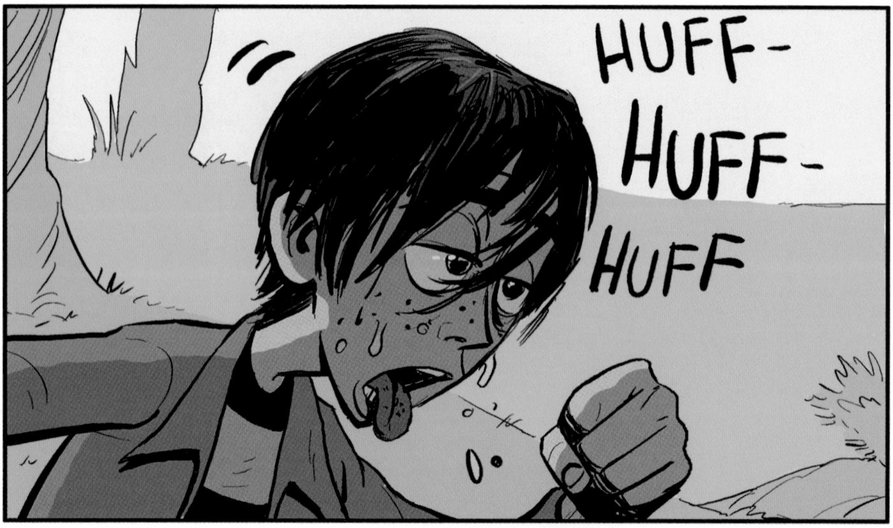
HUFF-
HUFF-
HUFF

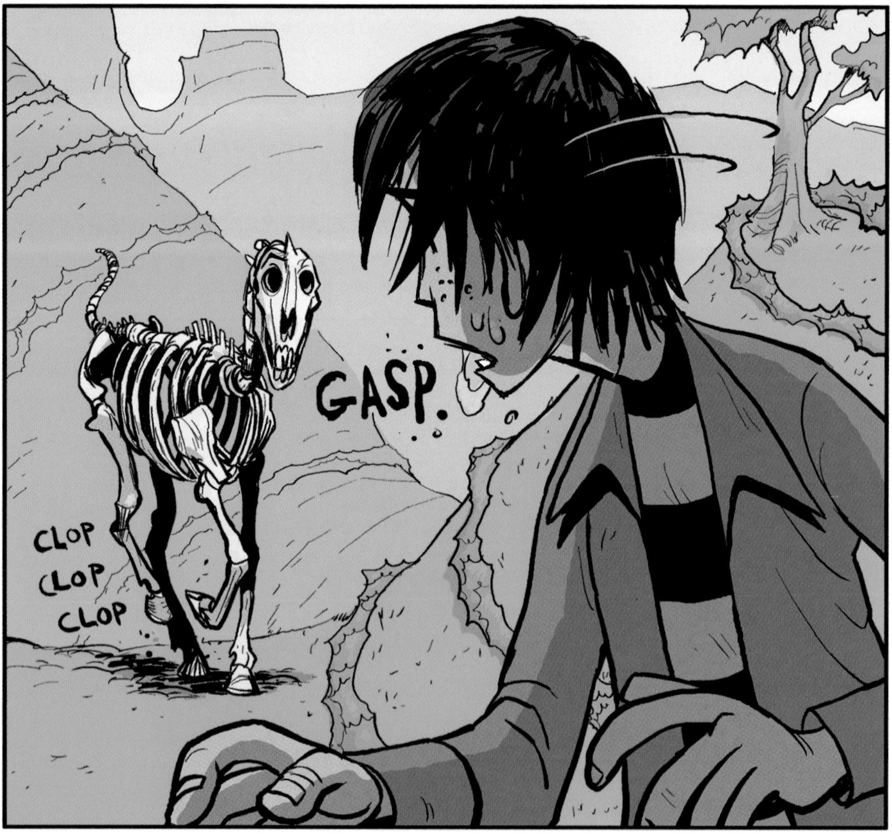
GASP.
CLOP
CLOP
CLOP

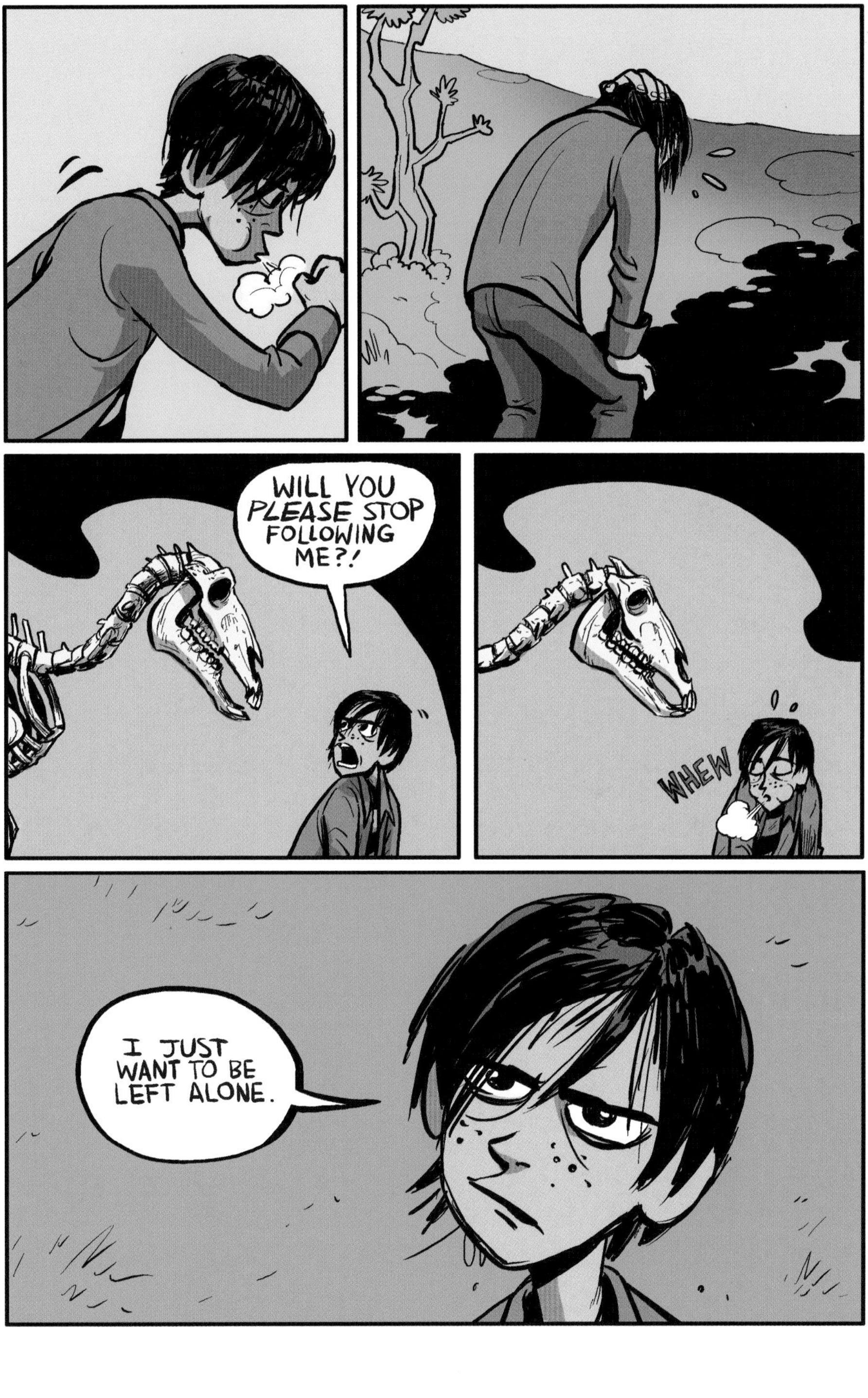
WILL YOU PLEASE STOP FOLLOWING ME?!
WHEW
I JUST WANT TO BE LEFT ALONE.

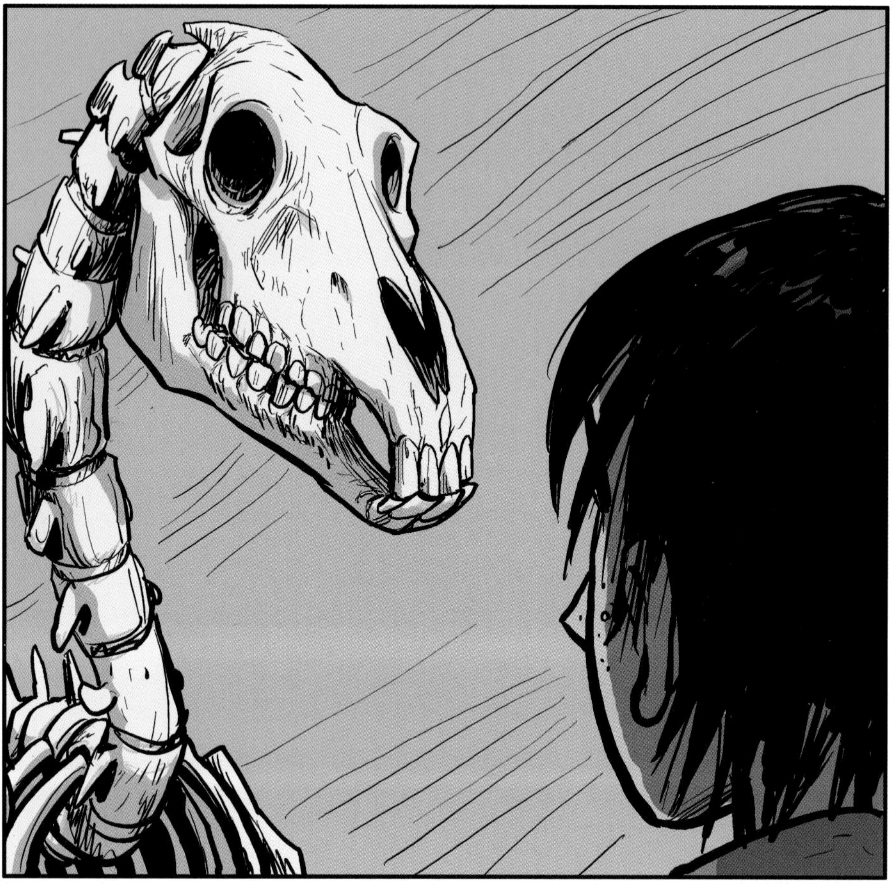

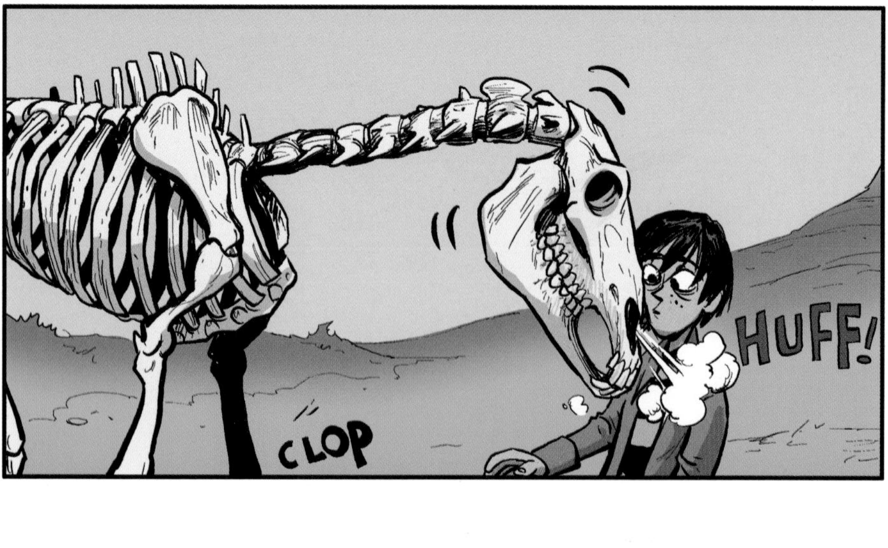
HUFF!
CLOP

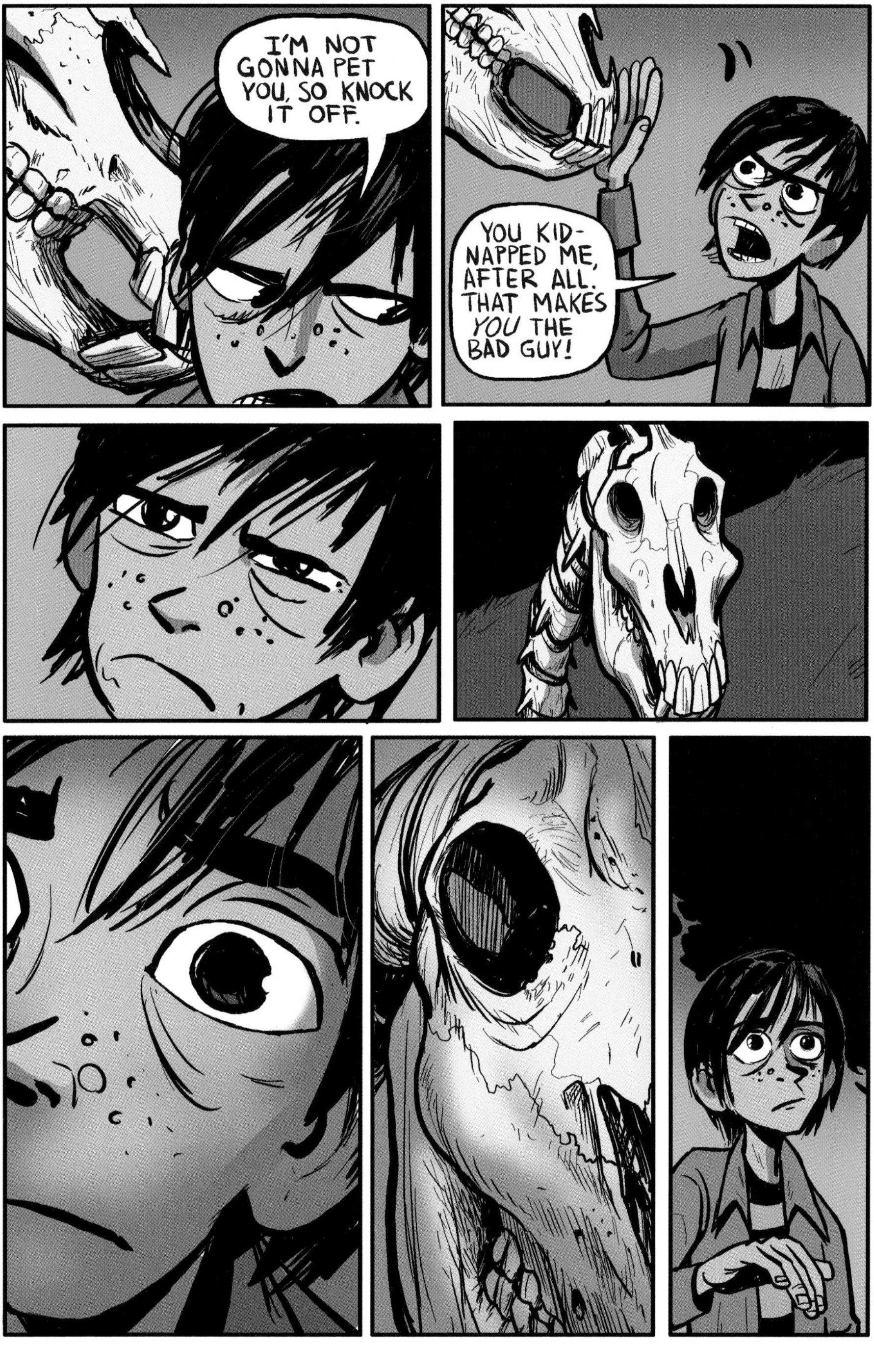
I'M NOT GONNA PET YOU, SO KNOCK IT OFF.
YOU KID-NAPPED ME, AFTER ALL. THAT MAKES *YOU* THE BAD GUY!

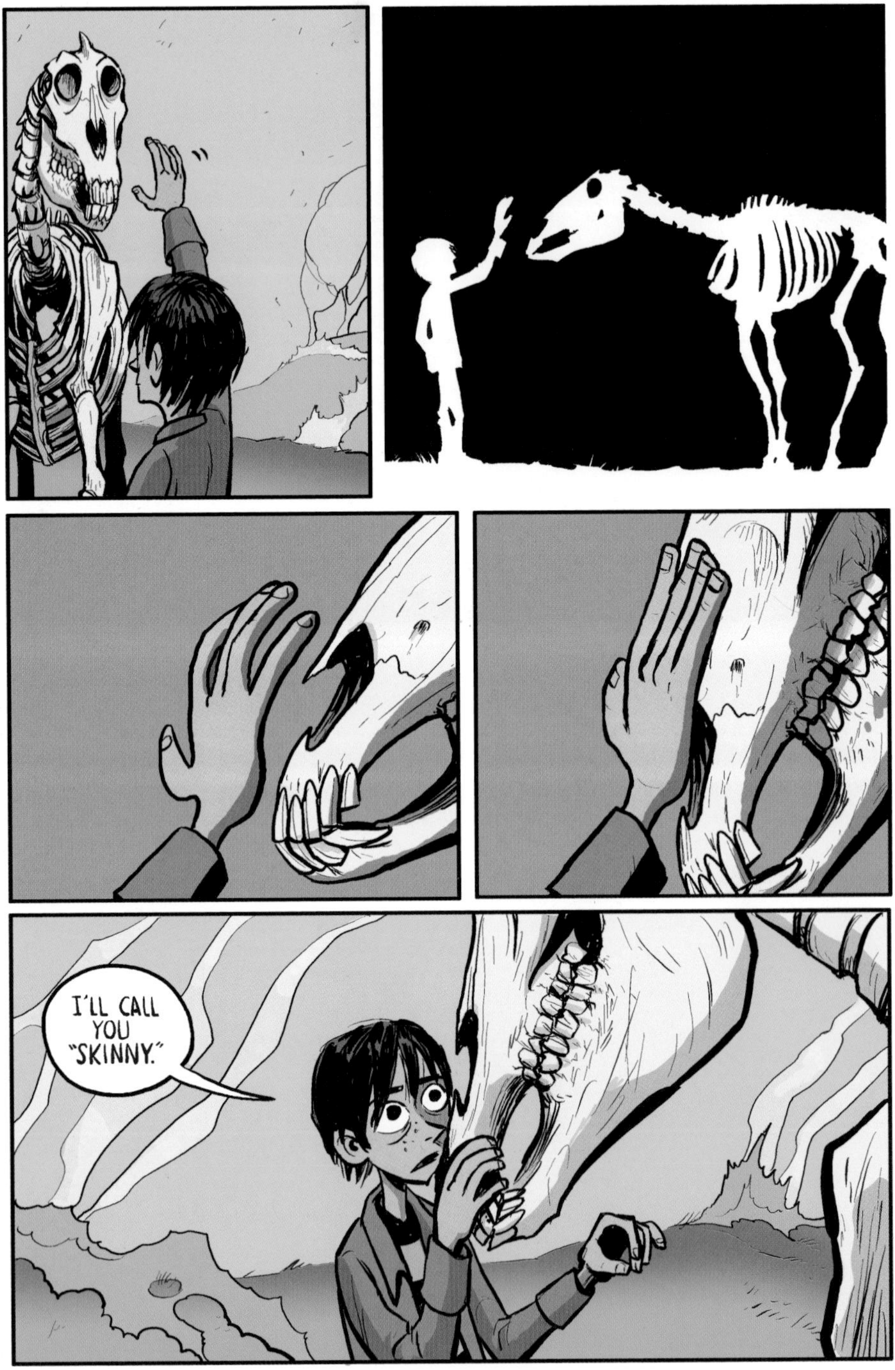
I'LL CALL YOU "SKINNY."

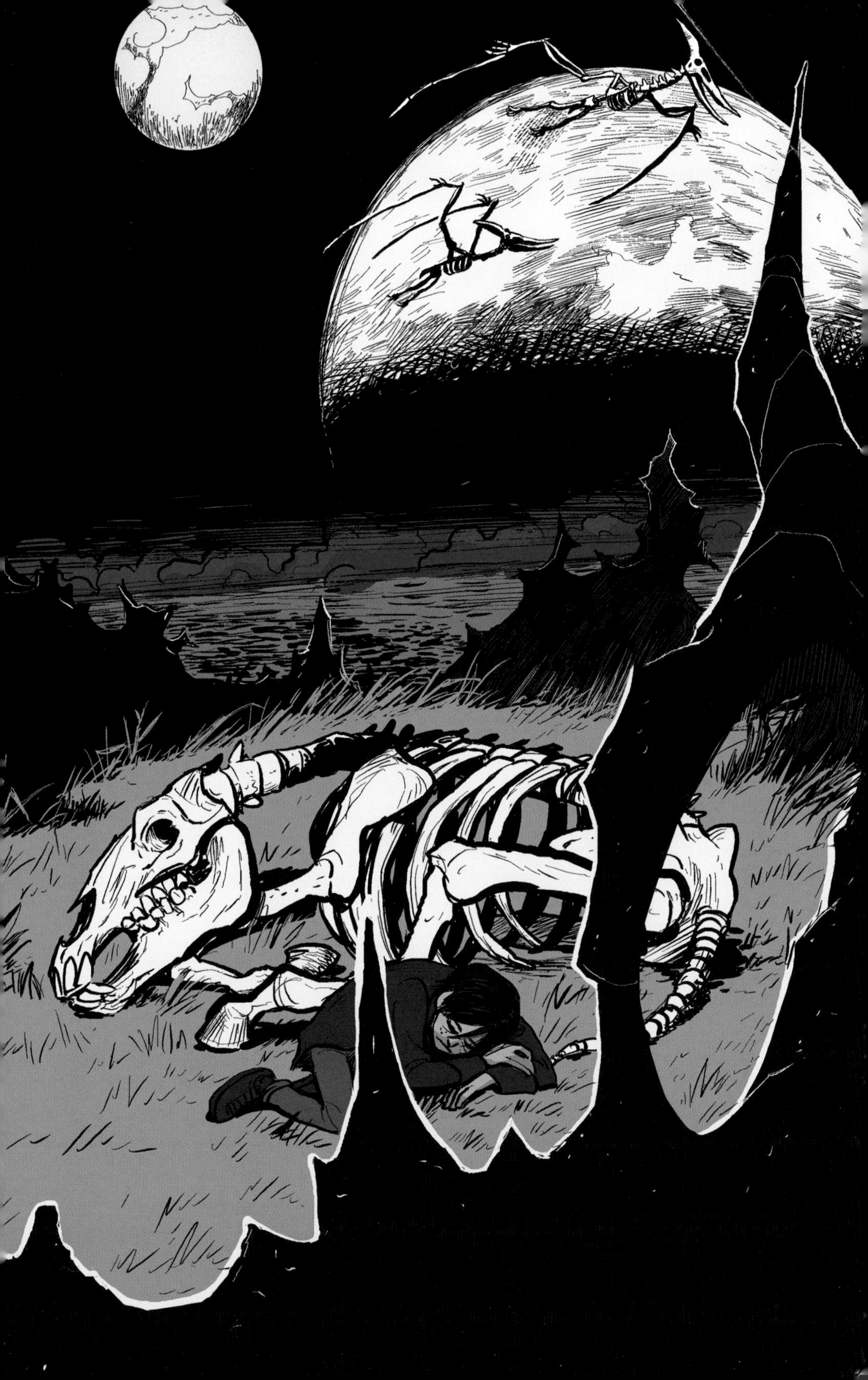

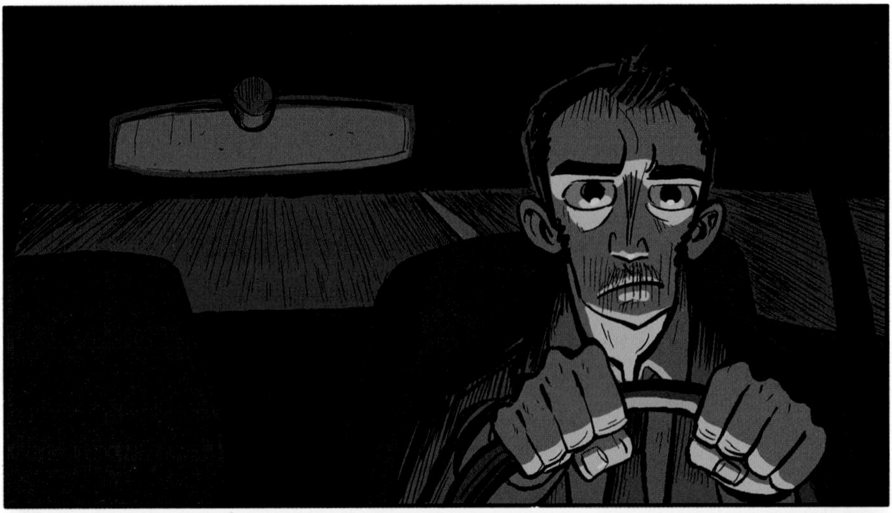

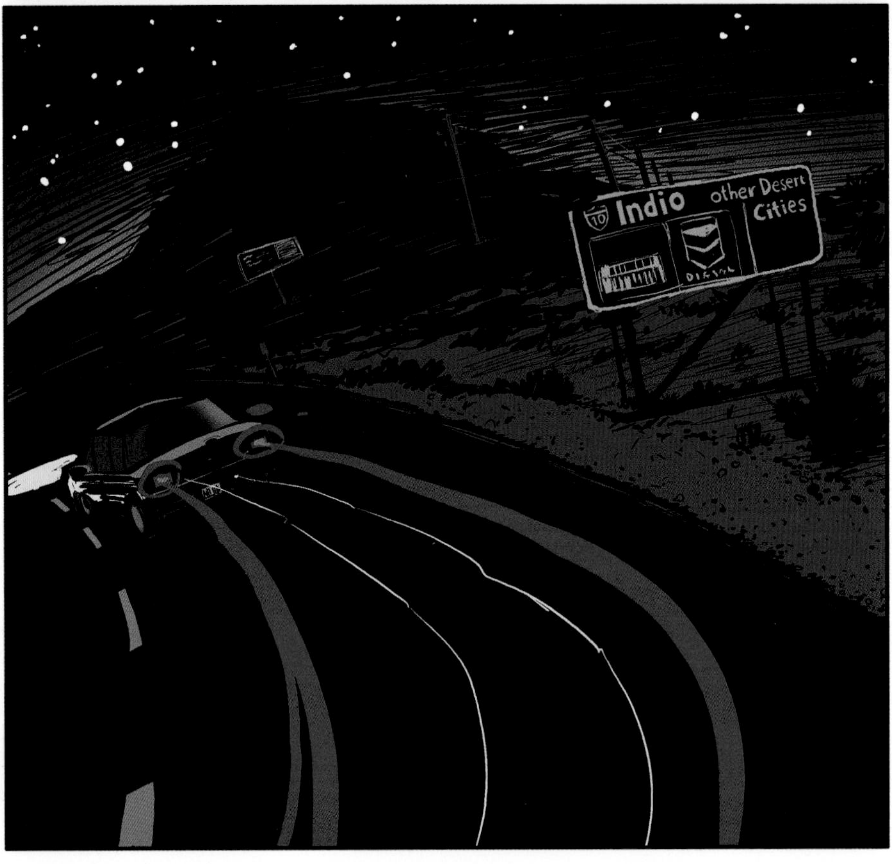
10 Indio other Desert Cities

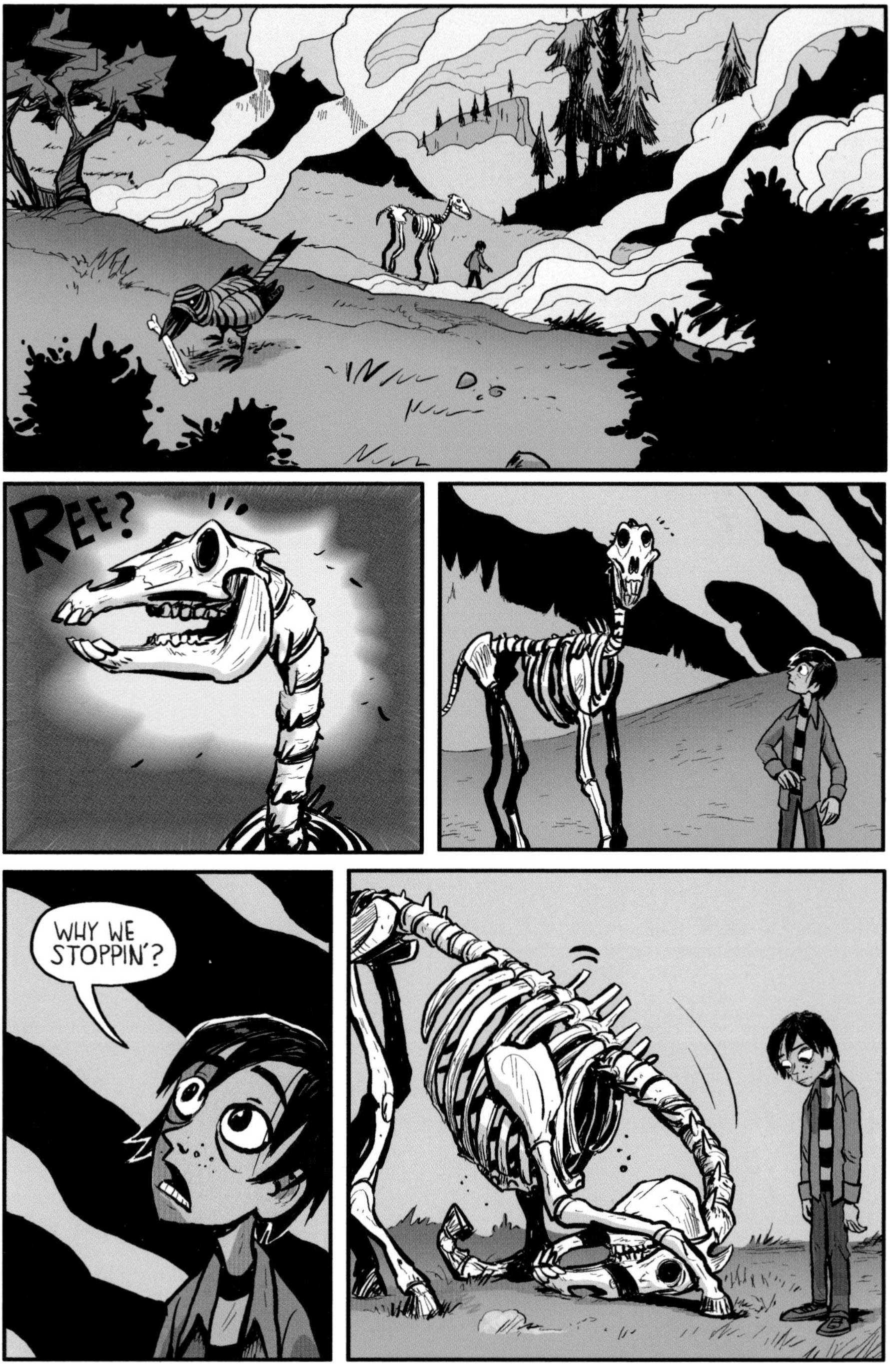
REE?
WHY WE STOPPIN'?

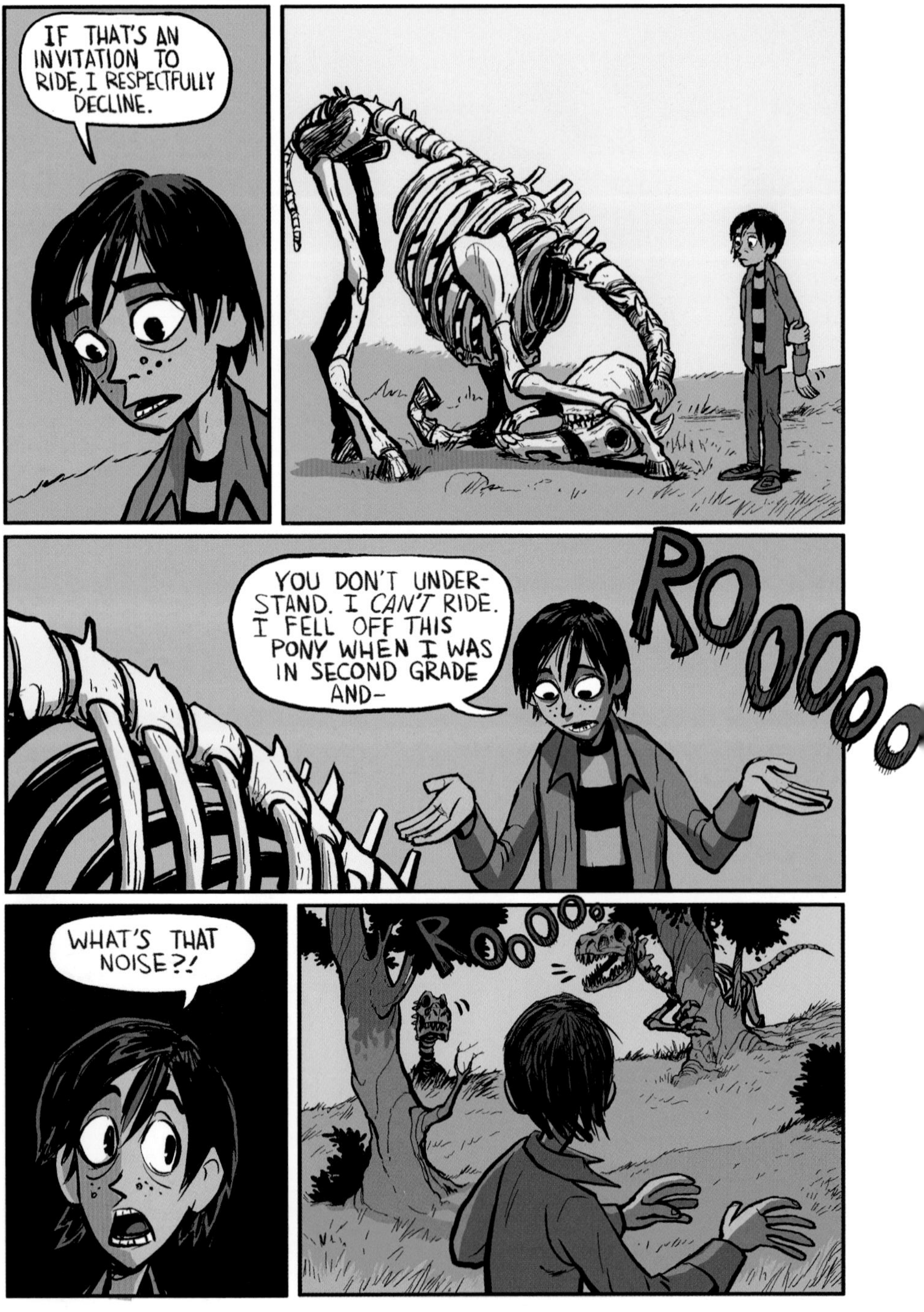
IF THAT'S AN INVITATION TO RIDE, I RESPECTFULLY DECLINE.
YOU DON'T UNDER-STAND. I *CAN'T* RIDE. I FELL OFF THIS PONY WHEN I WAS IN SECOND GRADE AND–
ROOOOO
WHAT'S THAT NOISE?!
ROOOOO

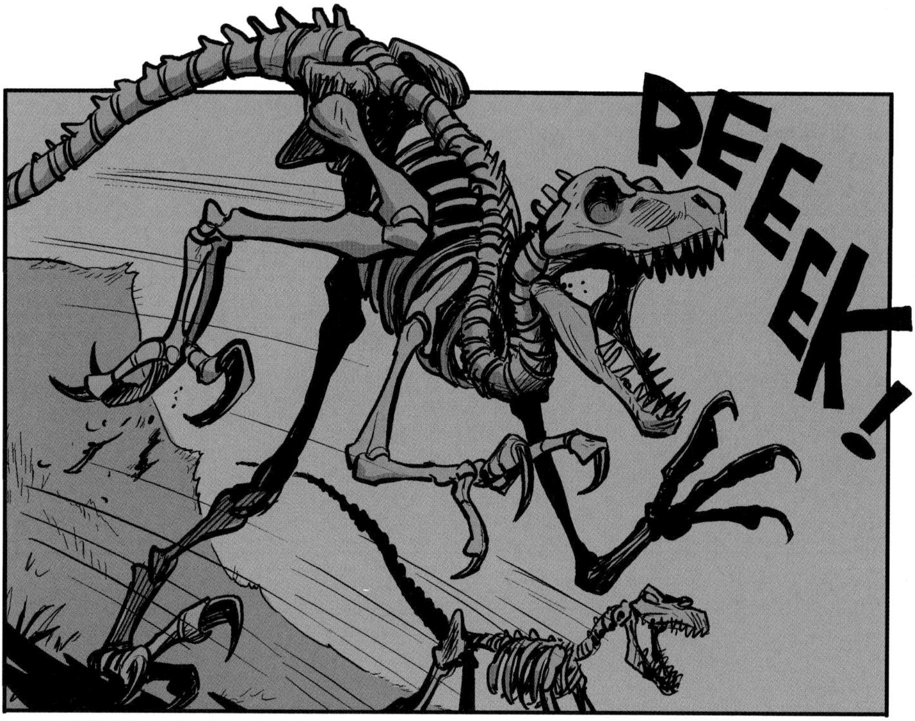
REEEK!

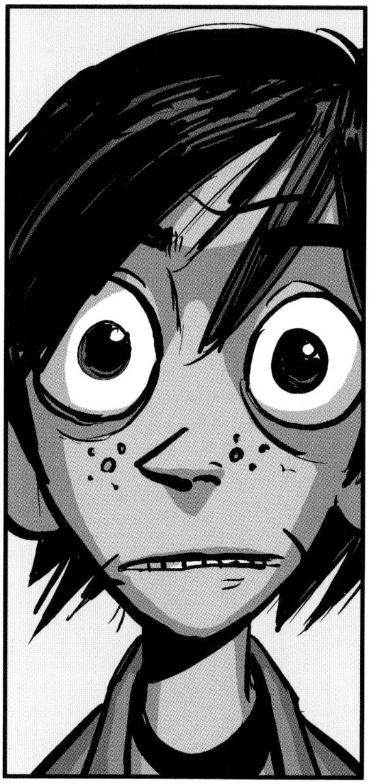

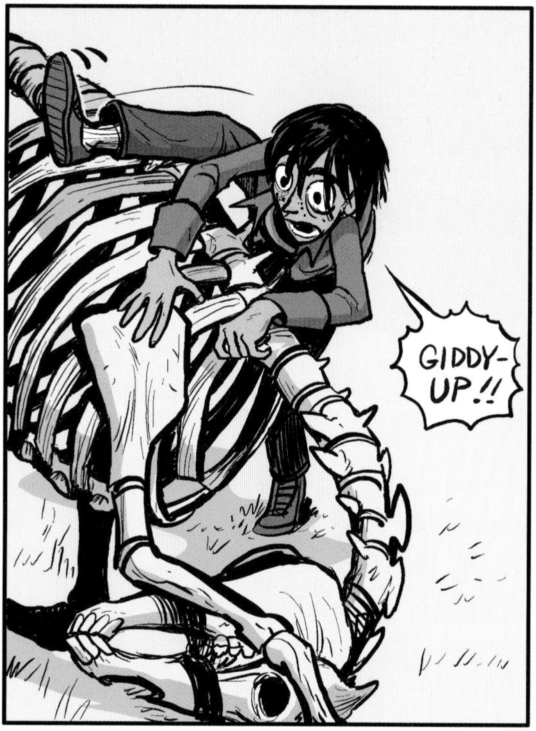
GIDDY-UP!!

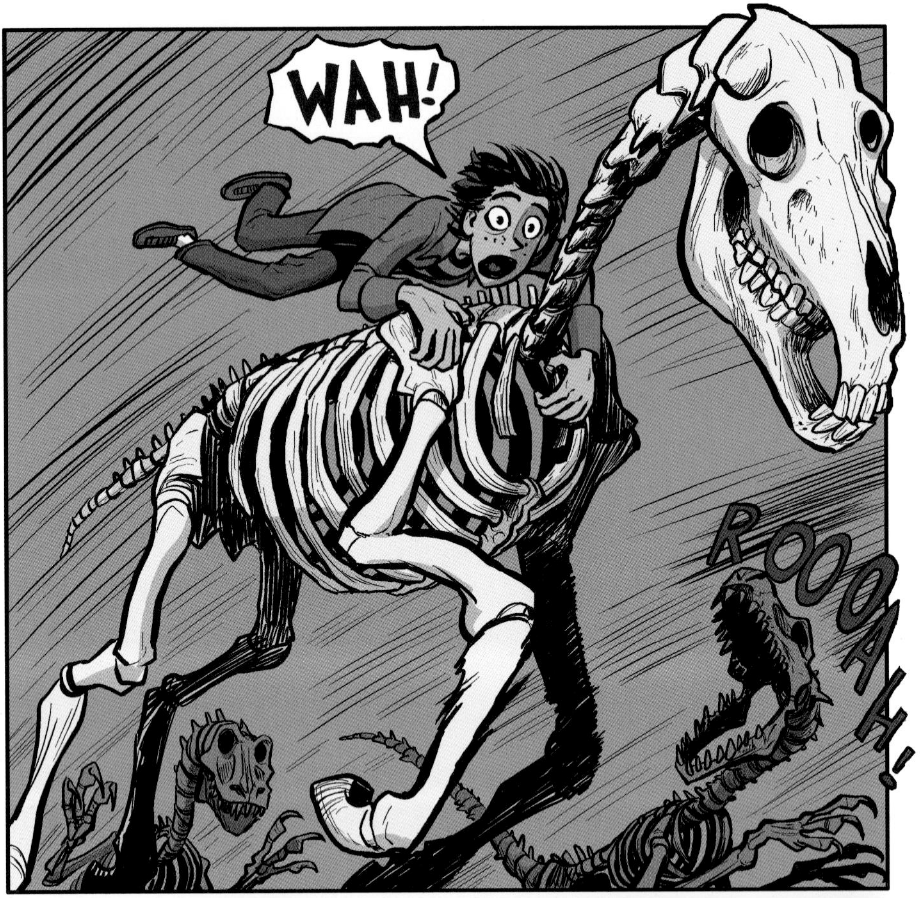
WAH!
ROOOAH!!

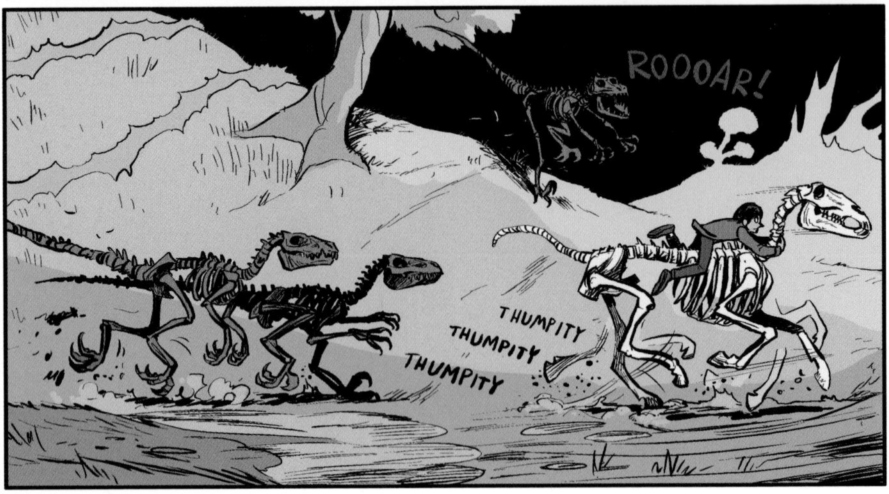
ROOOAR!
THUMPITY
THUMPITY
THUMPITY

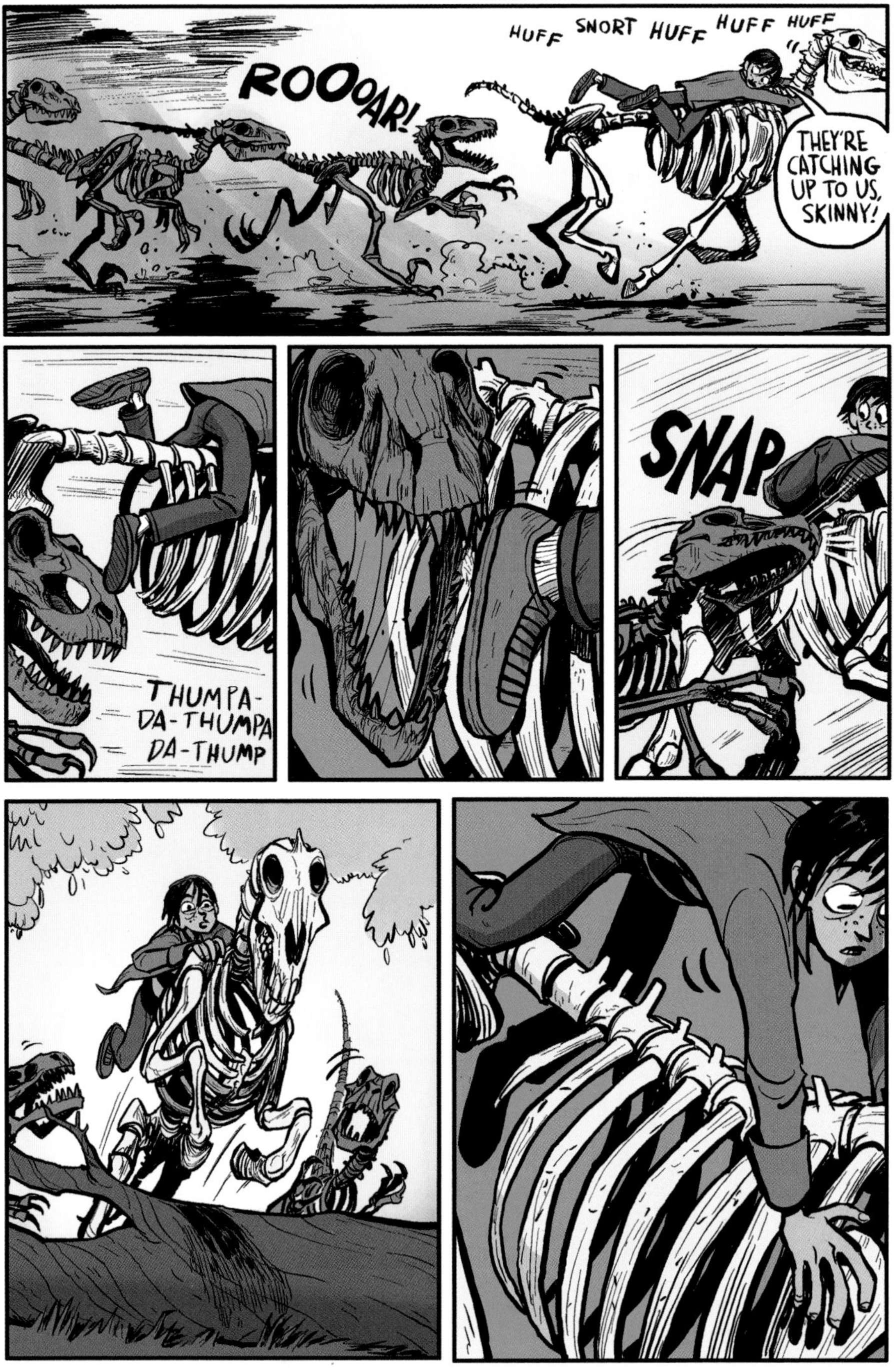
HUFF SNORT HUFF HUFF HUFF
ROOOAR!
THEY'RE CATCHING UP TO US, SKINNY!
THUMPA-DA-THUMPA DA-THUMP
SNAP

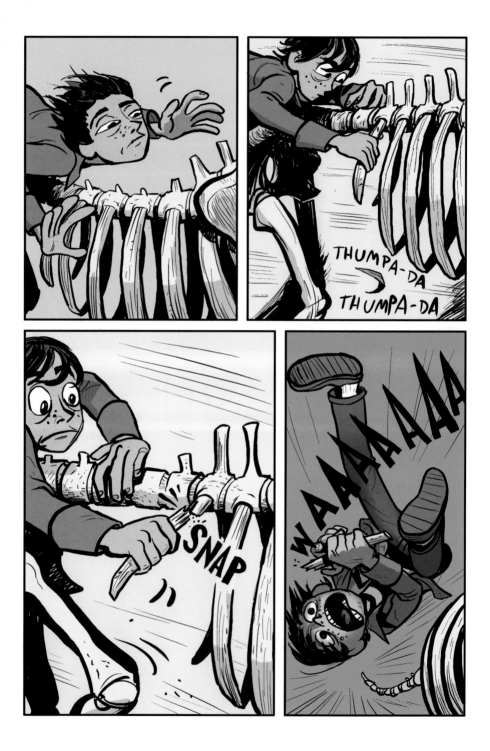

THUMPA-DA
THUMPA-DA

SNAP

WAAAAAAAA

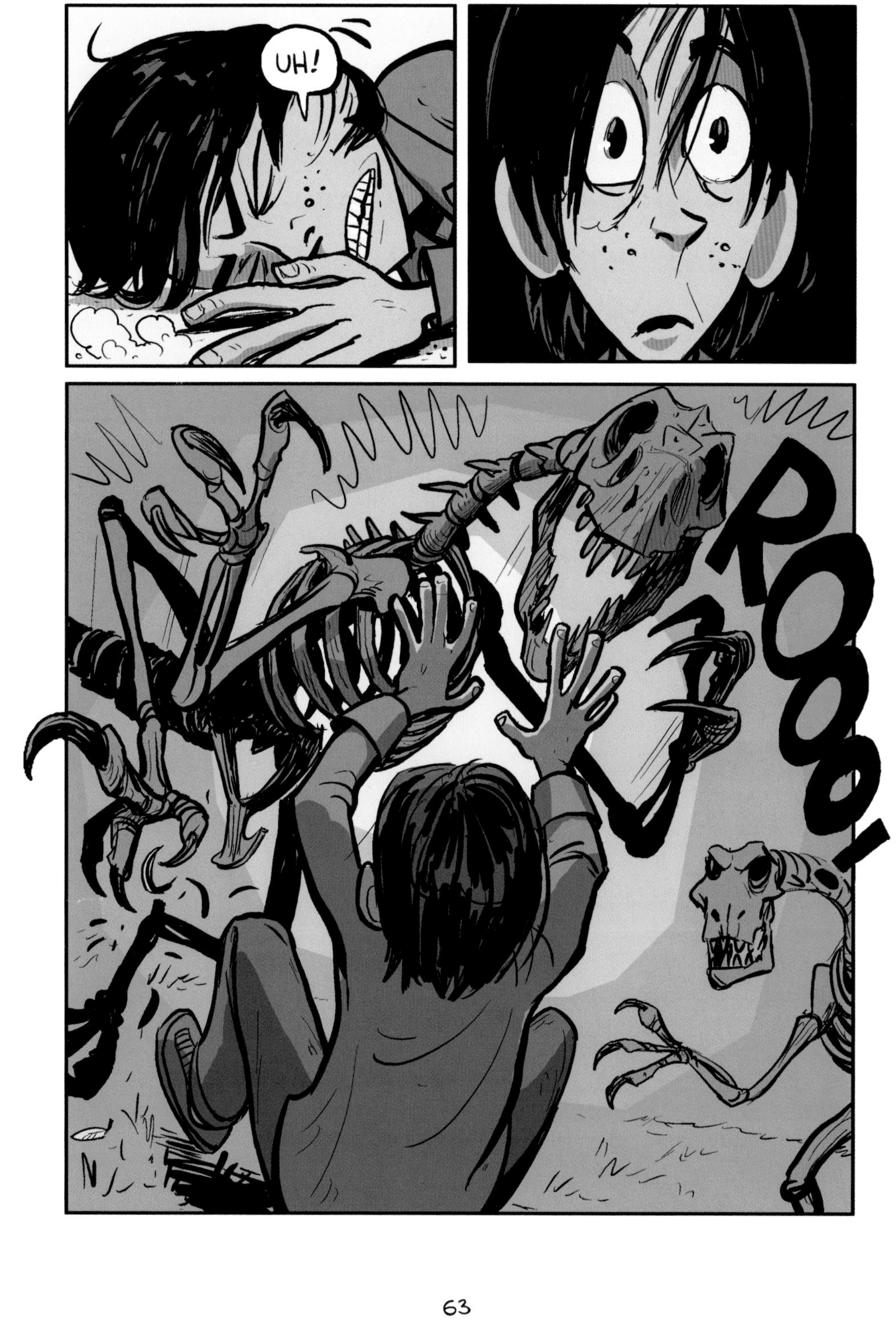
UH!
ROOO!

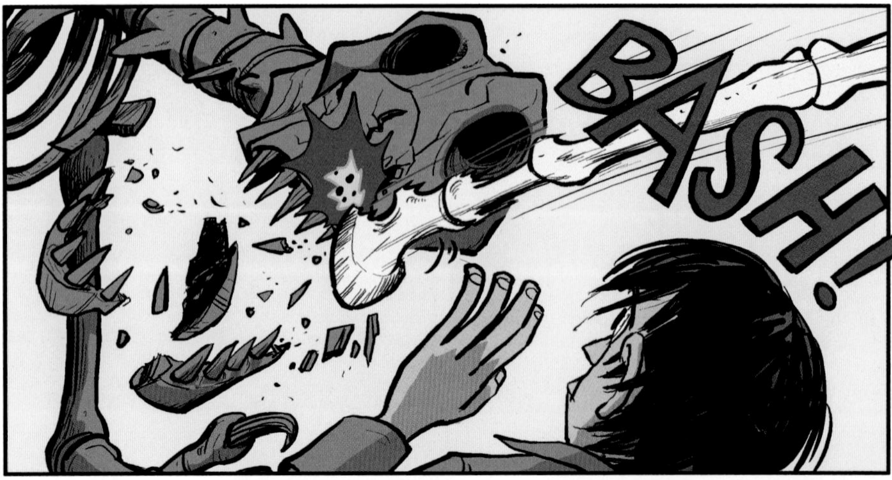
BASH!

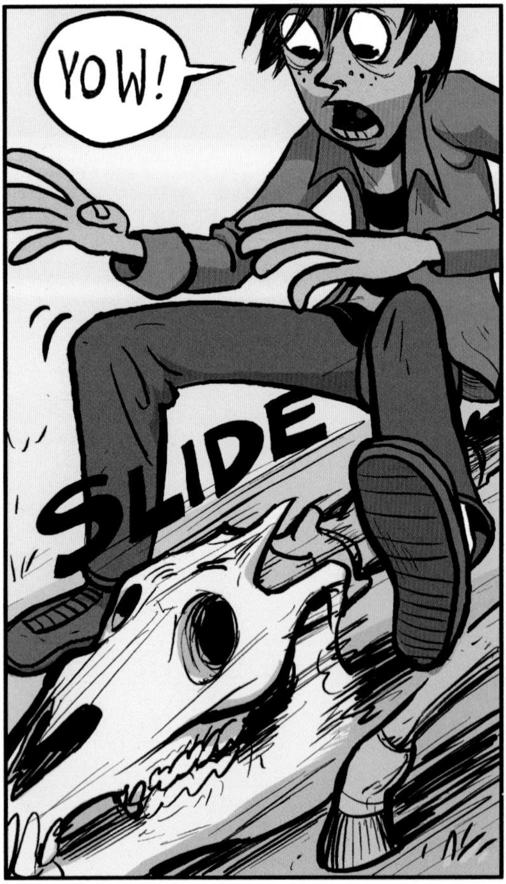
YOW!
SLIDE

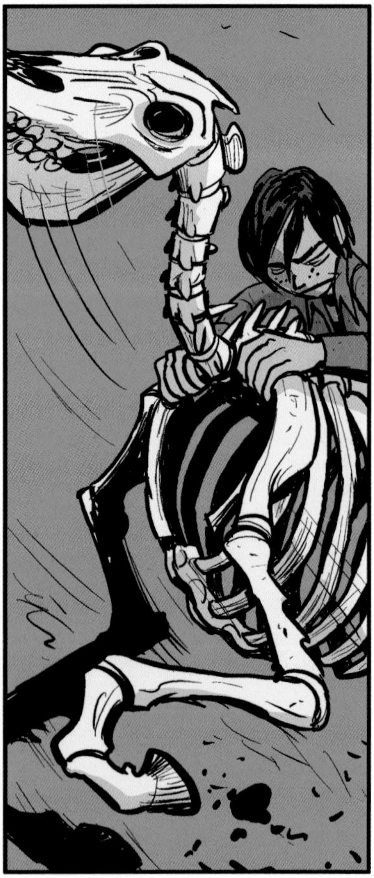

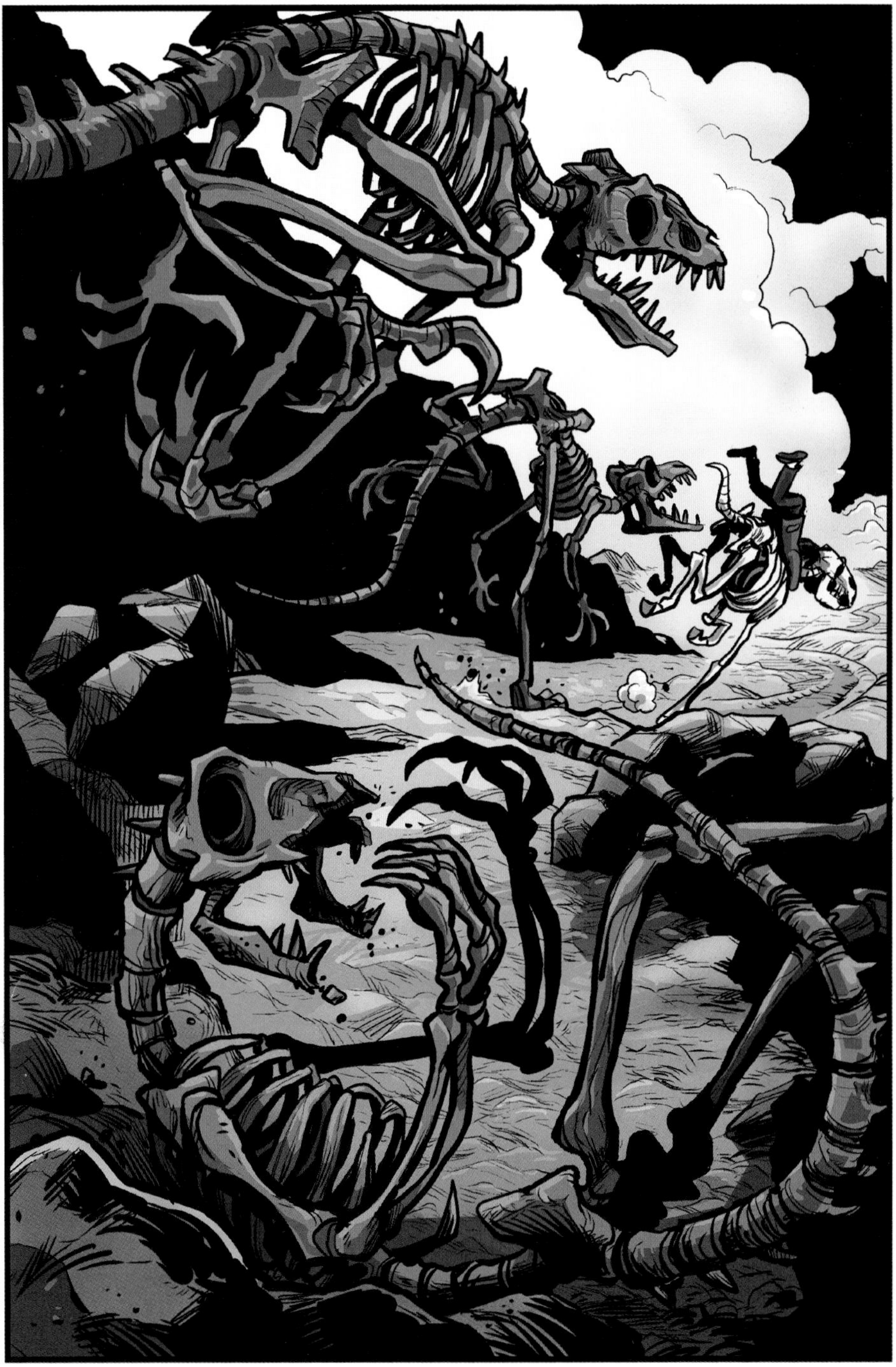

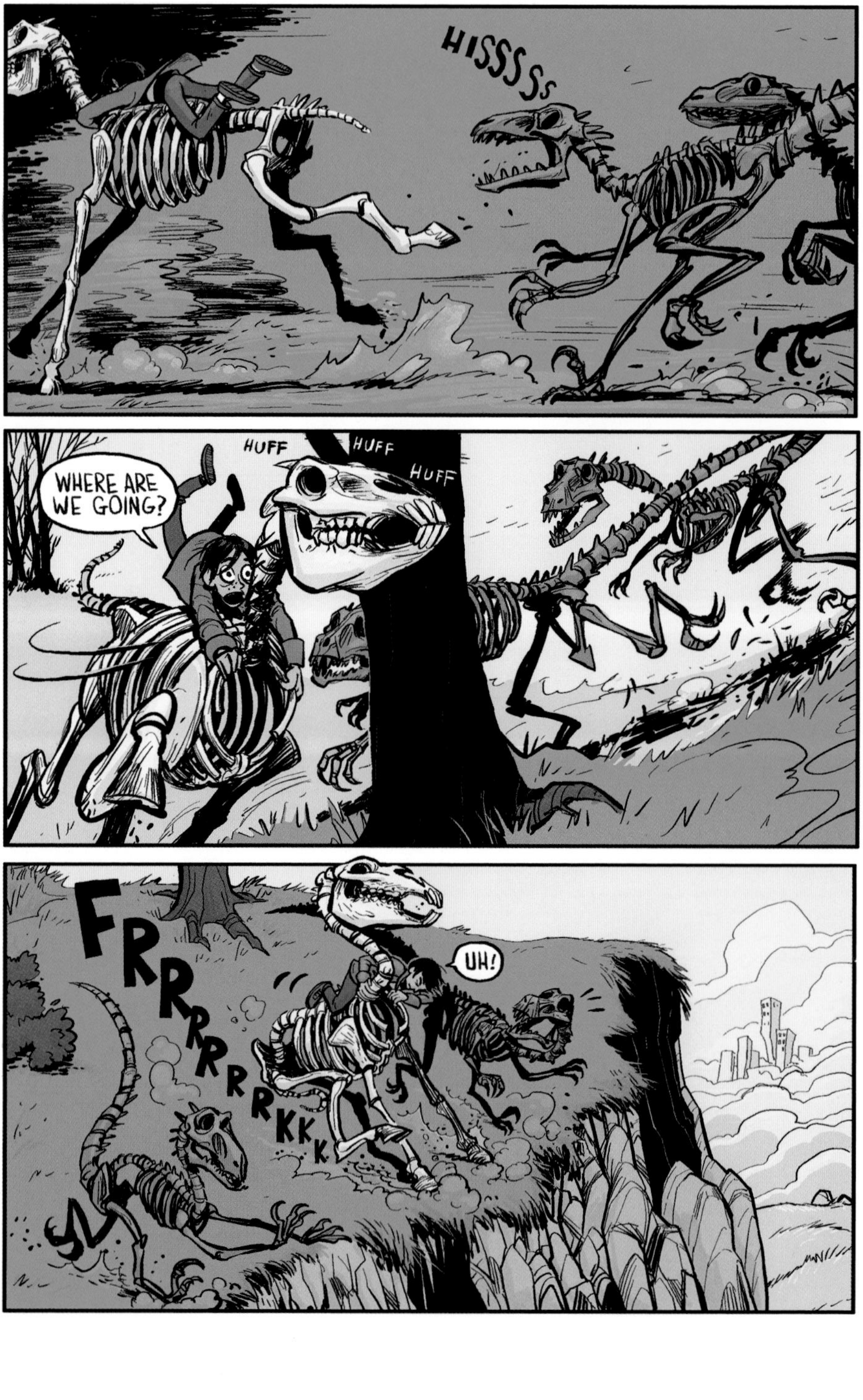
HISSSSs
HUFF
HUFF
HUFF
WHERE ARE WE GOING?
FRRRRRRRKKK
UH!

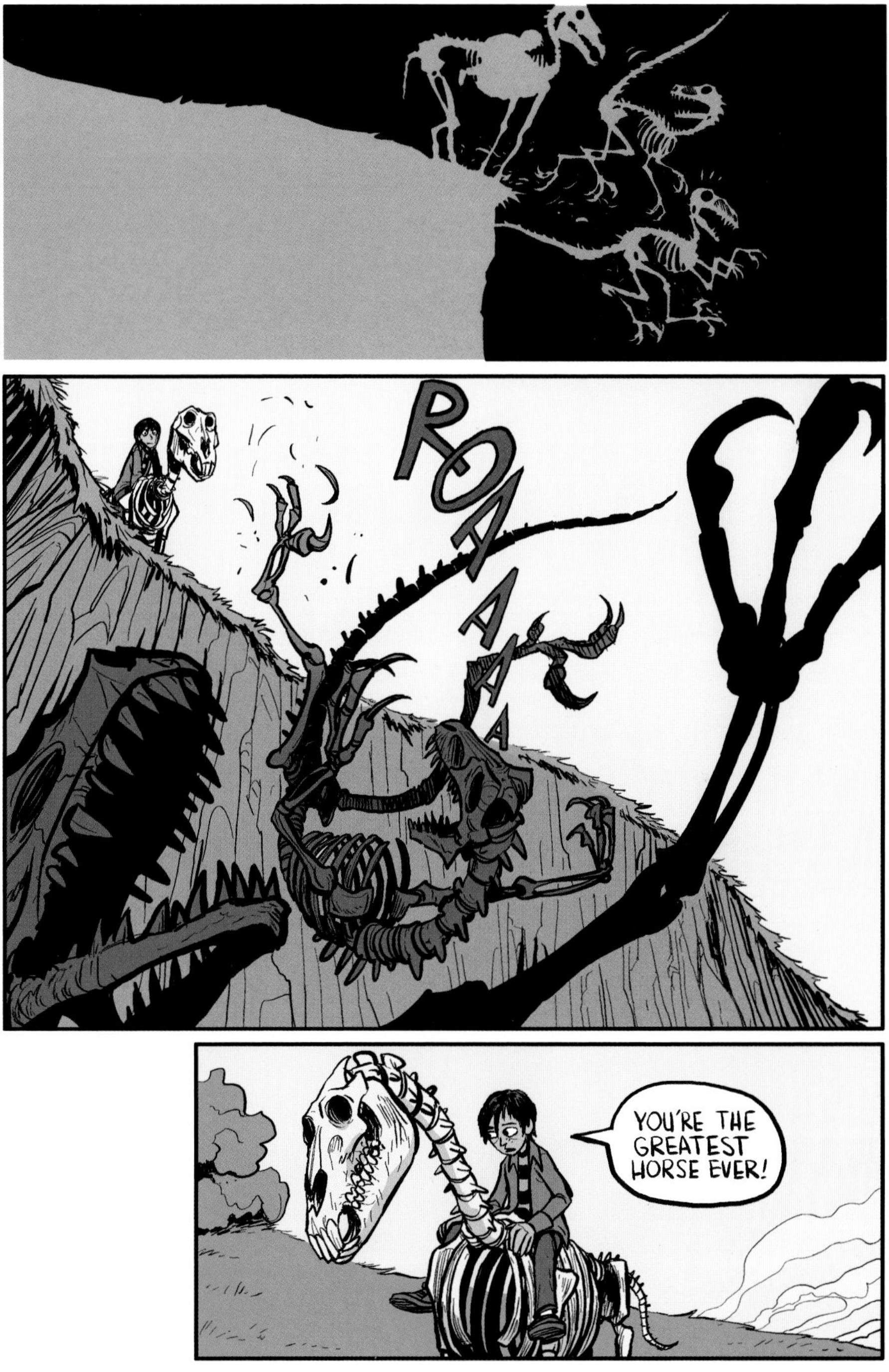
ROAAAAA
YOU'RE THE GREATEST HORSE EVER!

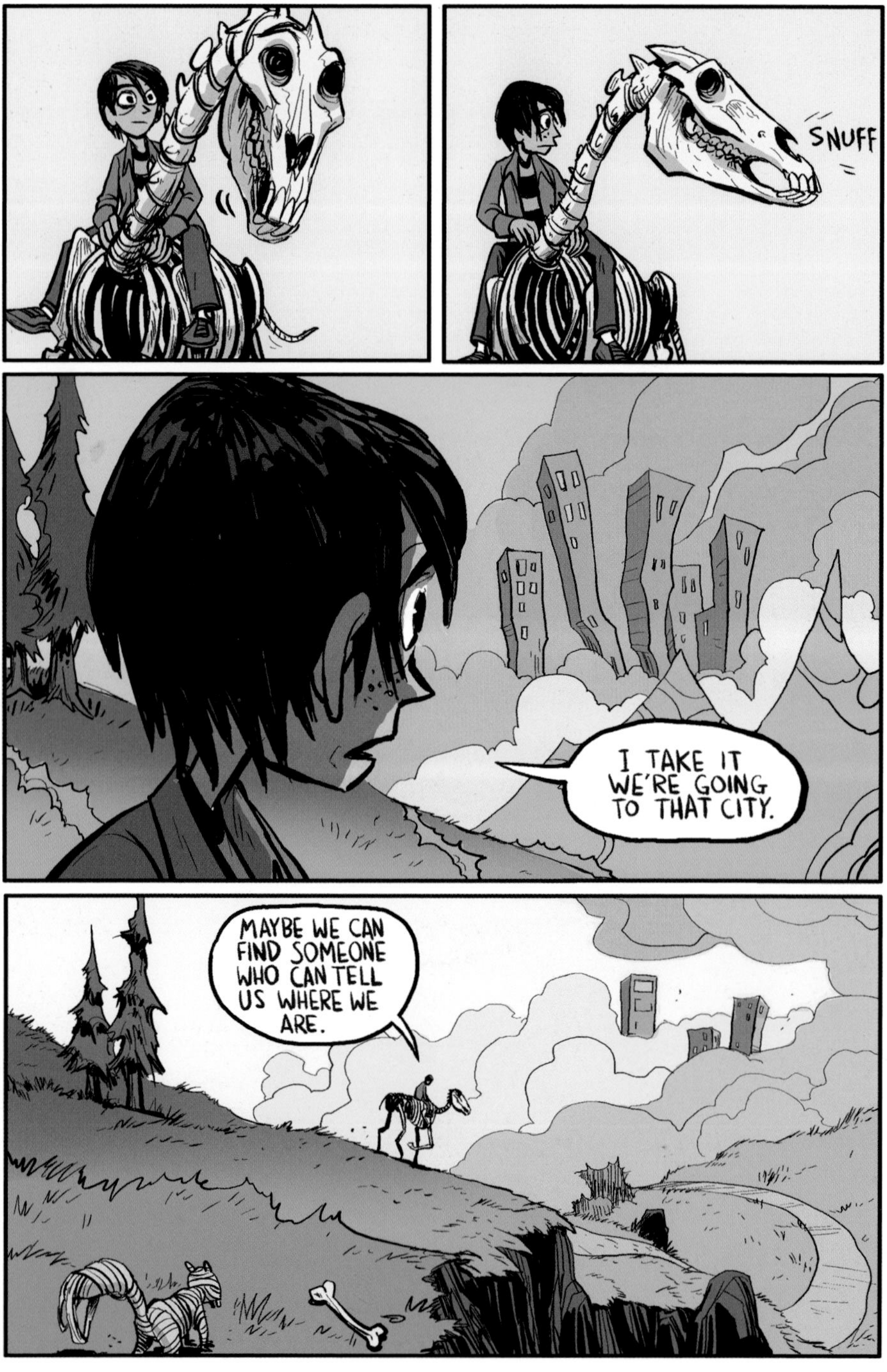
SNUFF
I TAKE IT WE'RE GOING TO THAT CITY.
MAYBE WE CAN FIND SOMEONE WHO CAN TELL US WHERE WE ARE.

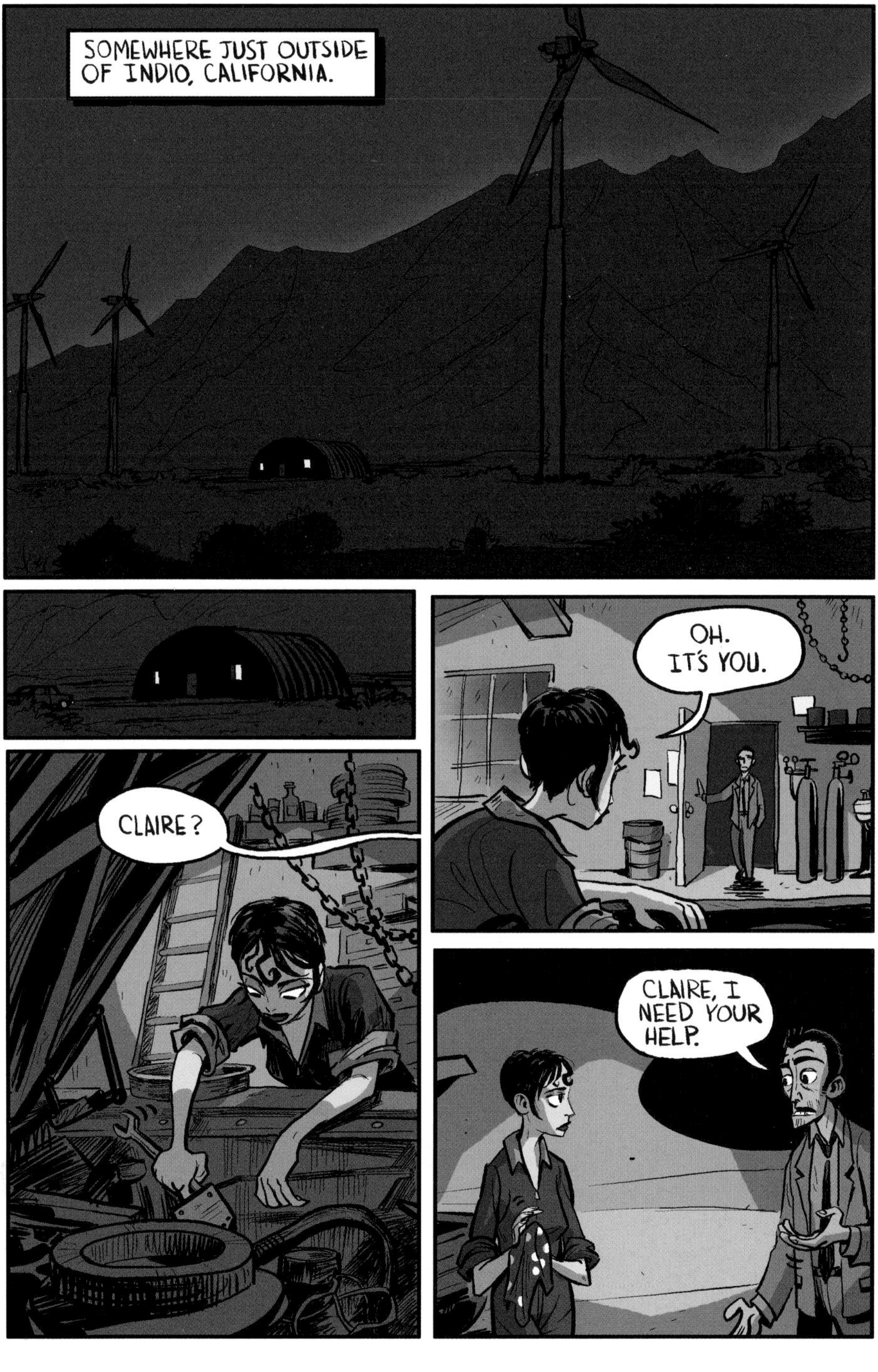
SOMEWHERE JUST OUTSIDE OF INDIO, CALIFORNIA.
CLAIRE?
OH. IT'S YOU.
CLAIRE, I NEED YOUR HELP.

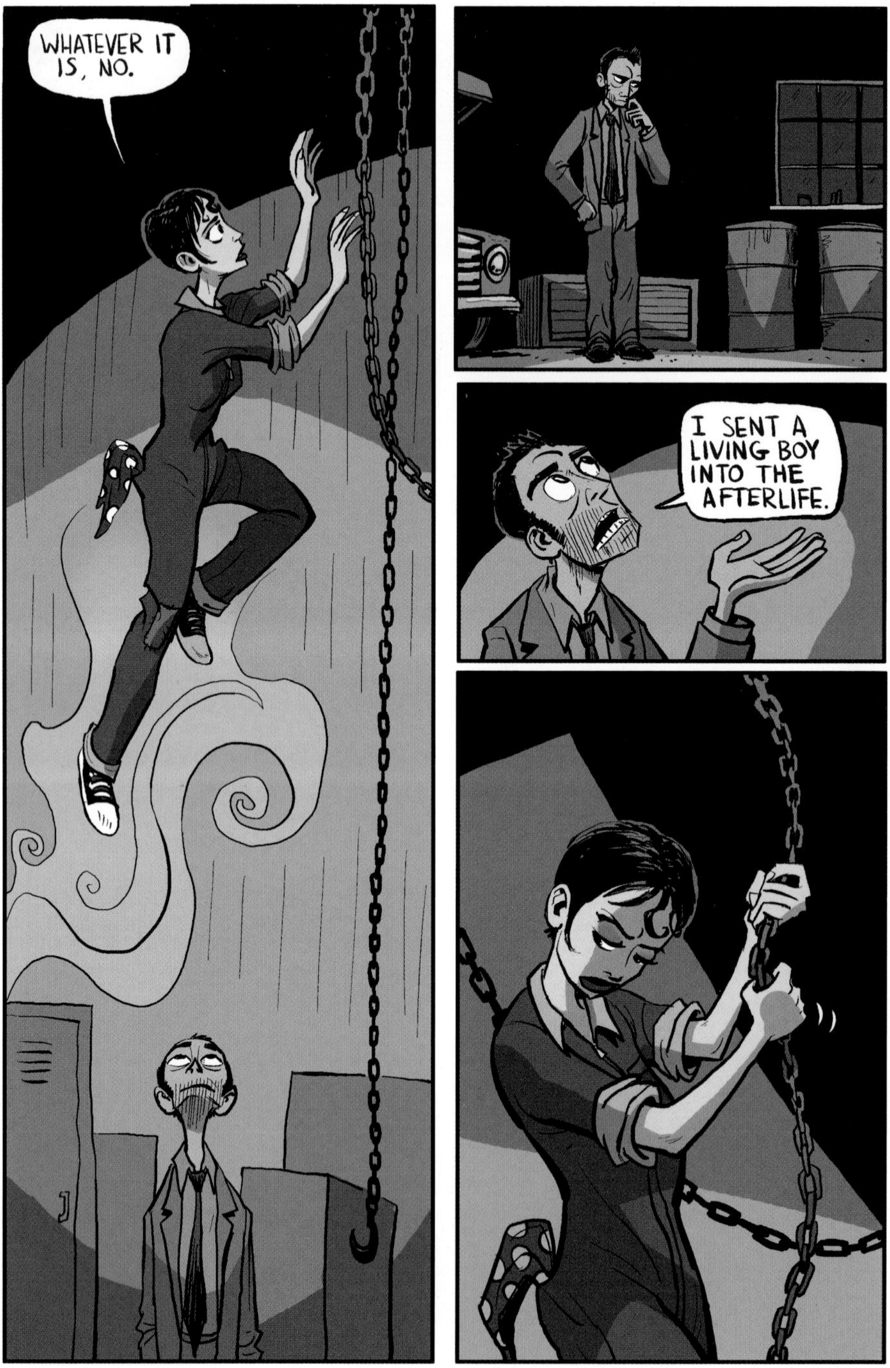
WHATEVER IT IS, NO.
I SENT A LIVING BOY INTO THE AFTERLIFE.

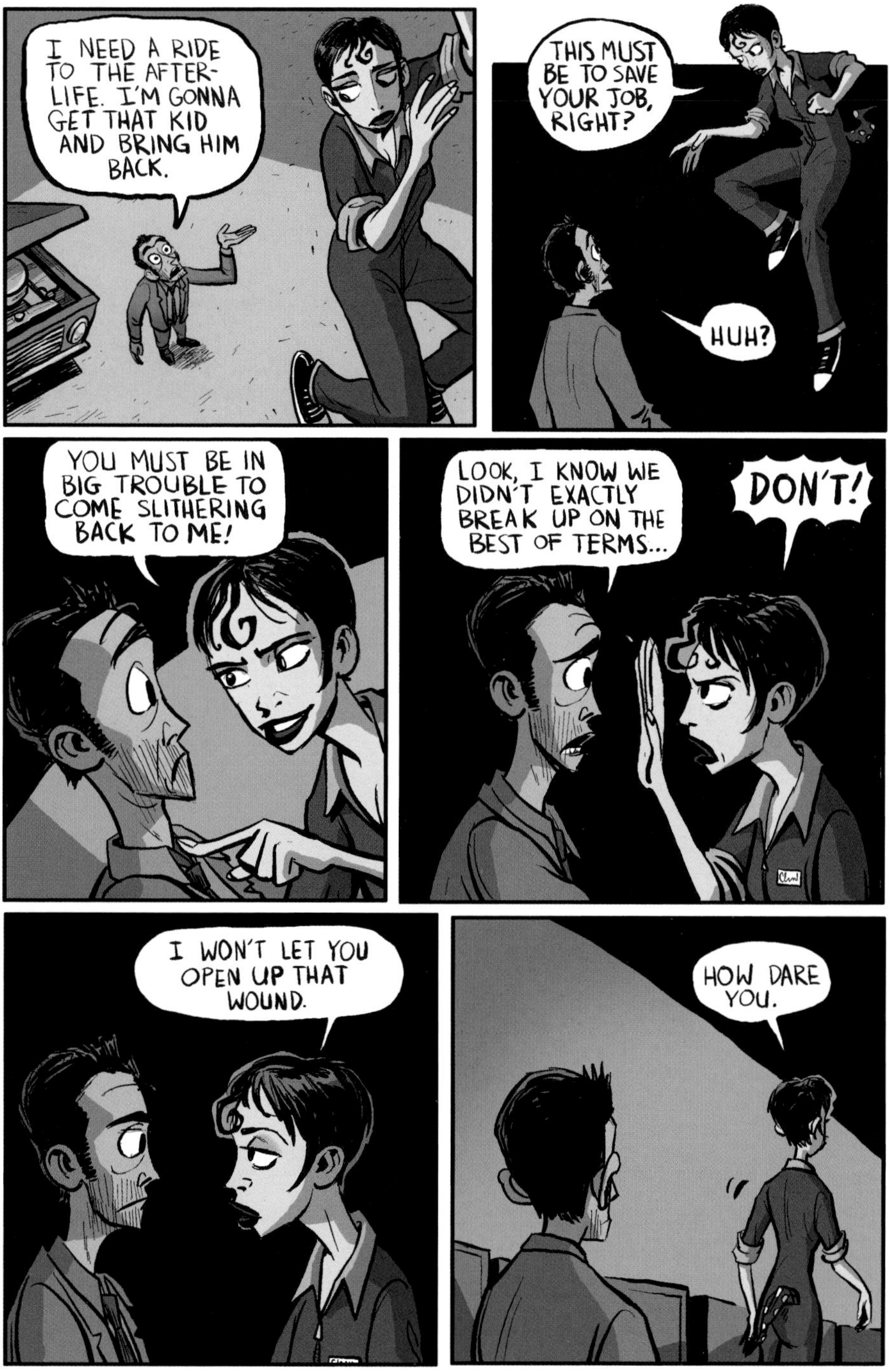
I NEED A RIDE TO THE AFTER-LIFE. I'M GONNA GET THAT KID AND BRING HIM BACK.
THIS MUST BE TO SAVE YOUR JOB, RIGHT?
HUH?
YOU MUST BE IN BIG TROUBLE TO COME SLITHERING BACK TO ME!
LOOK, I KNOW WE DIDN'T EXACTLY BREAK UP ON THE BEST OF TERMS...
DON'T!
I WON'T LET YOU OPEN UP THAT WOUND.
HOW DARE YOU.

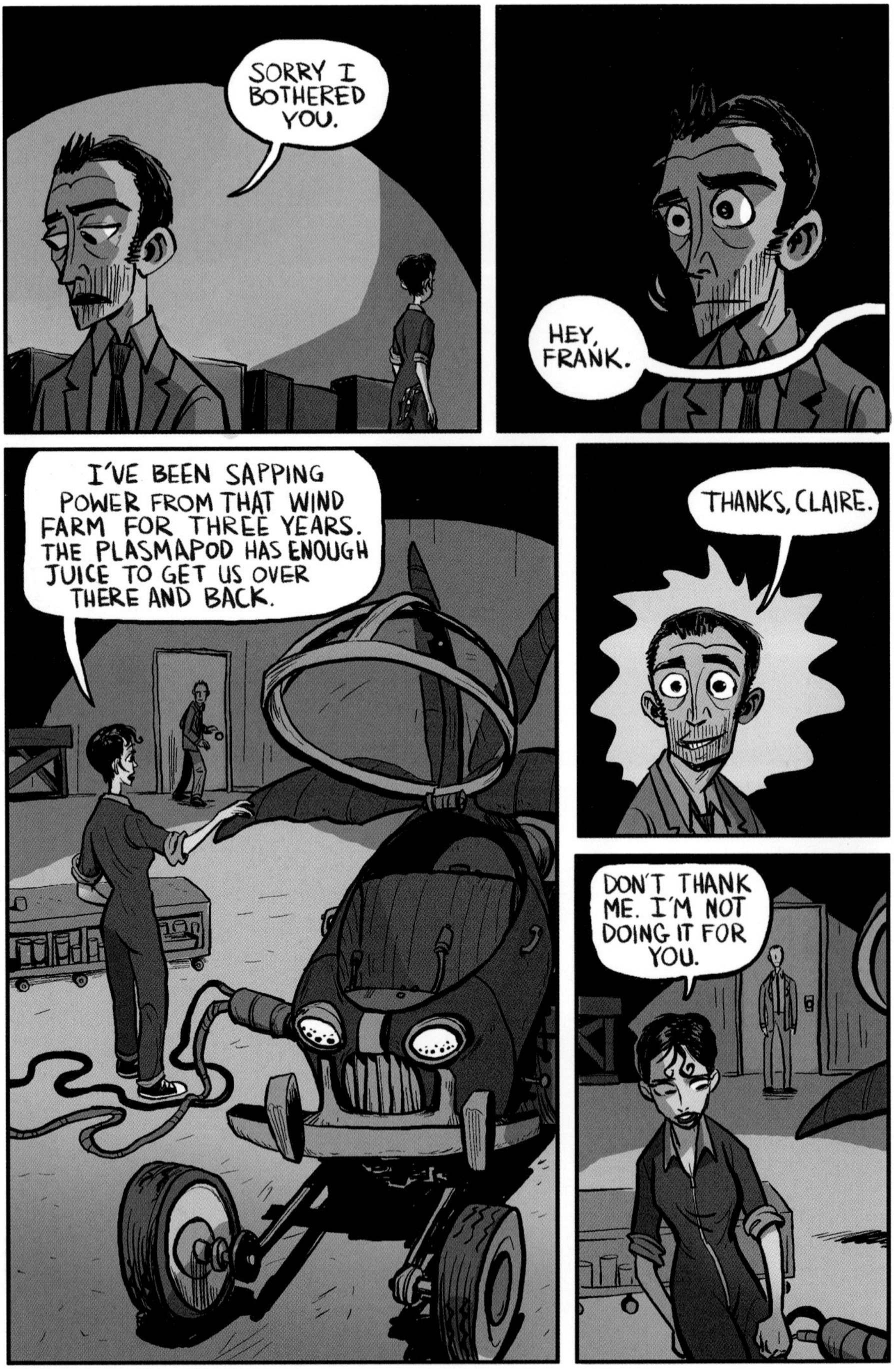
SORRY I BOTHERED YOU.
HEY, FRANK.
I'VE BEEN SAPPING POWER FROM THAT WIND FARM FOR THREE YEARS. THE PLASMAPOD HAS ENOUGH JUICE TO GET US OVER THERE AND BACK.
THANKS, CLAIRE.
DON'T THANK ME. I'M NOT DOING IT FOR YOU.

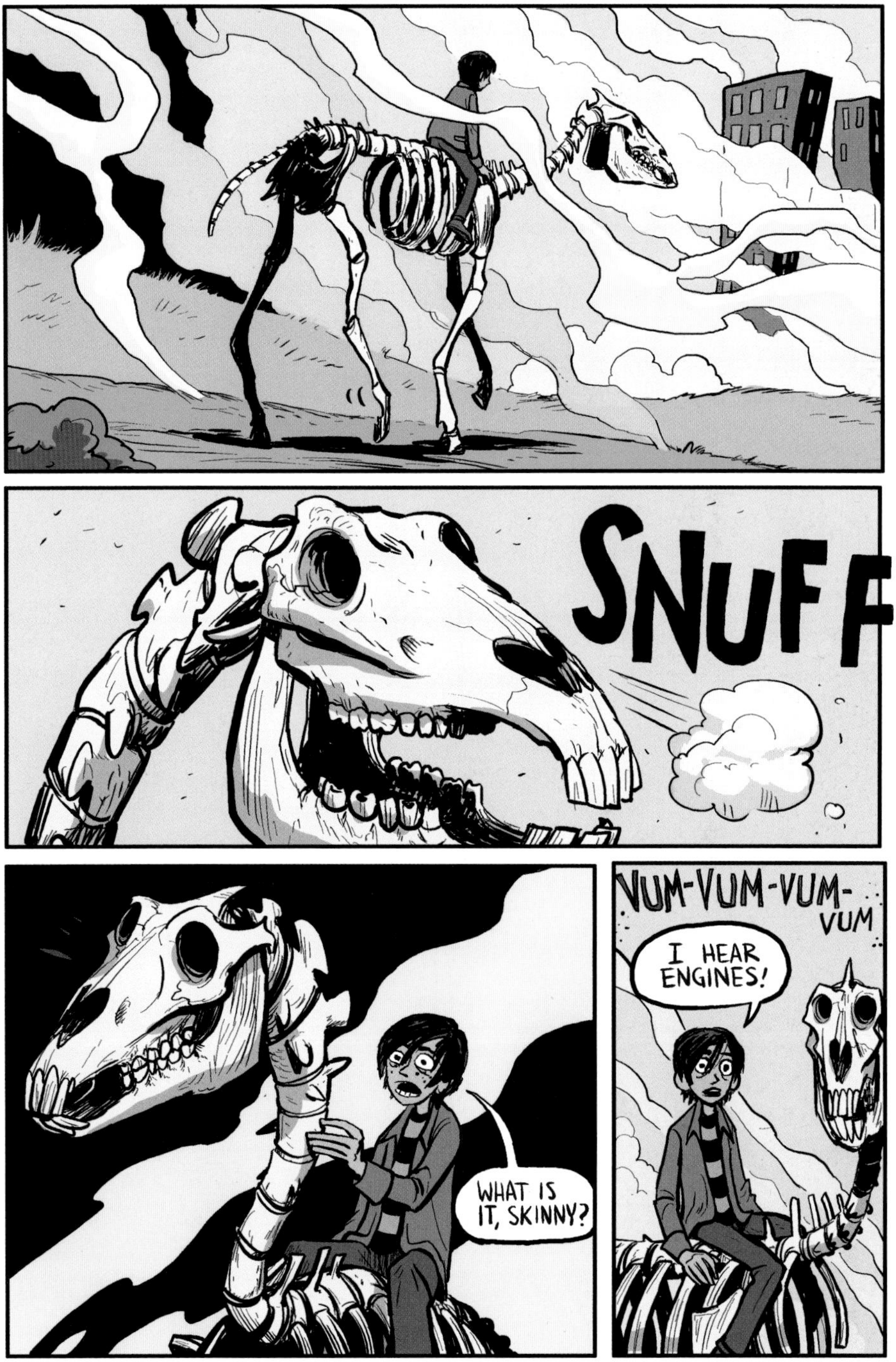
SNUFF
WHAT IS IT, SKINNY?
VUM-VUM-VUM-VUM
I HEAR ENGINES!

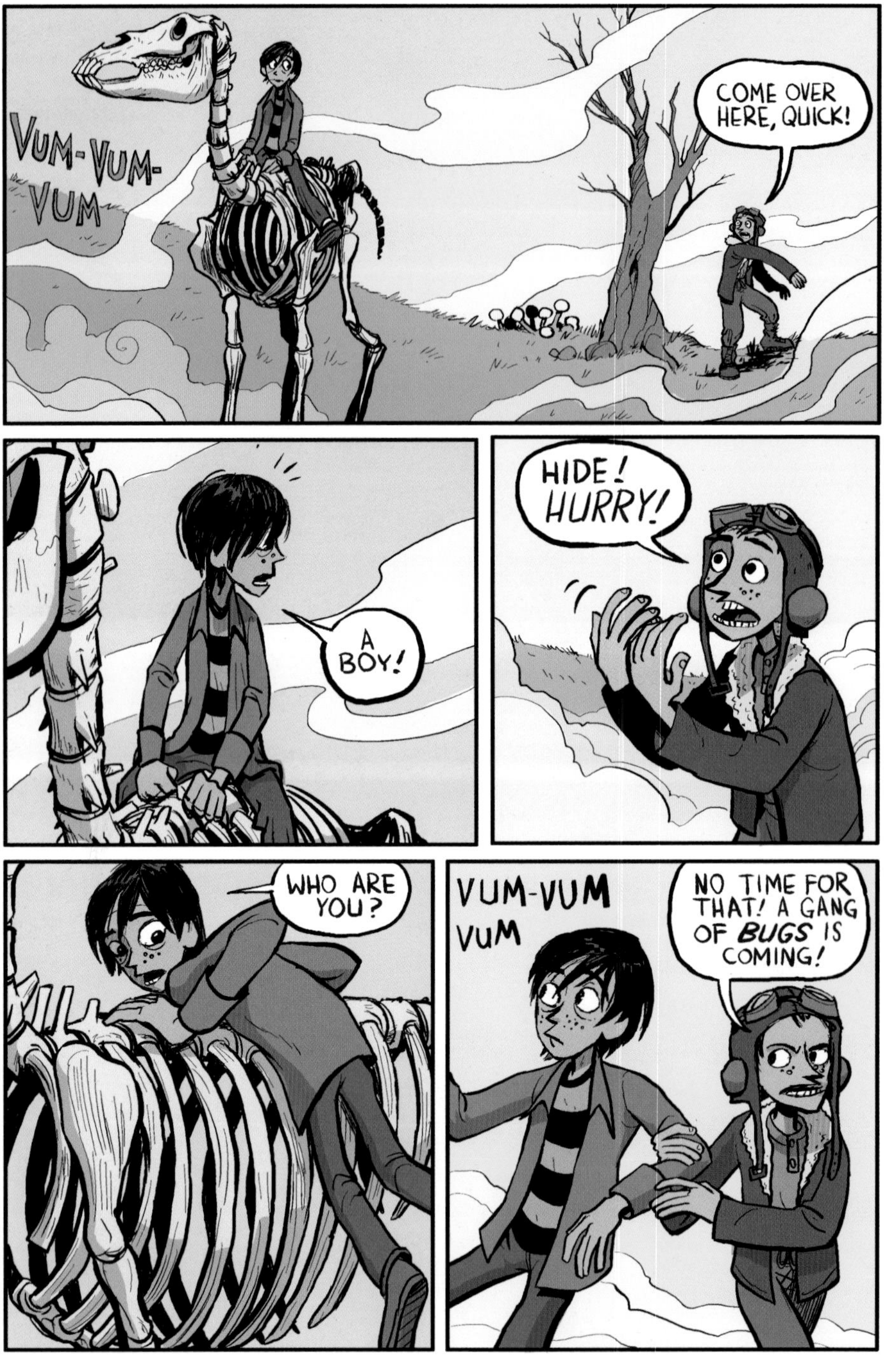
VUM-VUM-VUM
COME OVER HERE, QUICK!
A BOY!
HIDE! HURRY!
WHO ARE YOU?
VUM-VUM VUM
NO TIME FOR THAT! A GANG OF BUGS IS COMING!

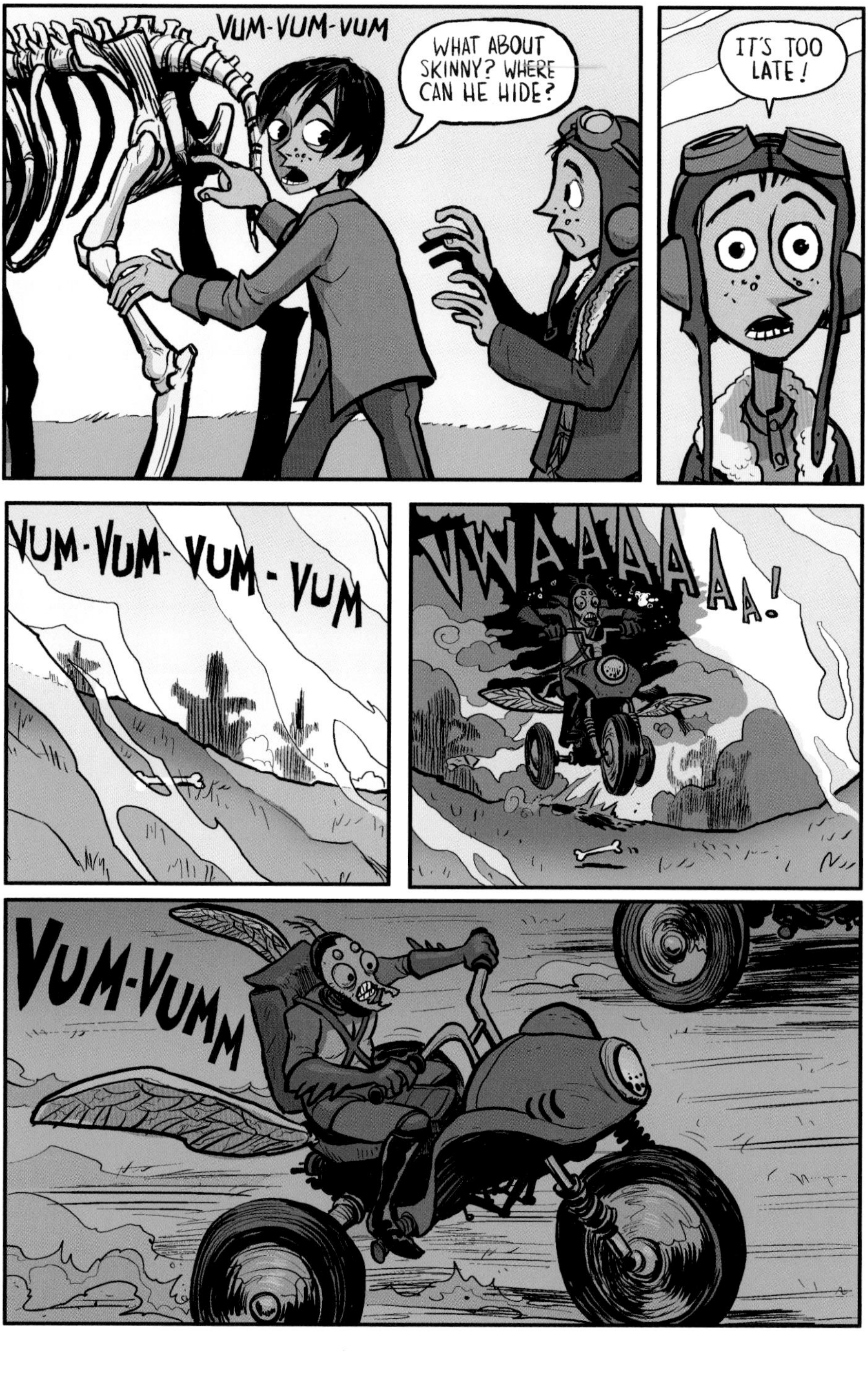
VUM-VUM-VUM
WHAT ABOUT SKINNY? WHERE CAN HE HIDE?
IT'S TOO LATE!
VUM-VUM-VUM-VUM
VWAAAAAAA!
VUM-VUMM

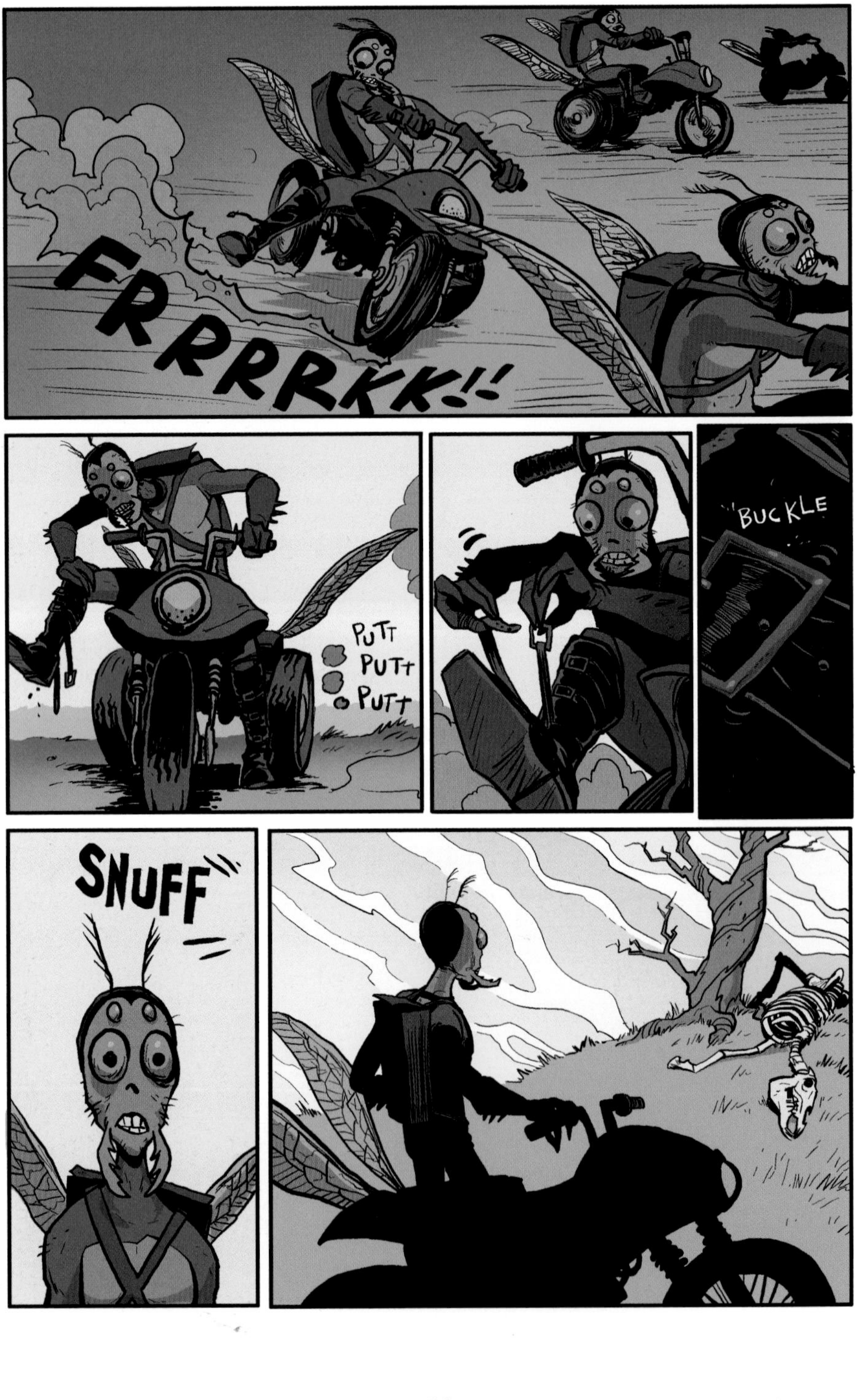
FRRRRKK!!
PUTT
PUTT
PUTT
BUCKLE
SNUFF

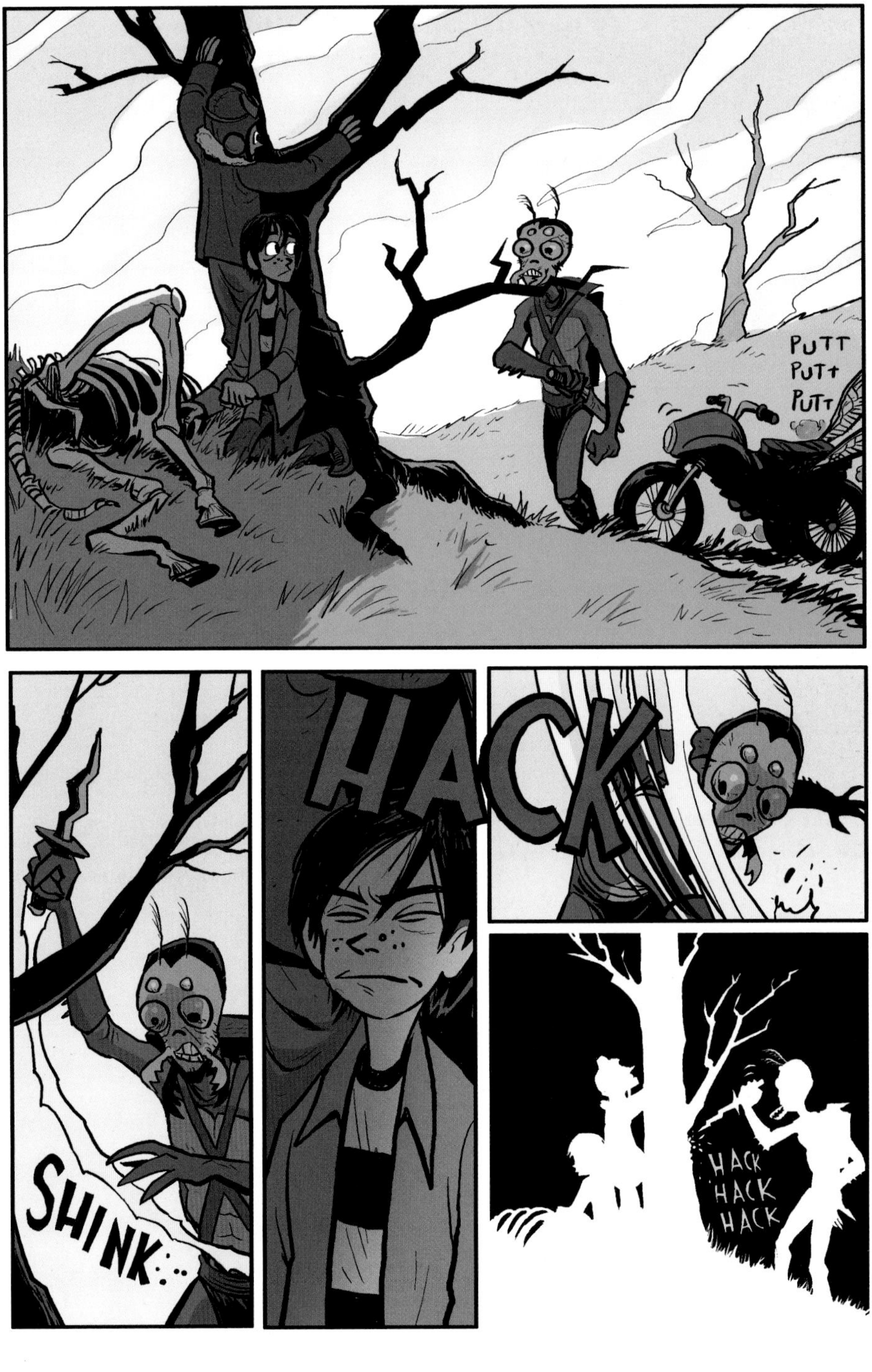
PUTT
PUTT
PUTT
SHINK
HACK
HACK
HACK
HACK

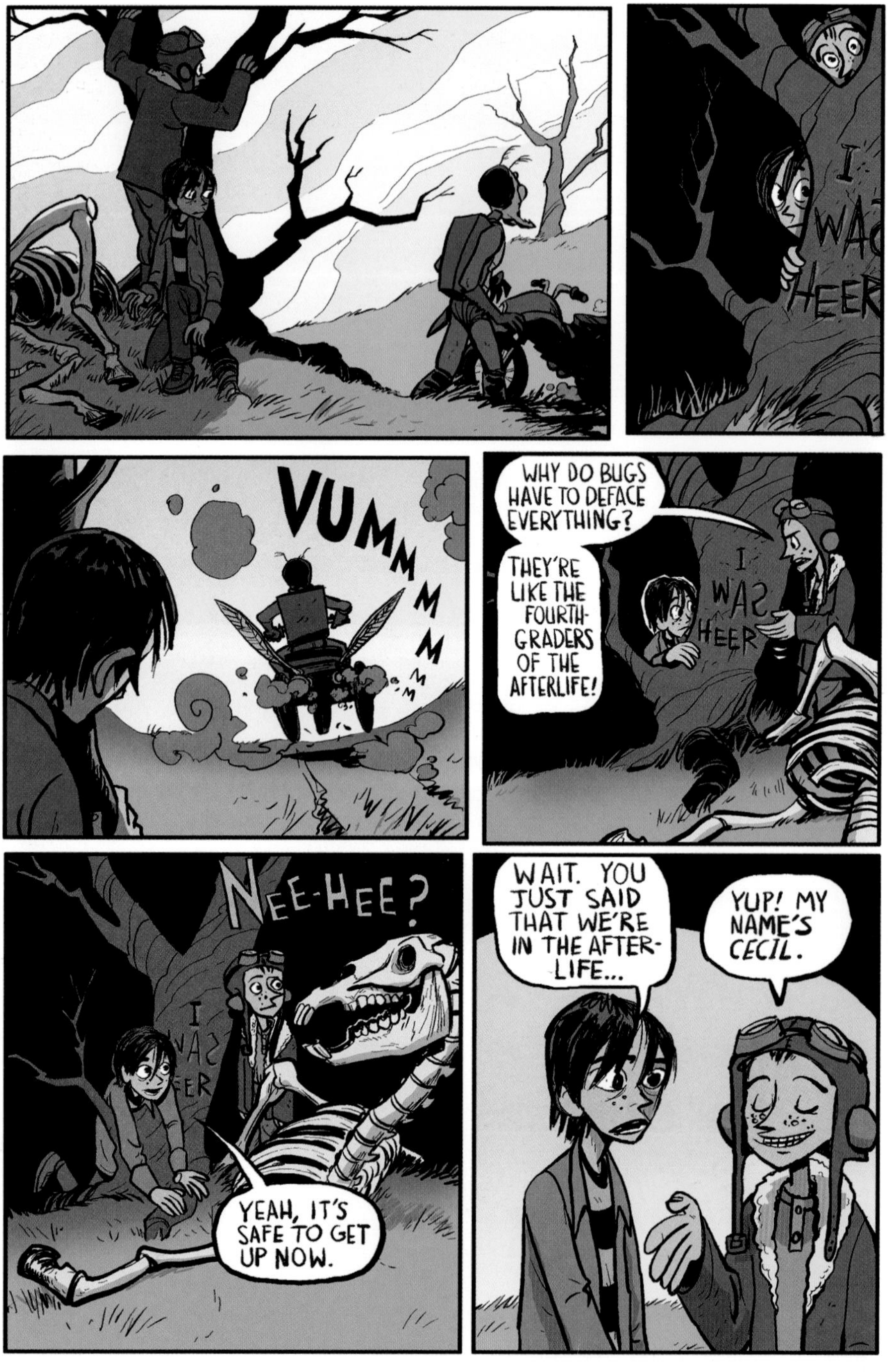
I WAS HEER
VUMMMMMM
WHY DO BUGS HAVE TO DEFACE EVERYTHING?
THEY'RE LIKE THE FOURTH-GRADERS OF THE AFTERLIFE!
I WAS HEER
NEE-HEE?
YEAH, IT'S SAFE TO GET UP NOW.
WAIT. YOU JUST SAID THAT WE'RE IN THE AFTER-LIFE...
YUP! MY NAME'S CECIL.

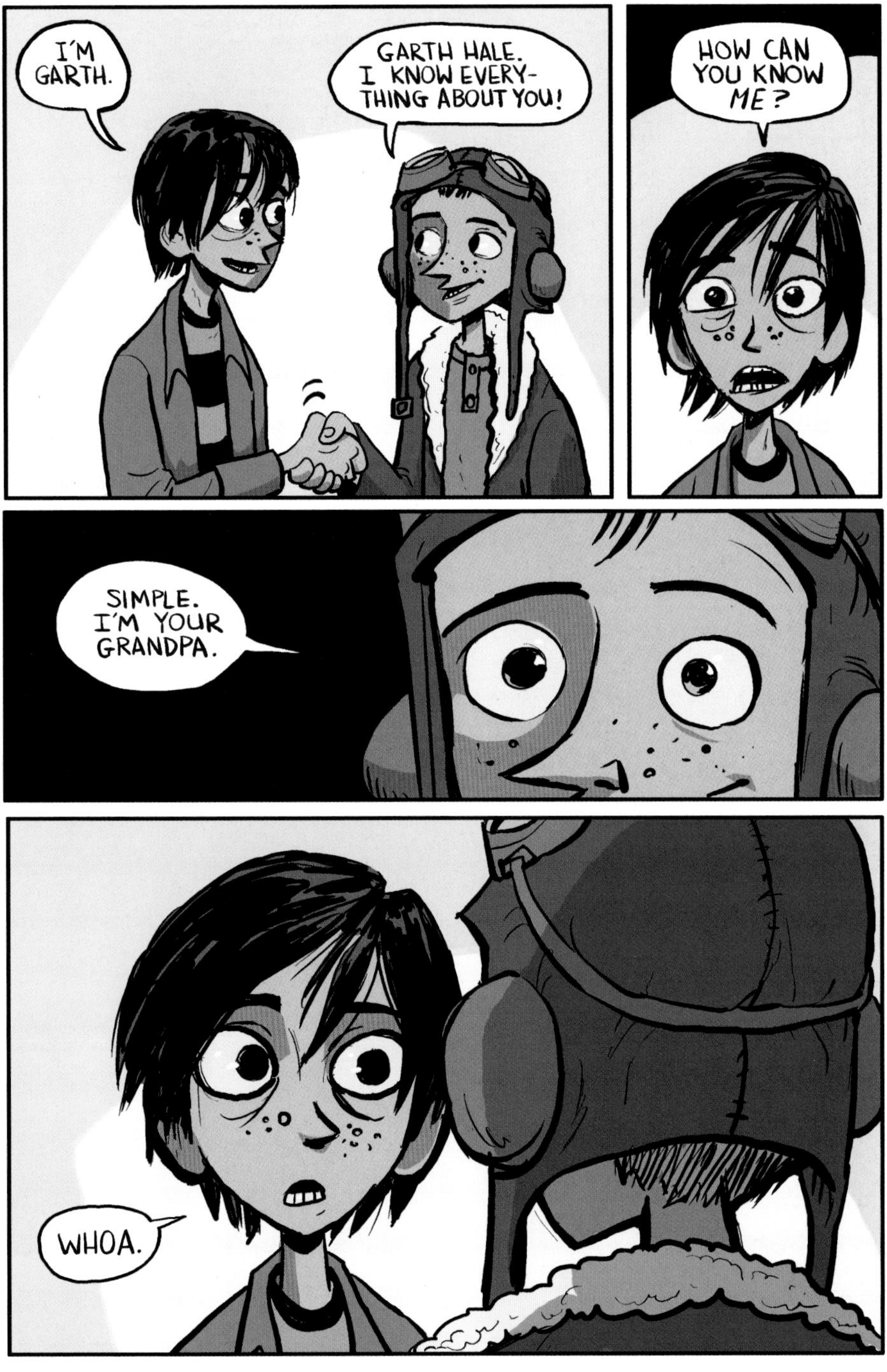
I'M GARTH.
GARTH HALE. I KNOW EVERYTHING ABOUT YOU!
HOW CAN YOU KNOW ME?
SIMPLE. I'M YOUR GRANDPA.
WHOA.

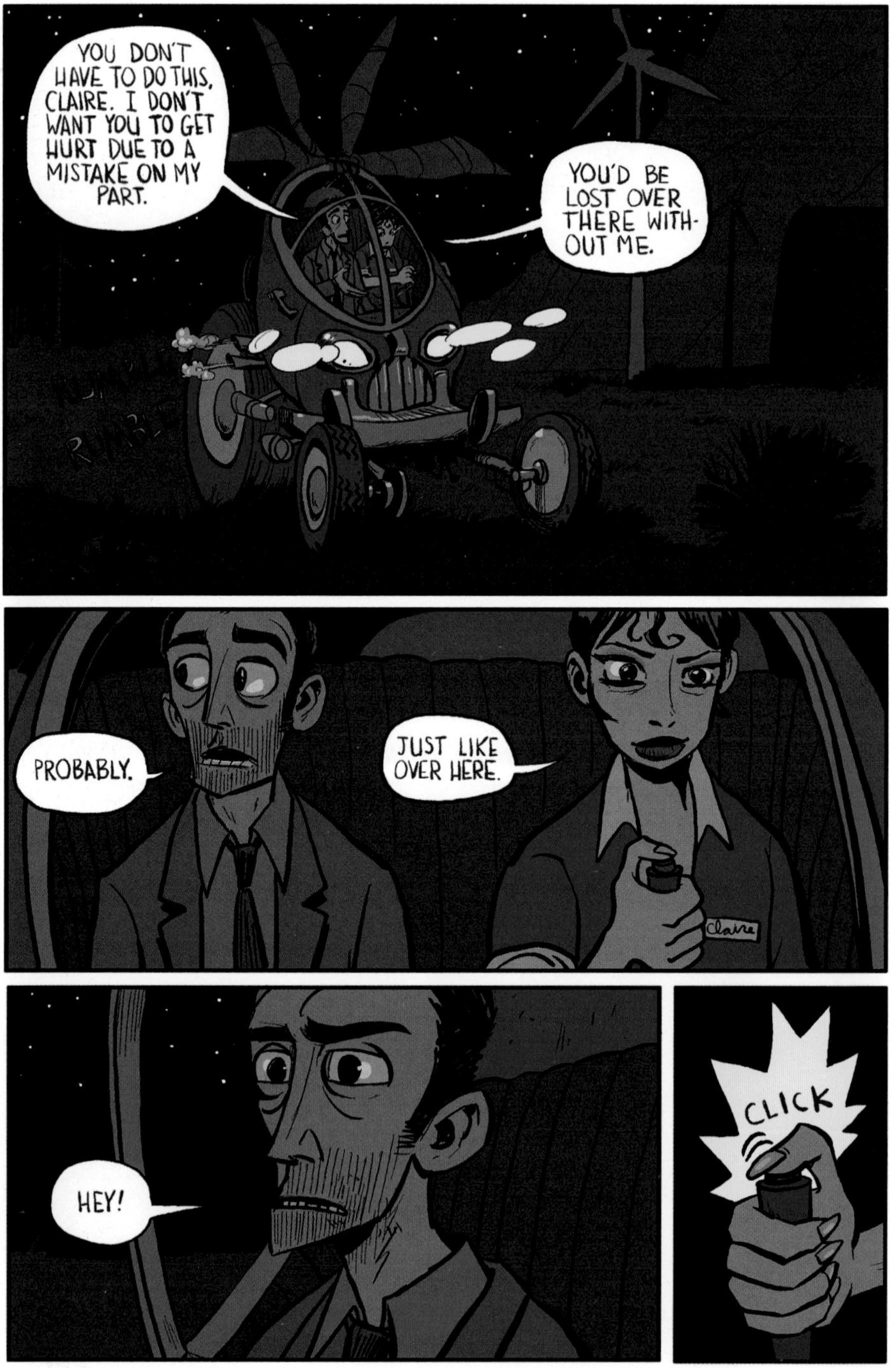
YOU DON'T HAVE TO DO THIS, CLAIRE. I DON'T WANT YOU TO GET HURT DUE TO A MISTAKE ON MY PART.
YOU'D BE LOST OVER THERE WITH-OUT ME.
PROBABLY.
JUST LIKE OVER HERE.
HEY!
CLICK

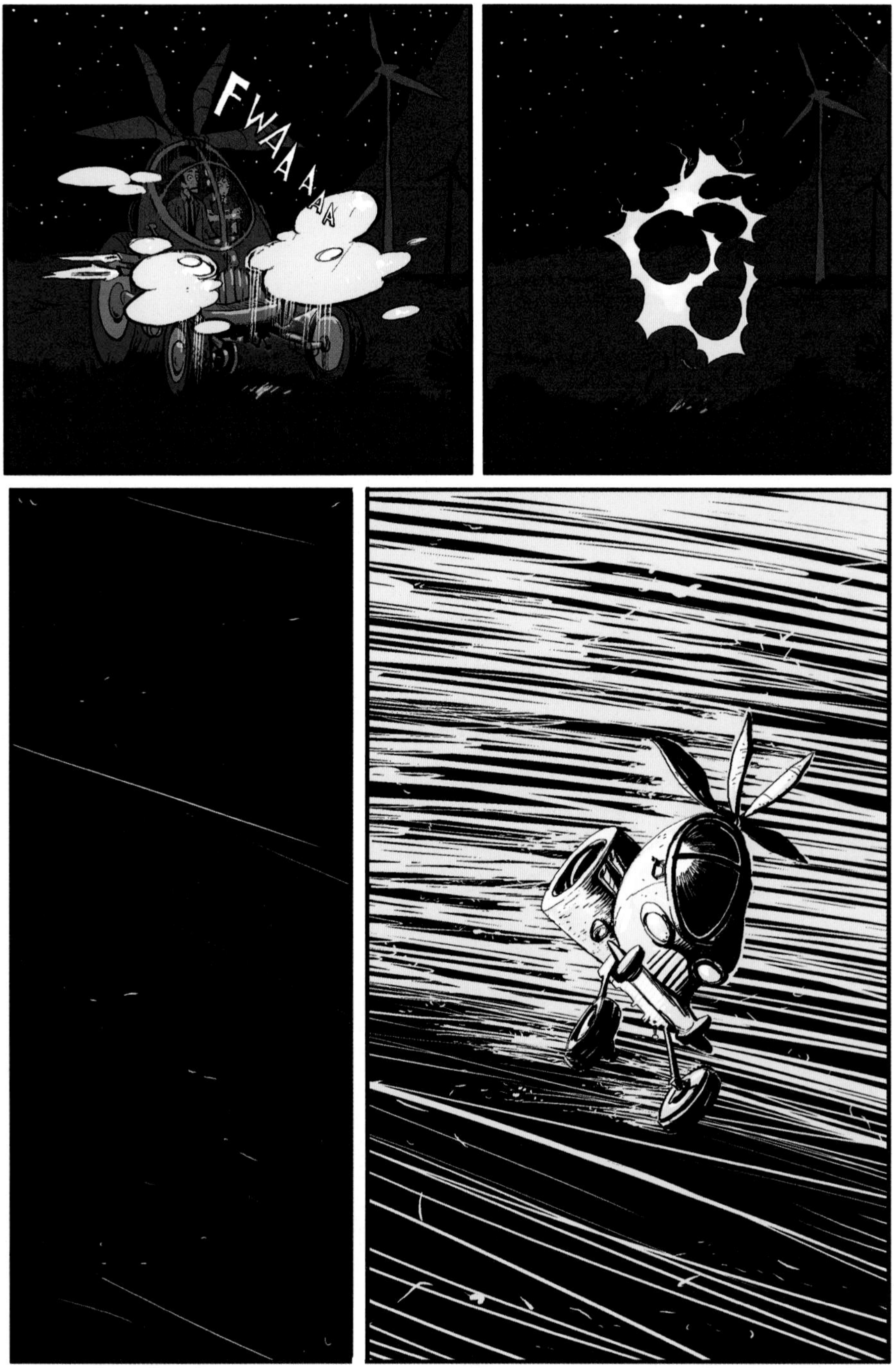
FWAAAAAA

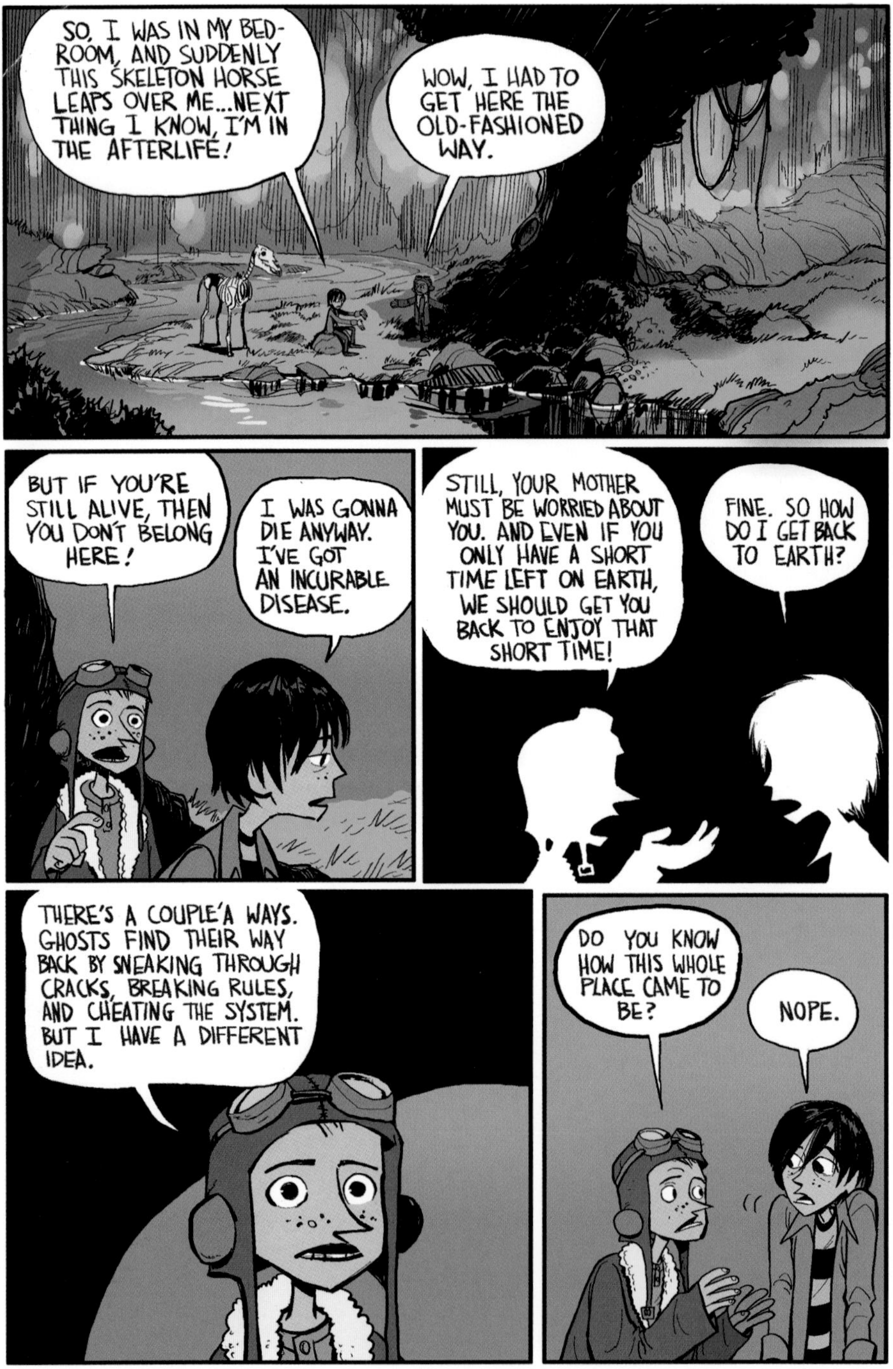
SO, I WAS IN MY BED-ROOM, AND SUDDENLY THIS SKELETON HORSE LEAPS OVER ME...NEXT THING I KNOW, I'M IN THE AFTERLIFE!
WOW, I HAD TO GET HERE THE OLD-FASHIONED WAY.
BUT IF YOU'RE STILL ALIVE, THEN YOU DON'T BELONG HERE!
I WAS GONNA DIE ANYWAY. I'VE GOT AN INCURABLE DISEASE.
STILL, YOUR MOTHER MUST BE WORRIED ABOUT YOU. AND EVEN IF YOU ONLY HAVE A SHORT TIME LEFT ON EARTH, WE SHOULD GET YOU BACK TO ENJOY THAT SHORT TIME!
FINE. SO HOW DO I GET BACK TO EARTH?
THERE'S A COUPLE'A WAYS. GHOSTS FIND THEIR WAY BACK BY SNEAKING THROUGH CRACKS, BREAKING RULES, AND CHEATING THE SYSTEM. BUT I HAVE A DIFFERENT IDEA.
DO YOU KNOW HOW THIS WHOLE PLACE CAME TO BE?
NOPE.

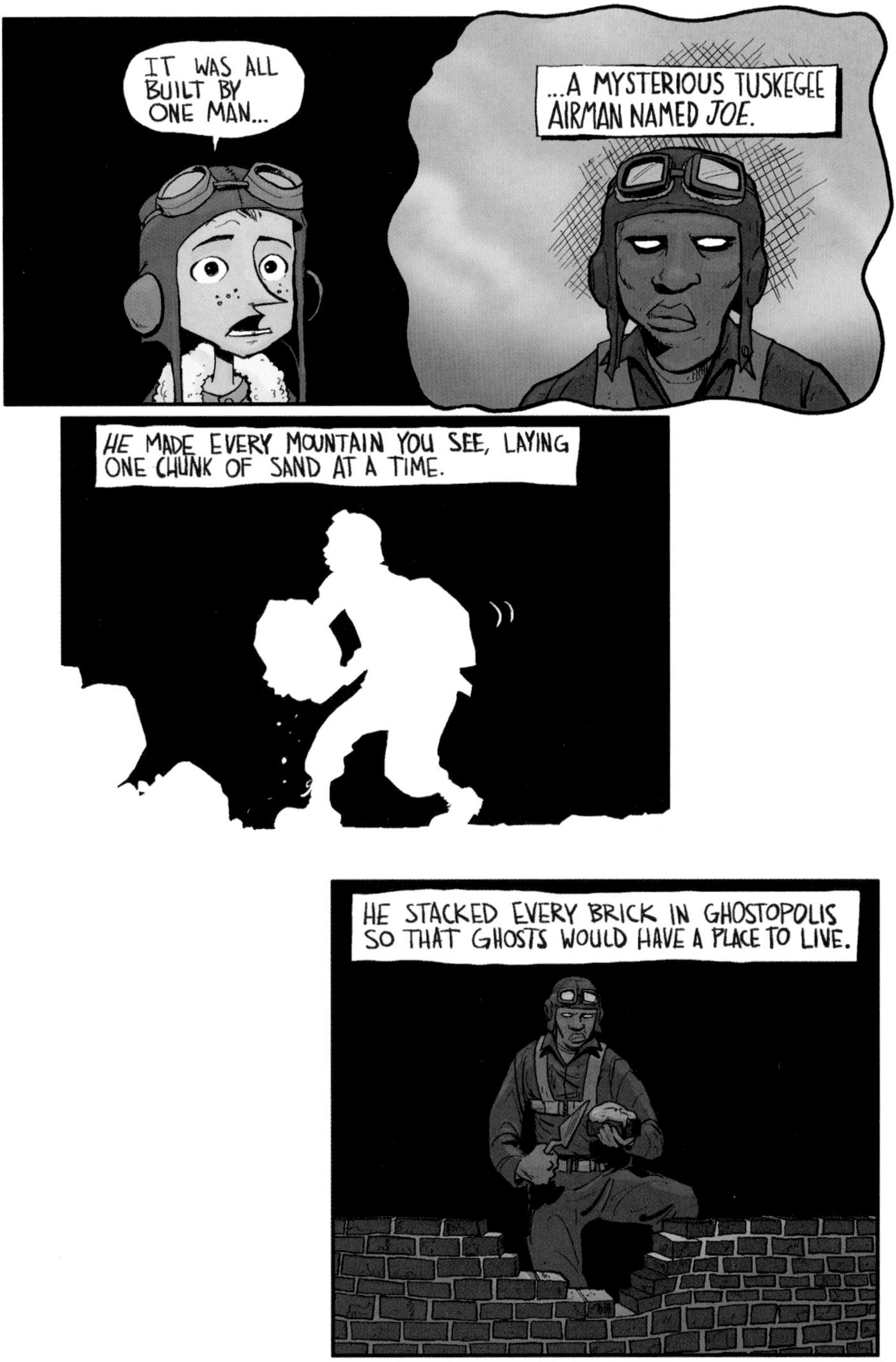
IT WAS ALL BUILT BY ONE MAN...
...A MYSTERIOUS TUSKEGEE AIRMAN NAMED JOE.
HE MADE EVERY MOUNTAIN YOU SEE, LAYING ONE CHUNK OF SAND AT A TIME.
HE STACKED EVERY BRICK IN GHOSTOPOLIS SO THAT GHOSTS WOULD HAVE A PLACE TO LIVE.

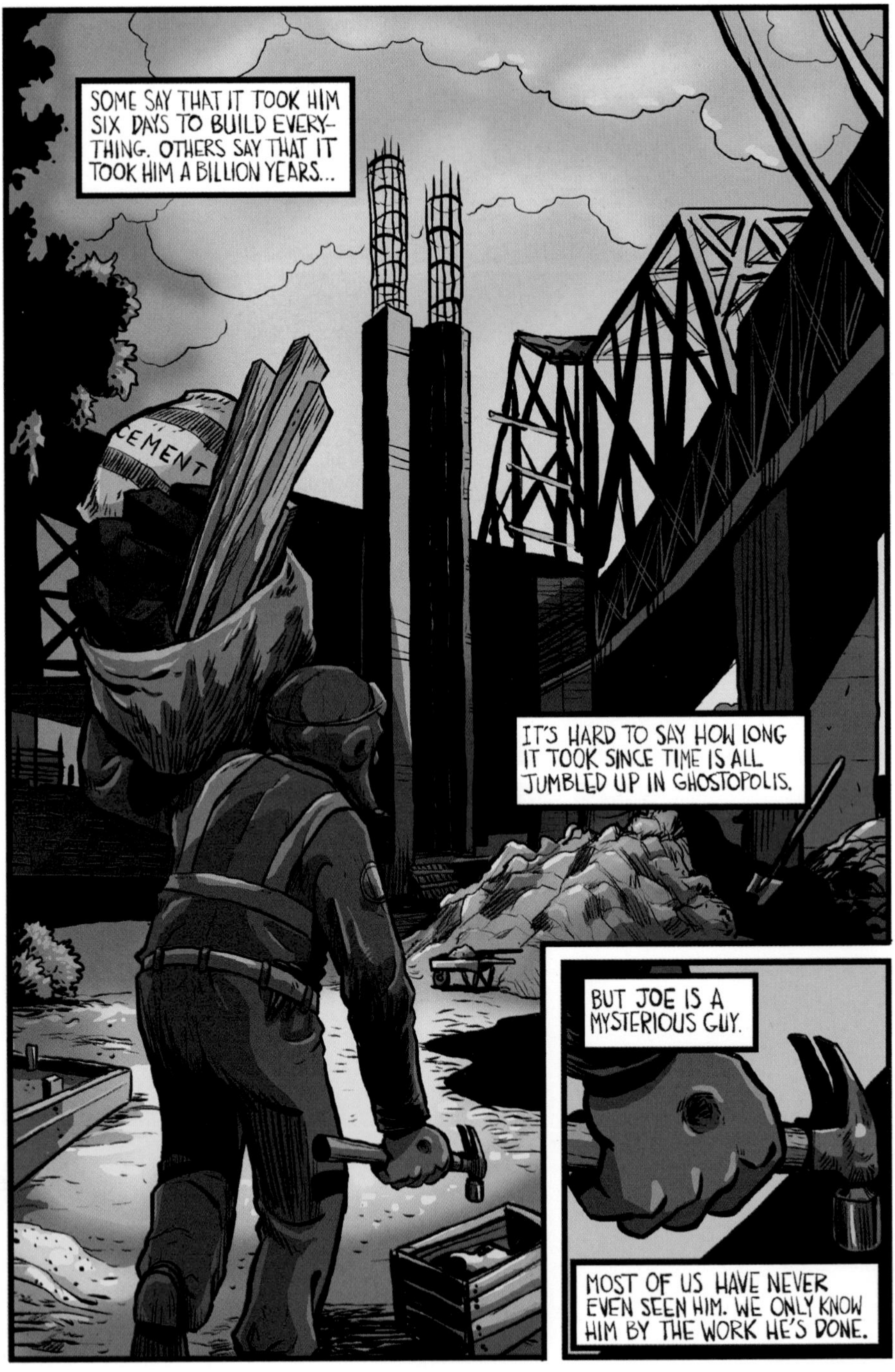
SOME SAY THAT IT TOOK HIM SIX DAYS TO BUILD EVERY-THING. OTHERS SAY THAT IT TOOK HIM A BILLION YEARS...
CEMENT
IT'S HARD TO SAY HOW LONG IT TOOK SINCE TIME IS ALL JUMBLED UP IN GHOSTOPOLIS.
BUT JOE IS A MYSTERIOUS GUY.
MOST OF US HAVE NEVER EVEN SEEN HIM. WE ONLY KNOW HIM BY THE WORK HE'S DONE.

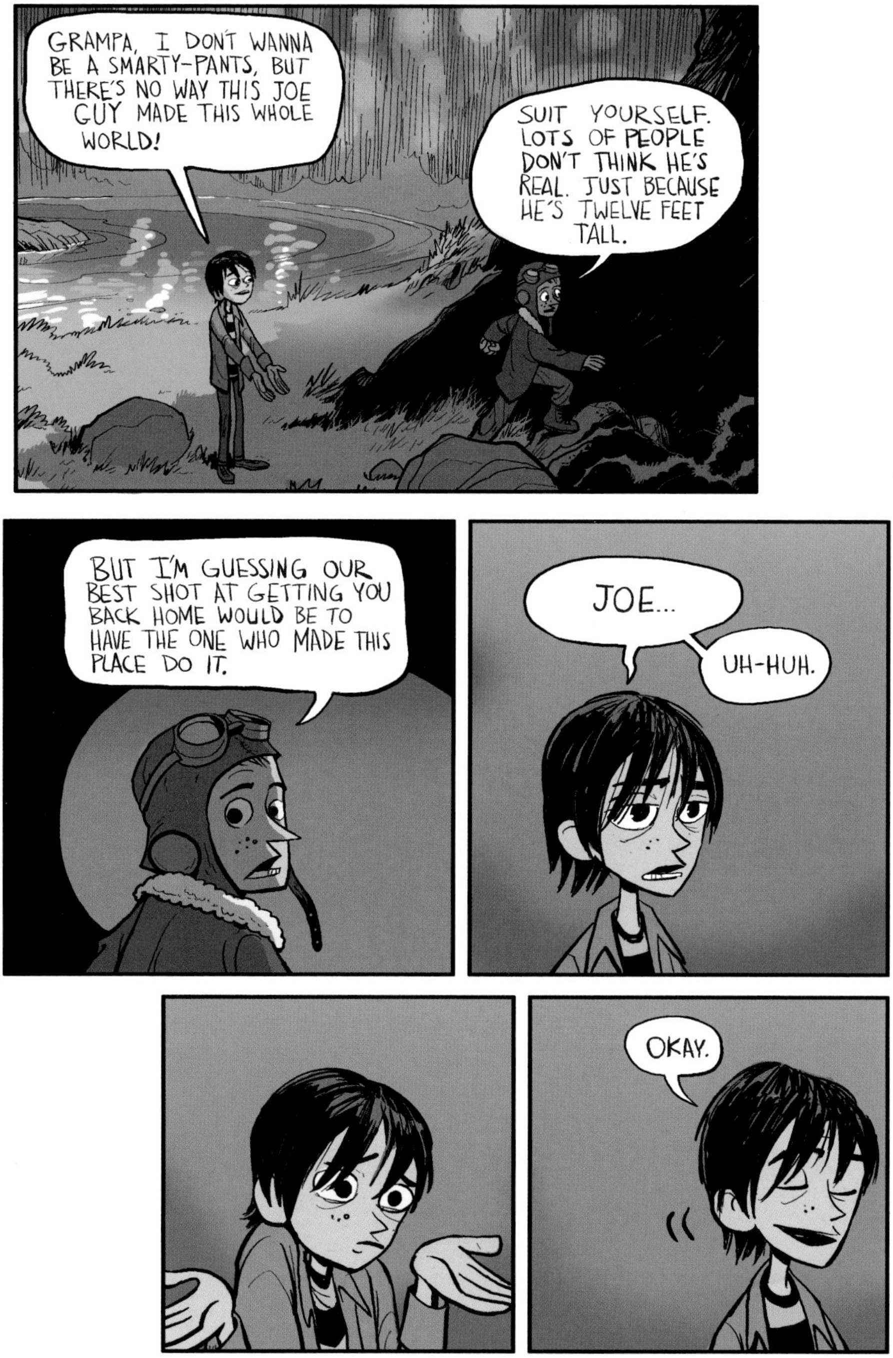
GRAMPA, I DON'T WANNA BE A SMARTY-PANTS, BUT THERE'S NO WAY THIS JOE GUY MADE THIS WHOLE WORLD!
SUIT YOURSELF. LOTS OF PEOPLE DON'T THINK HE'S REAL. JUST BECAUSE HE'S TWELVE FEET TALL.
BUT I'M GUESSING OUR BEST SHOT AT GETTING YOU BACK HOME WOULD BE TO HAVE THE ONE WHO MADE THIS PLACE DO IT.
JOE...
UH-HUH.
OKAY.

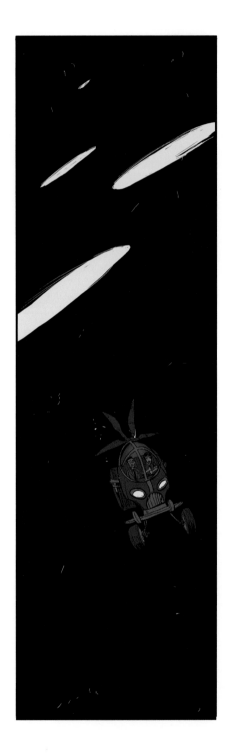

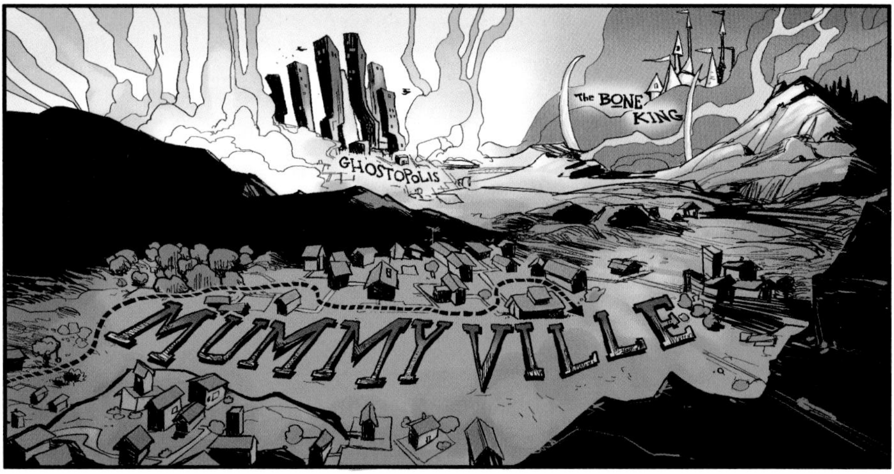
GHOSTOPOLIS
The BONE KING
MUMMY VILLE

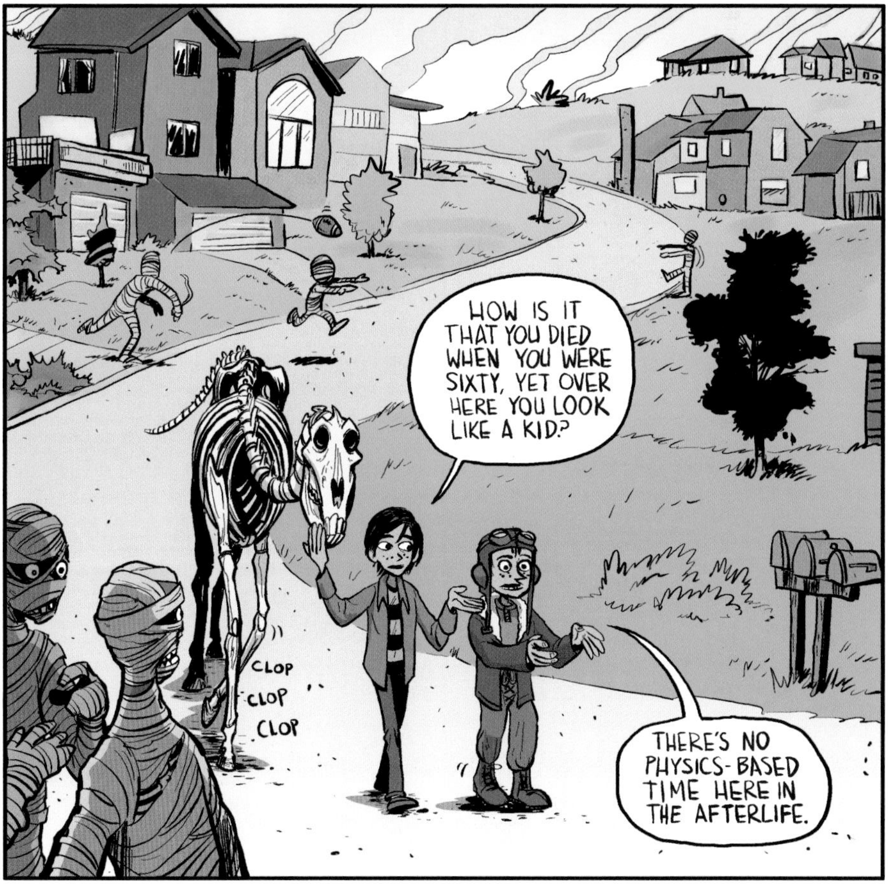
HOW IS IT THAT YOU DIED WHEN YOU WERE SIXTY, YET OVER HERE YOU LOOK LIKE A KID?
CLOP
CLOP
CLOP
THERE'S NO PHYSICS-BASED TIME HERE IN THE AFTERLIFE.

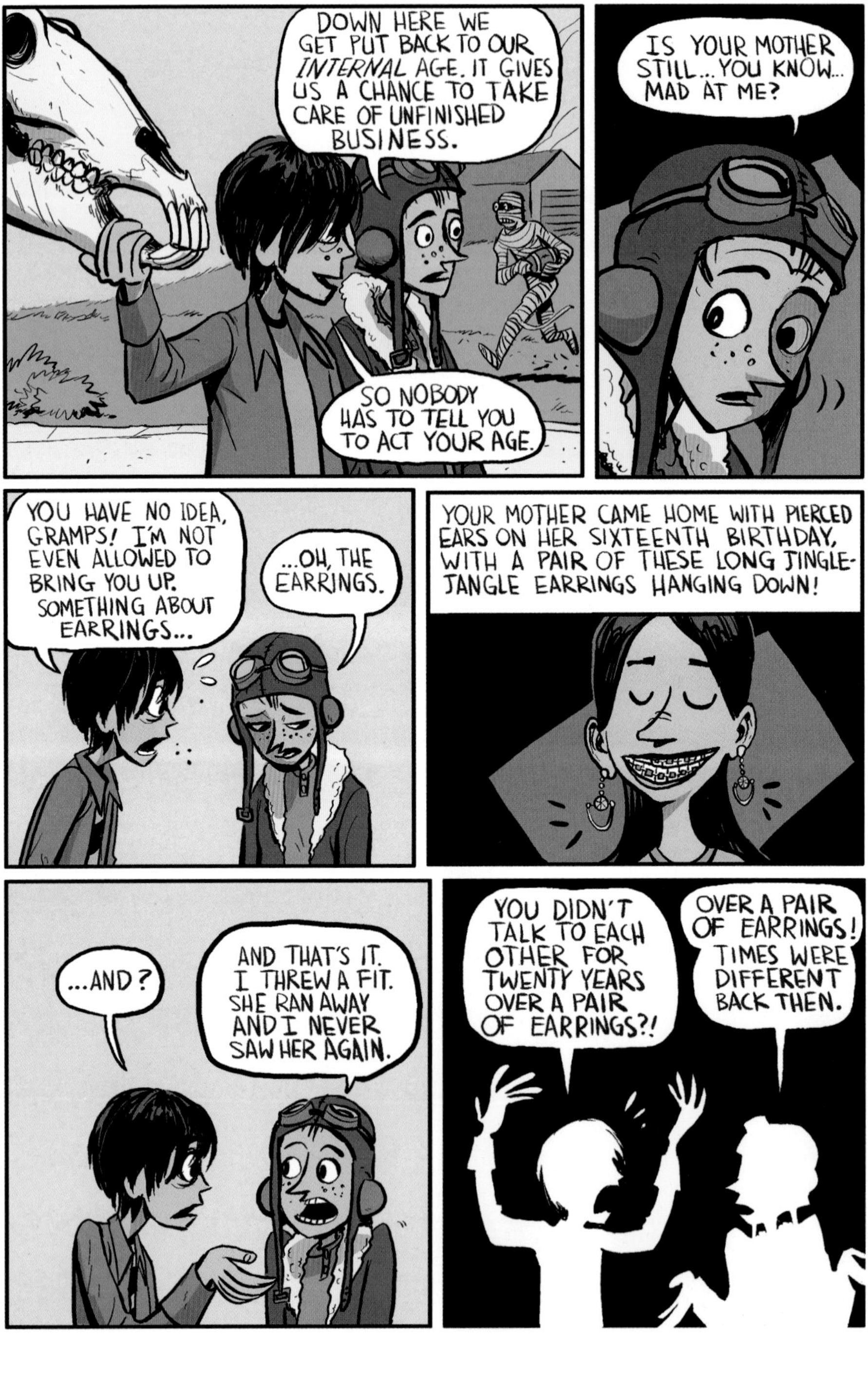
DOWN HERE WE GET PUT BACK TO OUR *INTERNAL* AGE. IT GIVES US A CHANCE TO TAKE CARE OF UNFINISHED BUSINESS.
SO NOBODY HAS TO TELL YOU TO ACT YOUR AGE.
IS YOUR MOTHER STILL... YOU KNOW... MAD AT ME?
YOU HAVE NO IDEA, GRAMPS! I'M NOT EVEN ALLOWED TO BRING YOU UP. SOMETHING ABOUT EARRINGS...
...OH, THE EARRINGS.
YOUR MOTHER CAME HOME WITH PIERCED EARS ON HER SIXTEENTH BIRTHDAY, WITH A PAIR OF THESE LONG JINGLE-JANGLE EARRINGS HANGING DOWN!
...AND?
AND THAT'S IT. I THREW A FIT. SHE RAN AWAY AND I NEVER SAW HER AGAIN.
YOU DIDN'T TALK TO EACH OTHER FOR TWENTY YEARS OVER A PAIR OF EARRINGS?!
OVER A PAIR OF EARRINGS! TIMES WERE DIFFERENT BACK THEN.

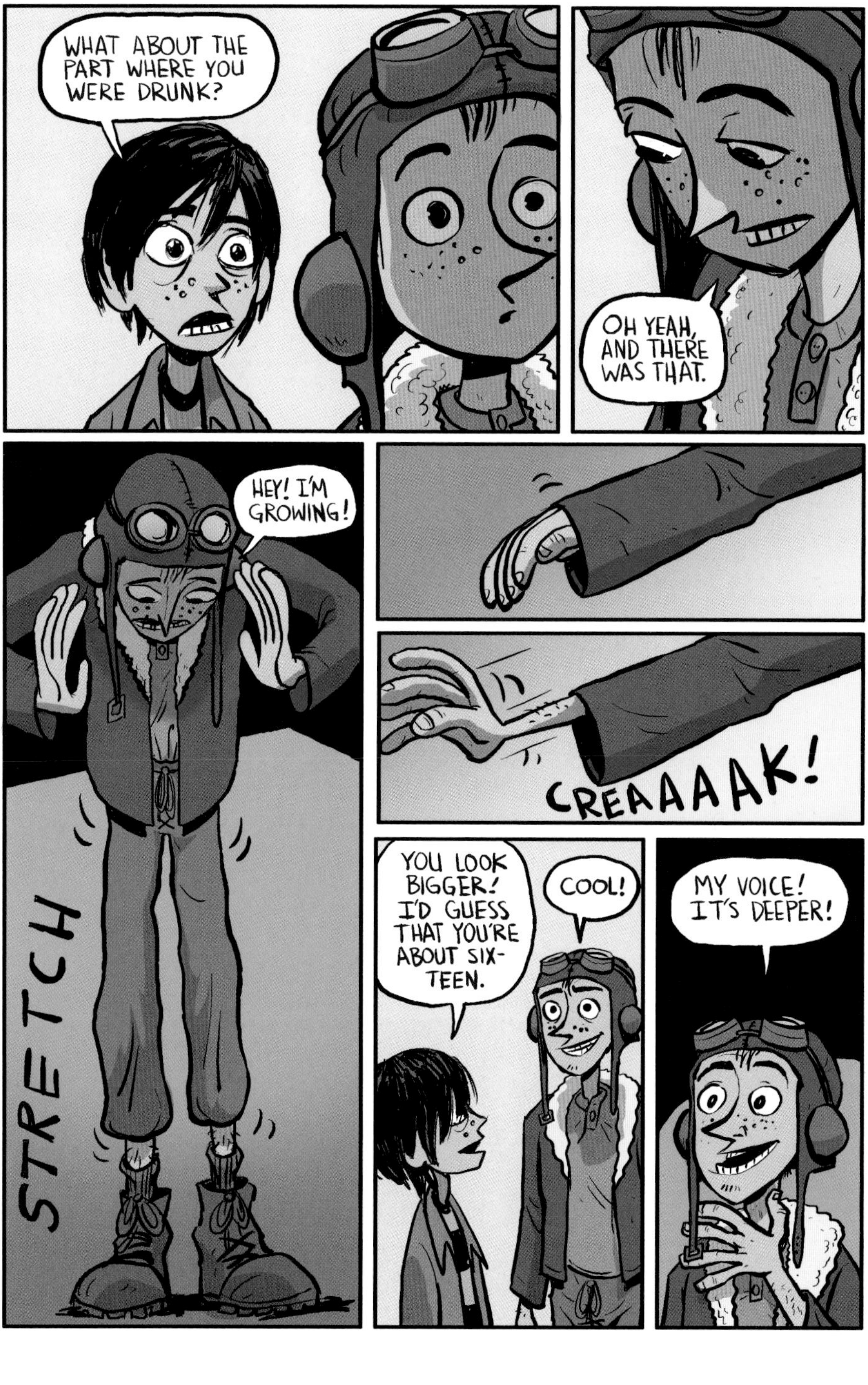

WHAT ABOUT THE PART WHERE YOU WERE DRUNK?
OH YEAH, AND THERE WAS THAT.
HEY! I'M GROWING!
STRETCH
CREAAAAK!
YOU LOOK BIGGER! I'D GUESS THAT YOU'RE ABOUT SIX-TEEN.
COOL!
MY VOICE! IT'S DEEPER!

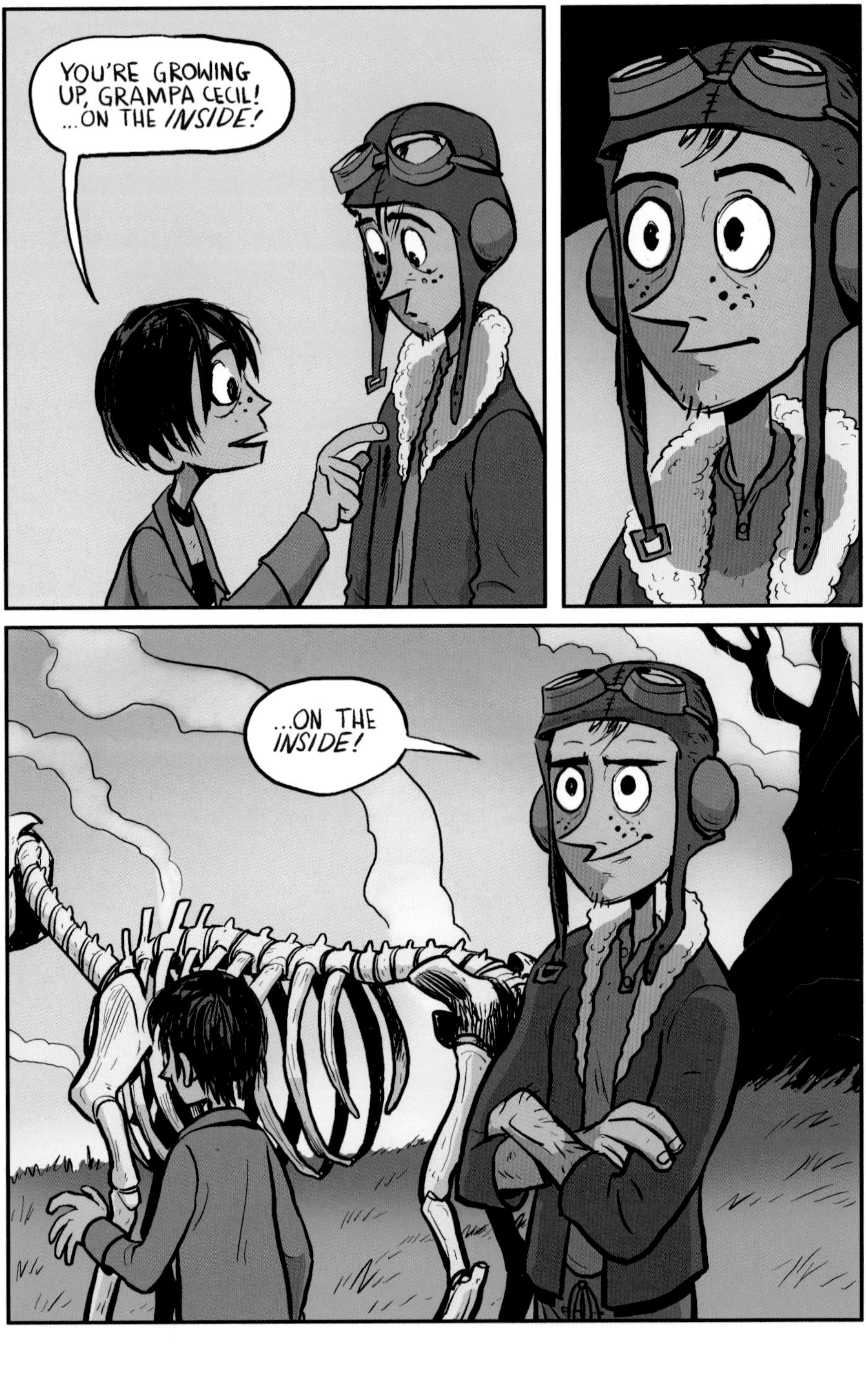
YOU'RE GROWING UP, GRAMPA CECIL! ...ON THE *INSIDE!*
...ON THE *INSIDE!*

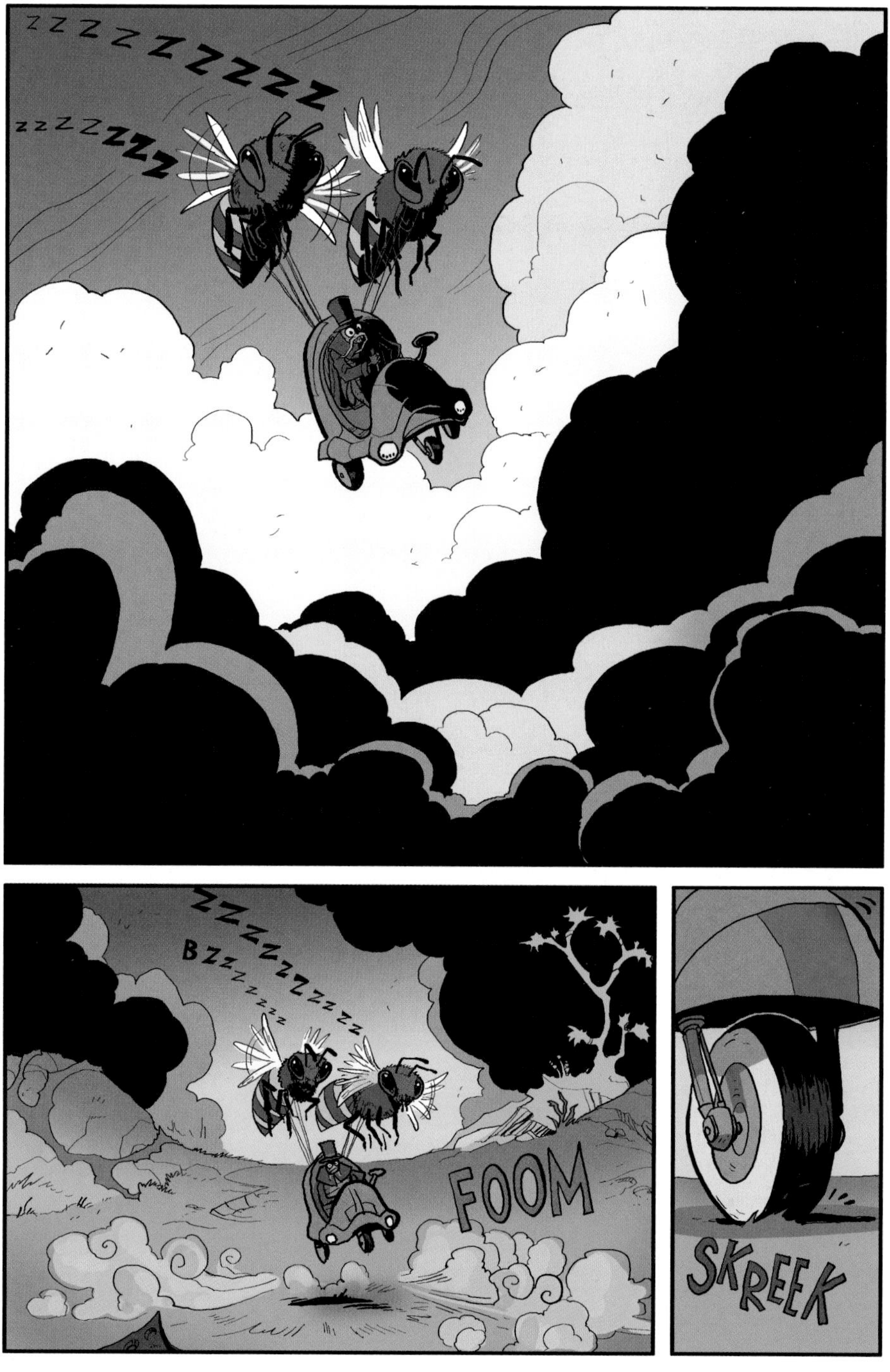

ZZZZZZZZZZZ
zzZZZZZ
ZZZZZ
BZzzzzzzzzzz
FOOM
SKREEK

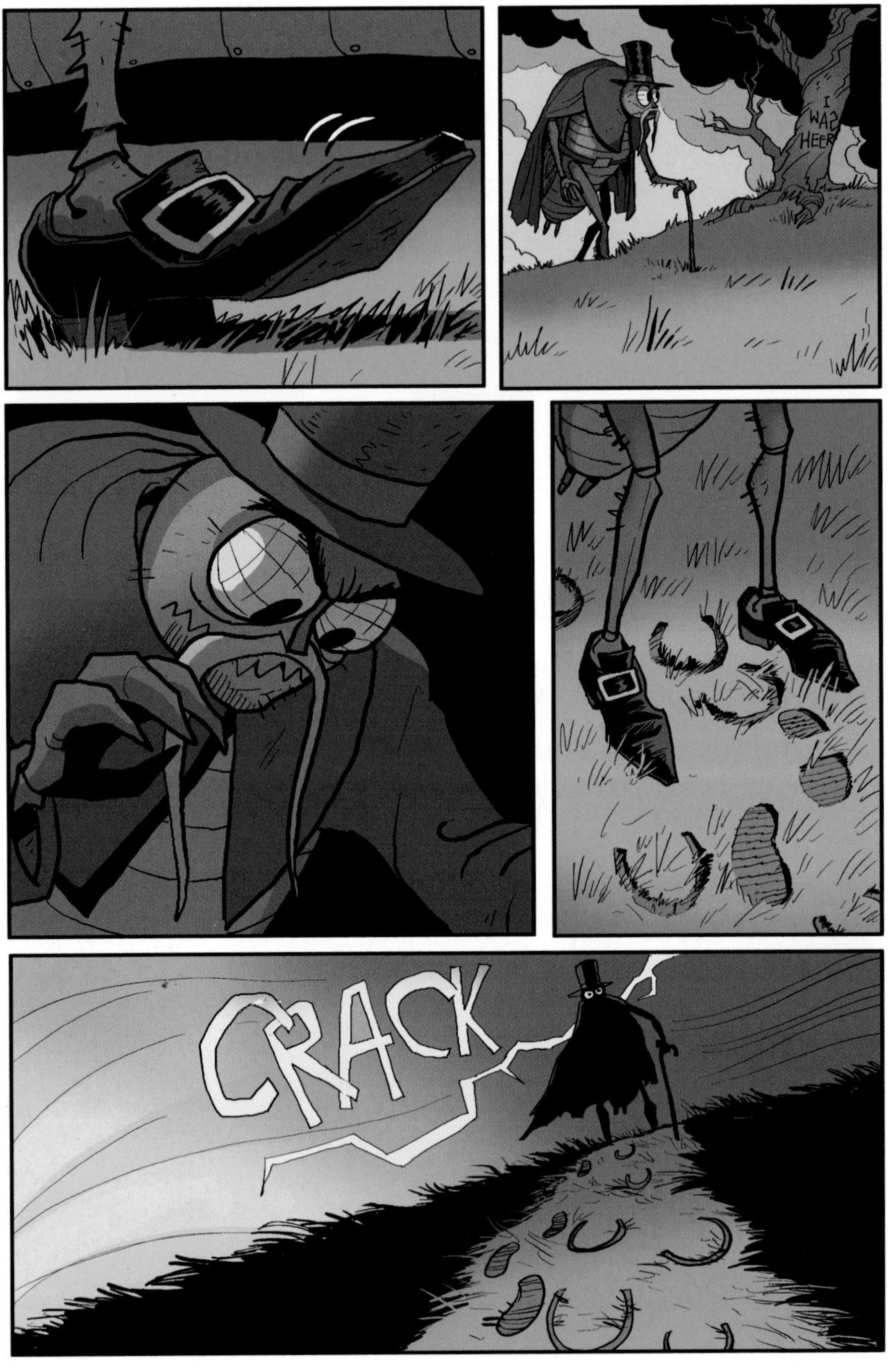
I WAS HEER
CRACK

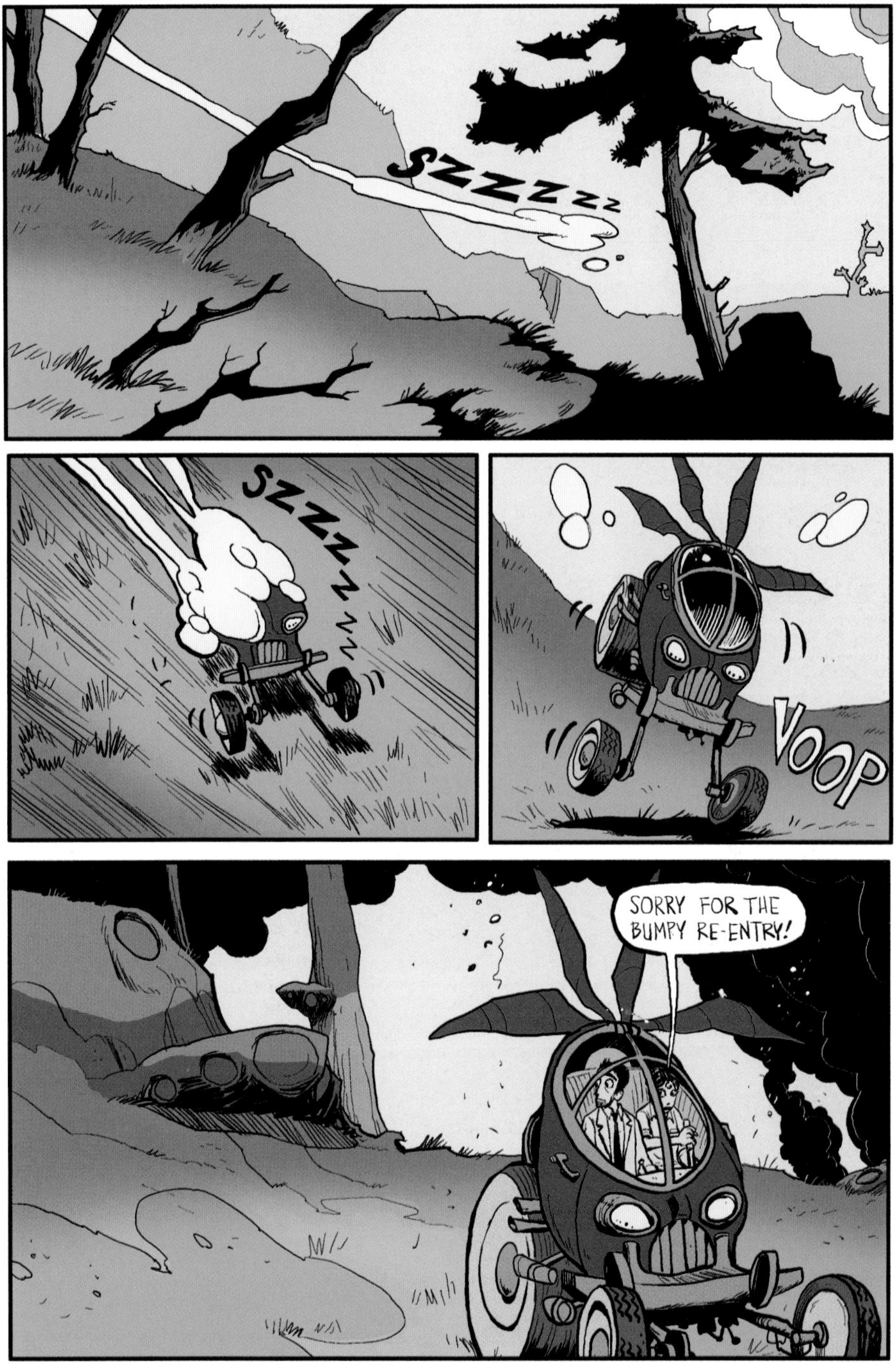
SZZZZZZZ
SZZZZZZZ
VOOP
SORRY FOR THE BUMPY RE-ENTRY!

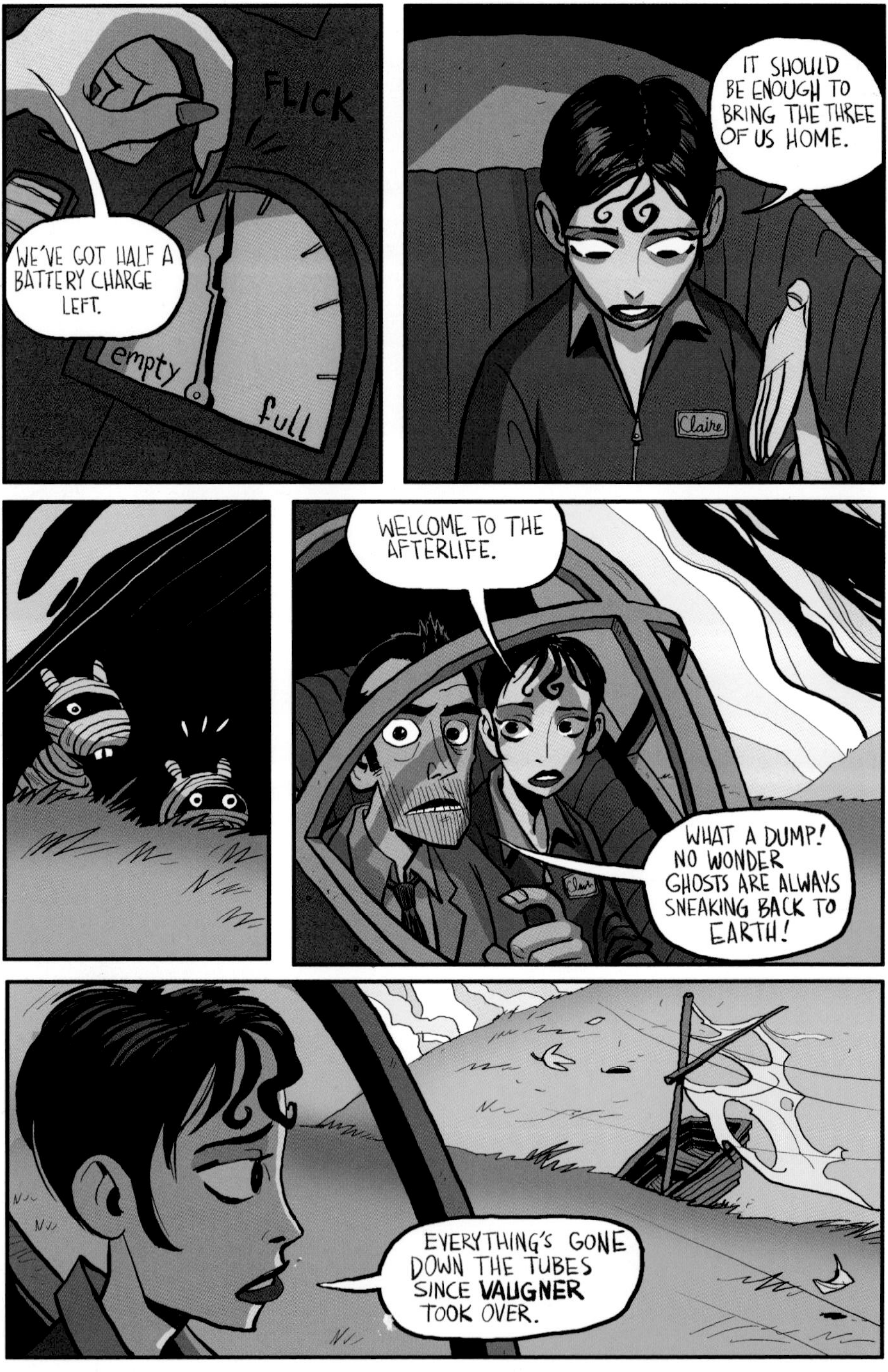
FLICK
WE'VE GOT HALF A BATTERY CHARGE LEFT.
empty
full
IT SHOULD BE ENOUGH TO BRING THE THREE OF US HOME.
Claire
WELCOME TO THE AFTERLIFE.
WHAT A DUMP! NO WONDER GHOSTS ARE ALWAYS SNEAKING BACK TO EARTH!
EVERYTHING'S GONE DOWN THE TUBES SINCE VAUGNER TOOK OVER.

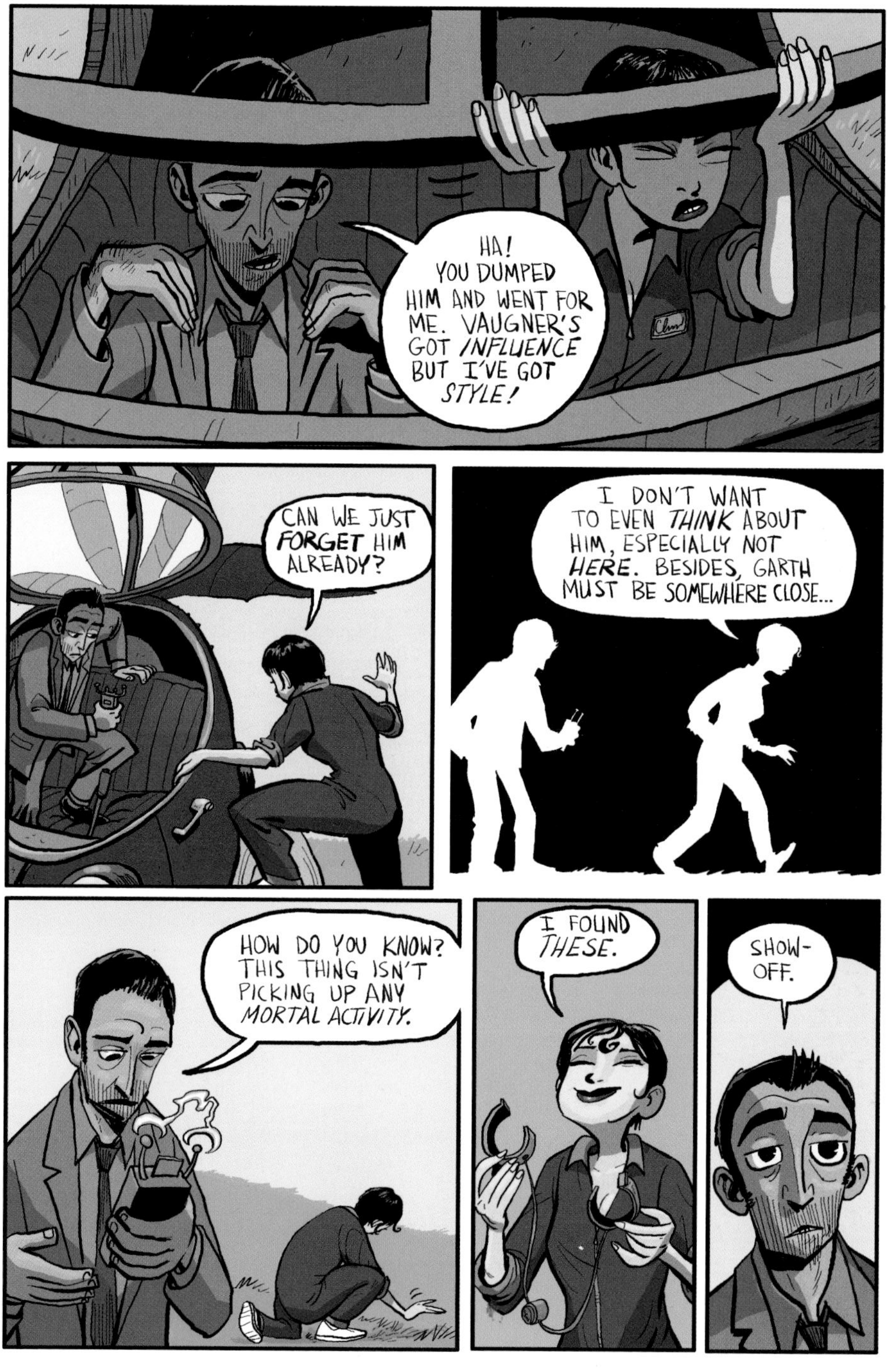
HA! YOU DUMPED HIM AND WENT FOR ME. VAUGNER'S GOT INFLUENCE BUT I'VE GOT STYLE!
CAN WE JUST FORGET HIM ALREADY?
I DON'T WANT TO EVEN THINK ABOUT HIM, ESPECIALLY NOT HERE. BESIDES, GARTH MUST BE SOMEWHERE CLOSE...
HOW DO YOU KNOW? THIS THING ISN'T PICKING UP ANY MORTAL ACTIVITY.
I FOUND THESE.
SHOW-OFF.

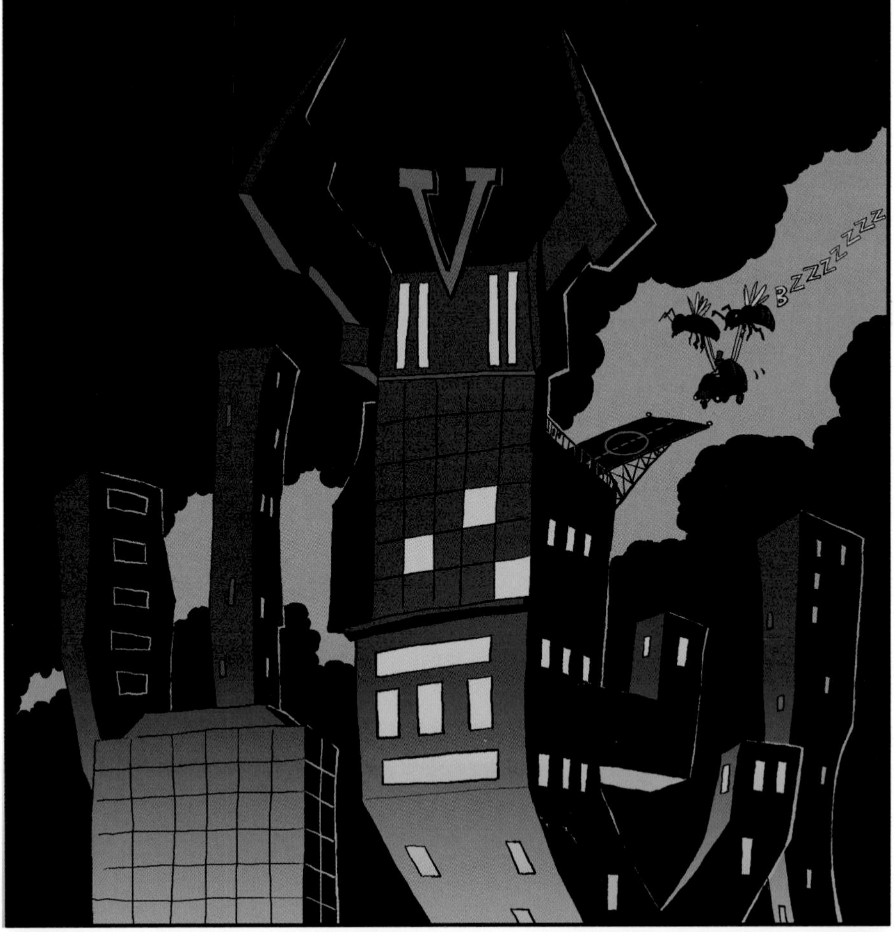
V
BZZZZZZZ

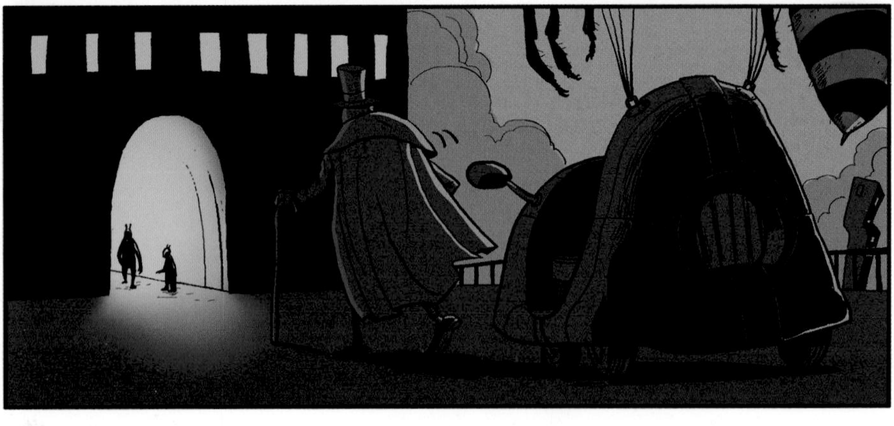

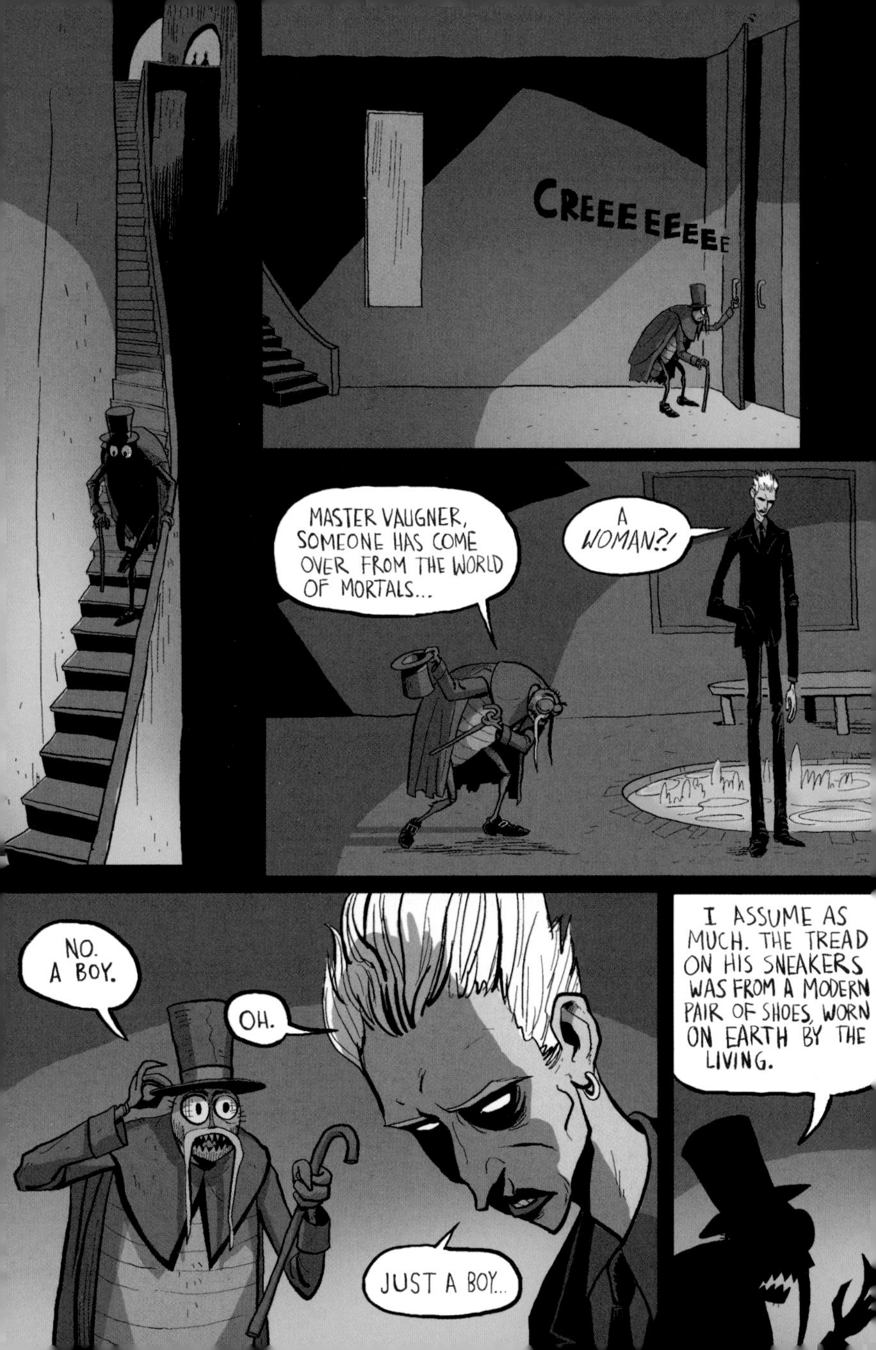
CREEEEEEEEE
MASTER VAUGNER, SOMEONE HAS COME OVER FROM THE WORLD OF MORTALS...
A *WOMAN?!*
NO. A BOY.
OH.
JUST A BOY...
I ASSUME AS MUCH. THE TREAD ON HIS SNEAKERS WAS FROM A MODERN PAIR OF SHOES, WORN ON EARTH BY THE LIVING.

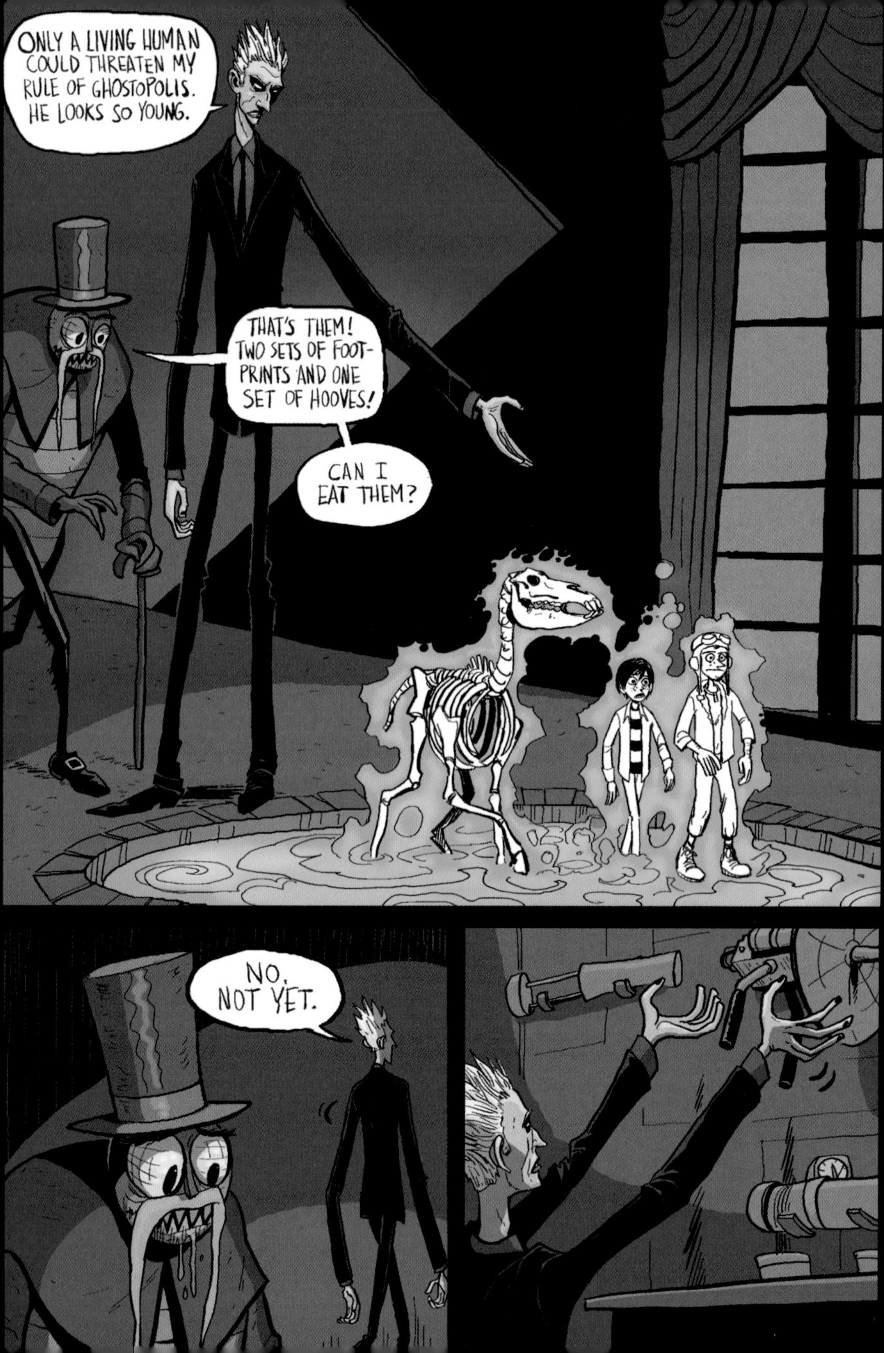
ONLY A LIVING HUMAN COULD THREATEN MY RULE OF GHOSTOPOLIS. HE LOOKS SO YOUNG.
THAT'S THEM! TWO SETS OF FOOT-PRINTS AND ONE SET OF HOOVES!
CAN I EAT THEM?
NO, NOT YET.

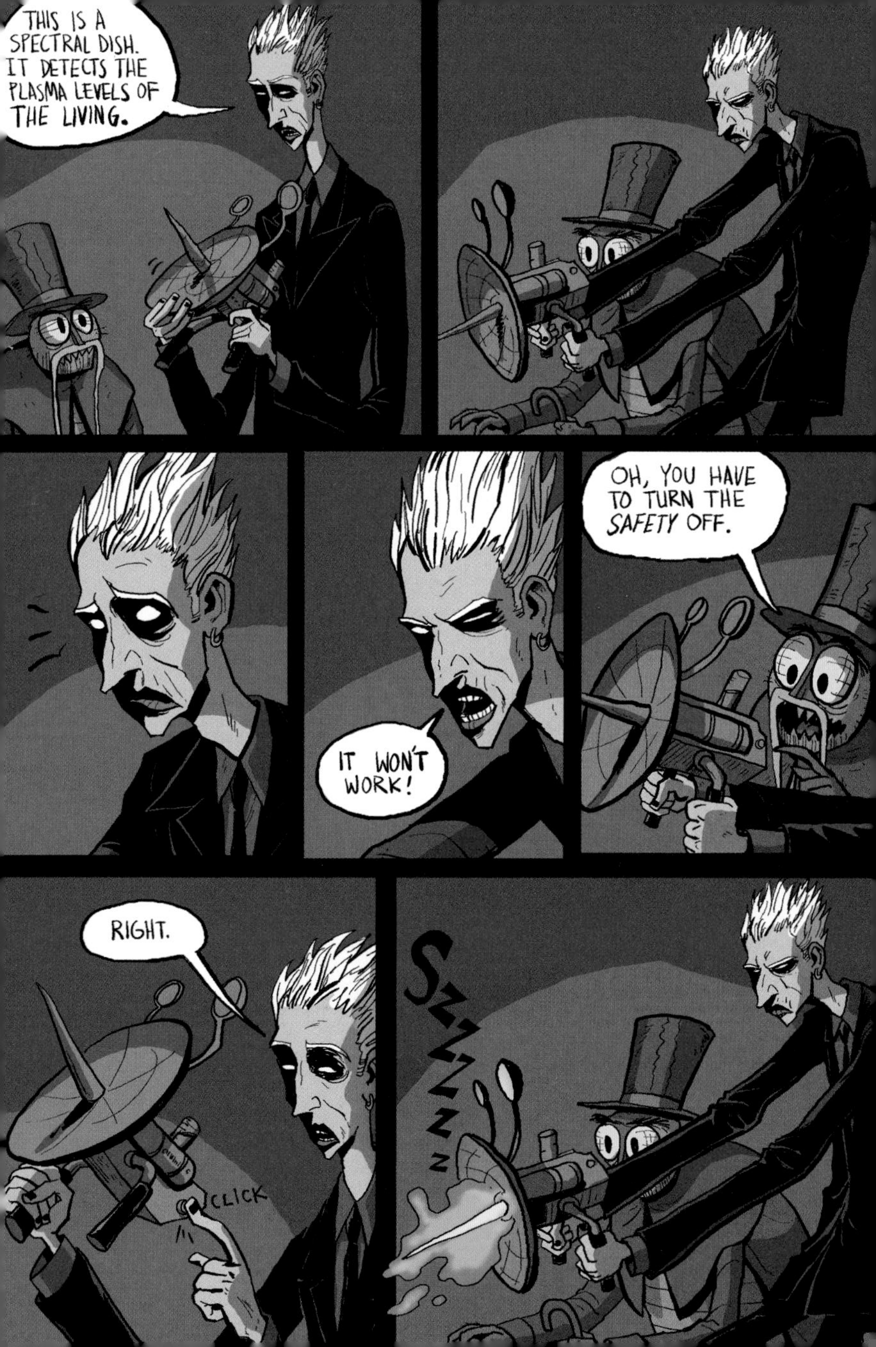
THIS IS A SPECTRAL DISH. IT DETECTS THE PLASMA LEVELS OF THE LIVING.
IT WON'T WORK!
OH, YOU HAVE TO TURN THE *SAFETY* OFF.
RIGHT.
CLICK
SZZZZZZ

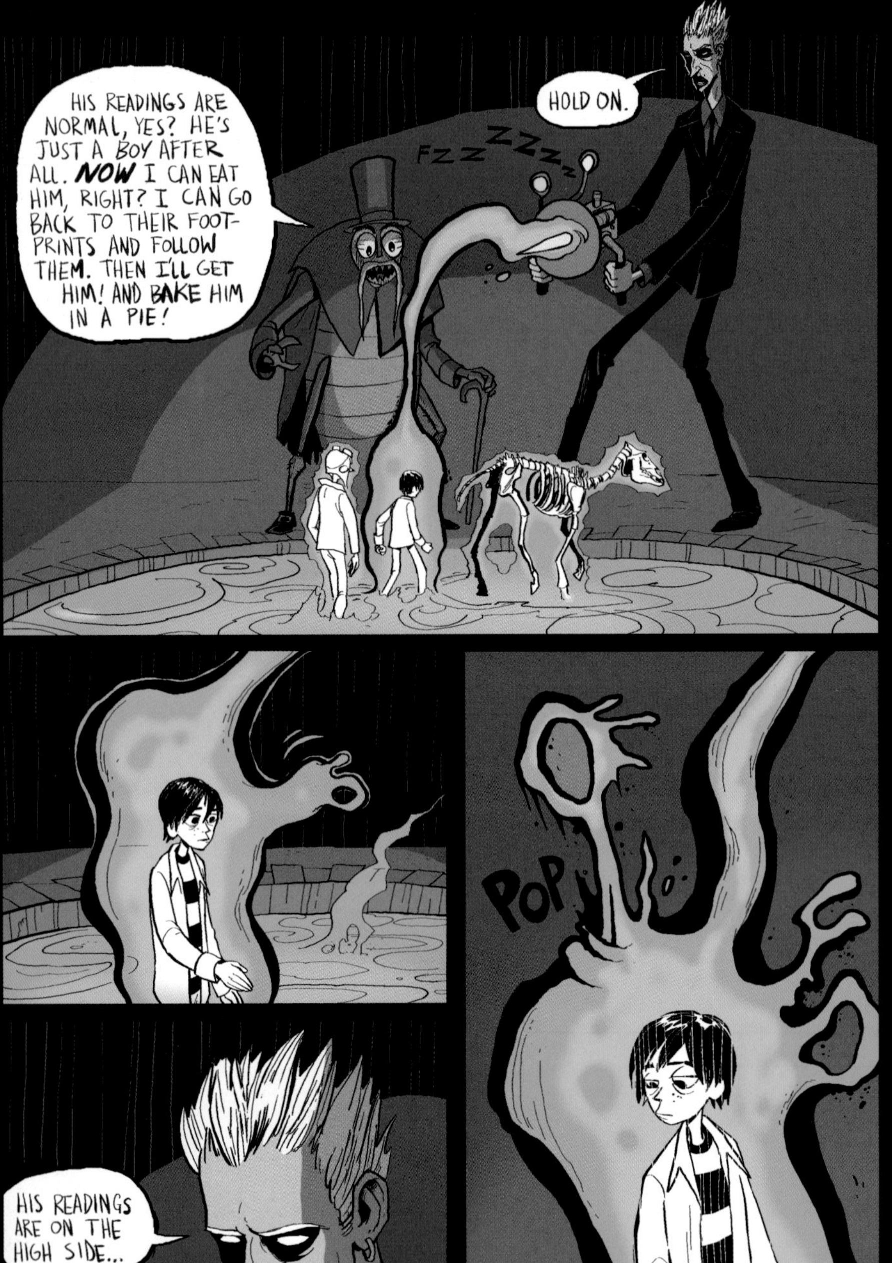
HIS READINGS ARE NORMAL, YES? HE'S JUST A BOY AFTER ALL. NOW I CAN EAT HIM, RIGHT? I CAN GO BACK TO THEIR FOOTPRINTS AND FOLLOW THEM. THEN I'LL GET HIM! AND BAKE HIM IN A PIE!
HOLD ON.
FZZ ZZZZZ
POP
HIS READINGS ARE ON THE HIGH SIDE...

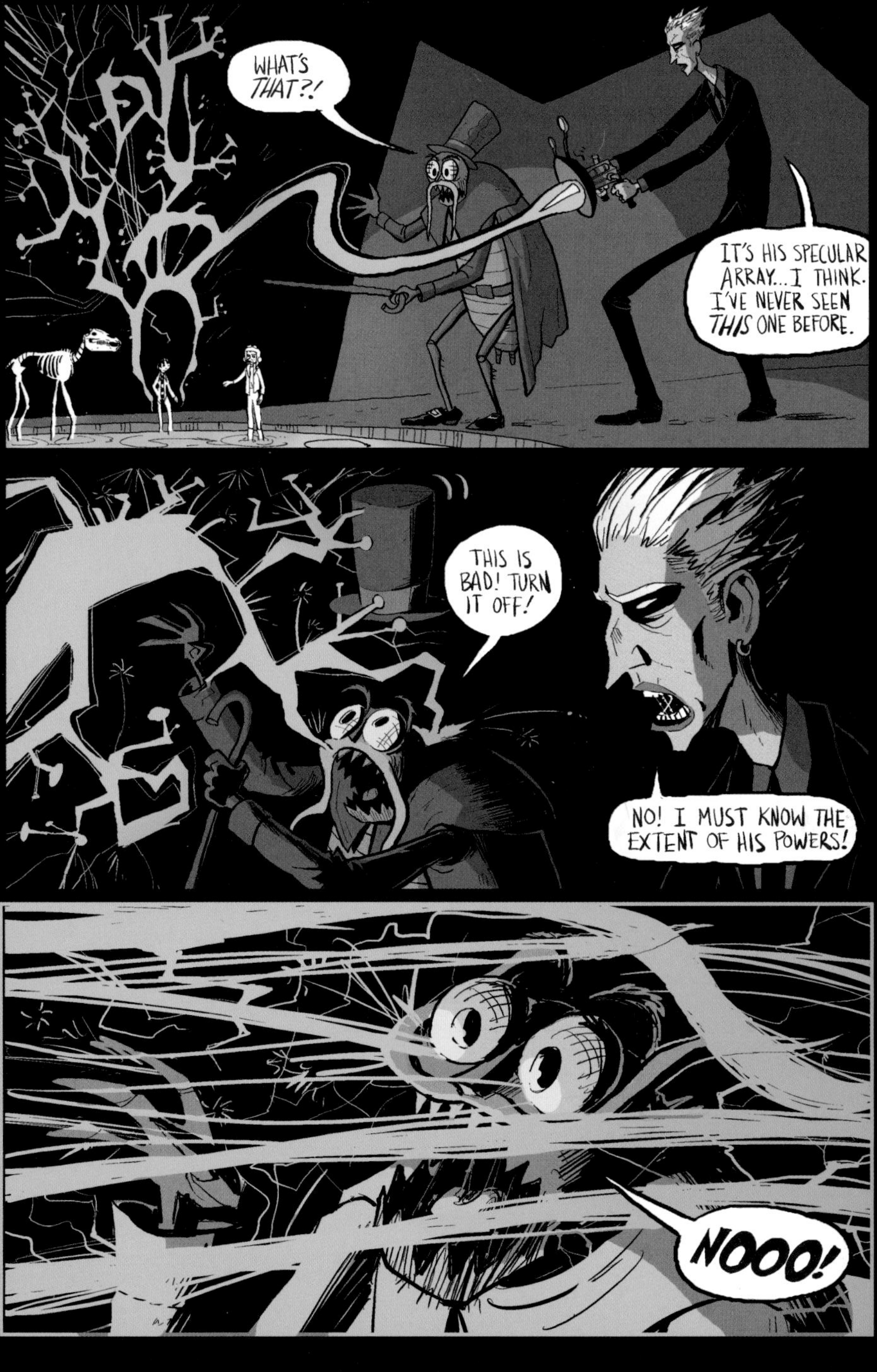
WHAT'S THAT?!
IT'S HIS SPECULAR ARRAY... I THINK. I'VE NEVER SEEN THIS ONE BEFORE.
THIS IS BAD! TURN IT OFF!
NO! I MUST KNOW THE EXTENT OF HIS POWERS!
NOOO!

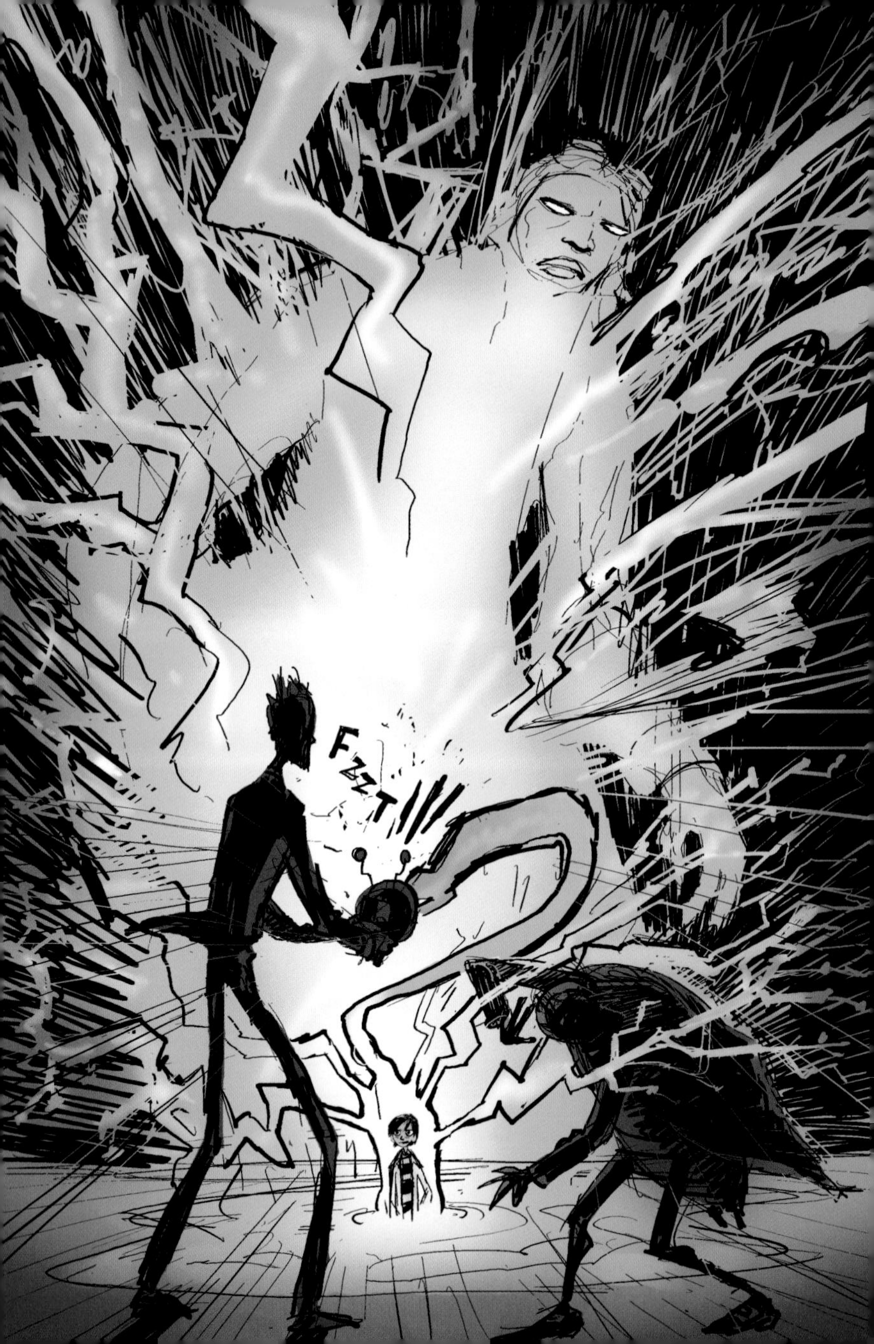
FZZT!!!

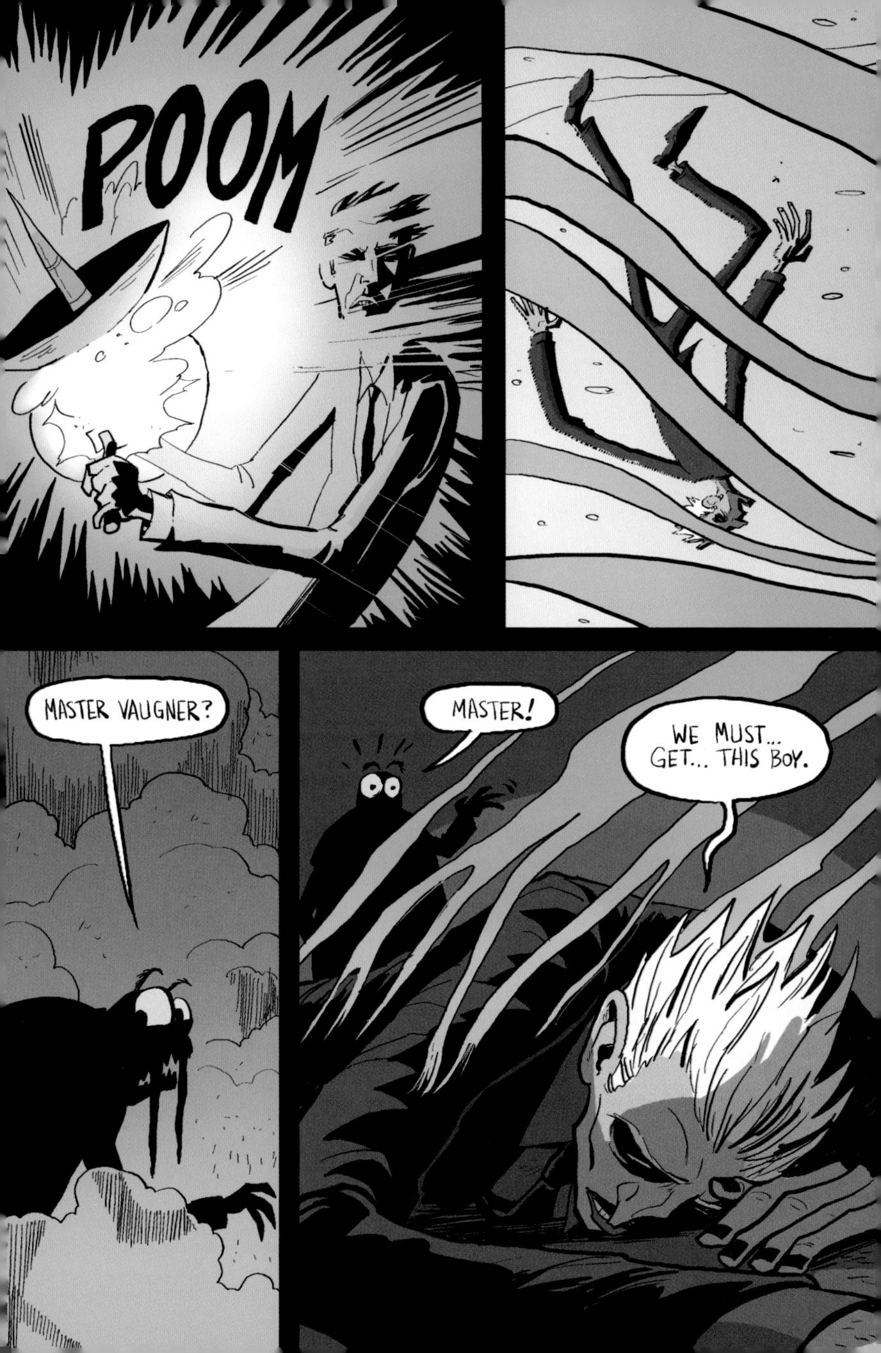
POOM
MASTER VAUGNER?
MASTER!
WE MUST... GET... THIS BOY.

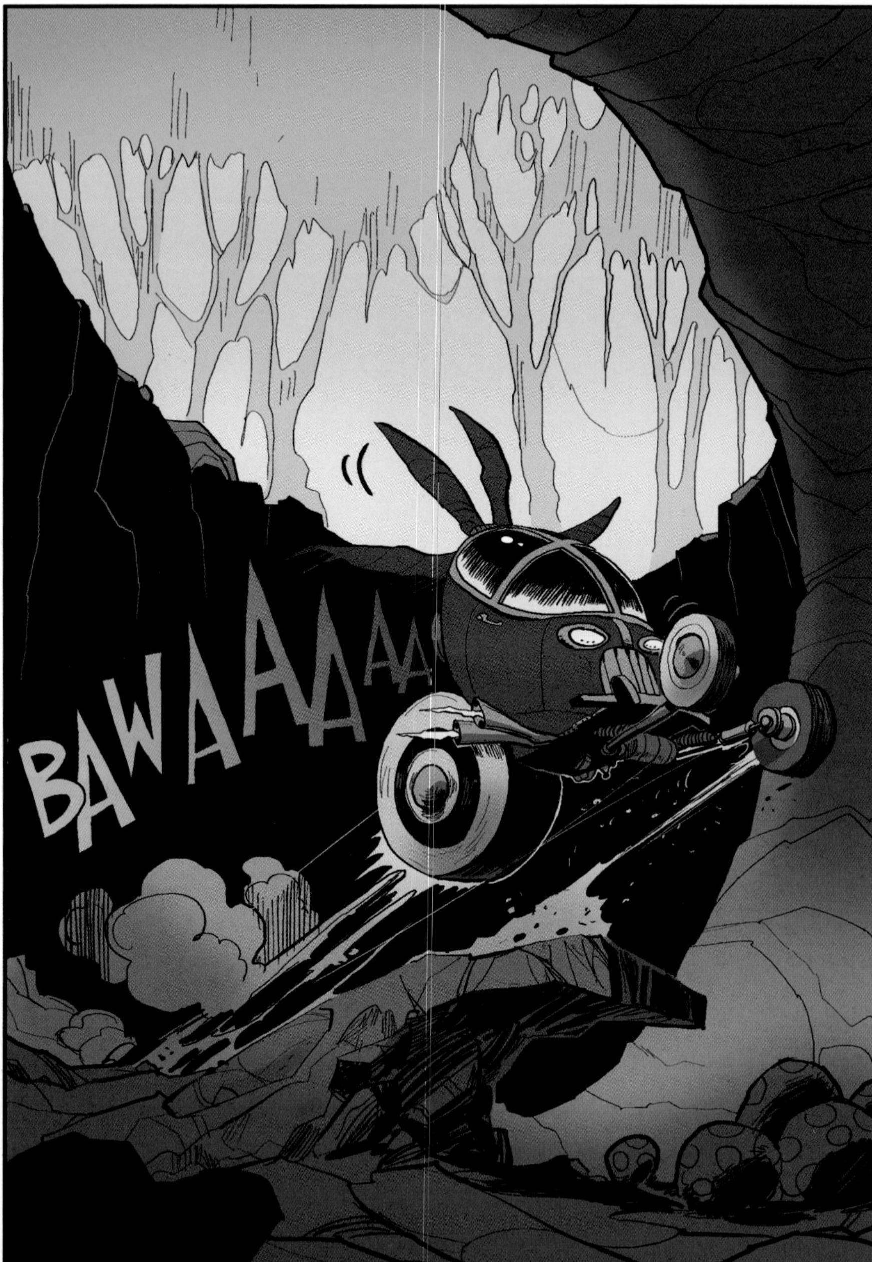
BAWAAAAAA

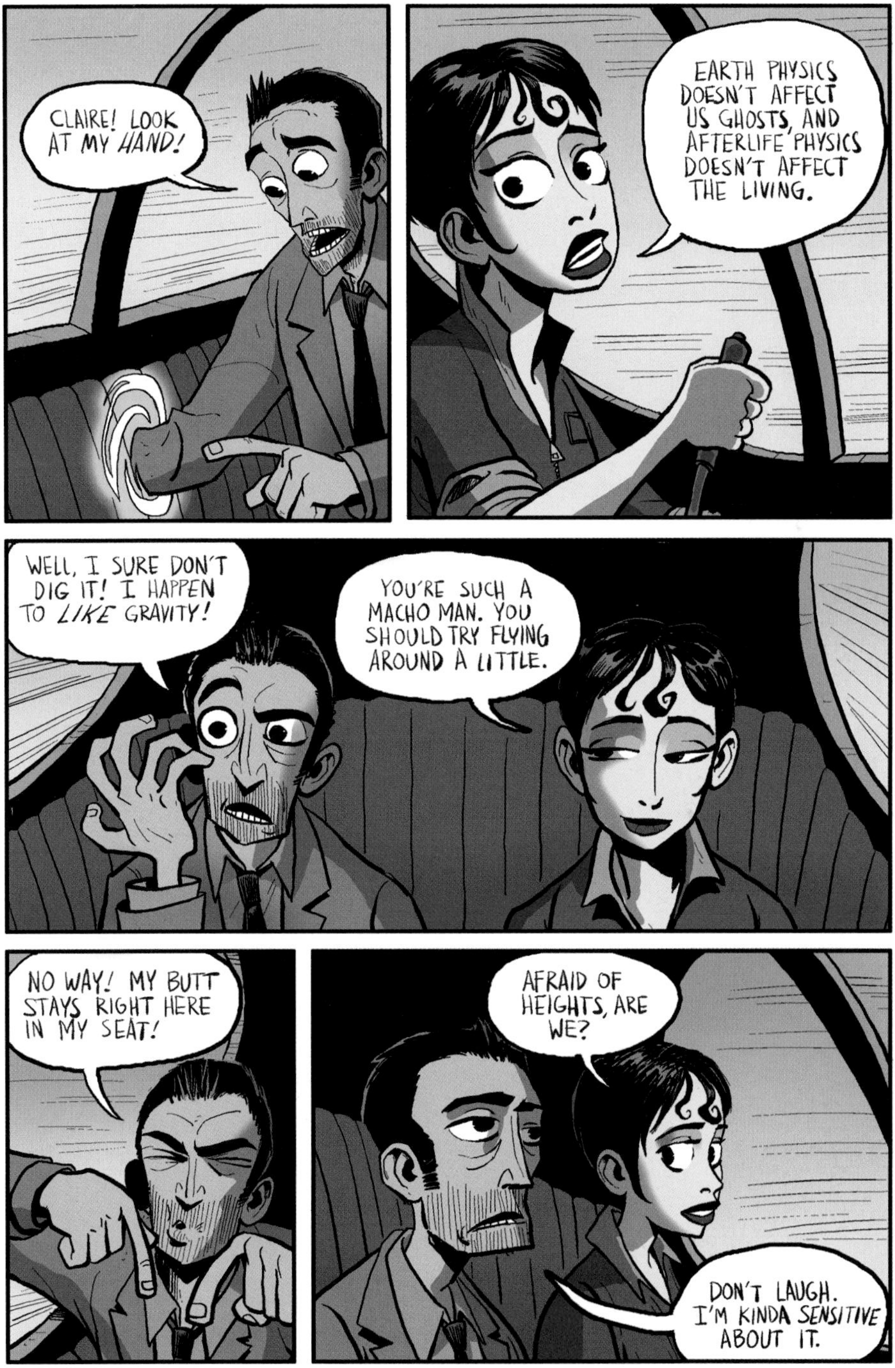
CLAIRE! LOOK AT MY *HAND!*
EARTH PHYSICS DOESN'T AFFECT US GHOSTS, AND AFTERLIFE PHYSICS DOESN'T AFFECT THE LIVING.
WELL, I SURE DON'T DIG IT! I HAPPEN TO *LIKE* GRAVITY!
YOU'RE SUCH A MACHO MAN. YOU SHOULD TRY FLYING AROUND A LITTLE.
NO WAY! MY BUTT STAYS RIGHT HERE IN MY SEAT!
AFRAID OF HEIGHTS, ARE WE?
DON'T LAUGH. I'M KINDA SENSITIVE ABOUT IT.

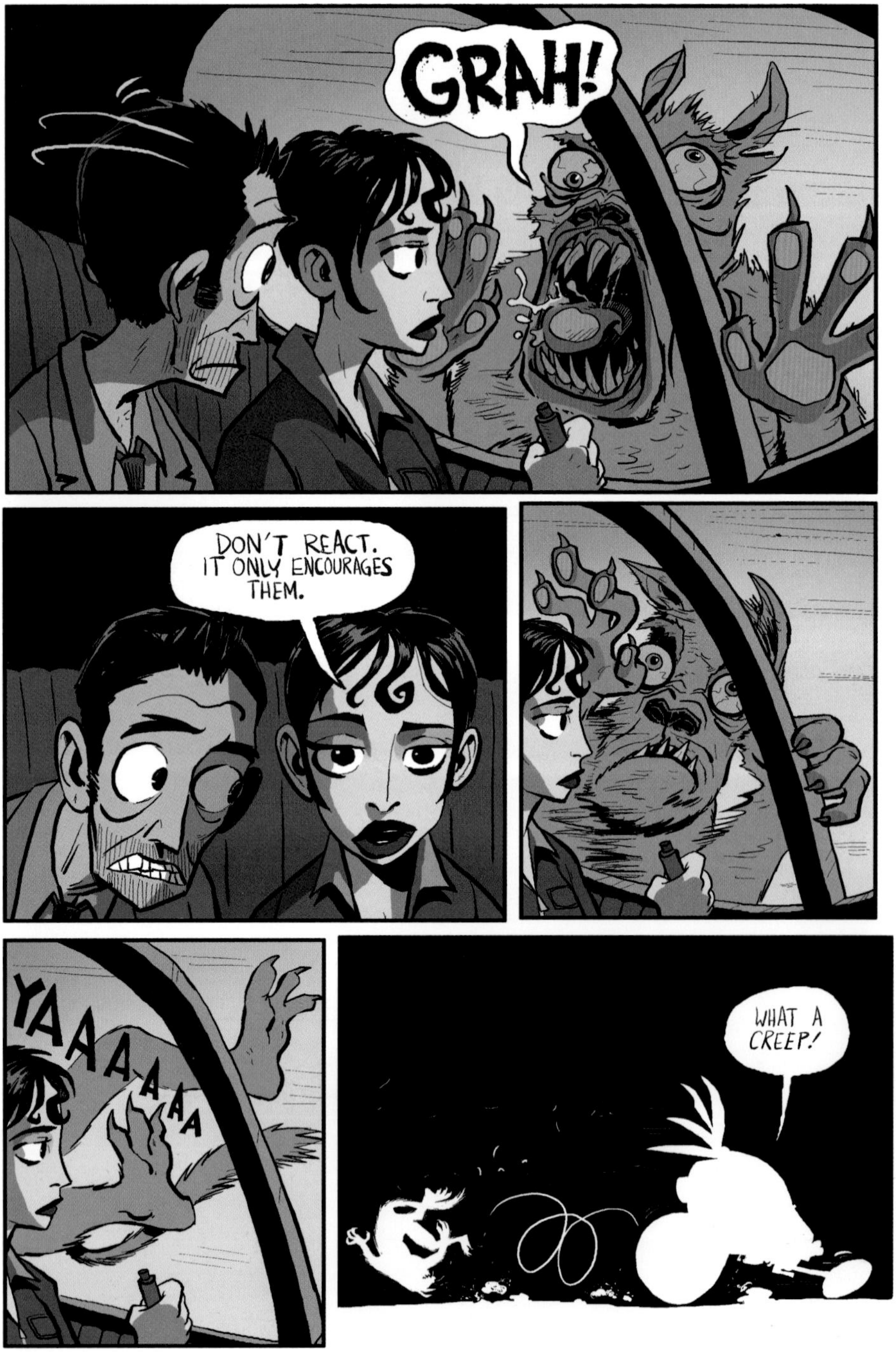
GRAH!
DON'T REACT. IT ONLY ENCOURAGES THEM.
YAAAAAAAA
WHAT A CREEP!

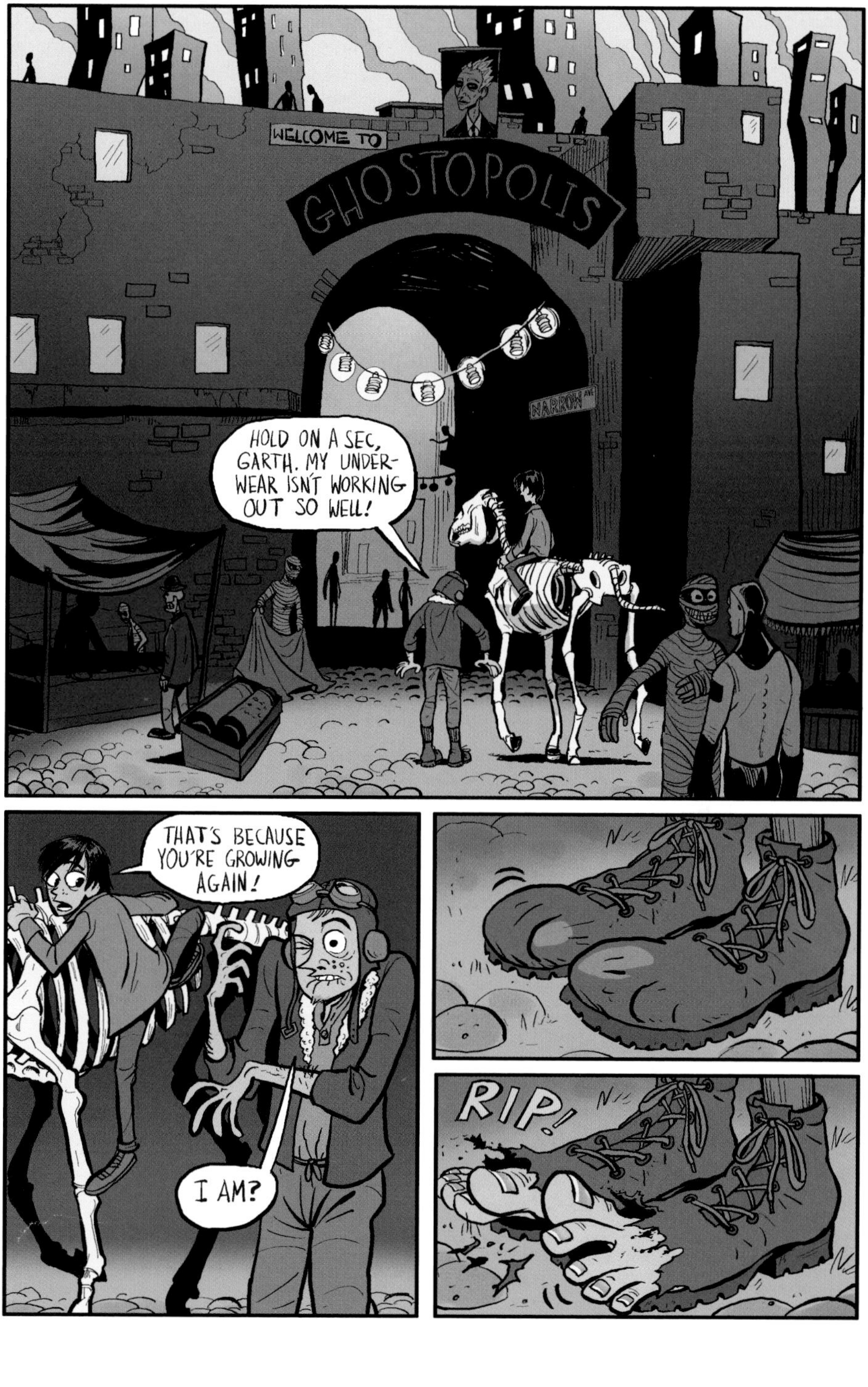
WELCOME TO
GHOSTOPOLIS
NARROW AVE
HOLD ON A SEC, GARTH. MY UNDERWEAR ISN'T WORKING OUT SO WELL!
THAT'S BECAUSE YOU'RE GROWING AGAIN!
I AM?
RIP!

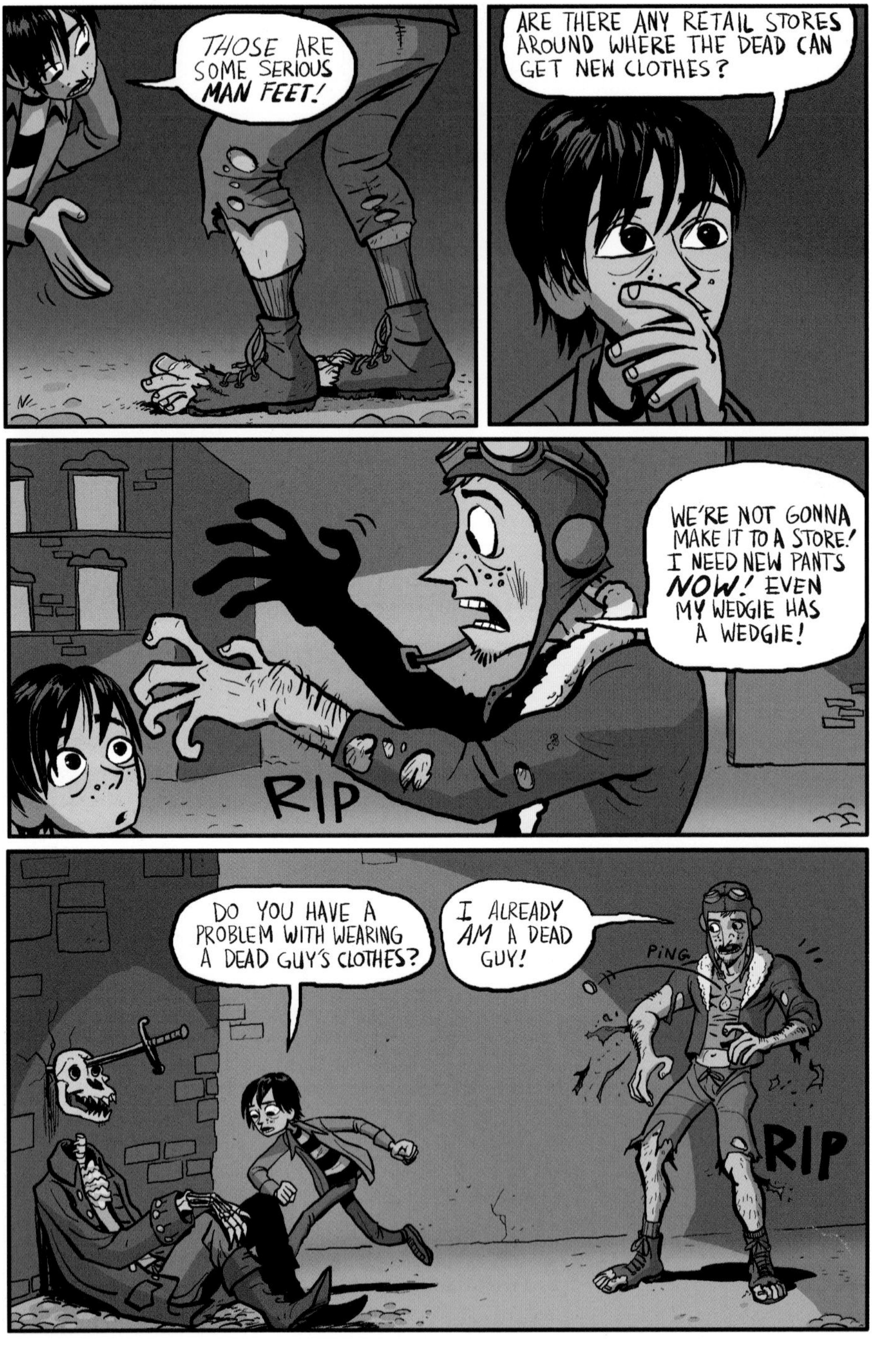
THOSE ARE SOME SERIOUS MAN FEET!
ARE THERE ANY RETAIL STORES AROUND WHERE THE DEAD CAN GET NEW CLOTHES?
WE'RE NOT GONNA MAKE IT TO A STORE! I NEED NEW PANTS NOW! EVEN MY WEDGIE HAS A WEDGIE!
RIP
DO YOU HAVE A PROBLEM WITH WEARING A DEAD GUY'S CLOTHES?
I ALREADY AM A DEAD GUY!
PING
RIP

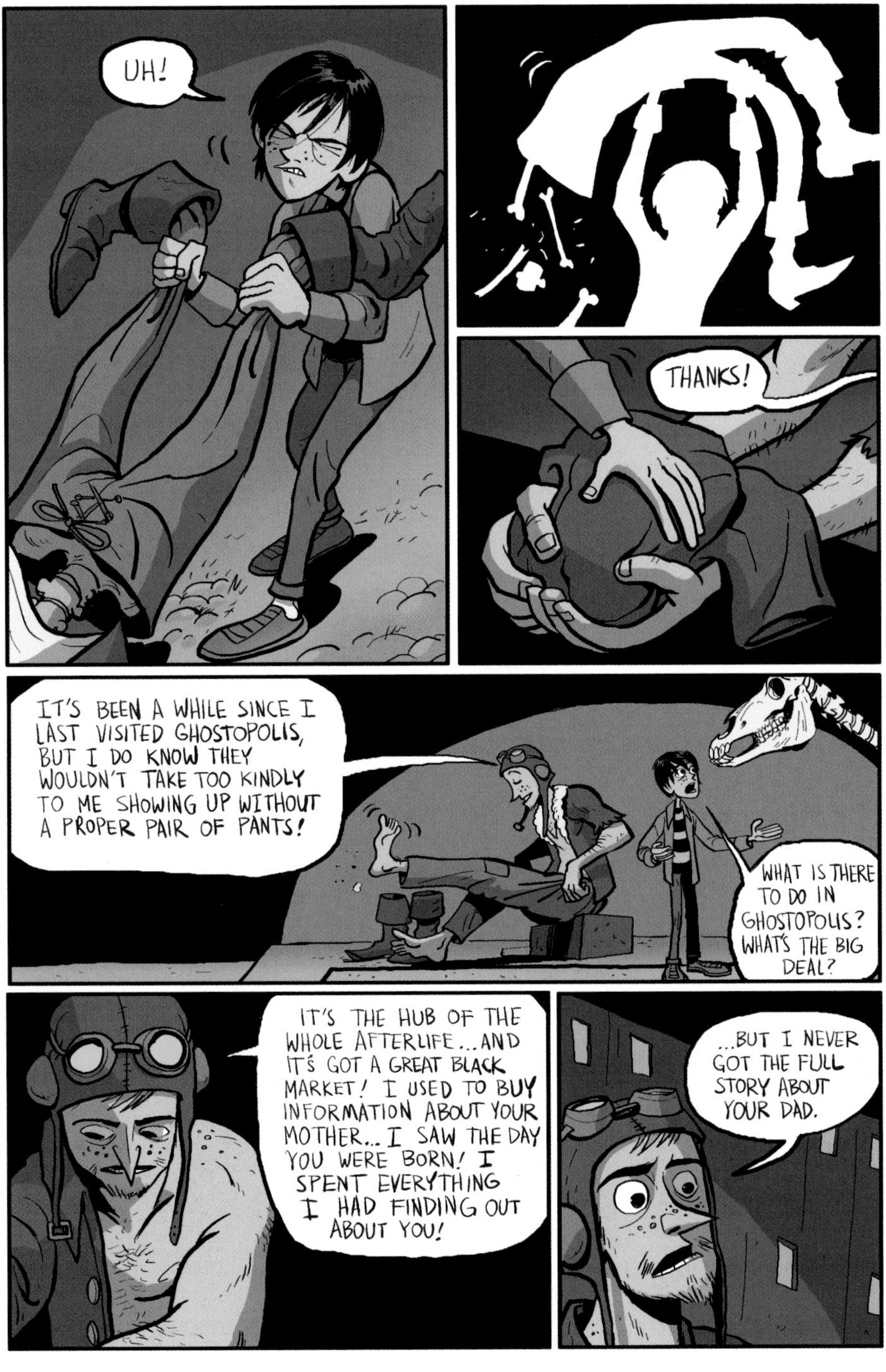
UH!
THANKS!
IT'S BEEN A WHILE SINCE I LAST VISITED GHOSTOPOLIS, BUT I DO KNOW THEY WOULDN'T TAKE TOO KINDLY TO ME SHOWING UP WITHOUT A PROPER PAIR OF PANTS!
WHAT IS THERE TO DO IN GHOSTOPOLIS? WHAT'S THE BIG DEAL?
IT'S THE HUB OF THE WHOLE AFTERLIFE... AND IT'S GOT A GREAT BLACK MARKET! I USED TO BUY INFORMATION ABOUT YOUR MOTHER... I SAW THE DAY YOU WERE BORN! I SPENT EVERYTHING I HAD FINDING OUT ABOUT YOU!
...BUT I NEVER GOT THE FULL STORY ABOUT YOUR DAD.

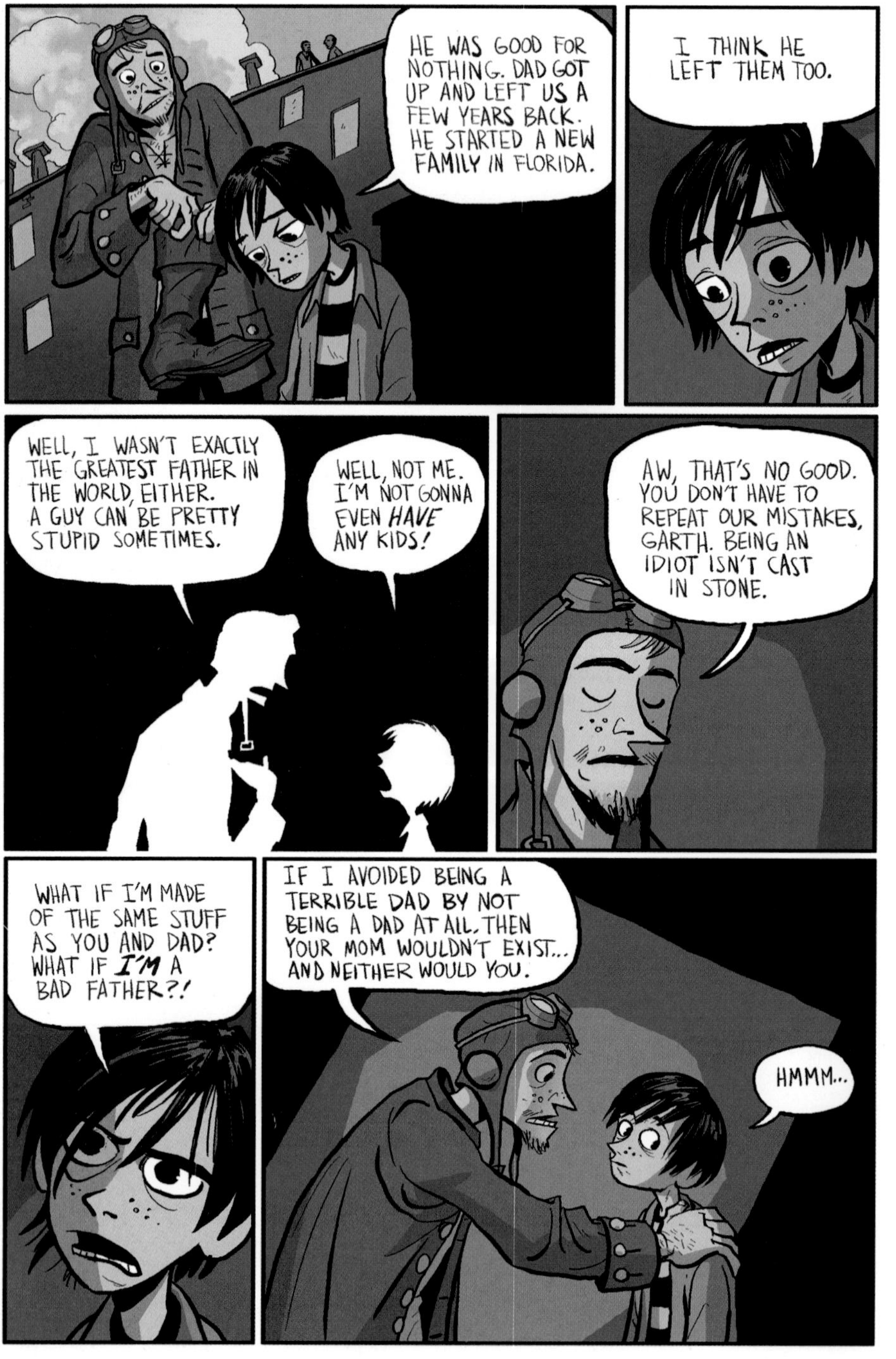
HE WAS GOOD FOR NOTHING. DAD GOT UP AND LEFT US A FEW YEARS BACK. HE STARTED A NEW FAMILY IN FLORIDA.
I THINK HE LEFT THEM TOO.
WELL, I WASN'T EXACTLY THE GREATEST FATHER IN THE WORLD, EITHER. A GUY CAN BE PRETTY STUPID SOMETIMES.
WELL, NOT ME. I'M NOT GONNA EVEN HAVE ANY KIDS!
AW, THAT'S NO GOOD. YOU DON'T HAVE TO REPEAT OUR MISTAKES, GARTH. BEING AN IDIOT ISN'T CAST IN STONE.
WHAT IF I'M MADE OF THE SAME STUFF AS YOU AND DAD? WHAT IF I'M A BAD FATHER?!
IF I AVOIDED BEING A TERRIBLE DAD BY NOT BEING A DAD AT ALL, THEN YOUR MOM WOULDN'T EXIST... AND NEITHER WOULD YOU.
HMMM...

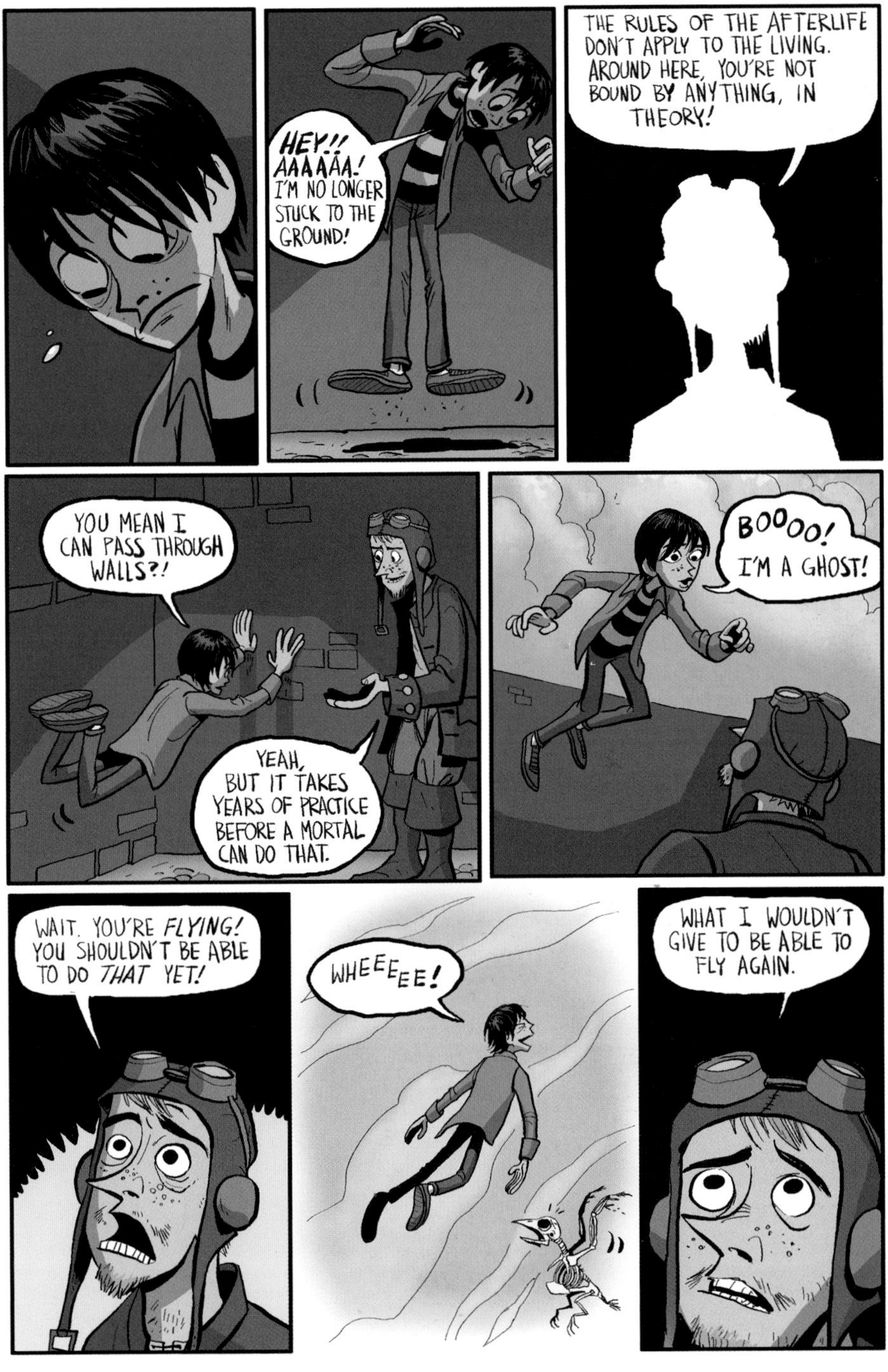
HEY!! AAAAAA! I'M NO LONGER STUCK TO THE GROUND!
THE RULES OF THE AFTERLIFE DON'T APPLY TO THE LIVING. AROUND HERE, YOU'RE NOT BOUND BY ANYTHING, IN THEORY!
YOU MEAN I CAN PASS THROUGH WALLS?!
YEAH, BUT IT TAKES YEARS OF PRACTICE BEFORE A MORTAL CAN DO THAT.
BOOOO! I'M A GHOST!
WAIT. YOU'RE FLYING! YOU SHOULDN'T BE ABLE TO DO THAT YET!
WHEEEEE!
WHAT I WOULDN'T GIVE TO BE ABLE TO FLY AGAIN.

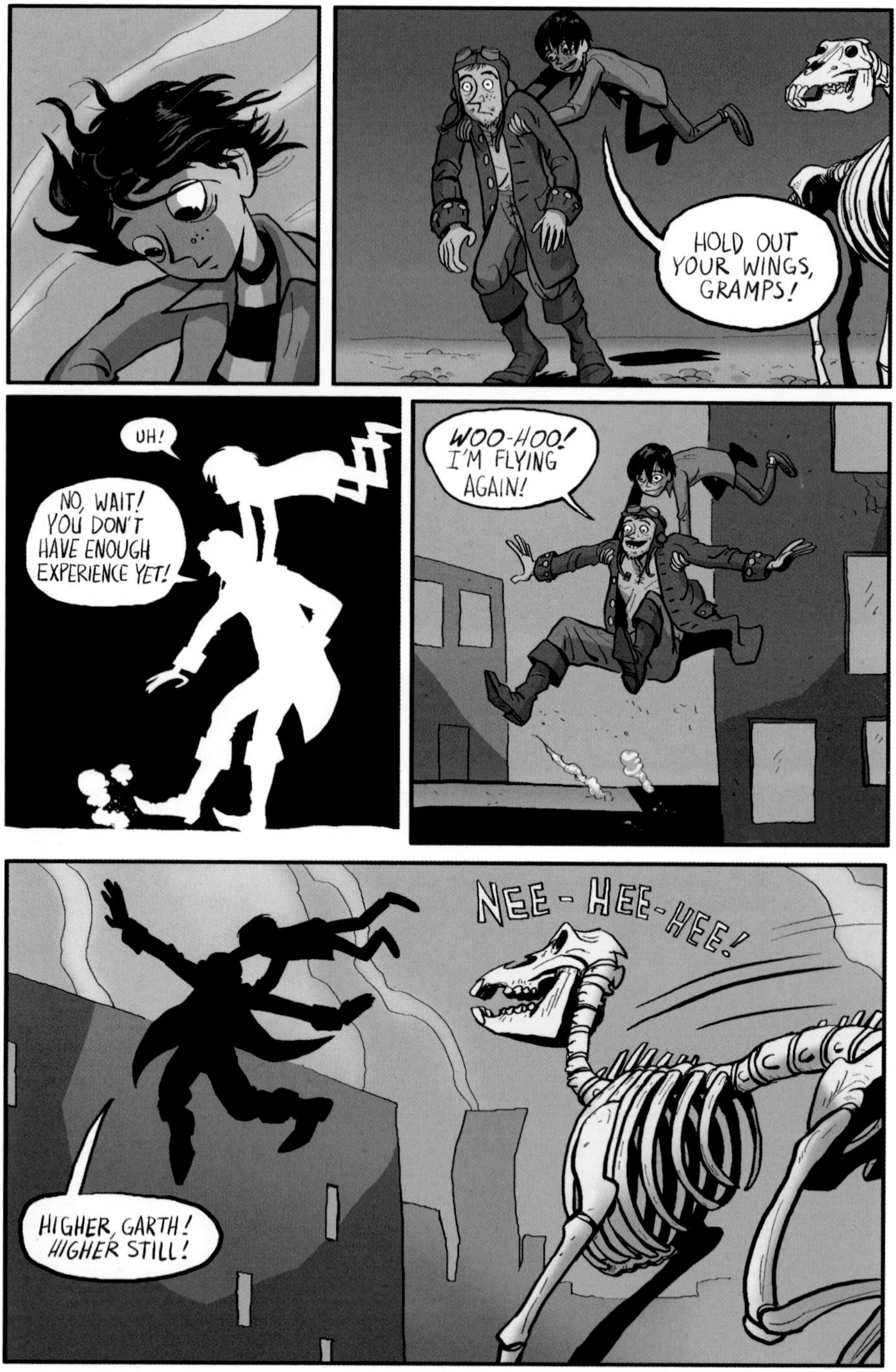
HOLD OUT YOUR WINGS, GRAMPS!
UH!
NO, WAIT! YOU DON'T HAVE ENOUGH EXPERIENCE YET!
WOO-HOO! I'M FLYING AGAIN!
NEE-HEE-HEE!
HIGHER, GARTH! HIGHER STILL!

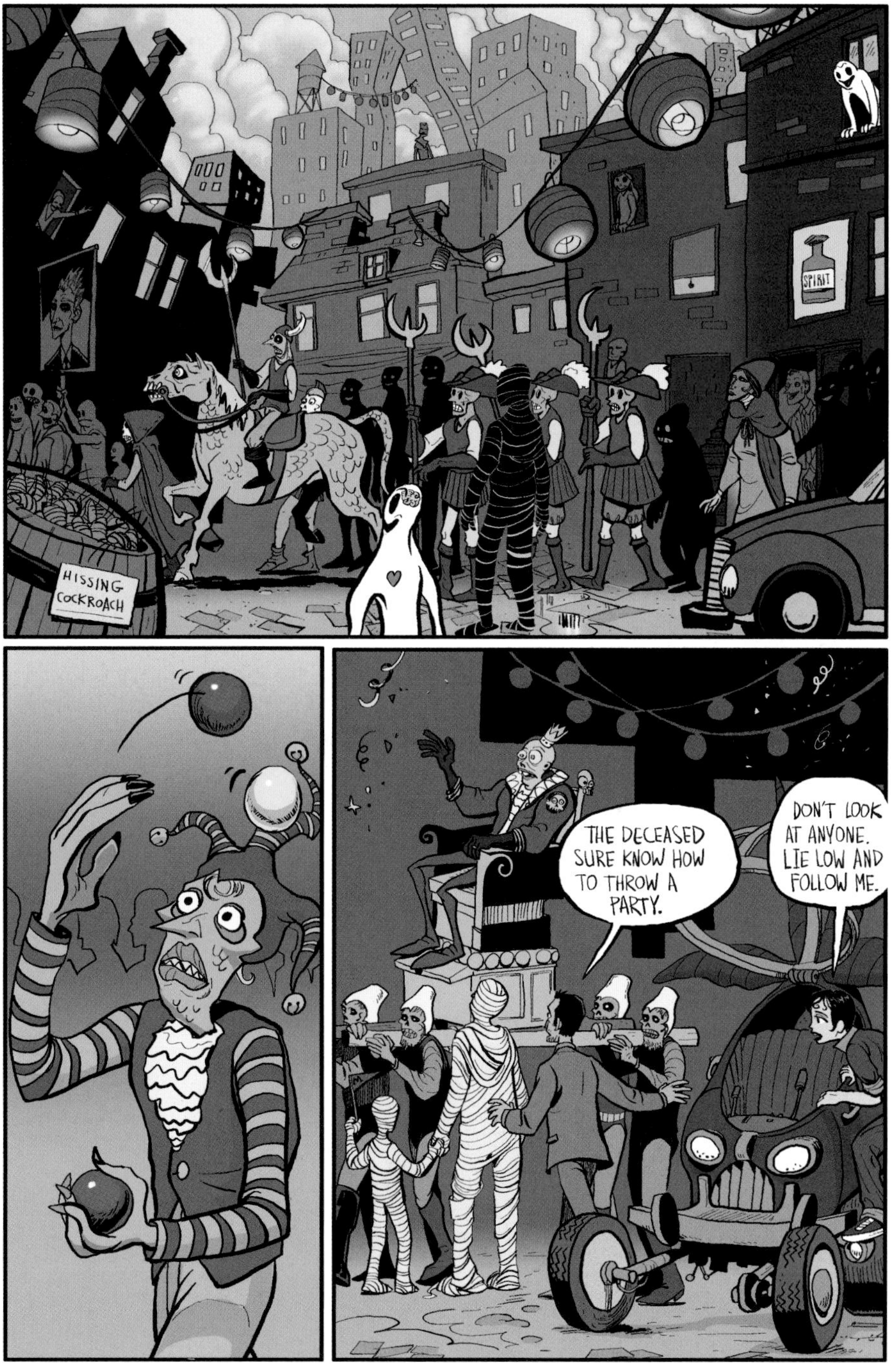
SPIRIT
HISSING COCKROACH
THE DECEASED SURE KNOW HOW TO THROW A PARTY.
DON'T LOOK AT ANYONE. LIE LOW AND FOLLOW ME.

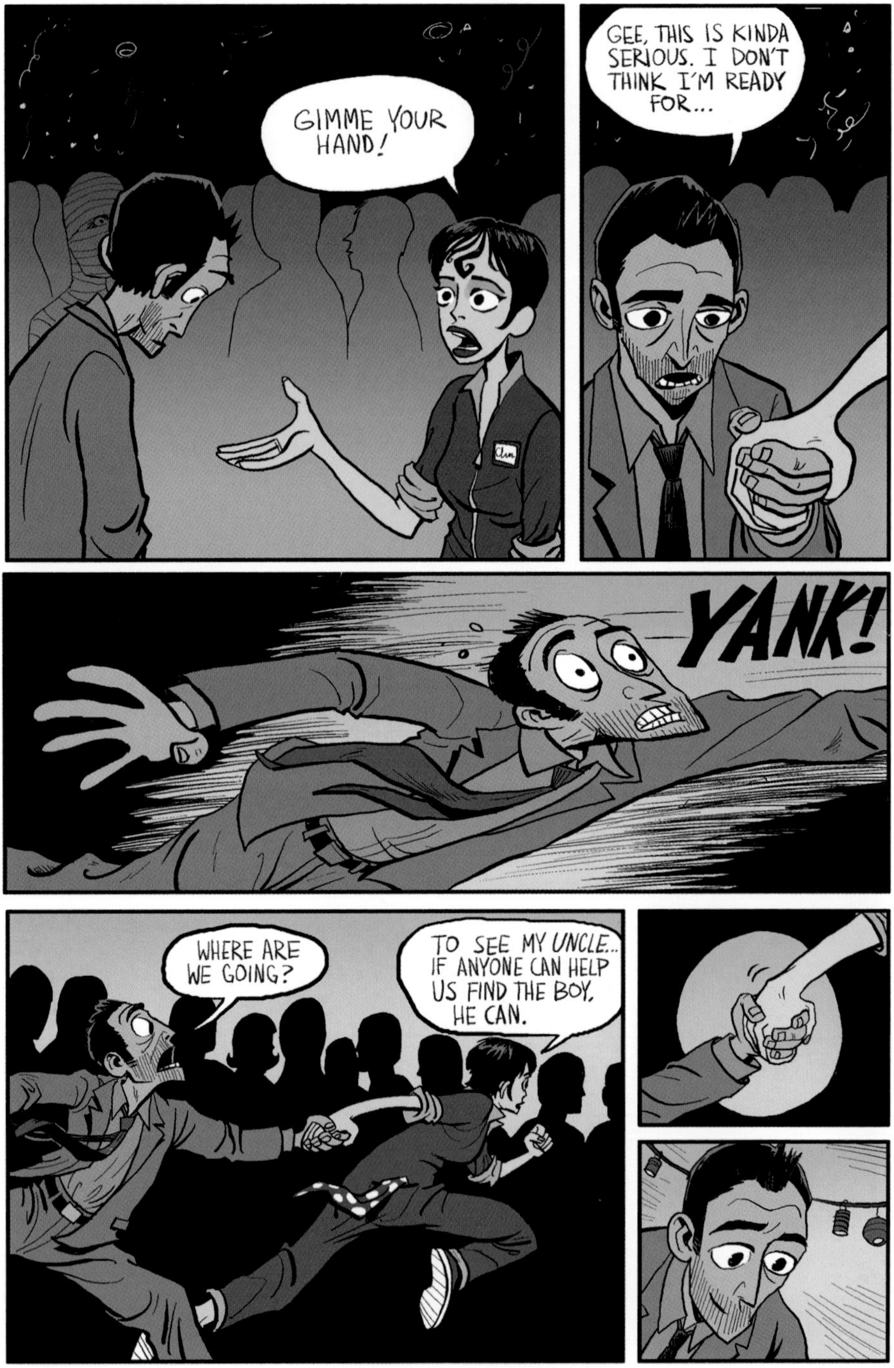
GIMME YOUR HAND!
GEE, THIS IS KINDA SERIOUS. I DON'T THINK I'M READY FOR...
YANK!
WHERE ARE WE GOING?
TO SEE MY UNCLE... IF ANYONE CAN HELP US FIND THE BOY, HE CAN.

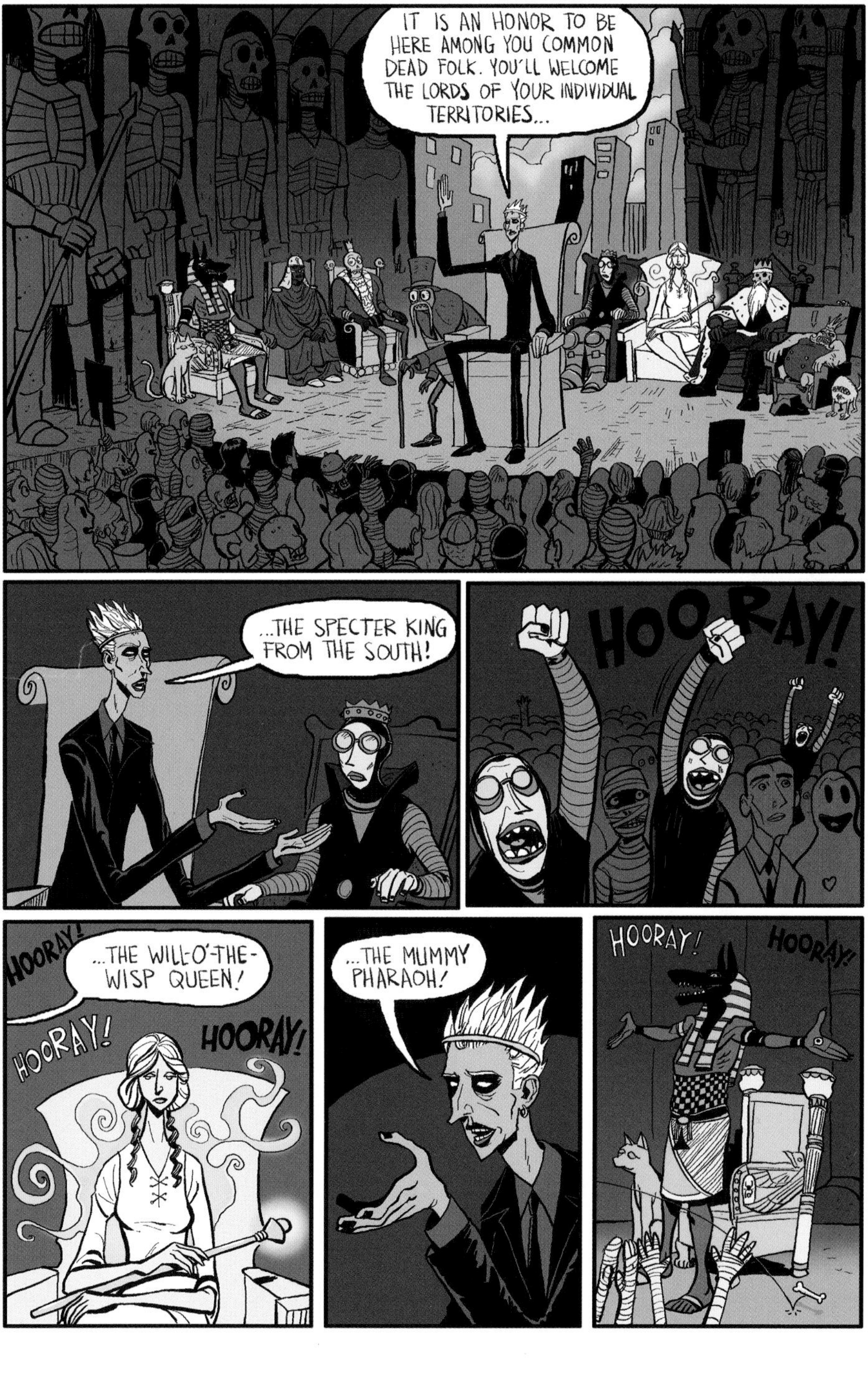
IT IS AN HONOR TO BE HERE AMONG YOU COMMON DEAD FOLK. YOU'LL WELCOME THE LORDS OF YOUR INDIVIDUAL TERRITORIES...
...THE SPECTER KING FROM THE SOUTH!
HOORAY!
HOORAY!
...THE WILL-O'-THE-WISP QUEEN!
HOORAY!
HOORAY!
...THE MUMMY PHARAOH!
HOORAY!
HOORAY!

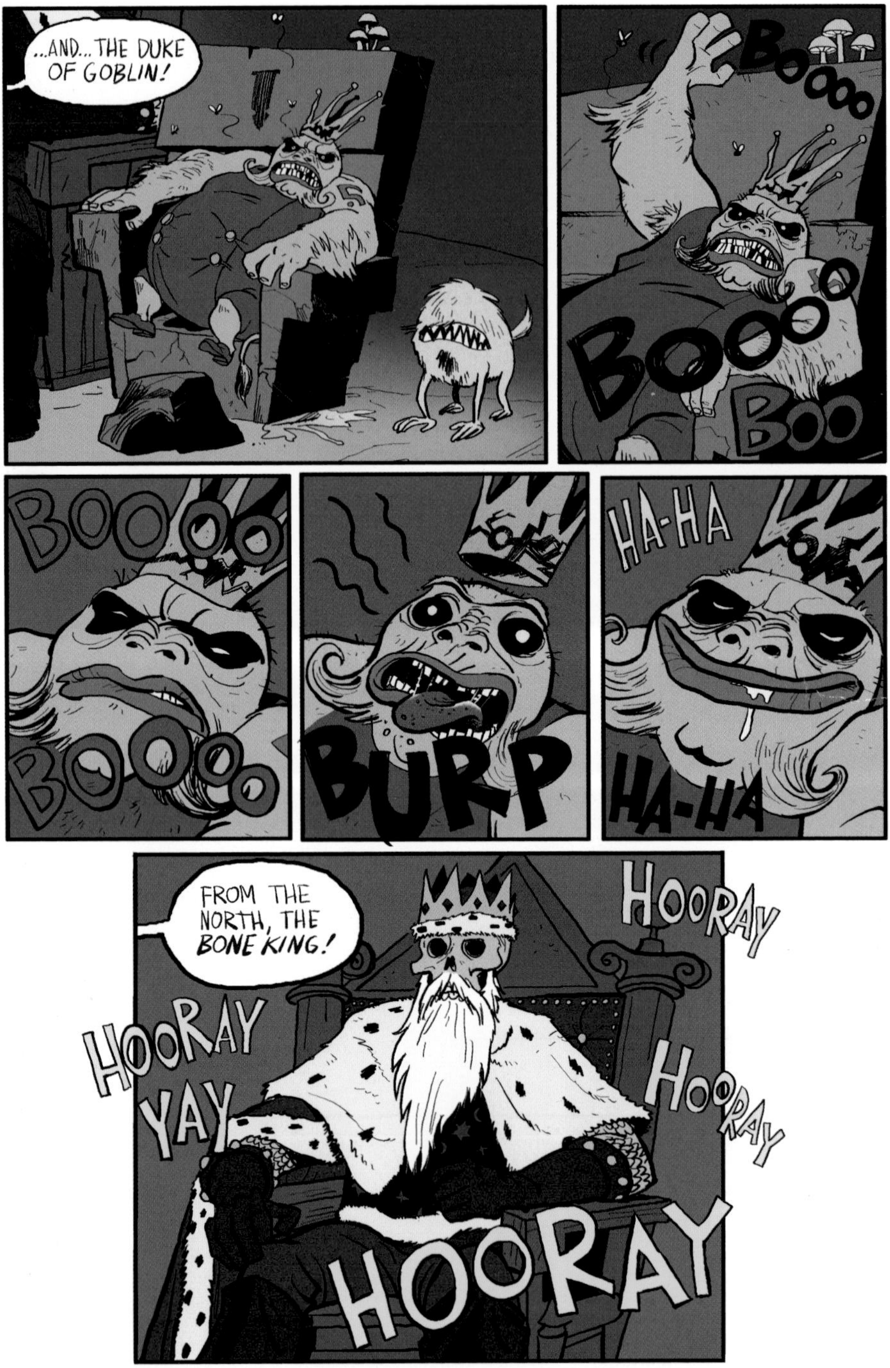
...AND... THE DUKE OF GOBLIN!
BOOOOO
BOOOOO
BOO
BOOOOO
BOOOOO
BURP
HA-HA
HA-HA
FROM THE NORTH, THE BONE KING!
HOORAY
HOORAY
YAY
HOORAY
HOORAY

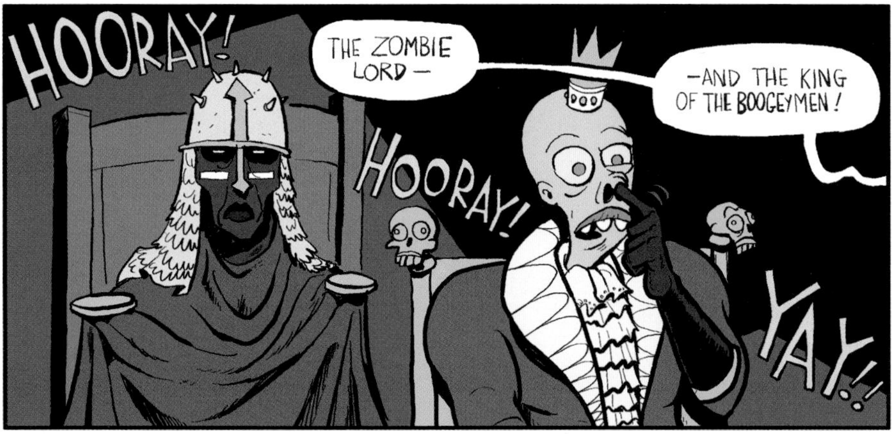
HOORAY!
THE ZOMBIE LORD—
—AND THE KING OF THE BOOGEYMEN!
HOORAY!
YAY!!

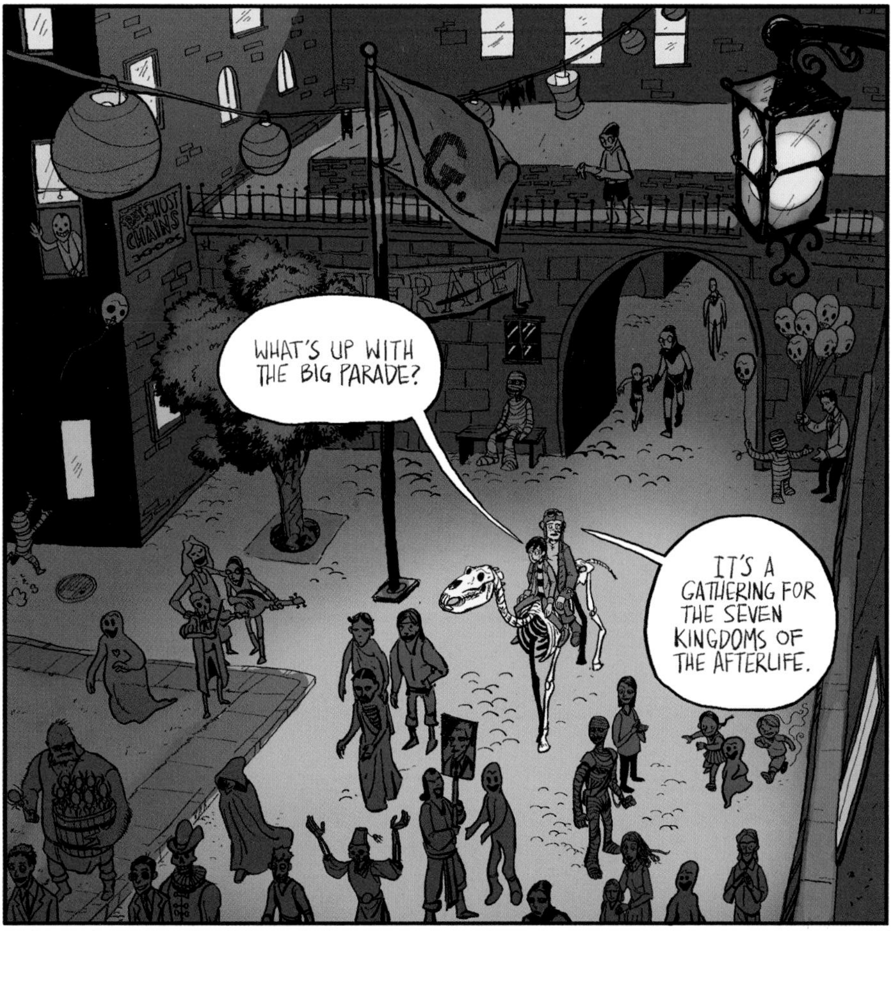
WHAT'S UP WITH THE BIG PARADE?
IT'S A GATHERING FOR THE SEVEN KINGDOMS OF THE AFTERLIFE.

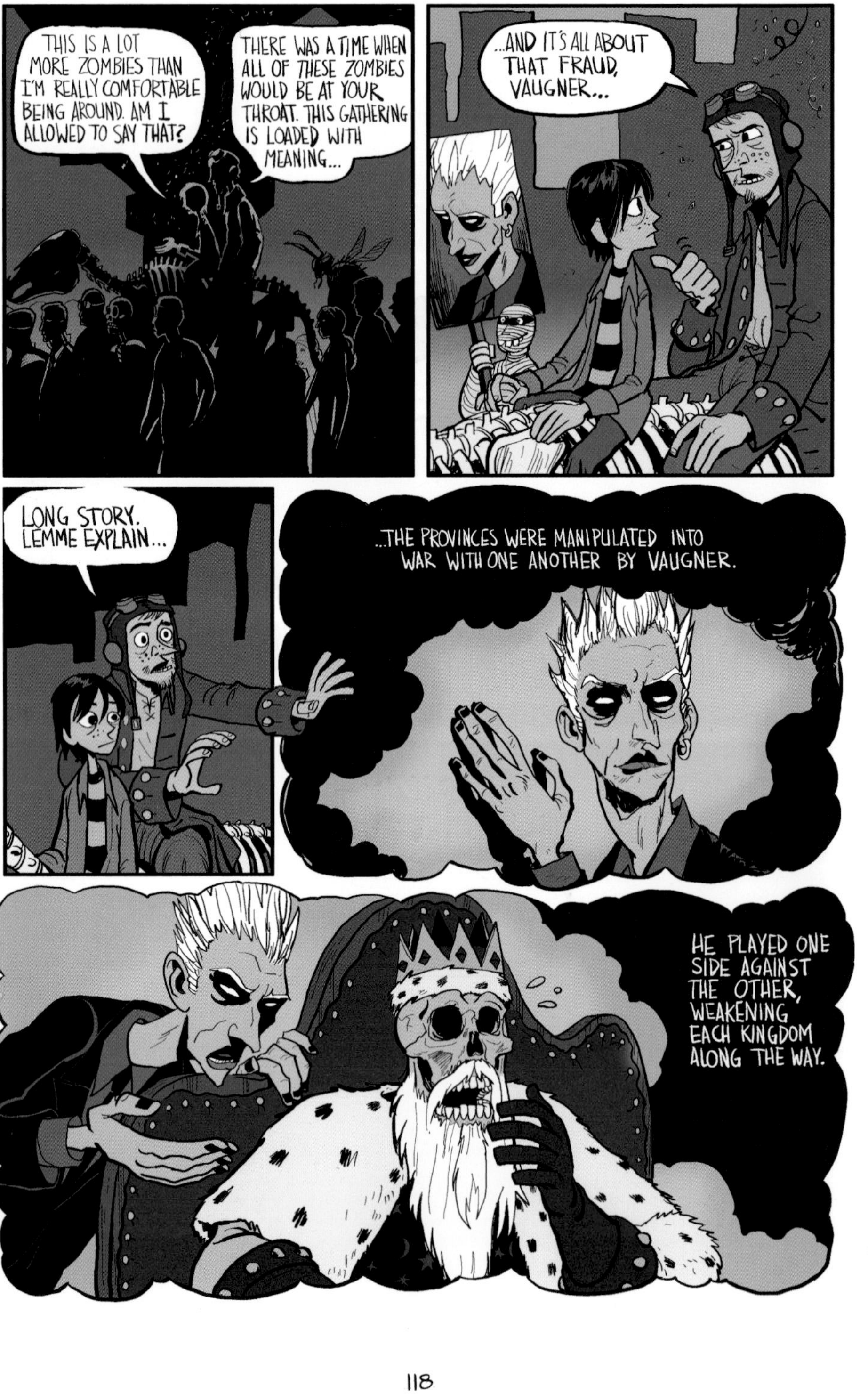
THIS IS A LOT MORE ZOMBIES THAN I'M REALLY COMFORTABLE BEING AROUND. AM I ALLOWED TO SAY THAT?
THERE WAS A TIME WHEN ALL OF THESE ZOMBIES WOULD BE AT YOUR THROAT. THIS GATHERING IS LOADED WITH MEANING...
...AND IT'S ALL ABOUT THAT FRAUD, VAUGNER...
LONG STORY. LEMME EXPLAIN...
...THE PROVINCES WERE MANIPULATED INTO WAR WITH ONE ANOTHER BY VAUGNER.
HE PLAYED ONE SIDE AGAINST THE OTHER, WEAKENING EACH KINGDOM ALONG THE WAY.

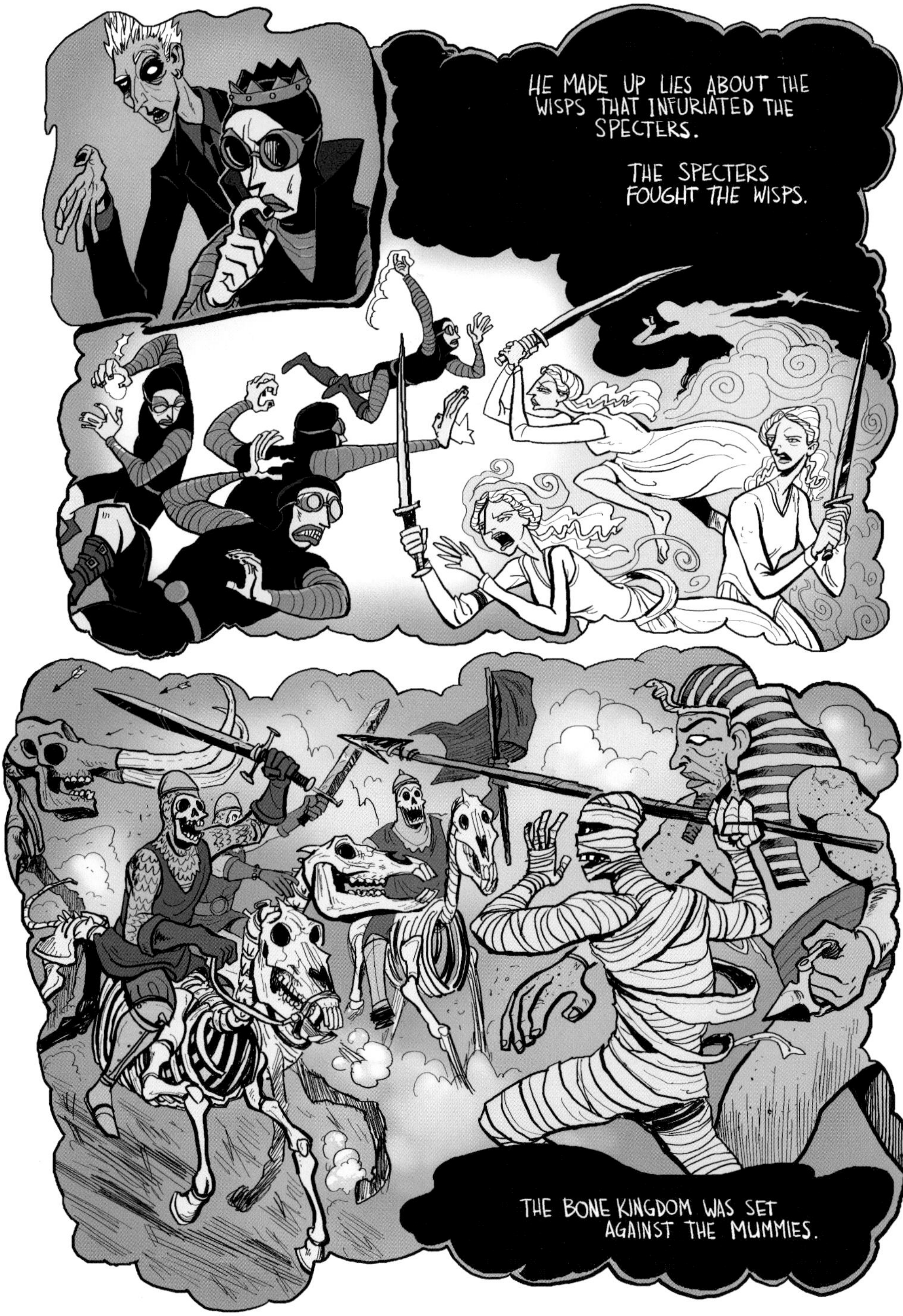
HE MADE UP LIES ABOUT THE WISPS THAT INFURIATED THE SPECTERS.
THE SPECTERS FOUGHT THE WISPS.
THE BONE KINGDOM WAS SET AGAINST THE MUMMIES.

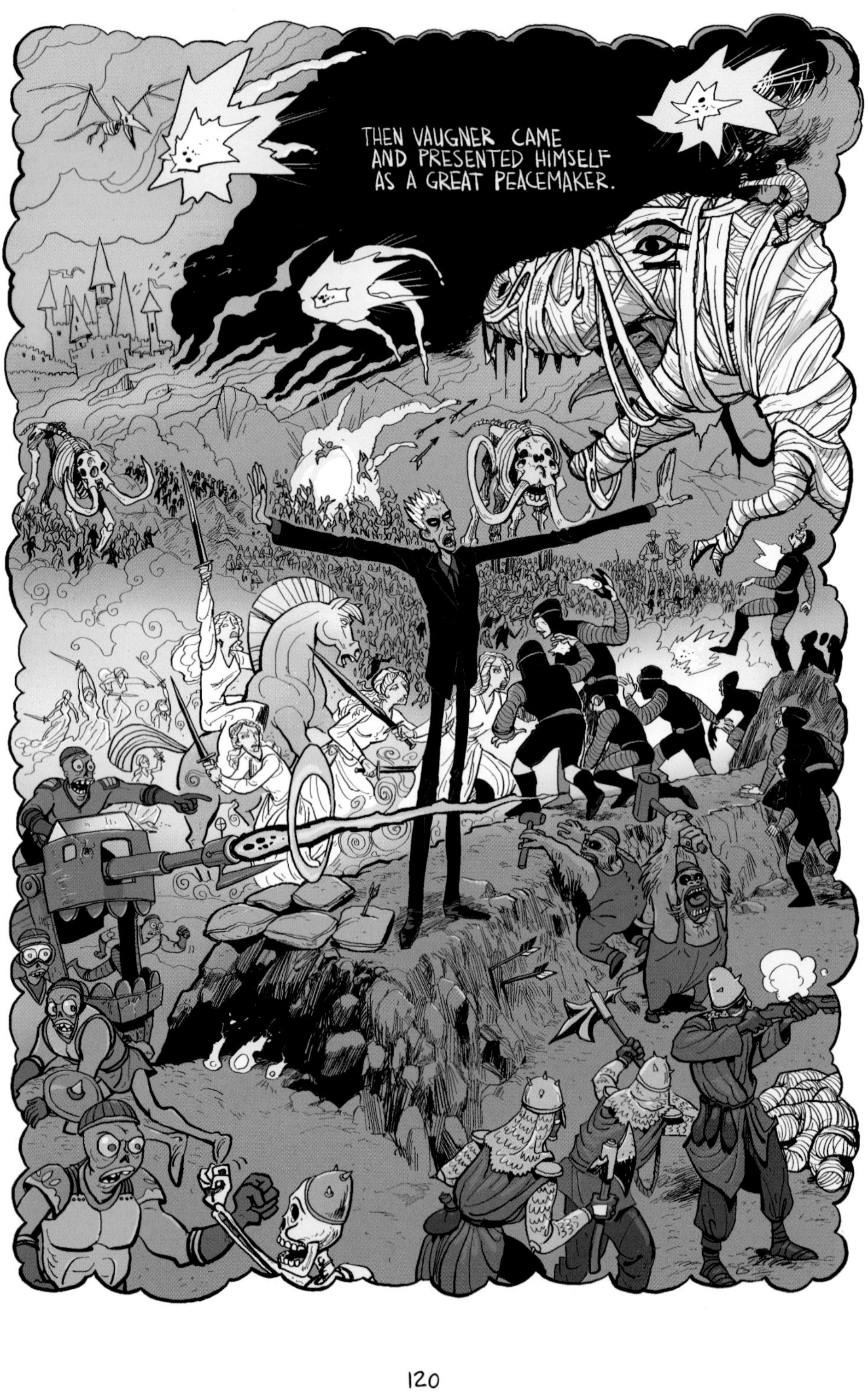
THEN VAUGNER CAME AND PRESENTED HIMSELF AS A GREAT PEACEMAKER.

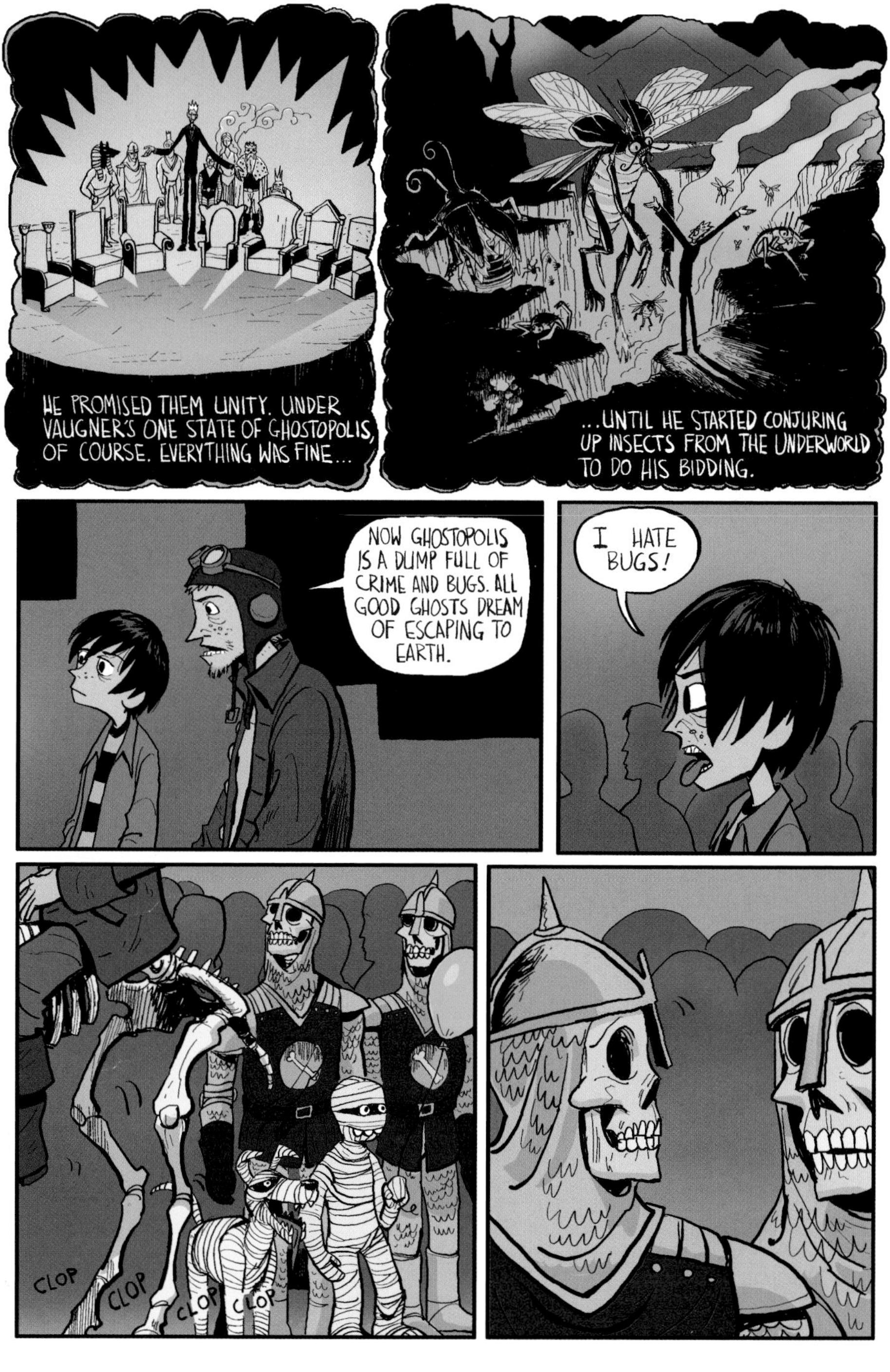
HE PROMISED THEM UNITY. UNDER VAUGNER'S ONE STATE OF GHOSTOPOLIS, OF COURSE. EVERYTHING WAS FINE...
...UNTIL HE STARTED CONJURING UP INSECTS FROM THE UNDERWORLD TO DO HIS BIDDING.
NOW GHOSTOPOLIS IS A DUMP FULL OF CRIME AND BUGS. ALL GOOD GHOSTS DREAM OF ESCAPING TO EARTH.
I HATE BUGS!
CLOP CLOP CLOP CLOP

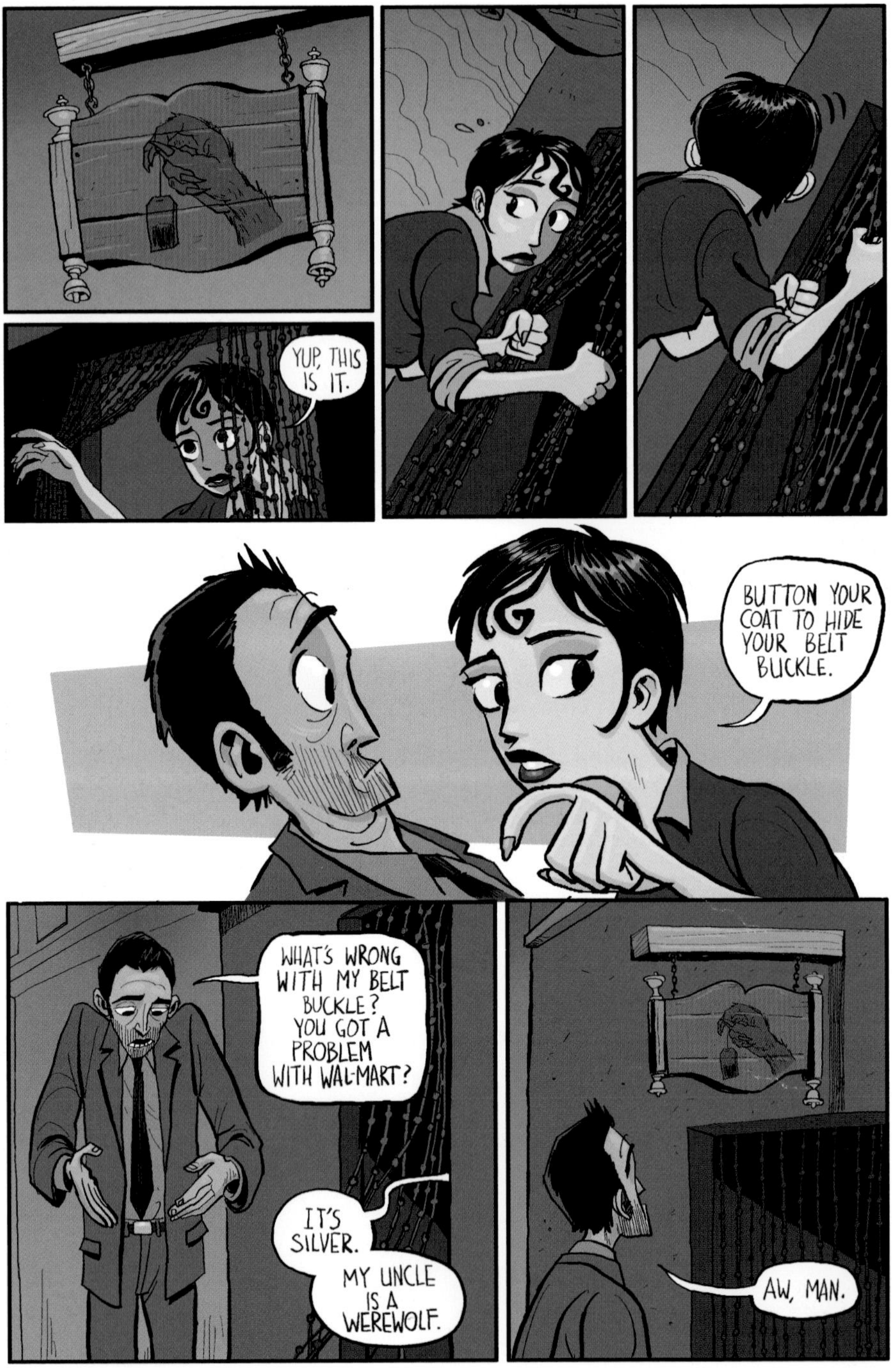
YUP, THIS IS IT.
BUTTON YOUR COAT TO HIDE YOUR BELT BUCKLE.
WHAT'S WRONG WITH MY BELT BUCKLE? YOU GOT A PROBLEM WITH WAL-MART?
IT'S SILVER.
MY UNCLE IS A WEREWOLF.
AW, MAN.

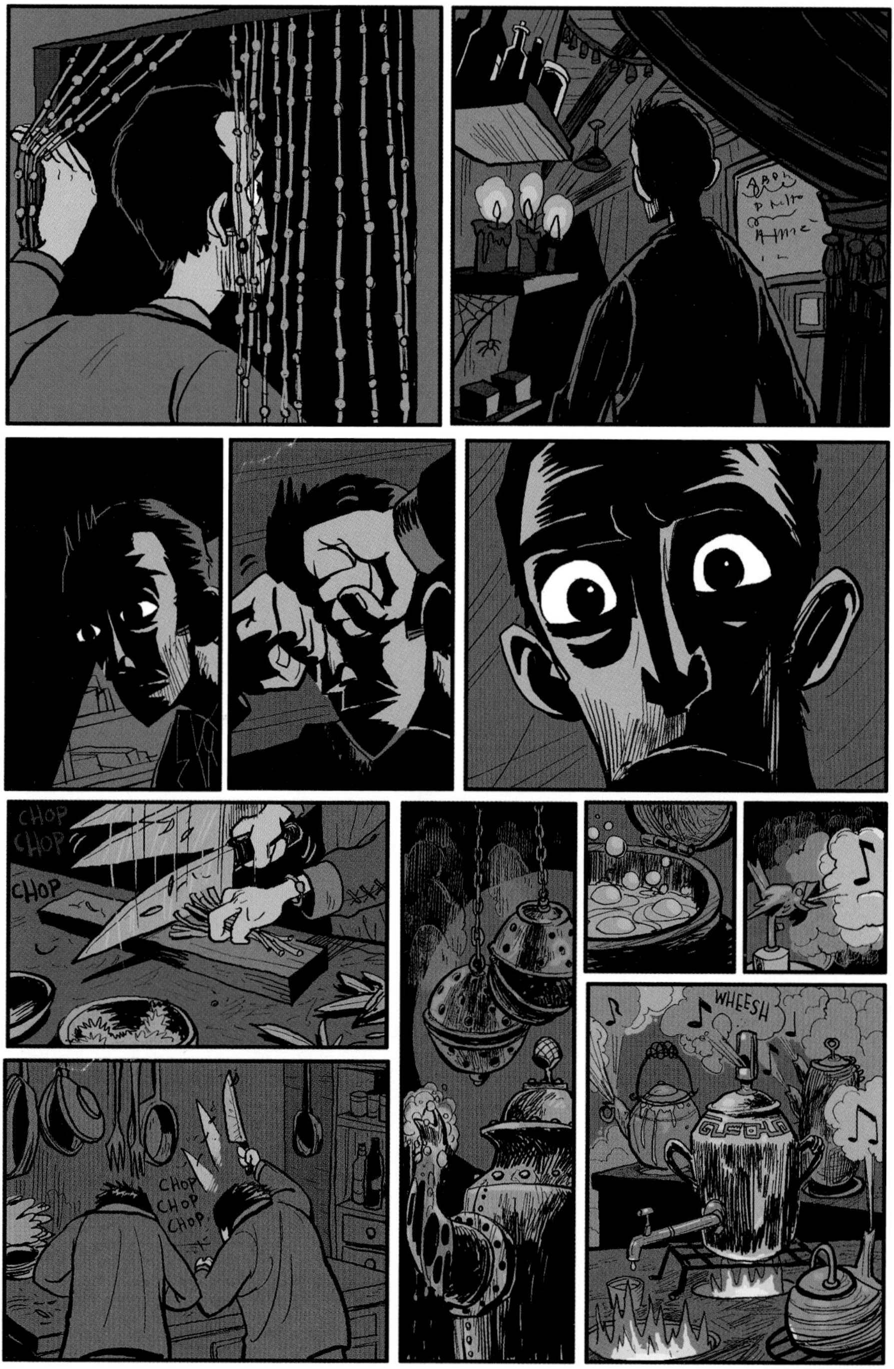
CHOP
CHOP
CHOP
CHOP
CHOP
CHOP
WHEESH

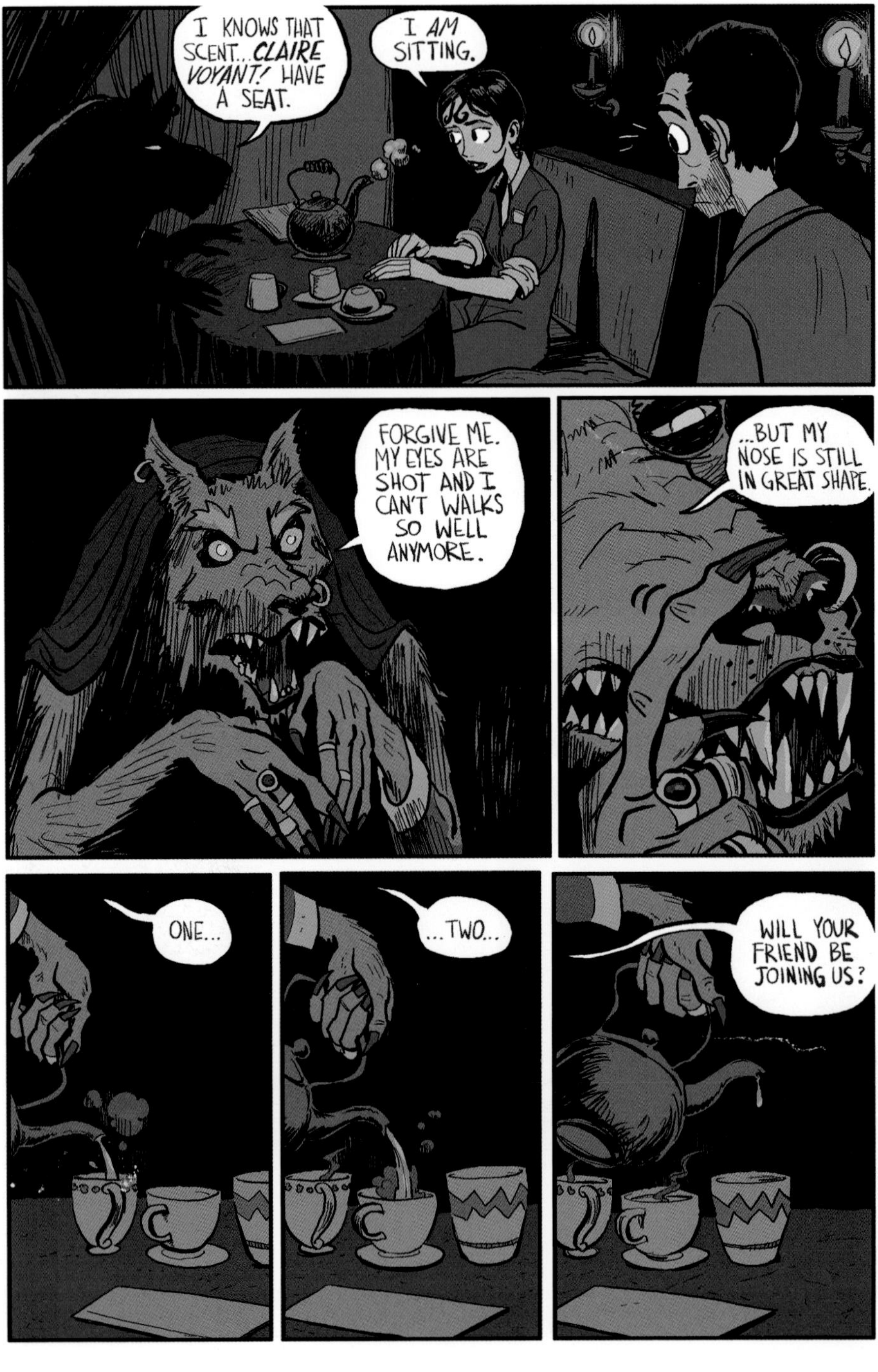

I KNOWS THAT SCENT... CLAIRE VOYANT! HAVE A SEAT.
I AM SITTING.
FORGIVE ME. MY EYES ARE SHOT AND I CAN'T WALKS SO WELL ANYMORE.
...BUT MY NOSE IS STILL IN GREAT SHAPE.
ONE...
...TWO...
WILL YOUR FRIEND BE JOINING US?

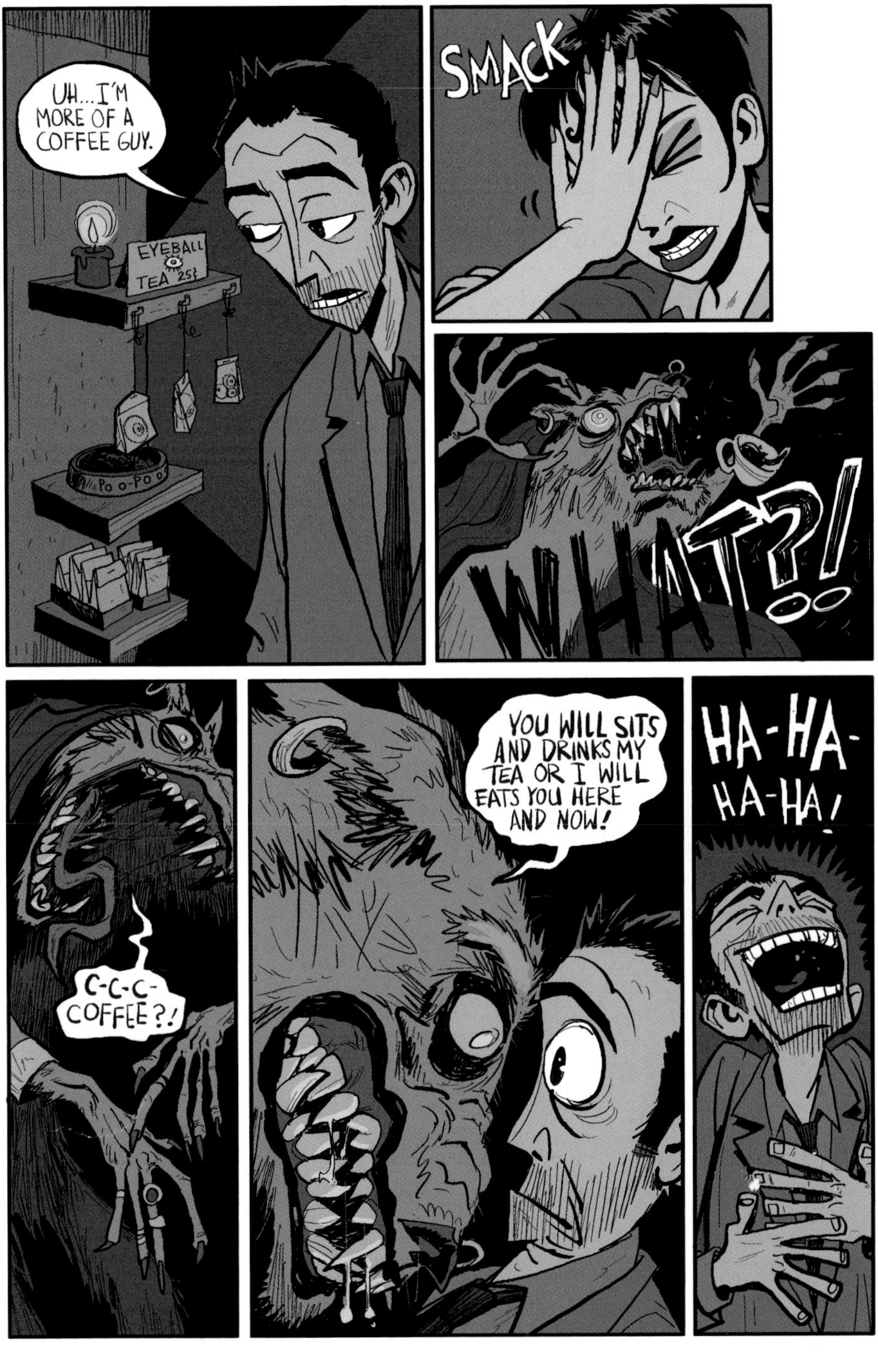
UH...I'M MORE OF A COFFEE GUY.
EYEBALL TEA 25¢
PO-PO
SMACK
WHAT?!
C-C-C-COFFEE?!
YOU WILL SITS AND DRINKS MY TEA OR I WILL EATS YOU HERE AND NOW!
HA-HA-HA-HA!

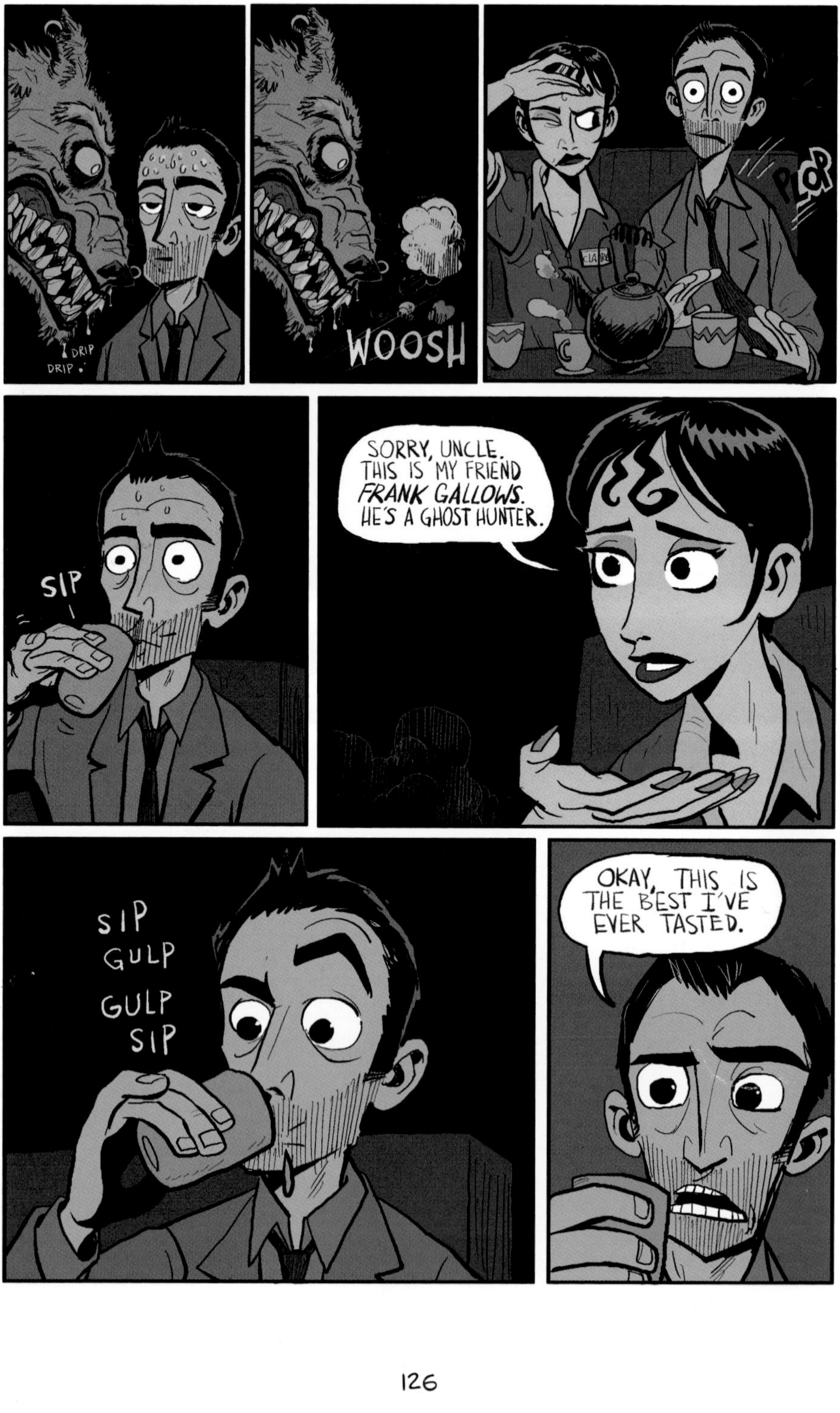
DRIP
DRIP
WOOSH
CLAIRE
PLOP
SIP
SORRY, UNCLE. THIS IS MY FRIEND *FRANK GALLOWS.* HE'S A GHOST HUNTER.
SIP
GULP
GULP
SIP
OKAY, THIS IS THE BEST I'VE EVER TASTED.

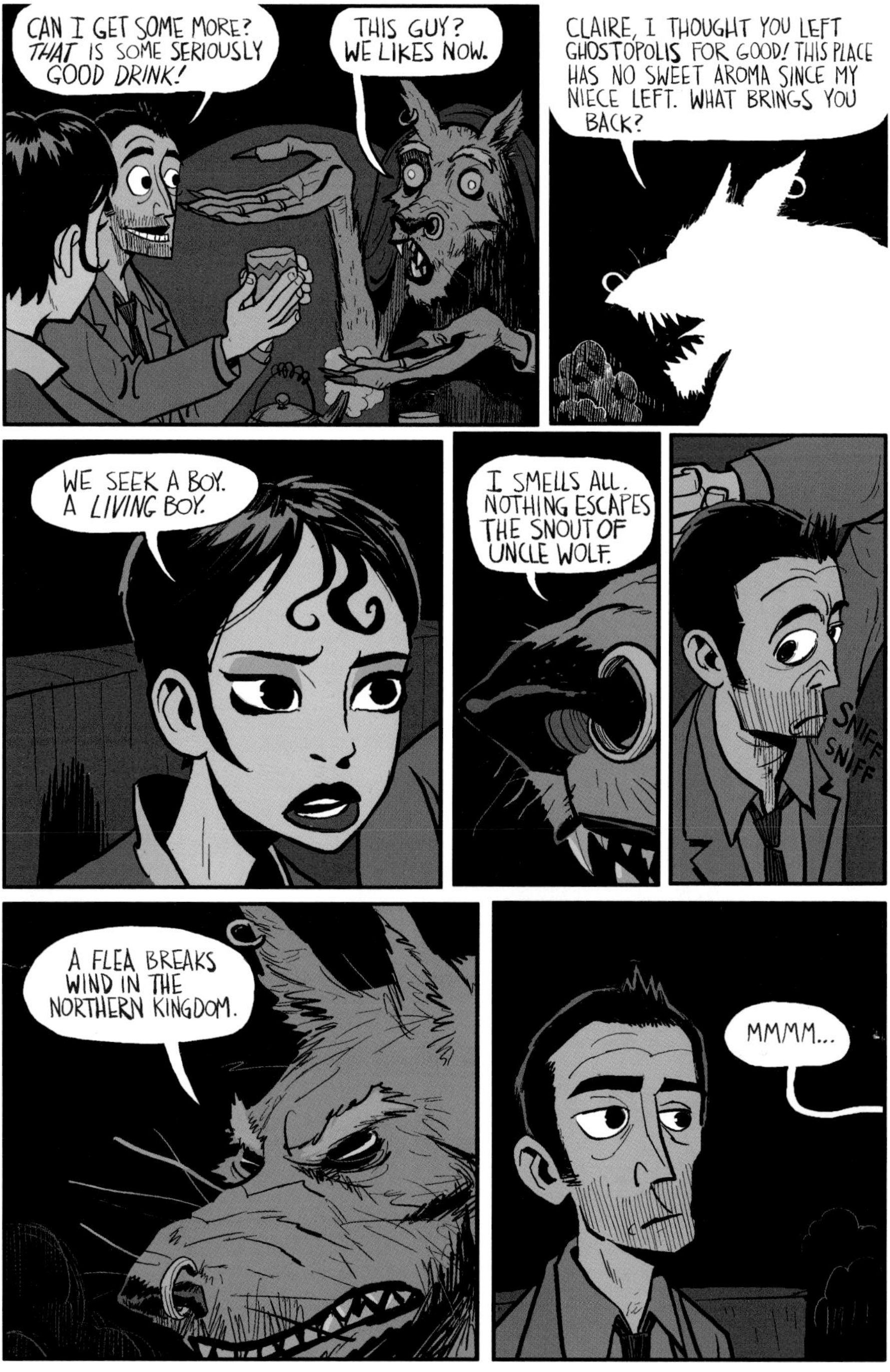

CAN I GET SOME MORE? *THAT* IS SOME SERIOUSLY GOOD *DRINK!*
THIS GUY? WE LIKES NOW.
CLAIRE, I THOUGHT YOU LEFT GHOSTOPOLIS FOR GOOD! THIS PLACE HAS NO SWEET AROMA SINCE MY NIECE LEFT. WHAT BRINGS YOU BACK?
WE SEEK A BOY. A *LIVING* BOY.
I SMELLS ALL. NOTHING ESCAPES THE SNOUT OF UNCLE WOLF.
SNIFF SNIFF
A FLEA BREAKS WIND IN THE NORTHERN KINGDOM.
MMMM...

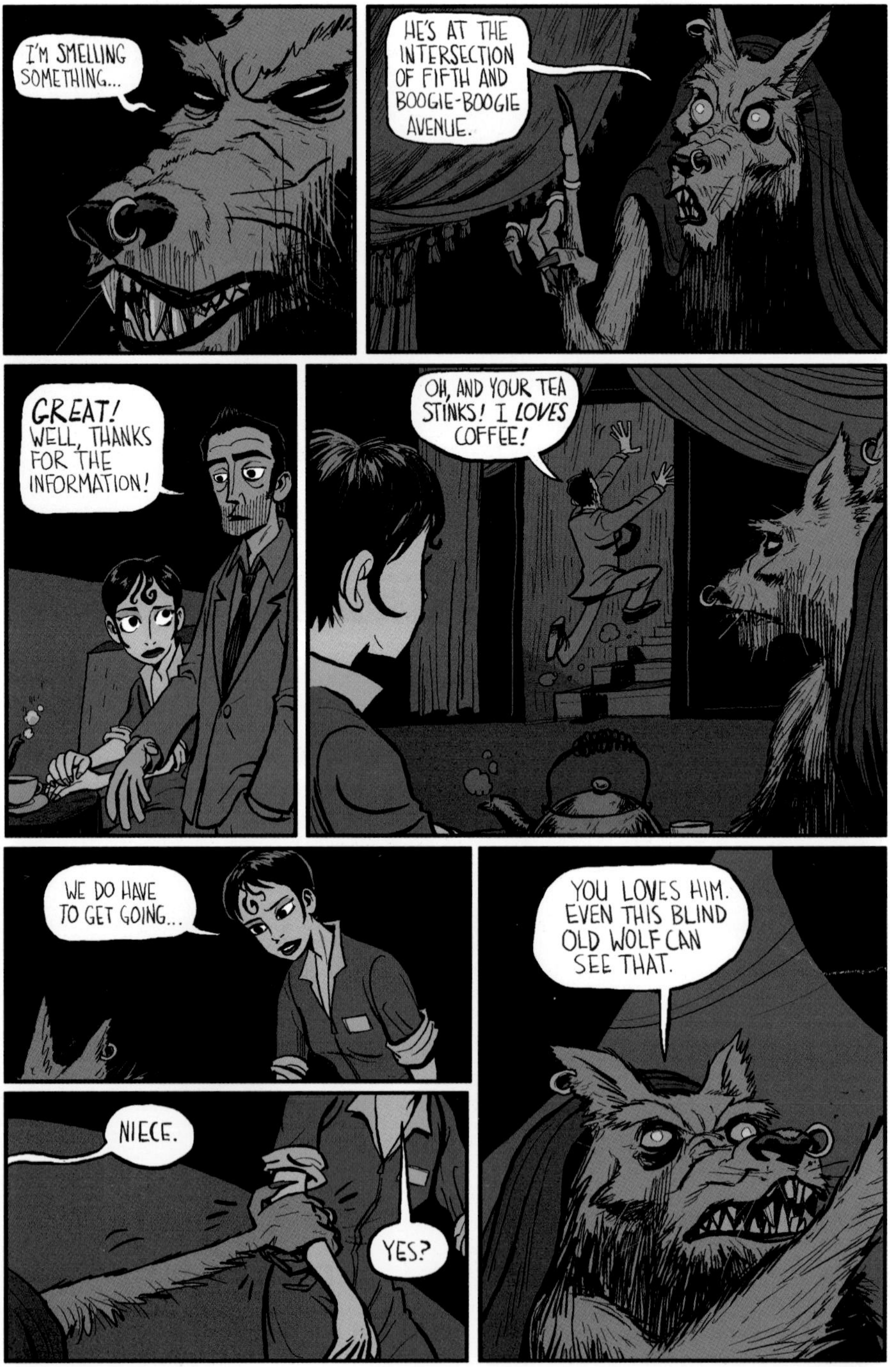
I'M SMELLING SOMETHING...
HE'S AT THE INTERSECTION OF FIFTH AND BOOGIE-BOOGIE AVENUE.
GREAT! WELL, THANKS FOR THE INFORMATION!
OH, AND YOUR TEA STINKS! I LOVES COFFEE!
WE DO HAVE TO GET GOING...
NIECE.
YES?
YOU LOVES HIM. EVEN THIS BLIND OLD WOLF CAN SEE THAT.

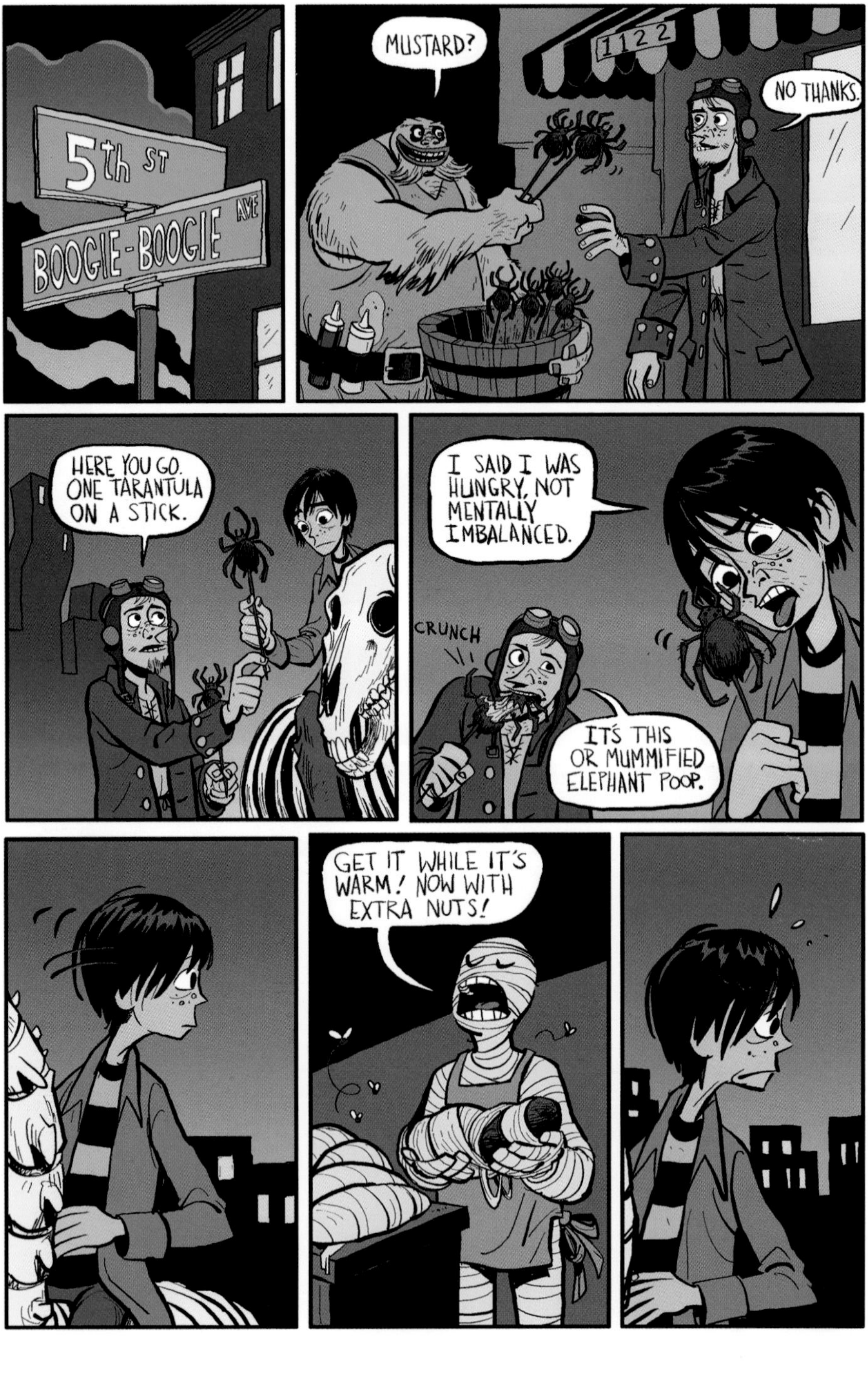
5th ST
BOOGIE-BOOGIE AVE
MUSTARD?
1122
NO THANKS.
HERE YOU GO. ONE TARANTULA ON A STICK.
I SAID I WAS HUNGRY, NOT MENTALLY IMBALANCED.
CRUNCH
IT'S THIS OR MUMMIFIED ELEPHANT POOP.
GET IT WHILE IT'S WARM! NOW WITH EXTRA NUTS!
!

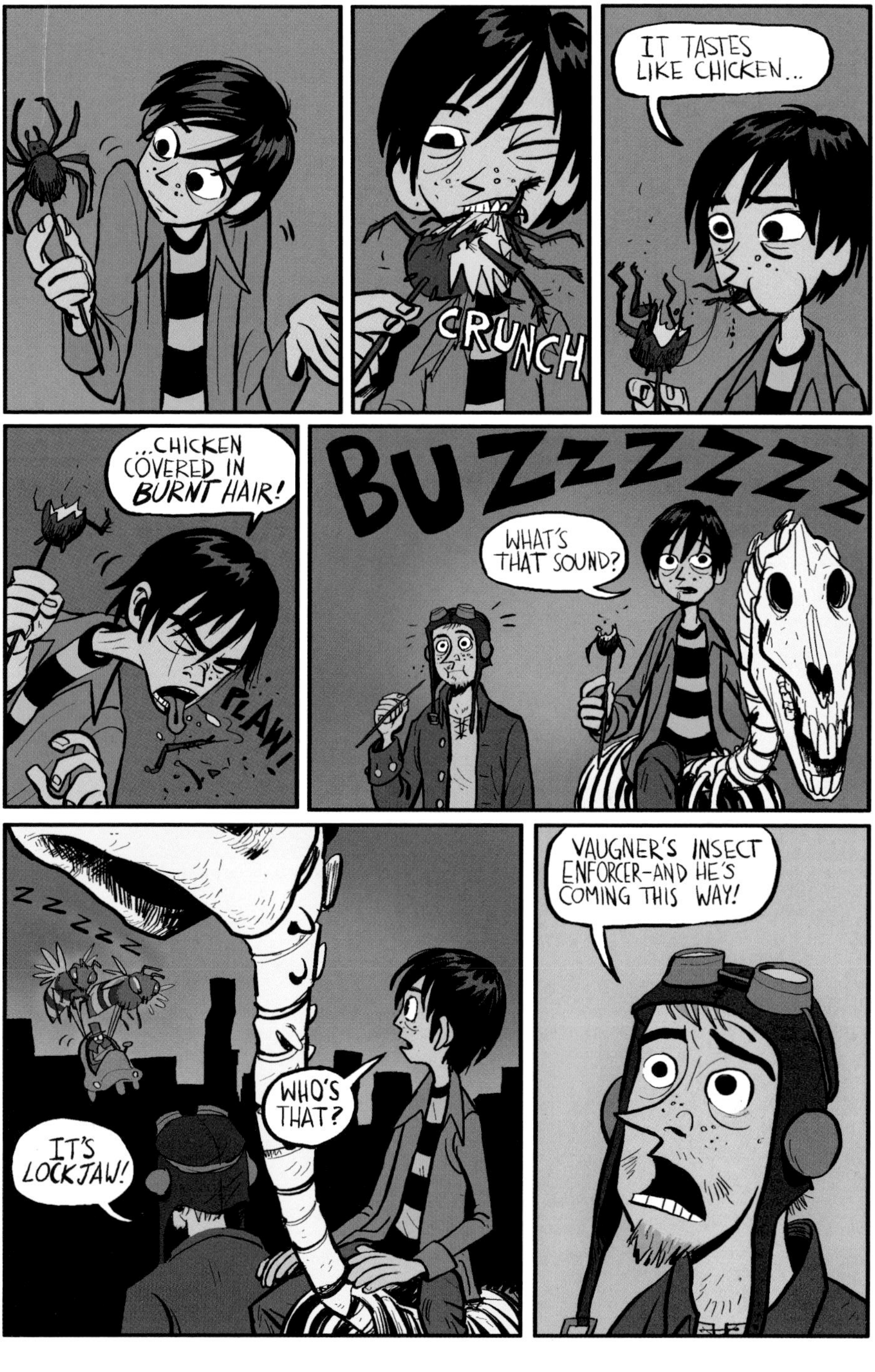

IT TASTES LIKE CHICKEN...
CRUNCH
...CHICKEN COVERED IN BURNT HAIR!
PLAW!
BUZZZZZZ
WHAT'S THAT SOUND?
ZZZZZ
WHO'S THAT?
IT'S LOCKJAW!
VAUGNER'S INSECT ENFORCER-AND HE'S COMING THIS WAY!

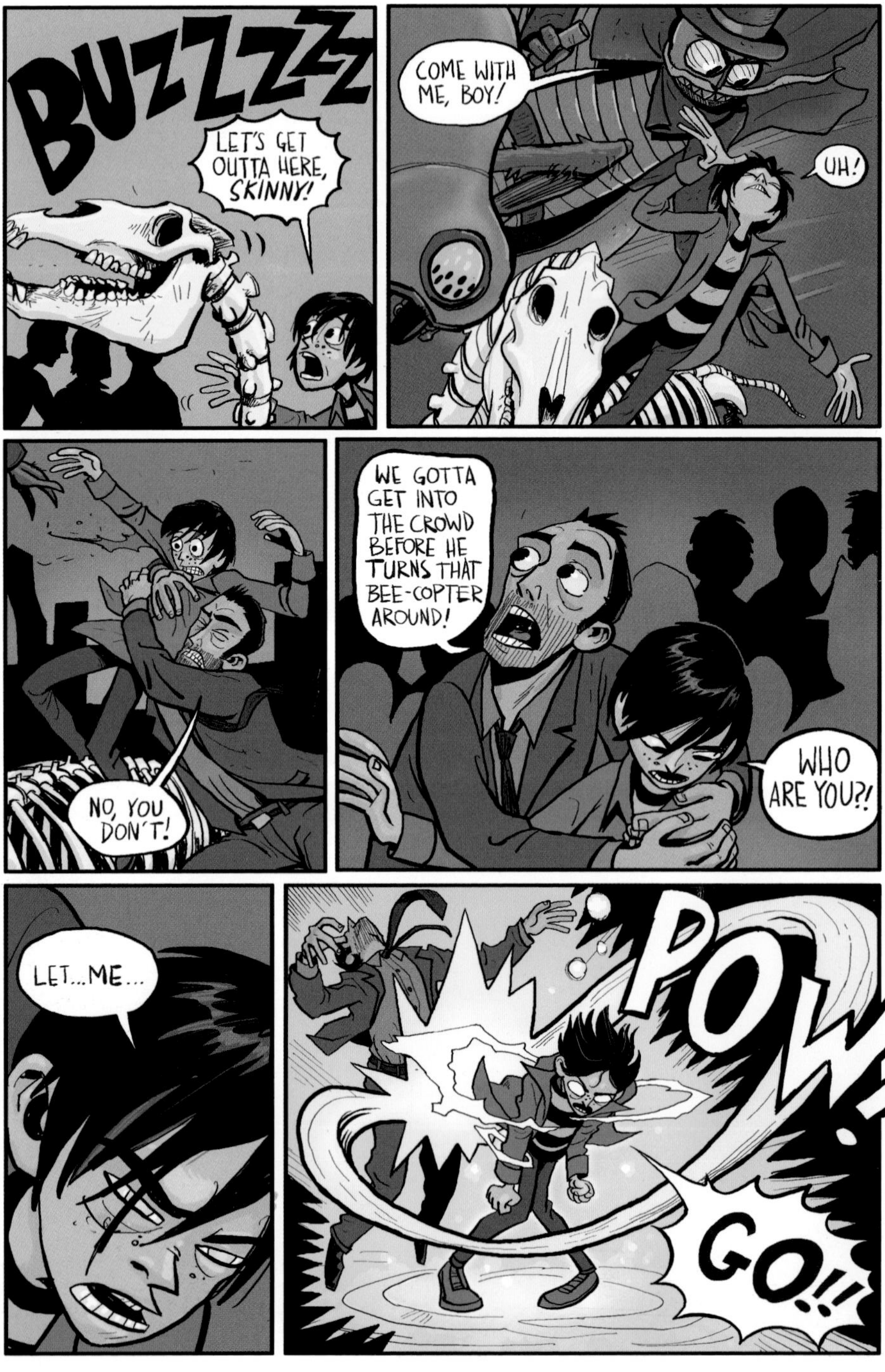
BUZZZZZ
LET'S GET OUTTA HERE, SKINNY!
COME WITH ME, BOY!
UH!
NO, YOU DON'T!
WE GOTTA GET INTO THE CROWD BEFORE HE TURNS THAT BEE-COPTER AROUND!
WHO ARE YOU?!
LET...ME...
POW!
GO!!

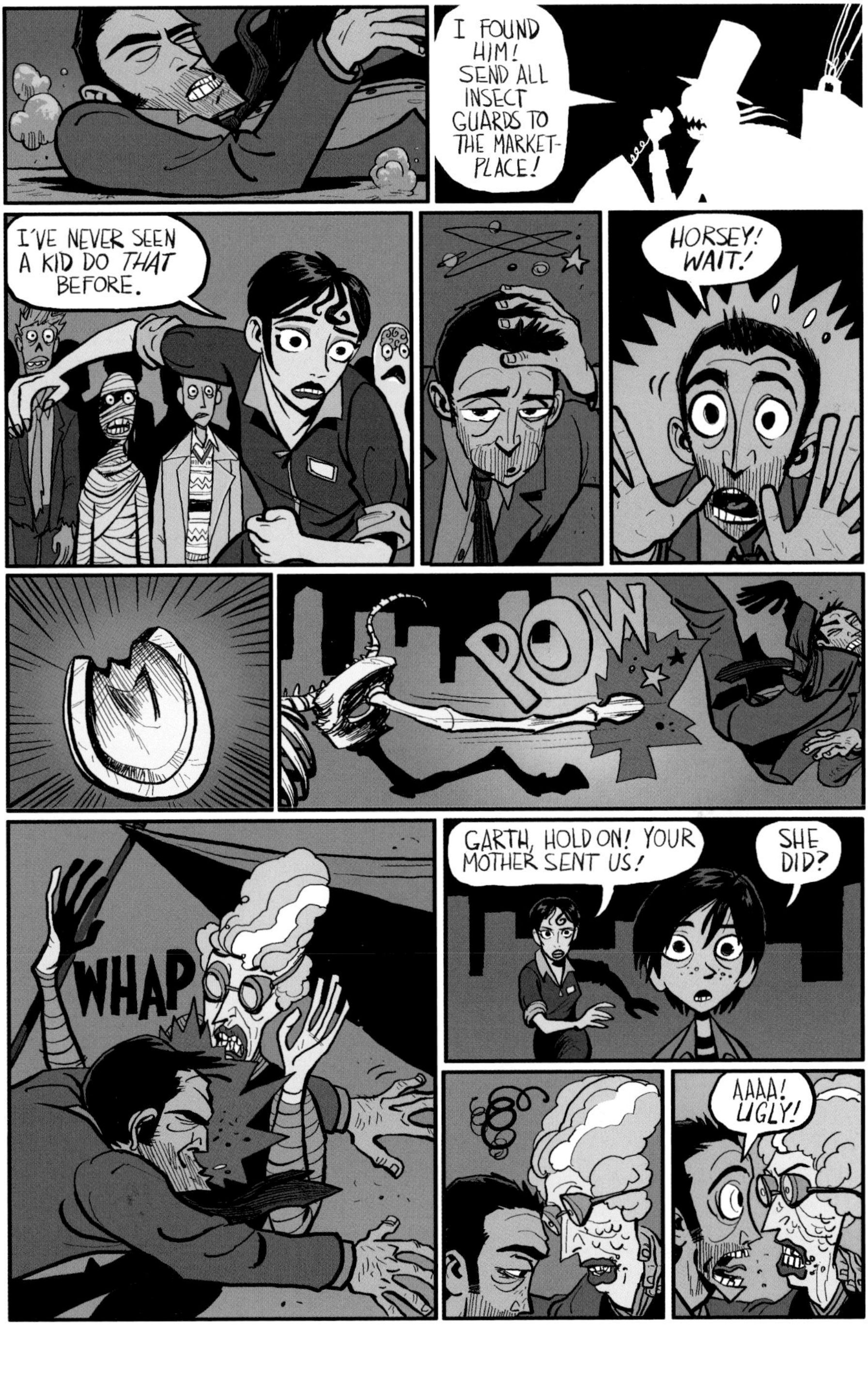

I FOUND HIM! SEND ALL INSECT GUARDS TO THE MARKET-PLACE!
I'VE NEVER SEEN A KID DO *THAT* BEFORE.
HORSEY! WAIT!
POW
WHAP
GARTH, HOLD ON! YOUR MOTHER SENT US!
SHE DID?
AAAA! UGLY!

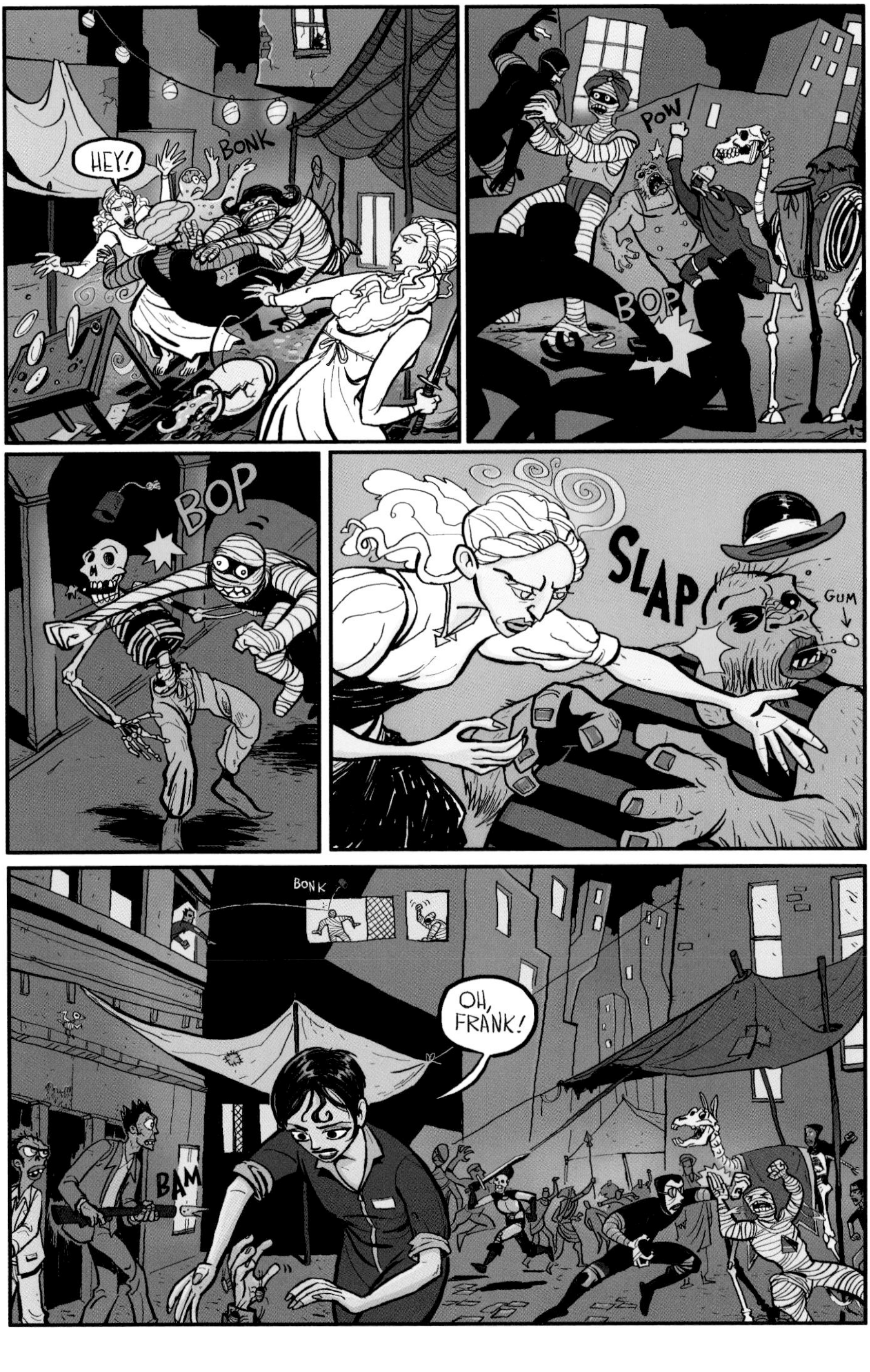
HEY!
BONK
POW
BOP
BOP
SLAP
GUM
BONK
BAM
OH, FRANK!

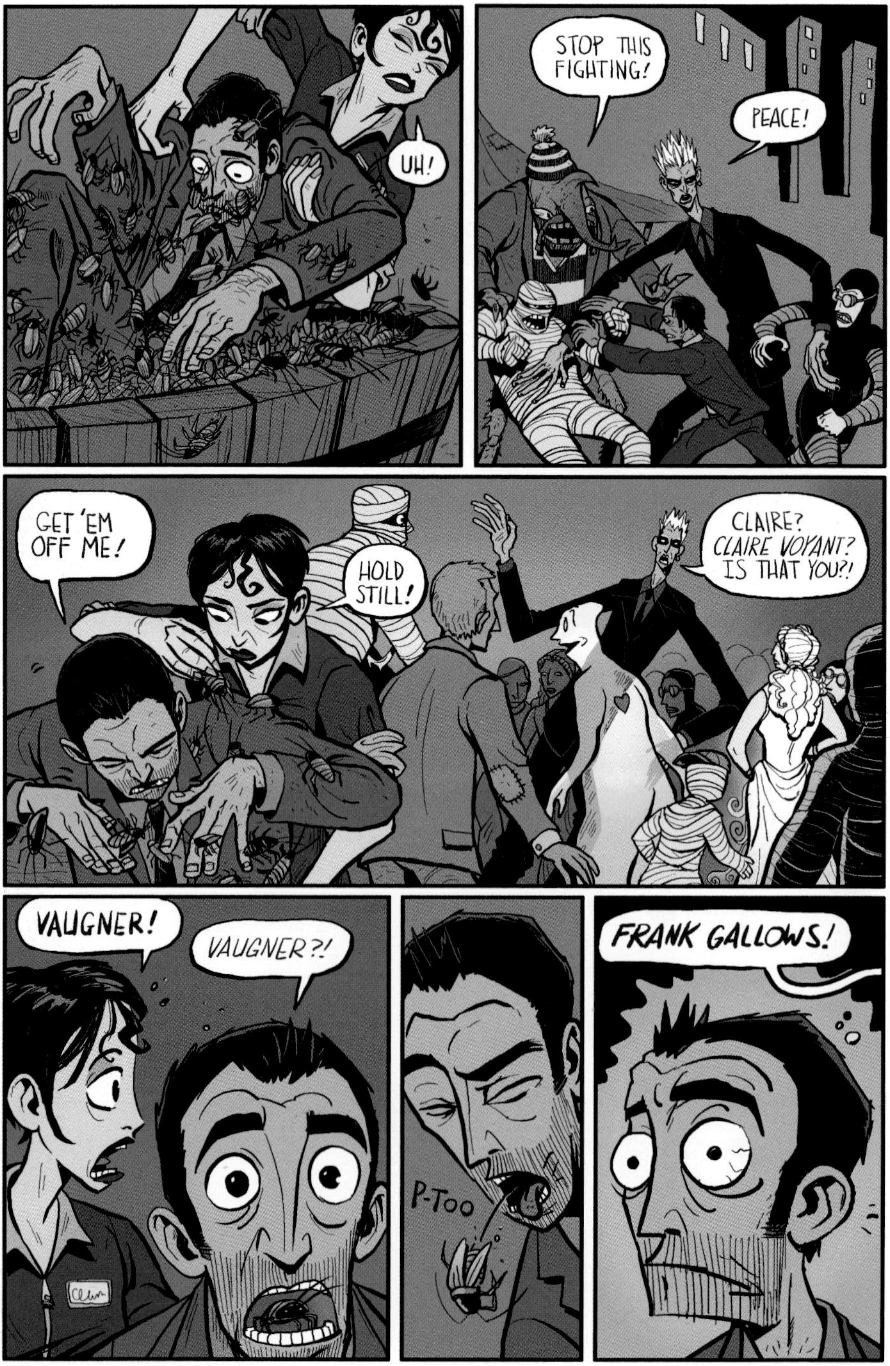
UH!
STOP THIS FIGHTING!
PEACE!
GET 'EM OFF ME!
HOLD STILL!
CLAIRE? CLAIRE VOYANT? IS THAT YOU?!
VAUGNER!
VAUGNER?!
P-TOO
FRANK GALLOWS!

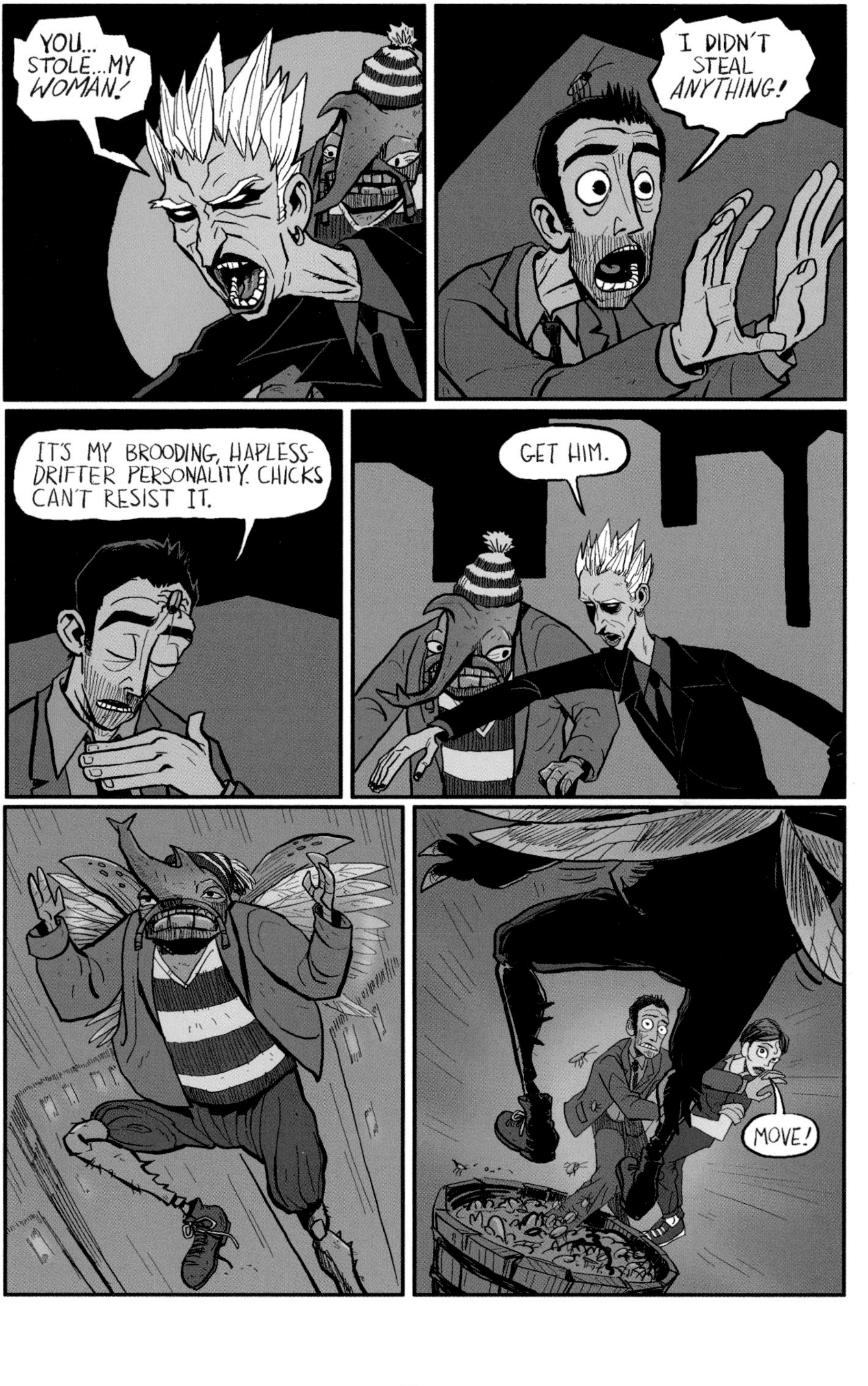
YOU... STOLE...MY WOMAN!
I DIDN'T STEAL ANYTHING!
IT'S MY BROODING, HAPLESS-DRIFTER PERSONALITY. CHICKS CAN'T RESIST IT.
GET HIM.
MOVE!

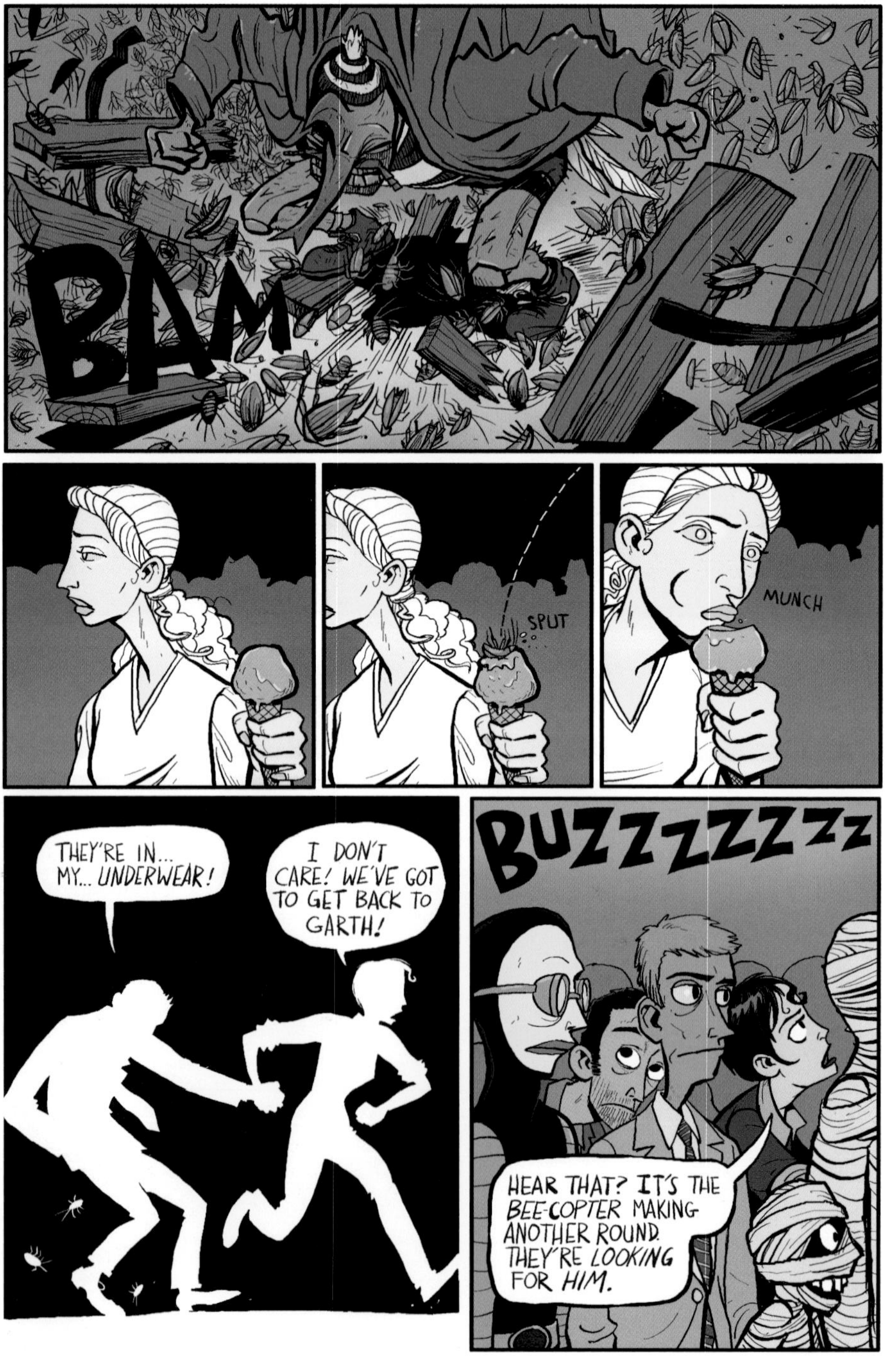
BAM
SPUT
MUNCH
THEY'RE IN... MY... UNDERWEAR!
I DON'T CARE! WE'VE GOT TO GET BACK TO GARTH!
BUZZZZZZzz
HEAR THAT? IT'S THE BEE-COPTER MAKING ANOTHER ROUND. THEY'RE LOOKING FOR HIM.

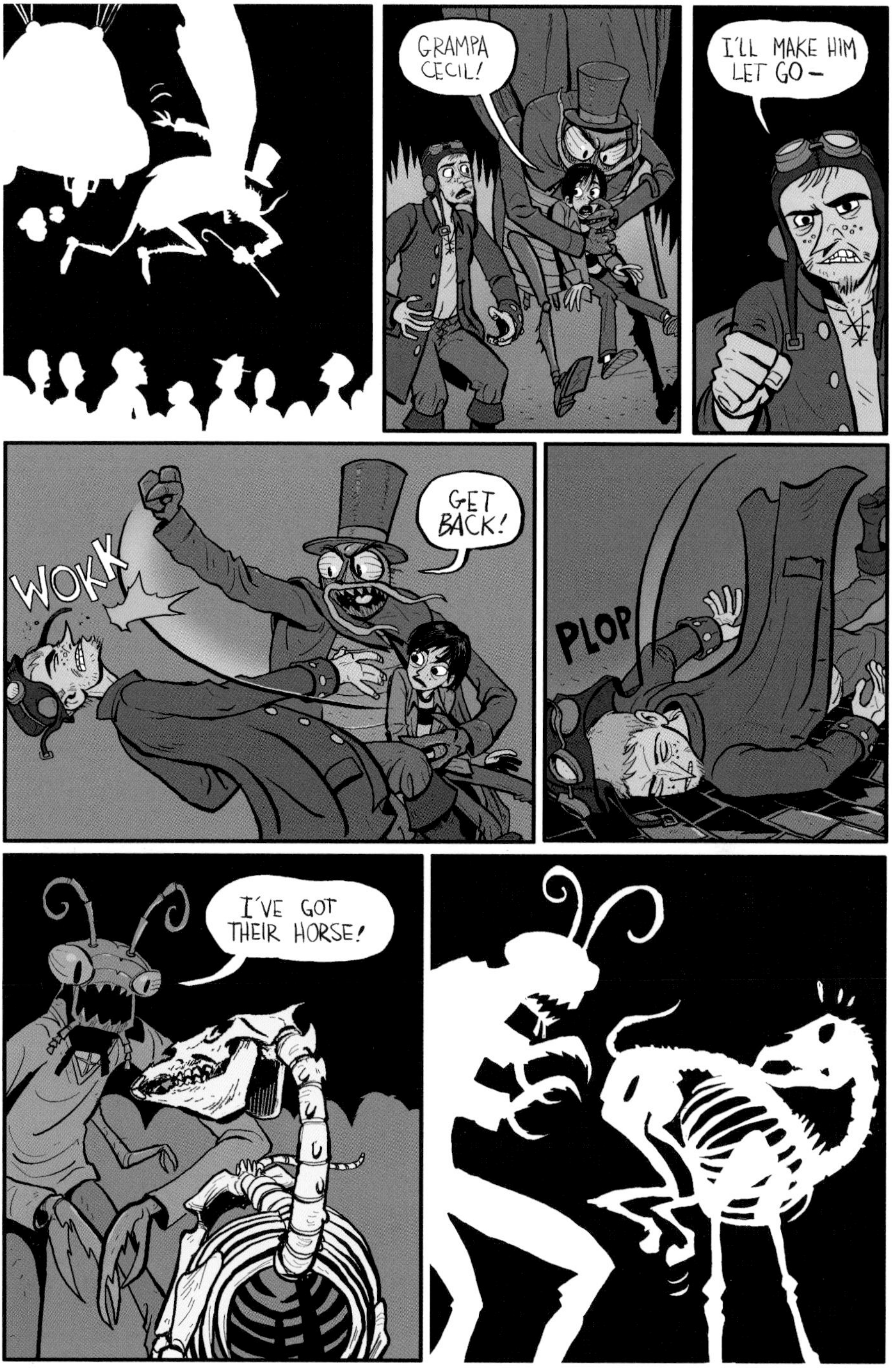
GRAMPA CECIL!
I'LL MAKE HIM LET GO—
WOKK
GET BACK!
PLOP
I'VE GOT THEIR HORSE!

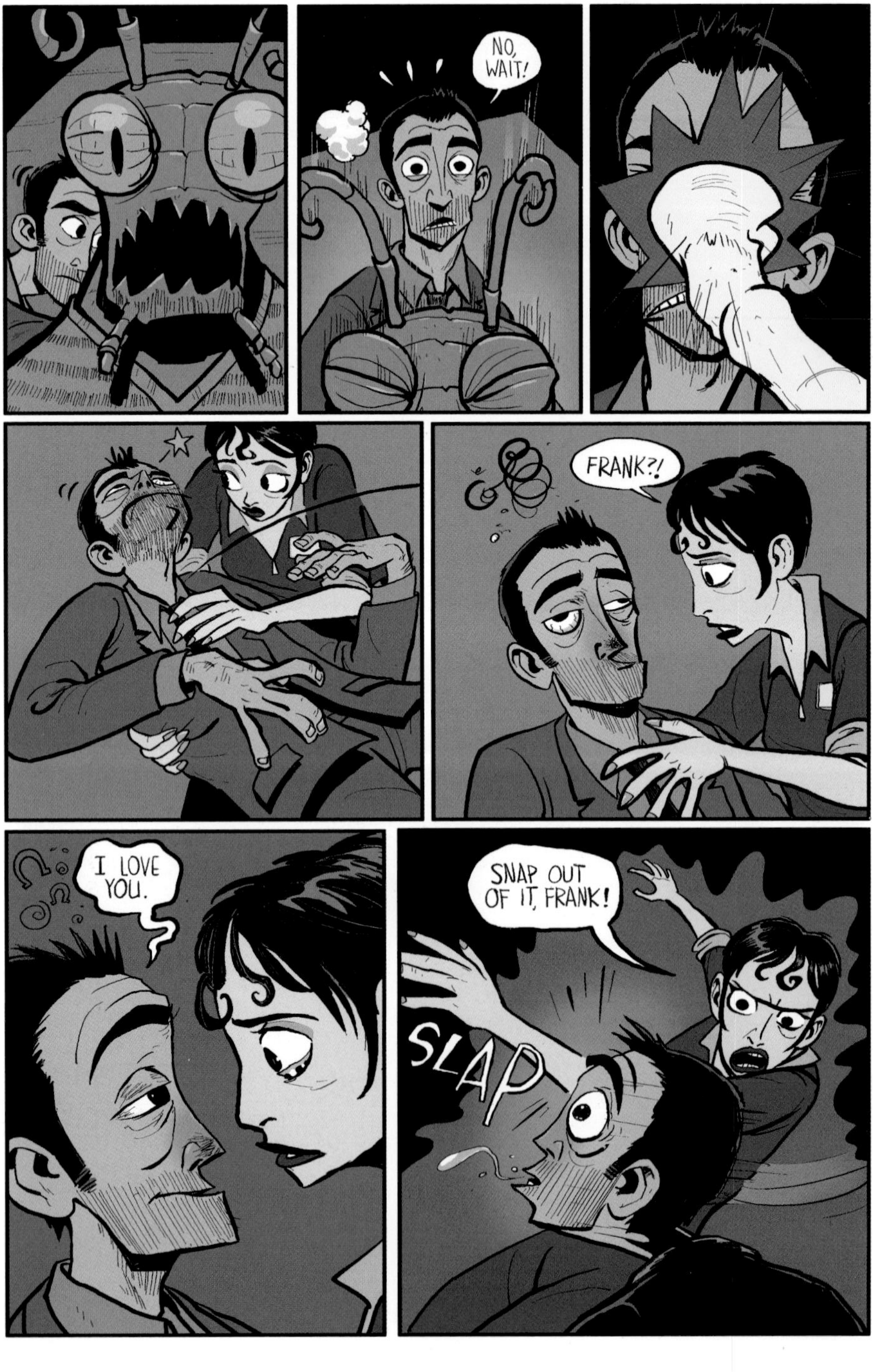
NO, WAIT!
FRANK?!
I LOVE YOU.
SNAP OUT OF IT, FRANK!
SLAP

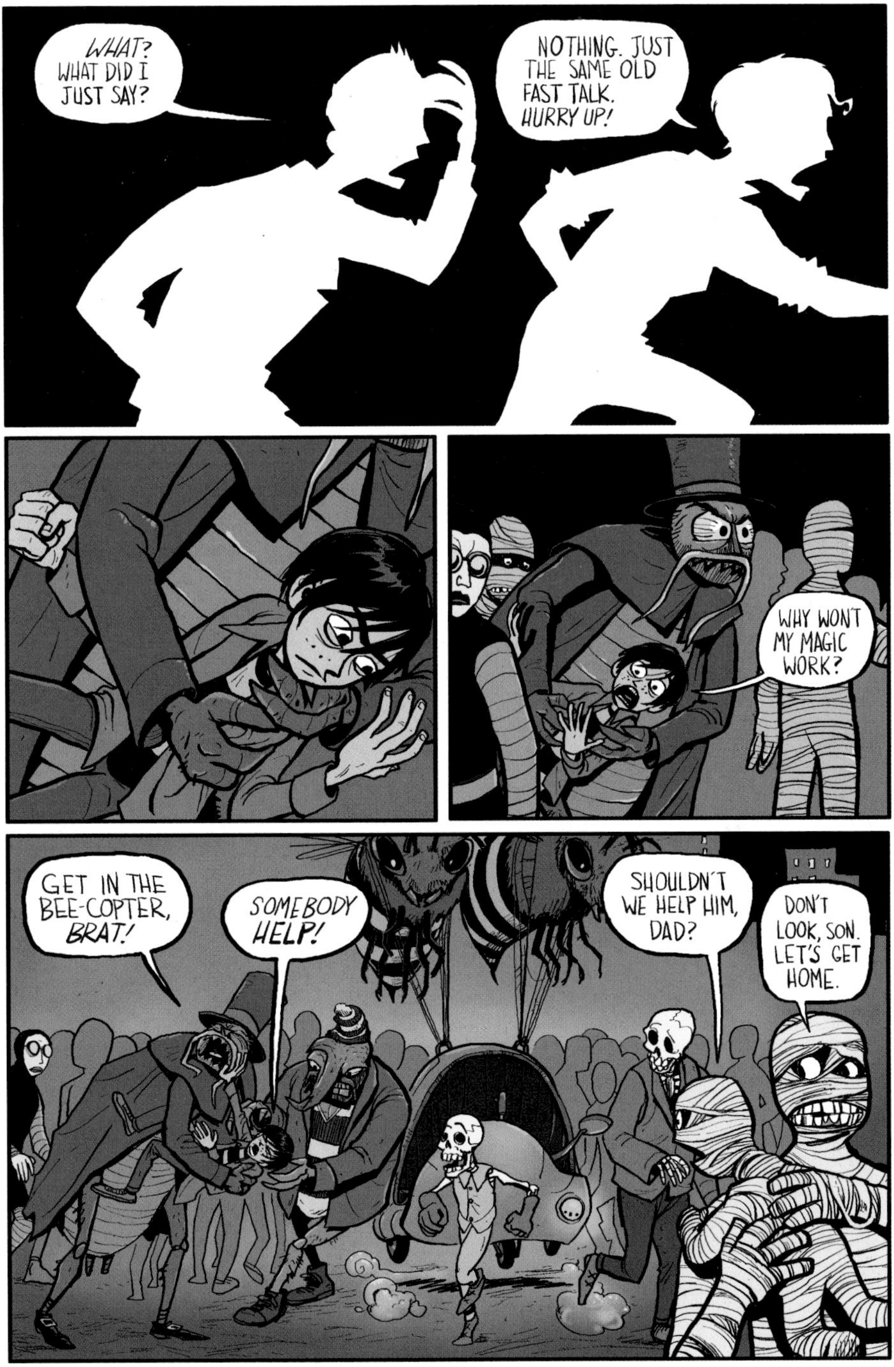
WHAT? WHAT DID I JUST SAY?
NOTHING. JUST THE SAME OLD FAST TALK. HURRY UP!
WHY WON'T MY MAGIC WORK?
GET IN THE BEE-COPTER, BRAT!
SOMEBODY HELP!
SHOULDN'T WE HELP HIM, DAD?
DON'T LOOK, SON. LET'S GET HOME.

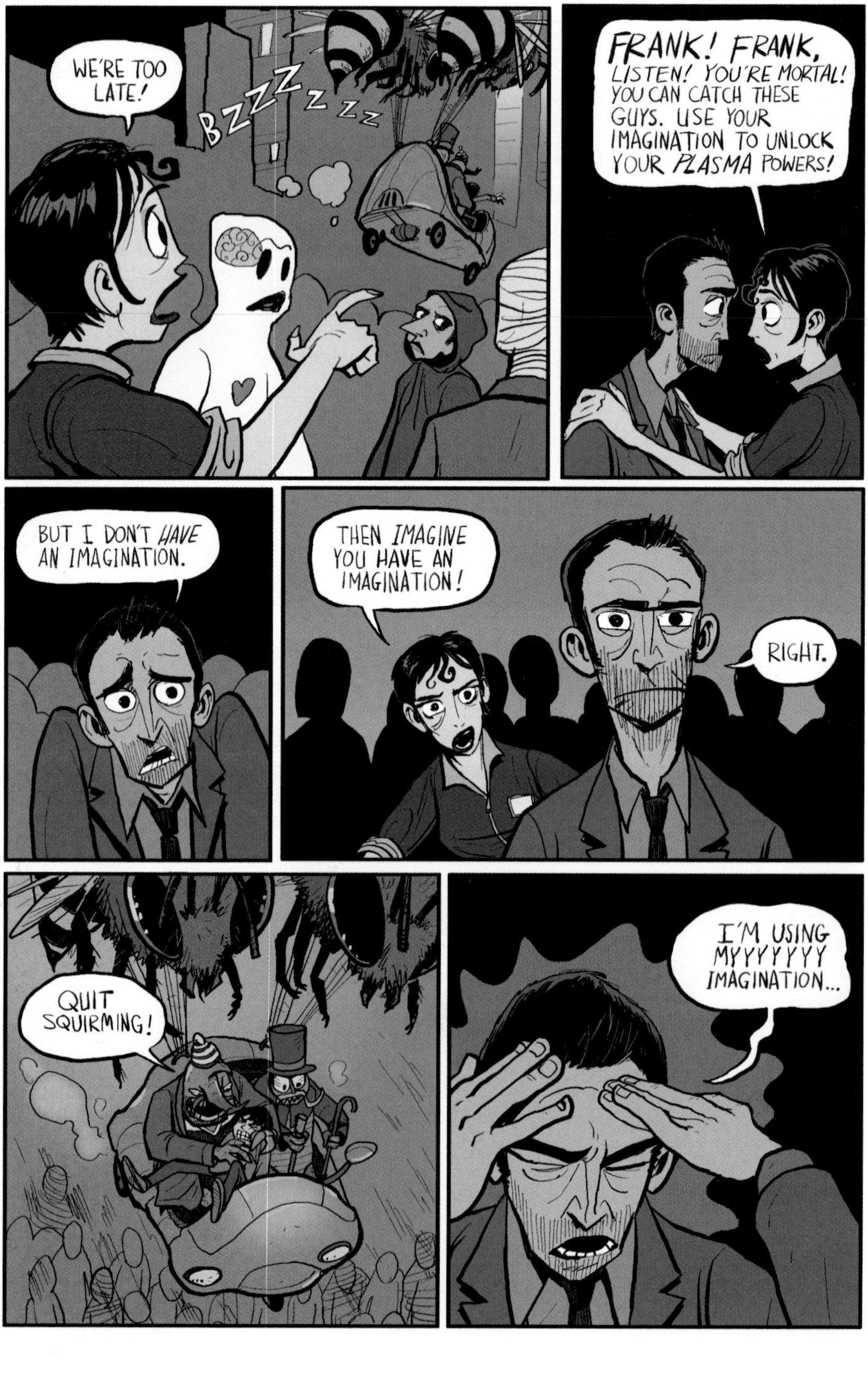
WE'RE TOO LATE!
BZZZZ Z Z Z
FRANK! FRANK, LISTEN! YOU'RE MORTAL! YOU CAN CATCH THESE GUYS. USE YOUR IMAGINATION TO UNLOCK YOUR PLASMA POWERS!
BUT I DON'T HAVE AN IMAGINATION.
THEN IMAGINE YOU HAVE AN IMAGINATION!
RIGHT.
QUIT SQUIRMING!
I'M USING MYYYYYYY IMAGINATION...

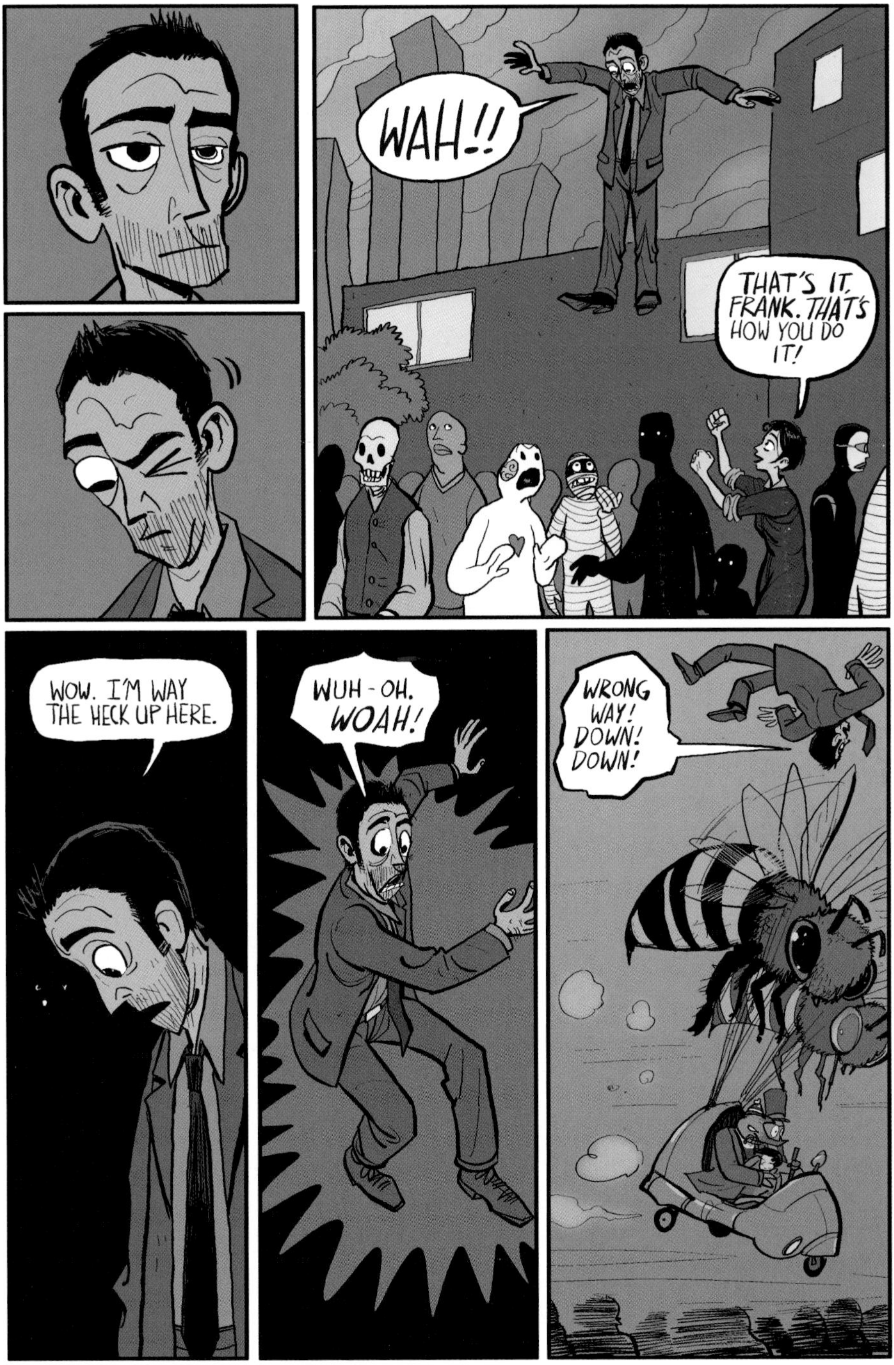
WAH!!
THAT'S IT, FRANK. THAT'S HOW YOU DO IT!
WOW. I'M WAY THE HECK UP HERE.
WUH-OH. WOAH!
WRONG WAY! DOWN! DOWN!

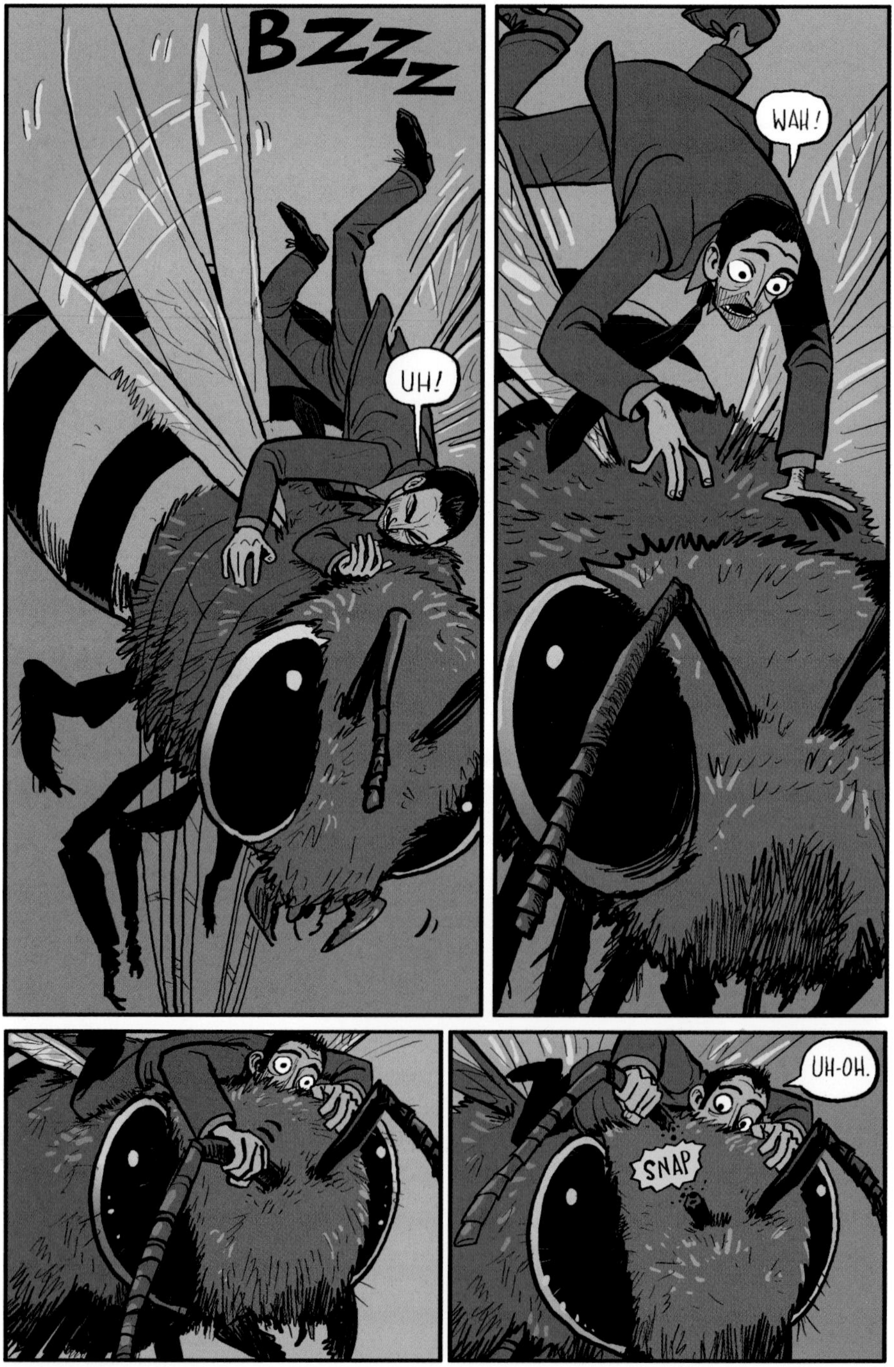
BZZZ
UH!
WAH!
UH-OH.
SNAP

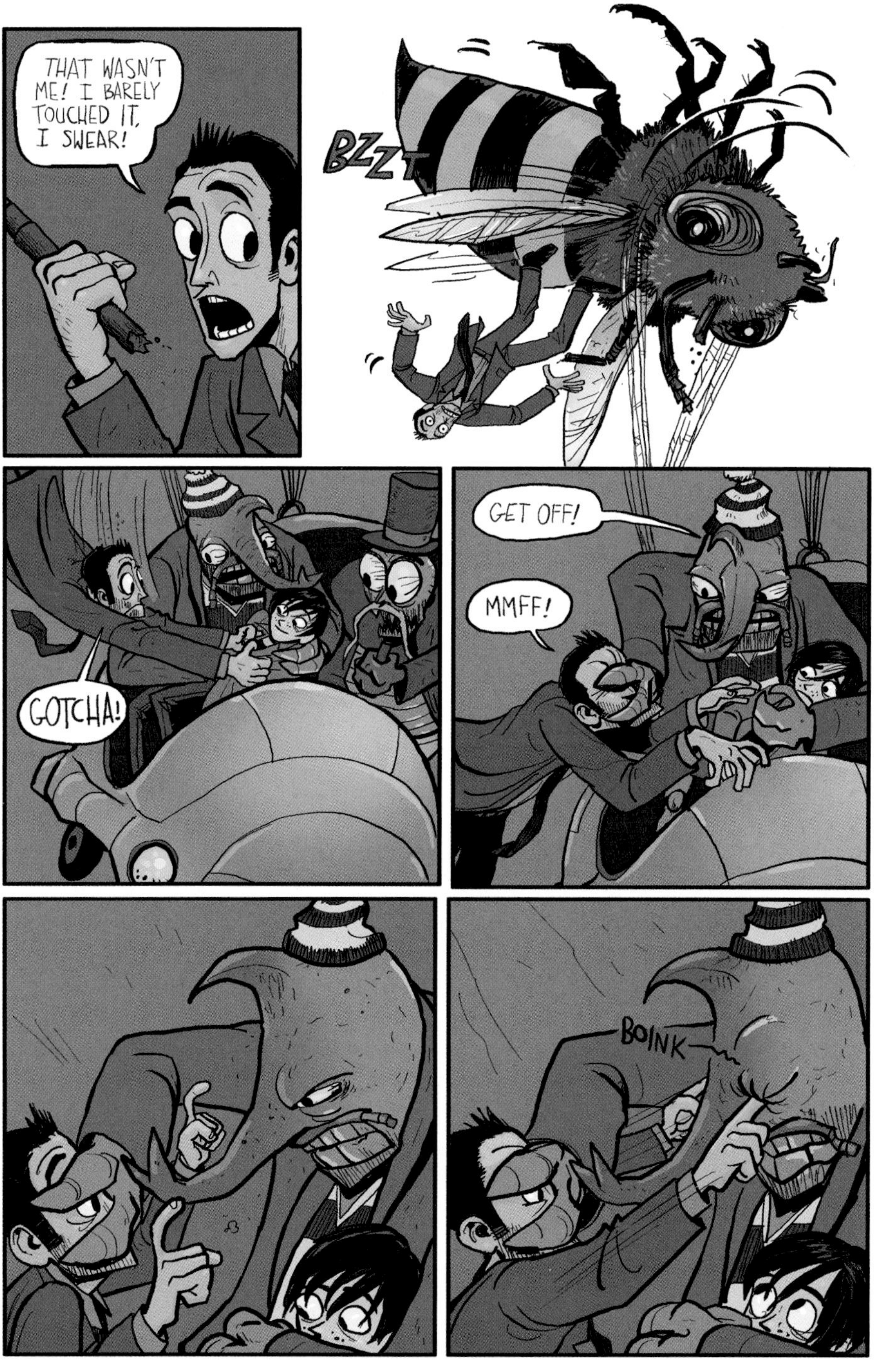
THAT WASN'T ME! I BARELY TOUCHED IT, I SWEAR!
BZZT
GOTCHA!
GET OFF!
MMFF!
BOINK

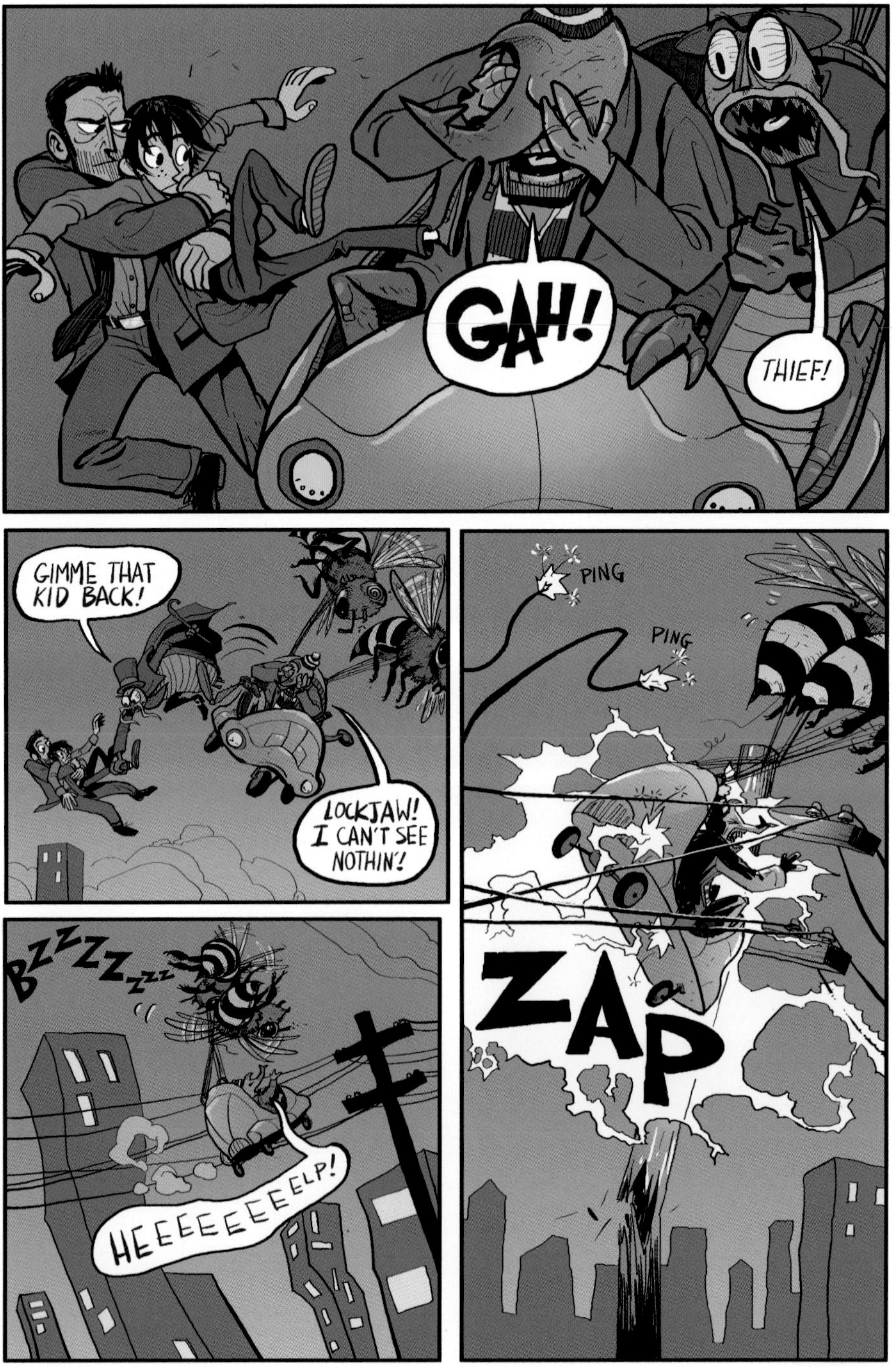
GAH!
THIEF!
GIMME THAT KID BACK!
LOCKJAW! I CAN'T SEE NOTHIN'!
PING
PING
ZAP
BZZZZZzzz
HEEEEEEEELP!

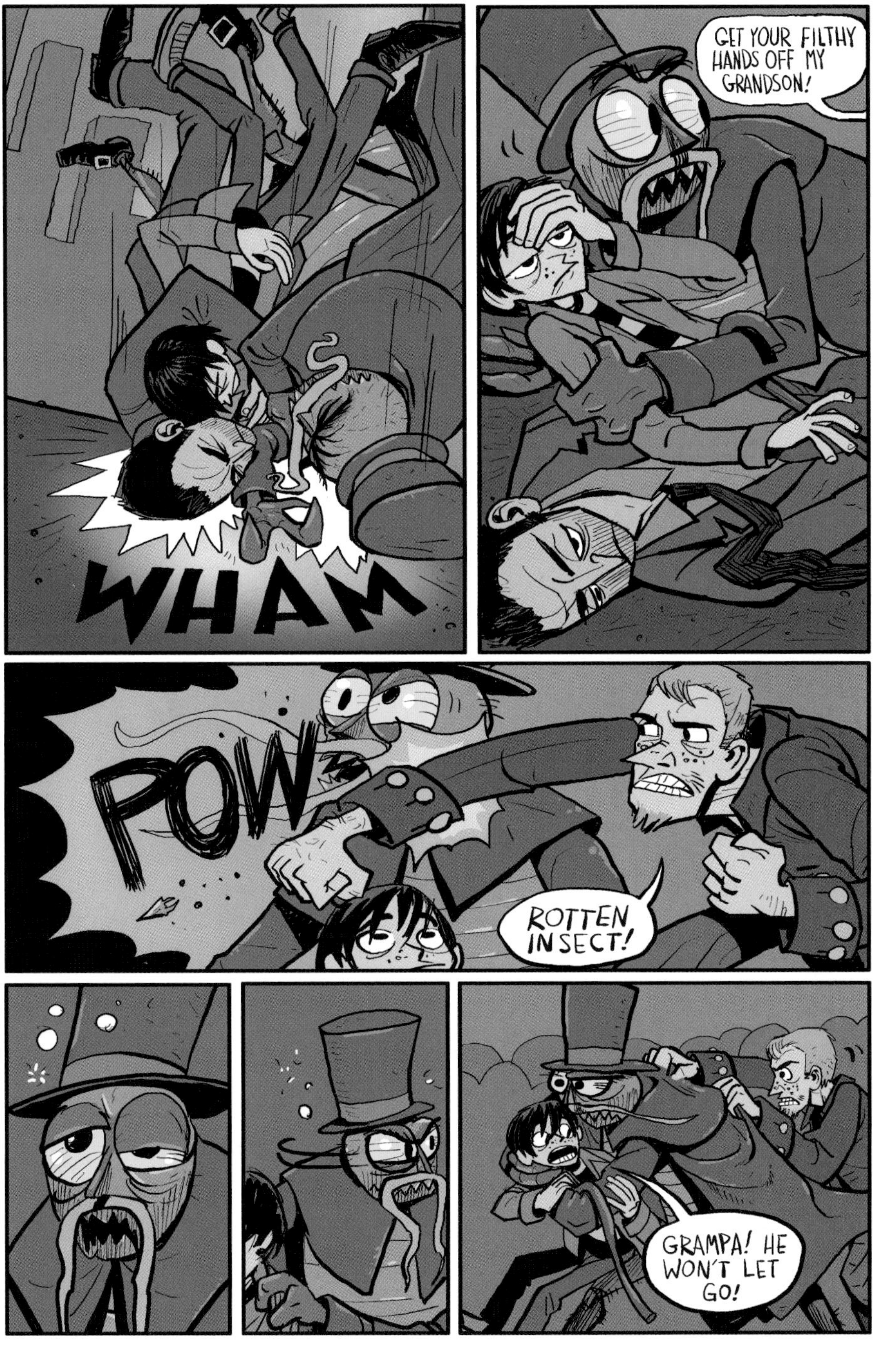
WHAM
GET YOUR FILTHY HANDS OFF MY GRANDSON!
POW
ROTTEN INSECT!
GRAMPA! HE WON'T LET GO!

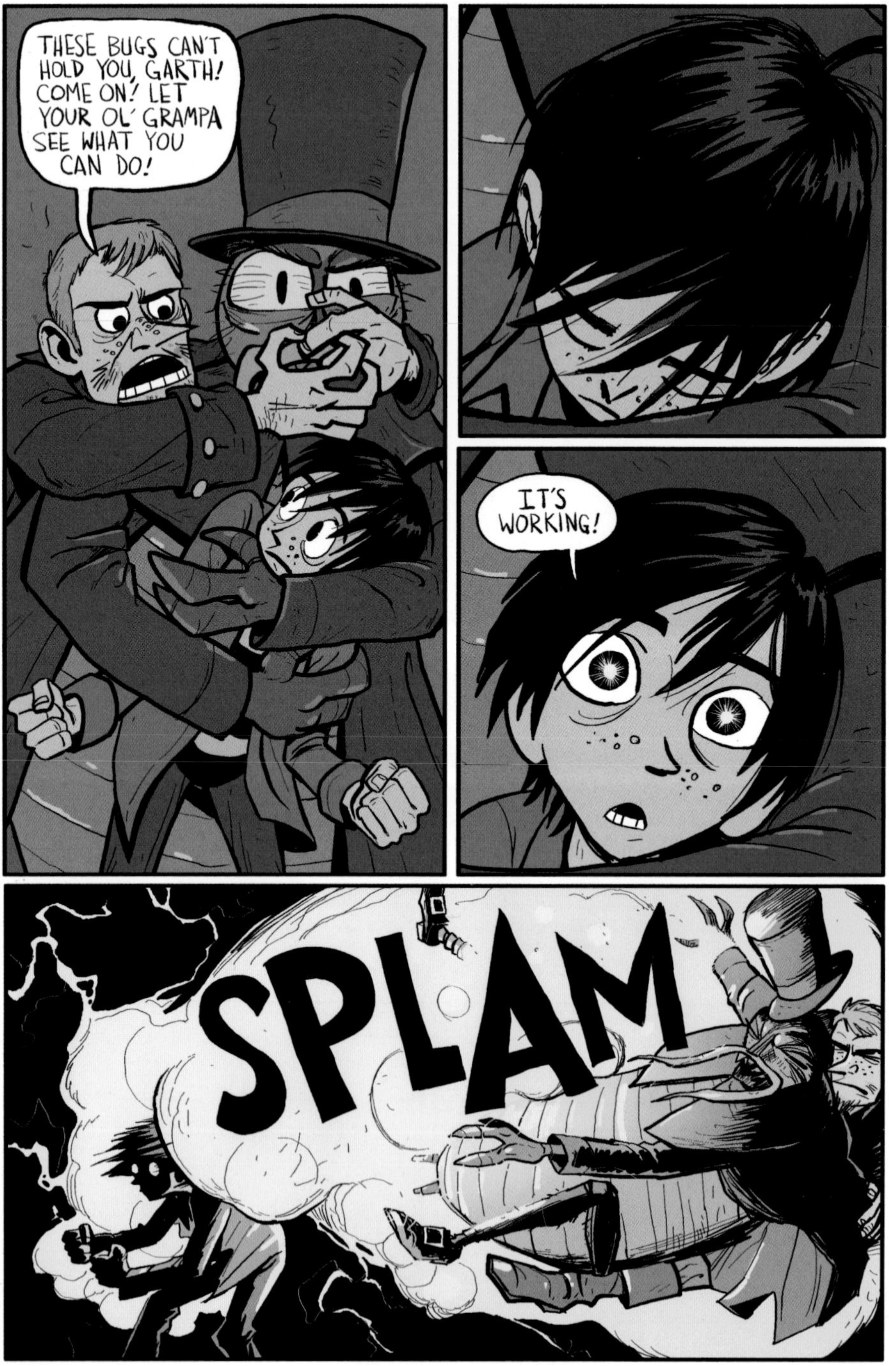
THESE BUGS CAN'T HOLD YOU, GARTH! COME ON! LET YOUR OL' GRAMPA SEE WHAT YOU CAN DO!
IT'S WORKING!
SPLAM

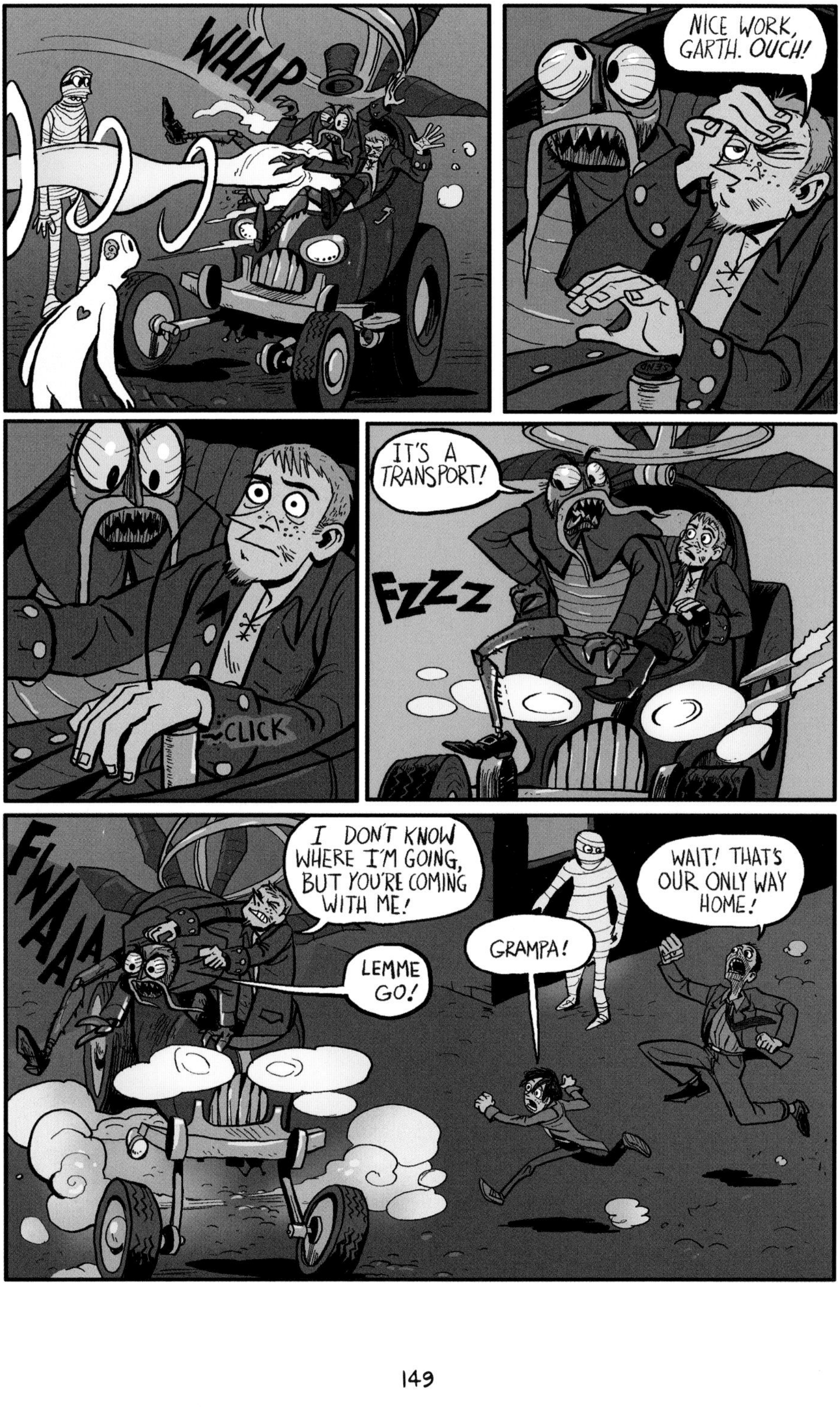
WHAP
NICE WORK, GARTH. OUCH!
CLICK
IT'S A TRANSPORT!
FZZZ
FWAAAA
I DON'T KNOW WHERE I'M GOING, BUT YOU'RE COMING WITH ME!
LEMME GO!
GRAMPA!
WAIT! THAT'S OUR ONLY WAY HOME!

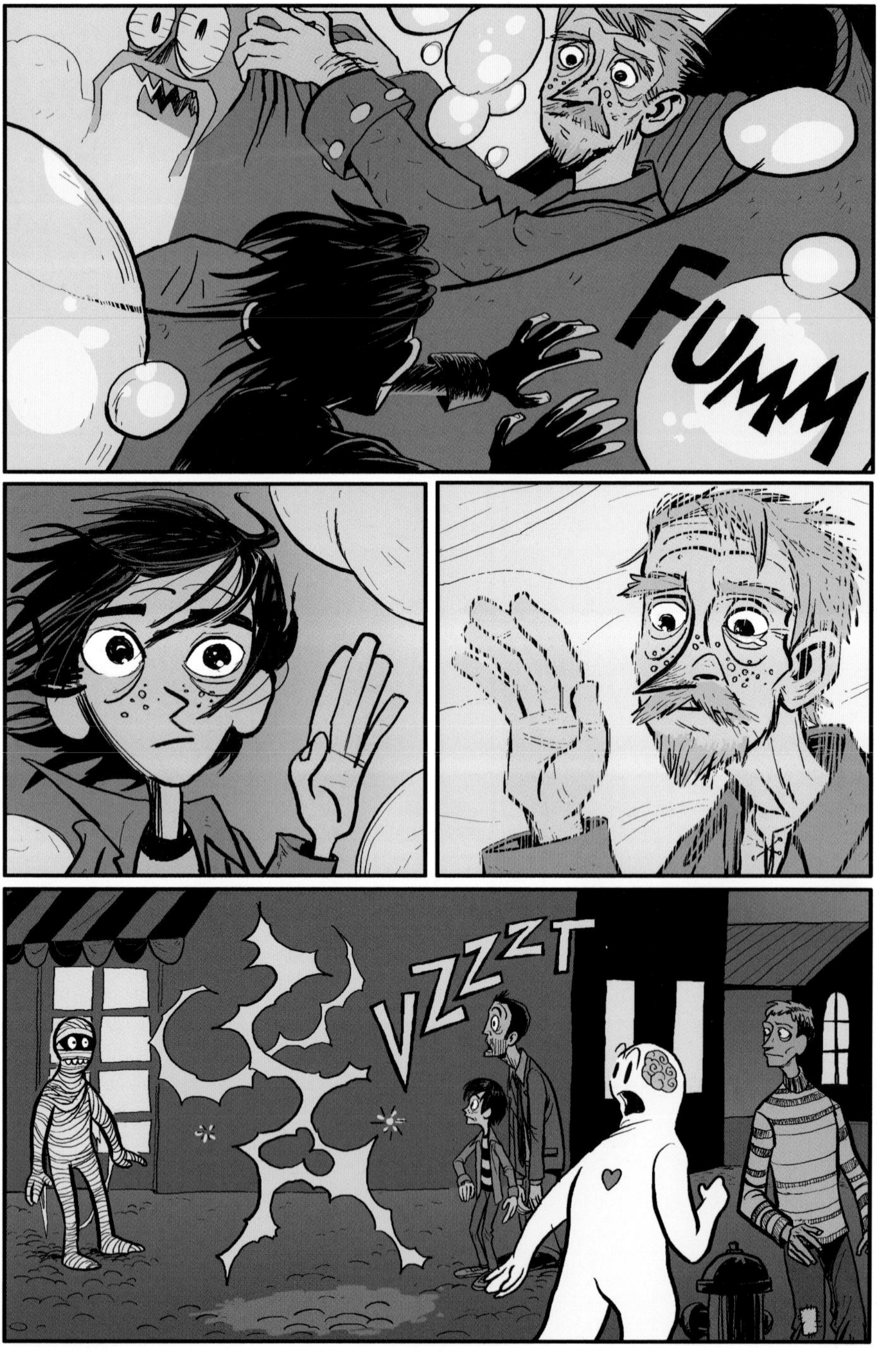
FUMM
VZZZZT

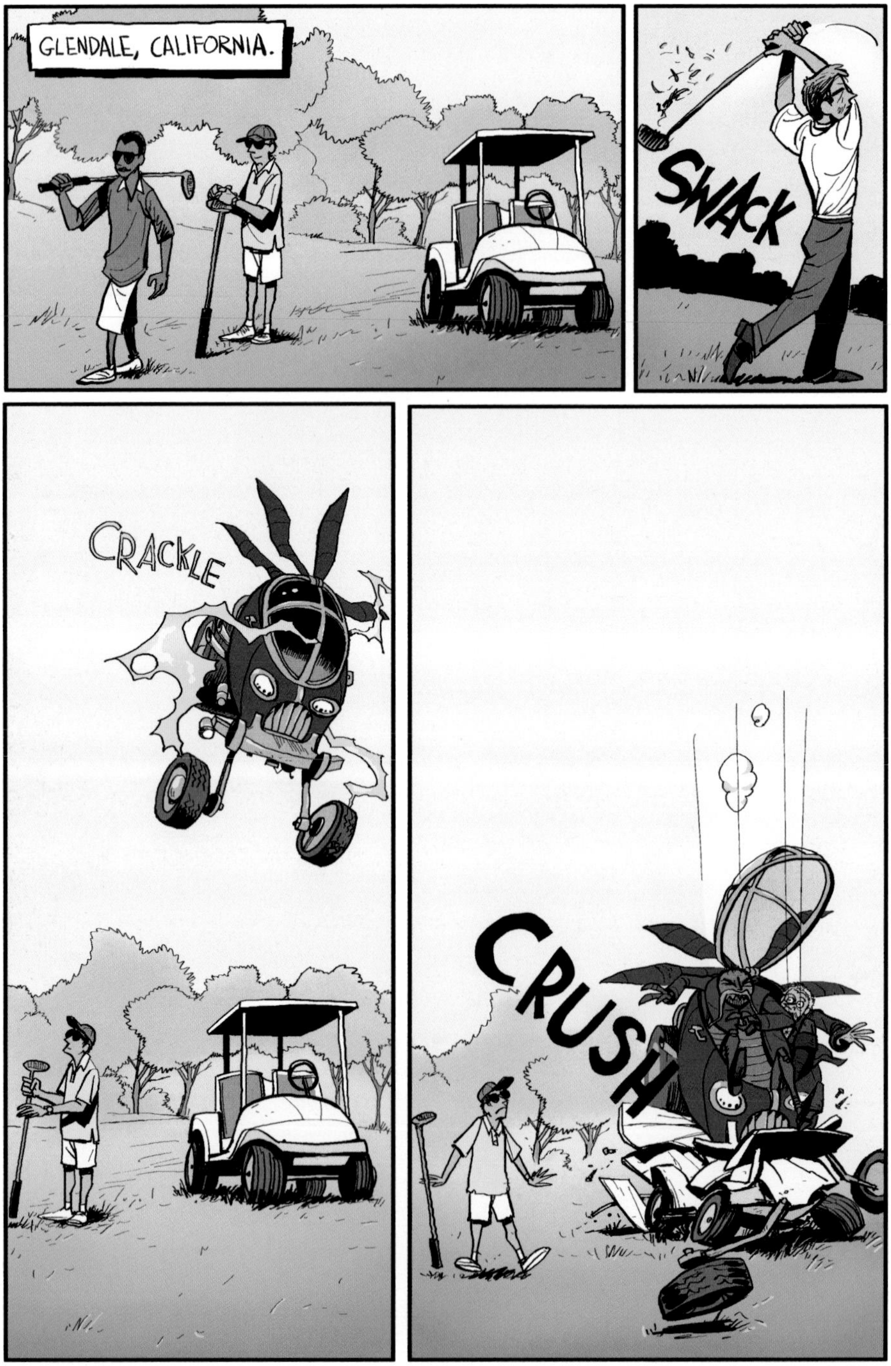
GLENDALE, CALIFORNIA.
SWACK
CRACKLE
CRUSH

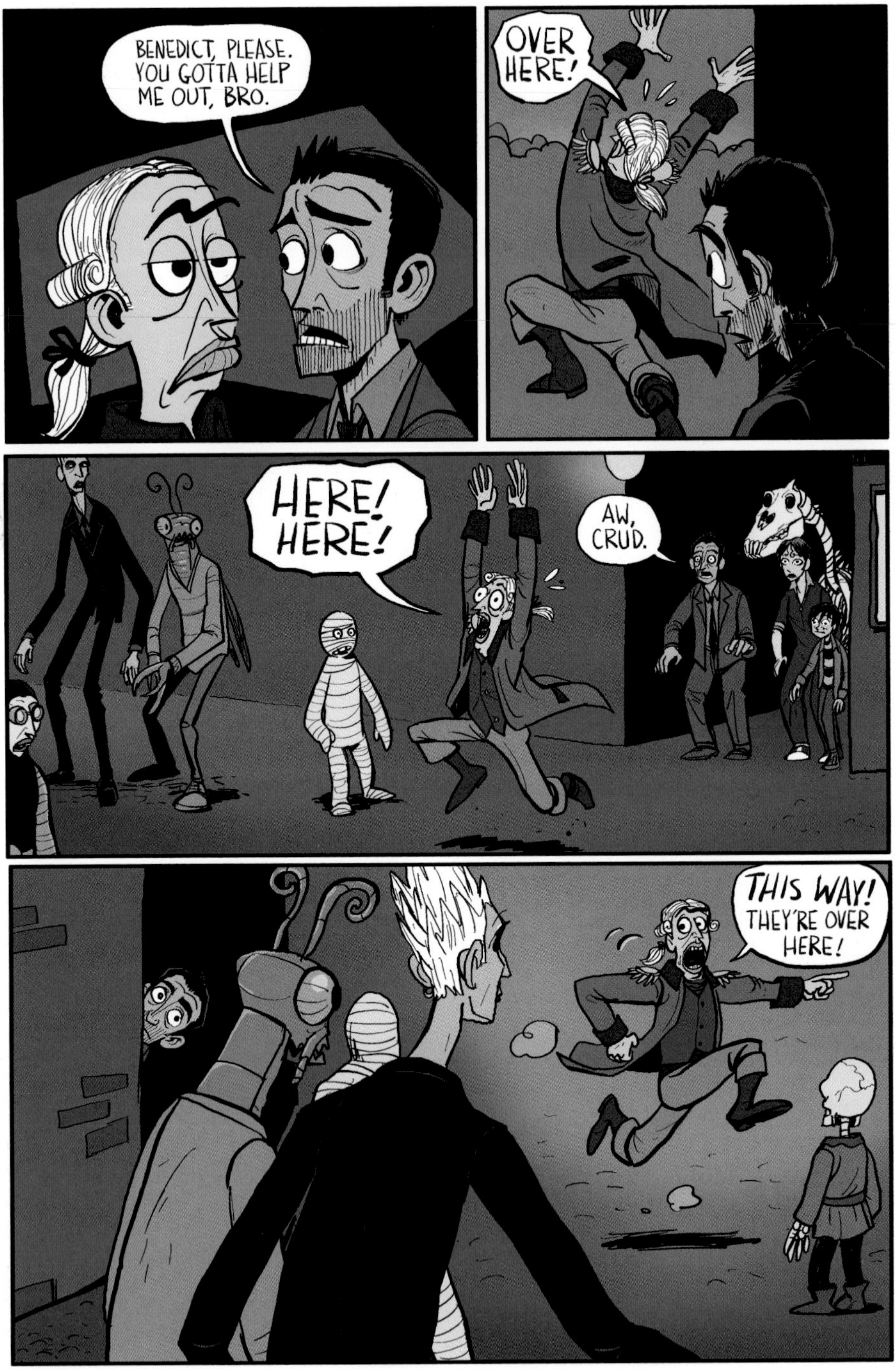
BENEDICT, PLEASE. YOU GOTTA HELP ME OUT, BRO.
OVER HERE!
HERE! HERE!
AW, CRUD.
THIS WAY! THEY'RE OVER HERE!

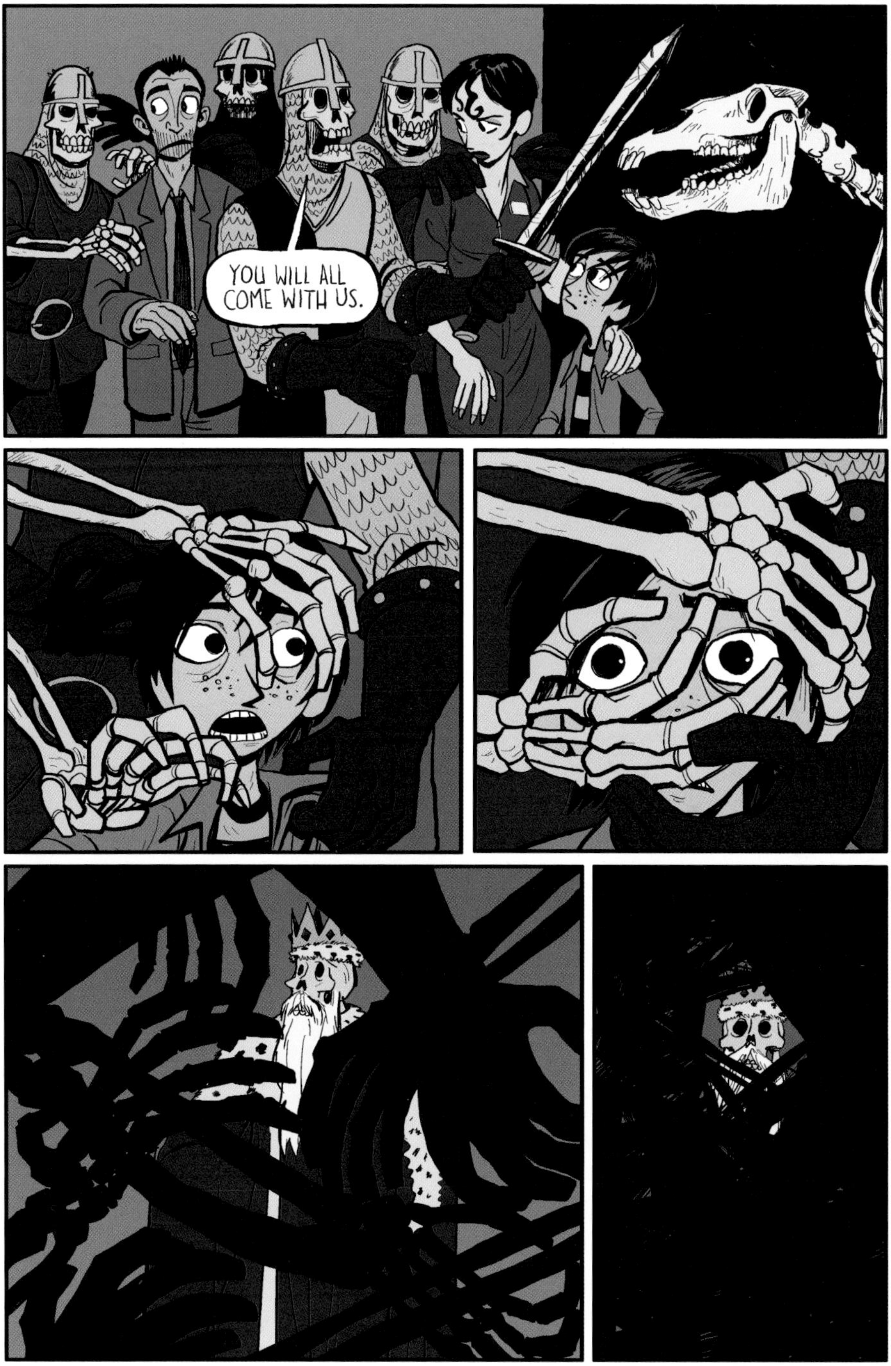
YOU WILL ALL COME WITH US.

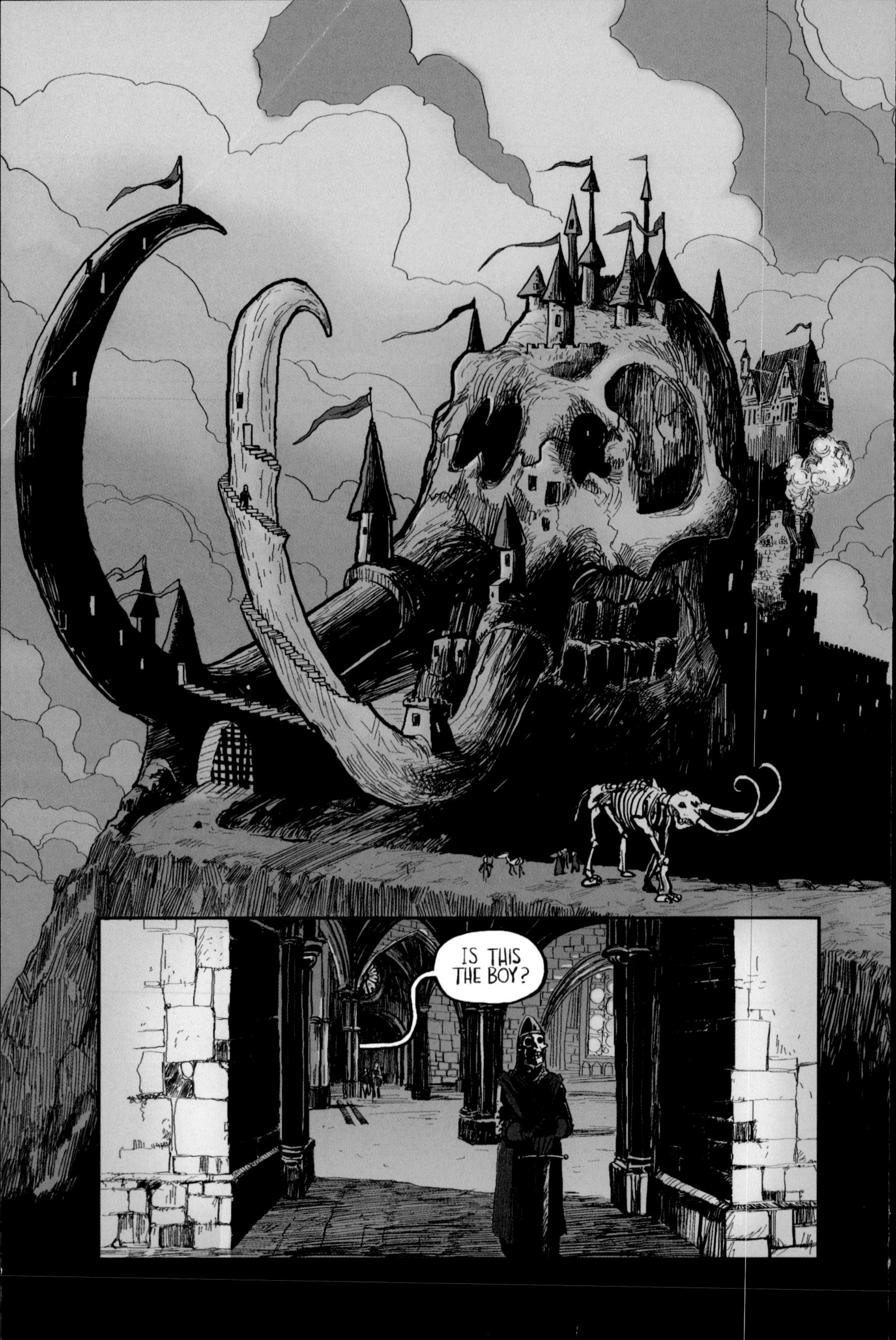
IS THIS THE BOY?

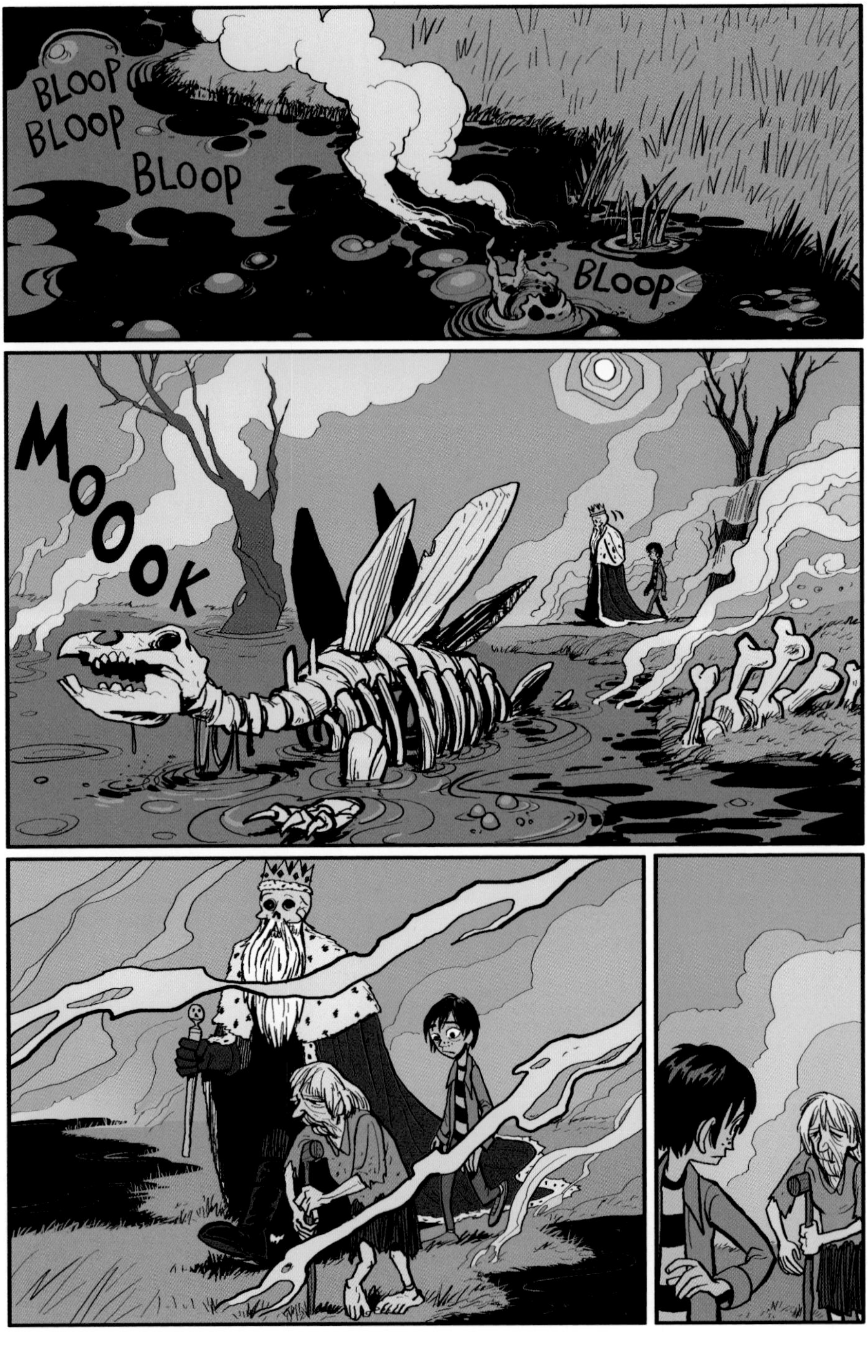
BLOOP
BLOOP
BLOOP
BLOOP
MOOOOK

169

172

173

177

179

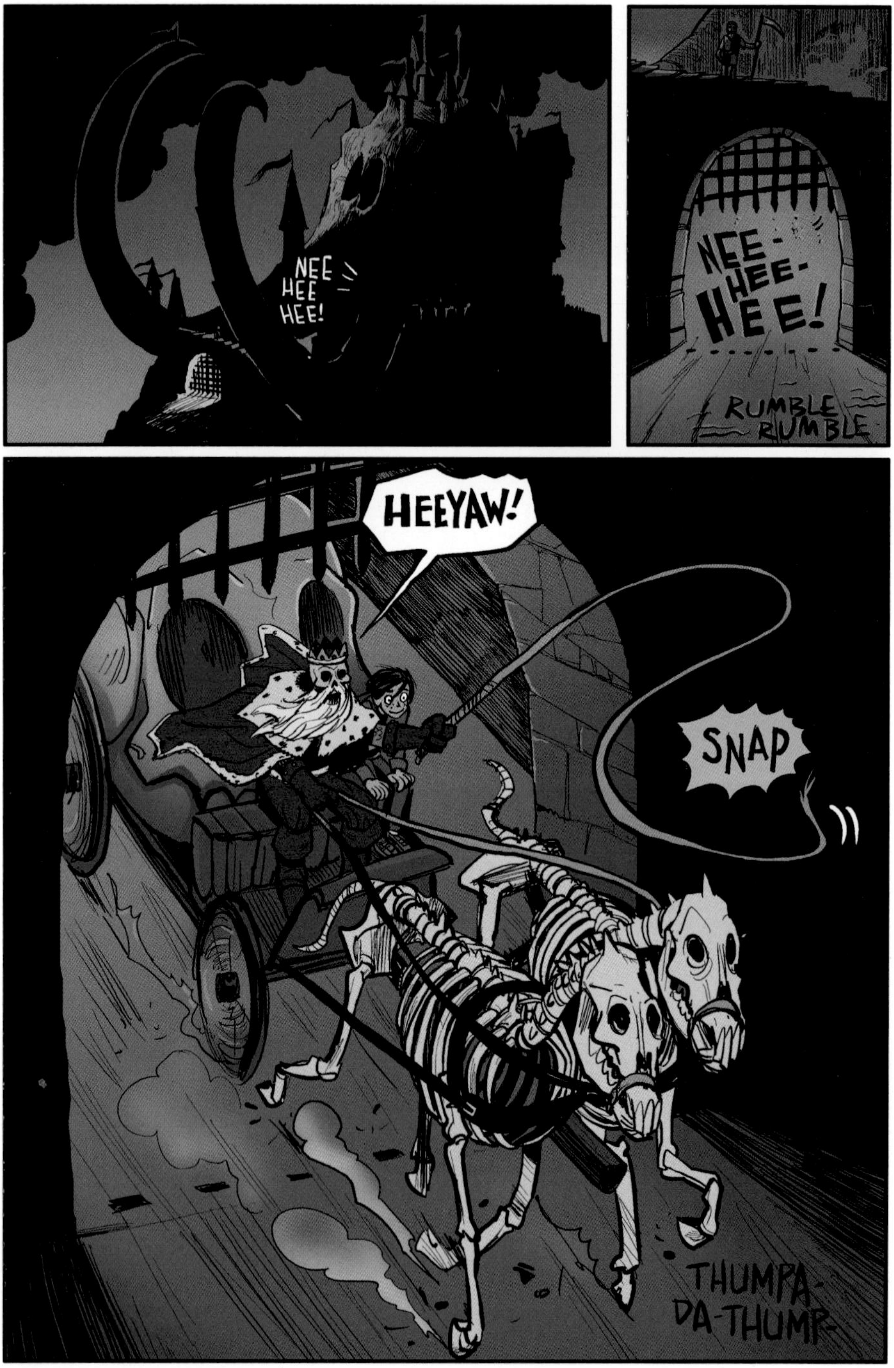
NEE
HEE
HEE!
NEE-
HEE-
HEE!
RUMBLE
RUMBLE
HEEYAW!
SNAP
THUMPA-
DA-THUMP-

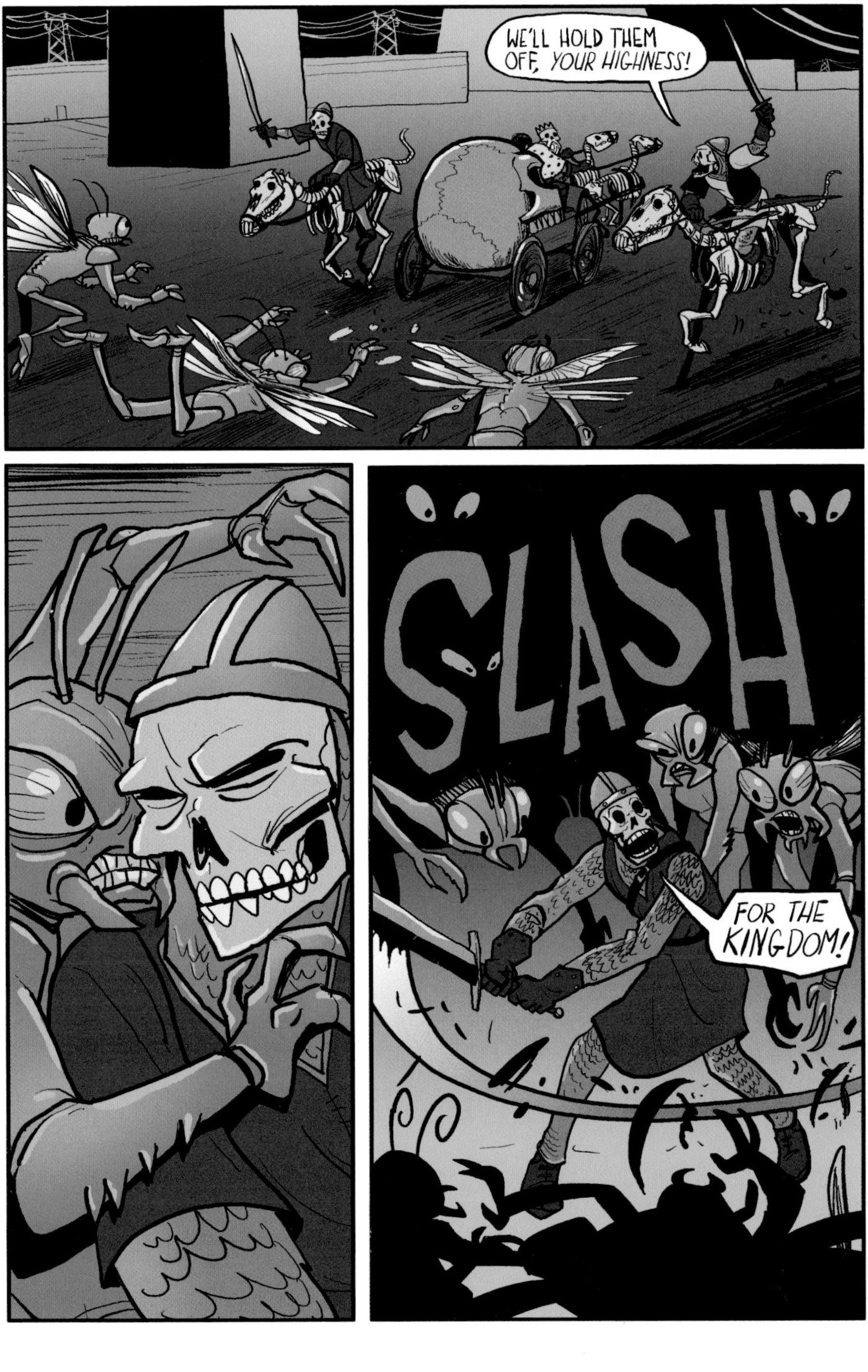
WE'LL HOLD THEM OFF, *YOUR HIGHNESS!*
SLASH
FOR THE KINGDOM!

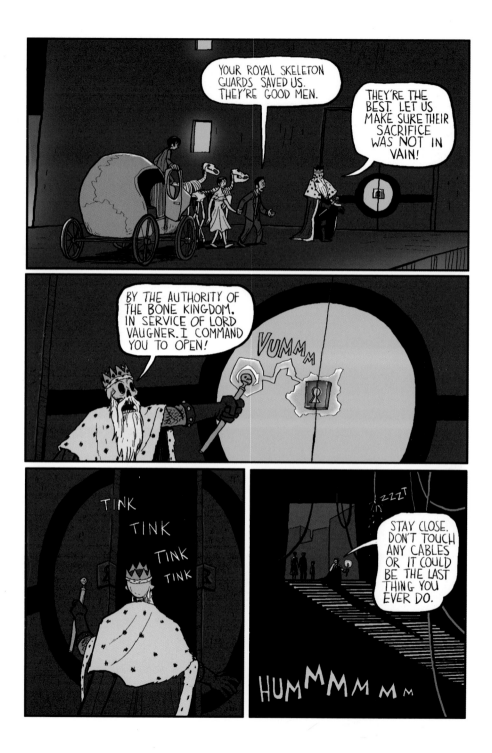

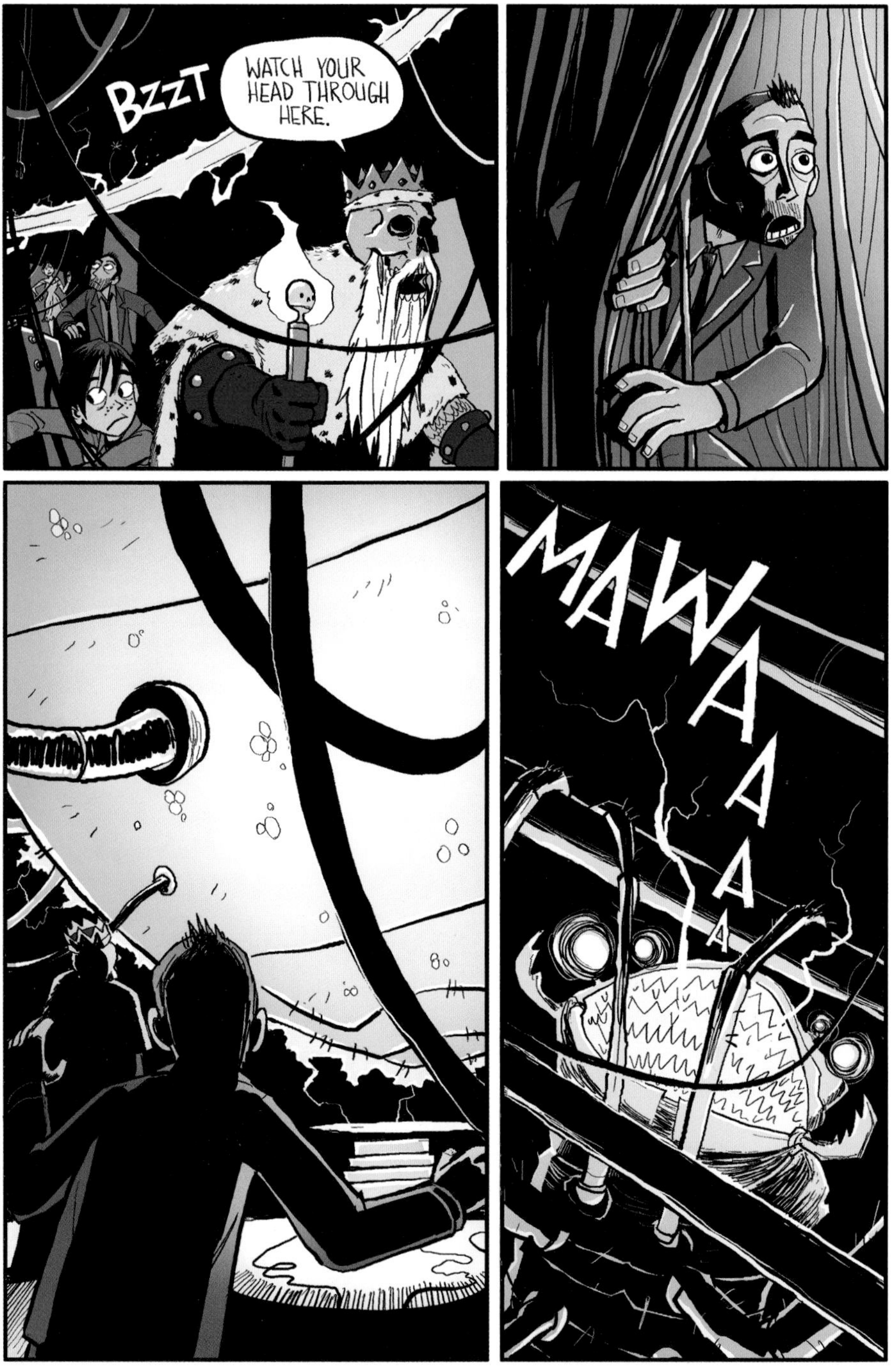
BZZT
WATCH YOUR HEAD THROUGH HERE.
MAWAAAAA

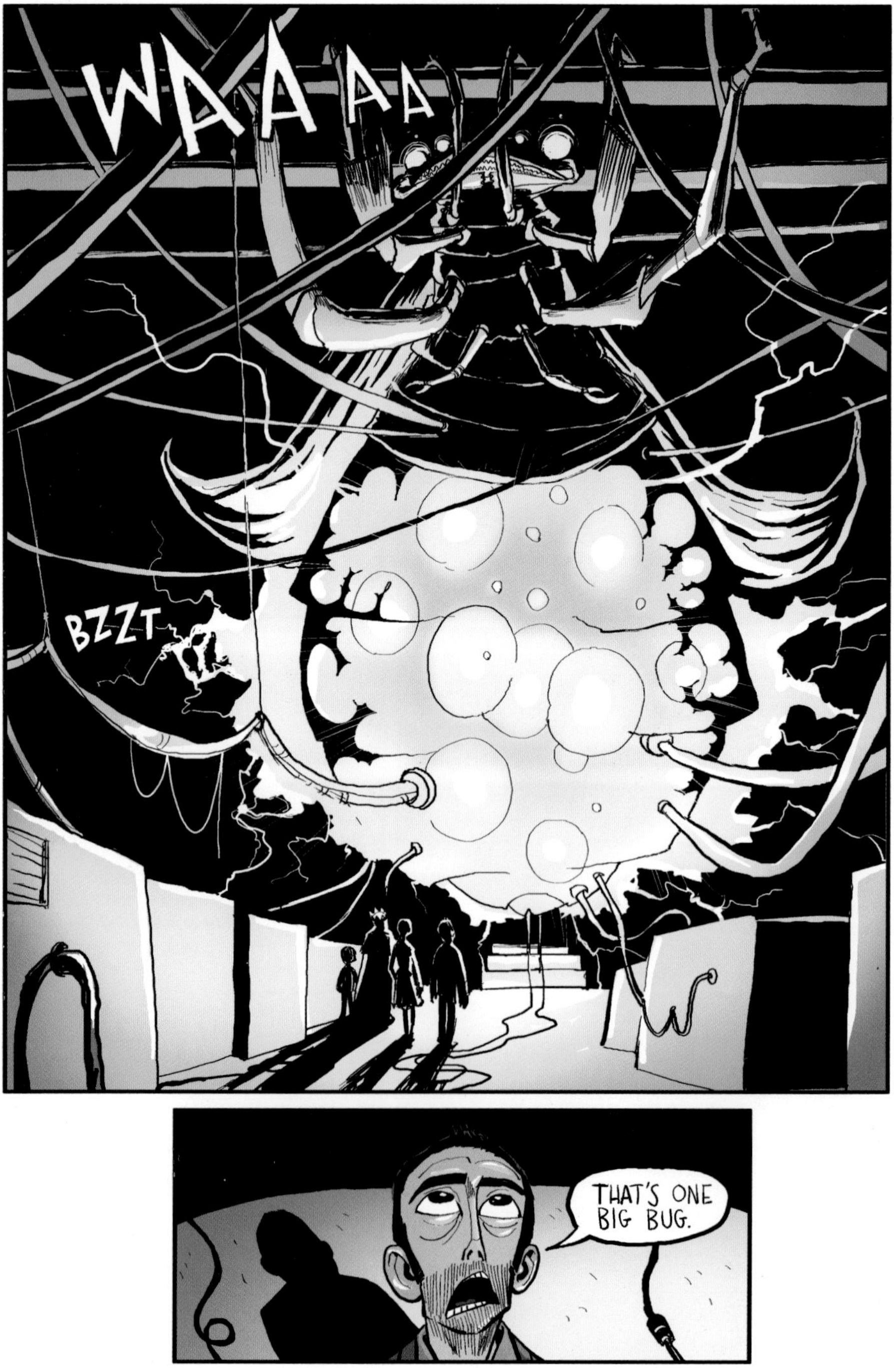
WAAAA
BZZT
THAT'S ONE BIG BUG.

199

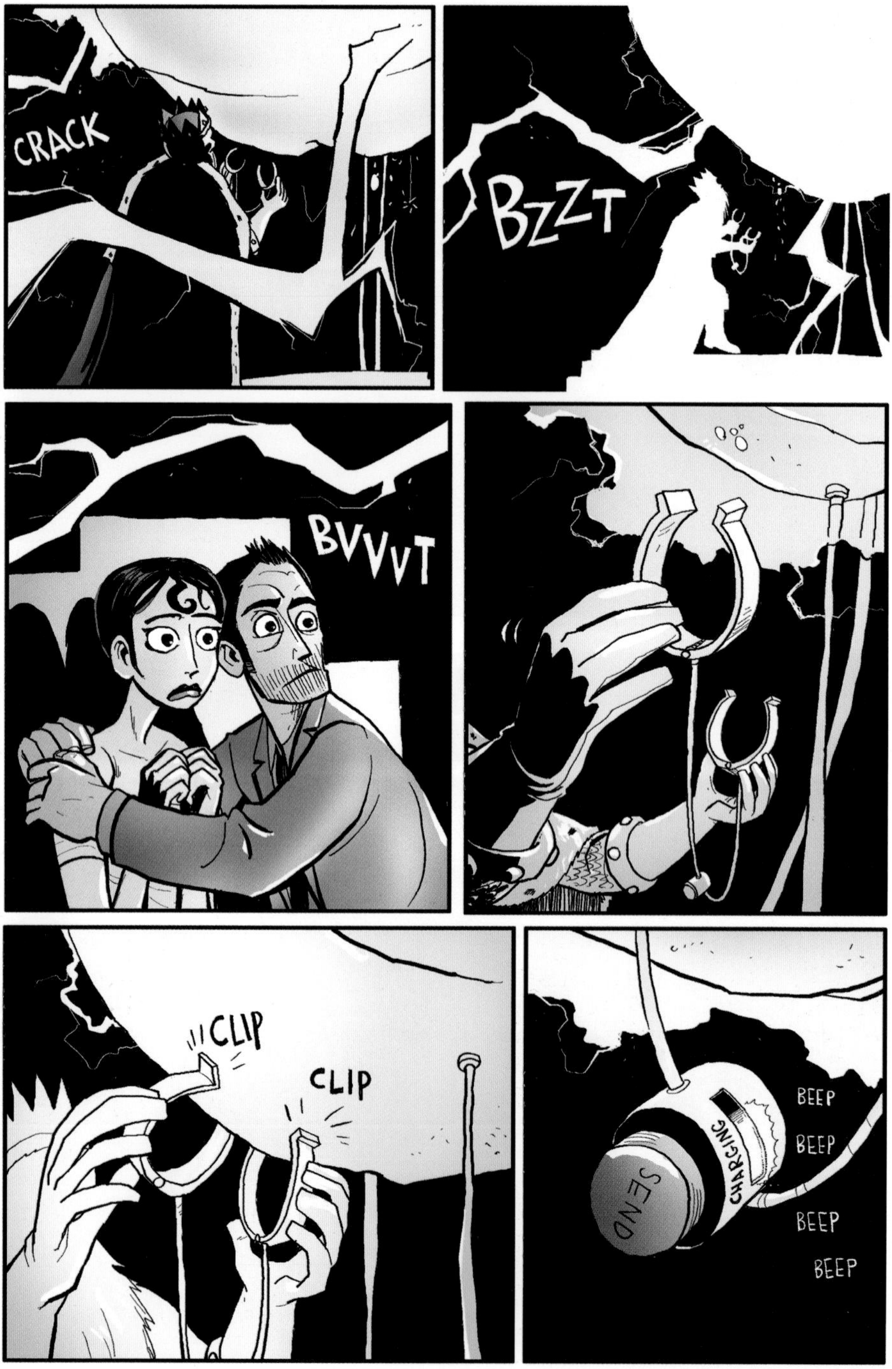
CRACK
BZZT
BVVVT
CLIP
CLIP
CHARGING
SEND
BEEP
BEEP
BEEP
BEEP

202

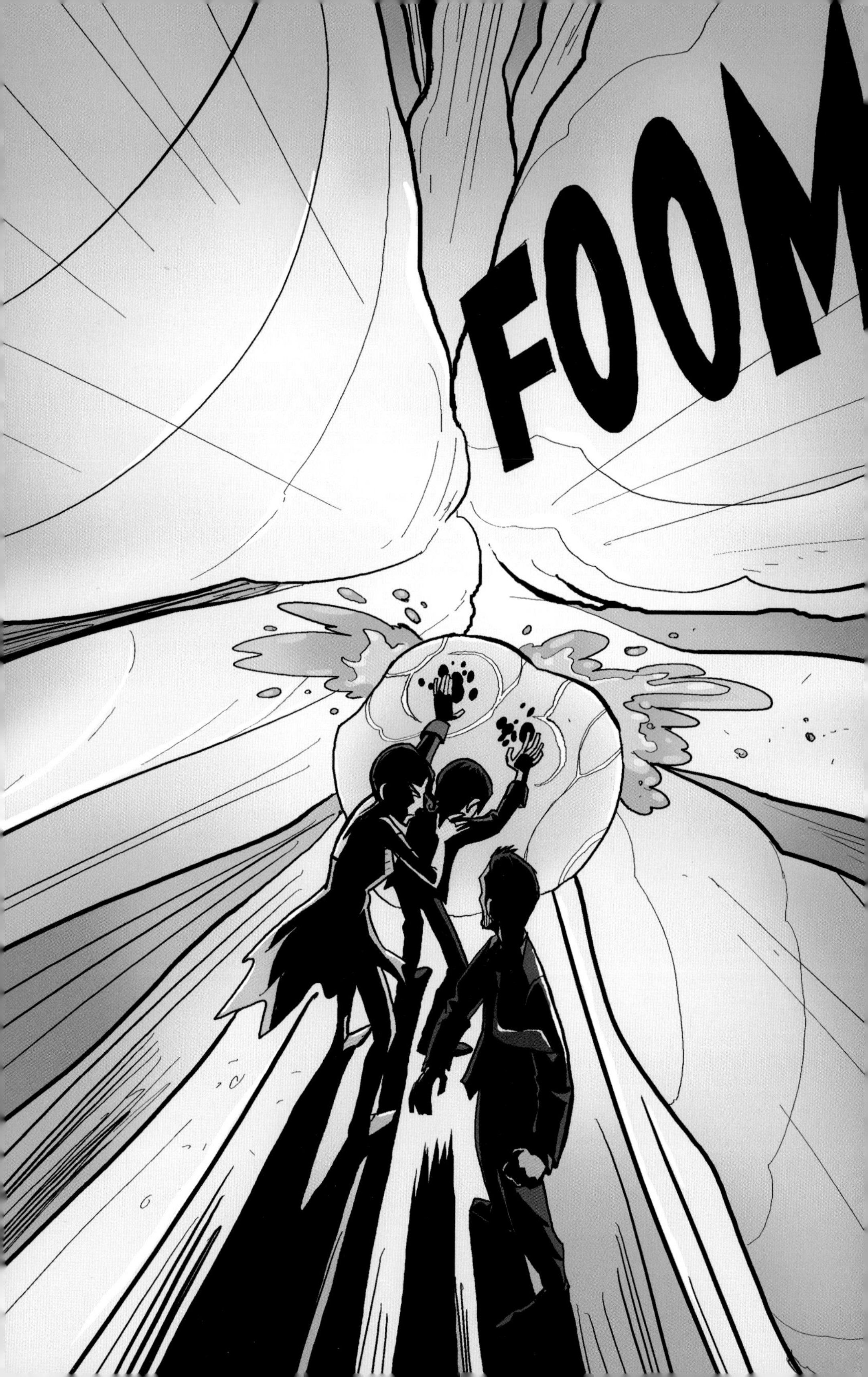
FOOM

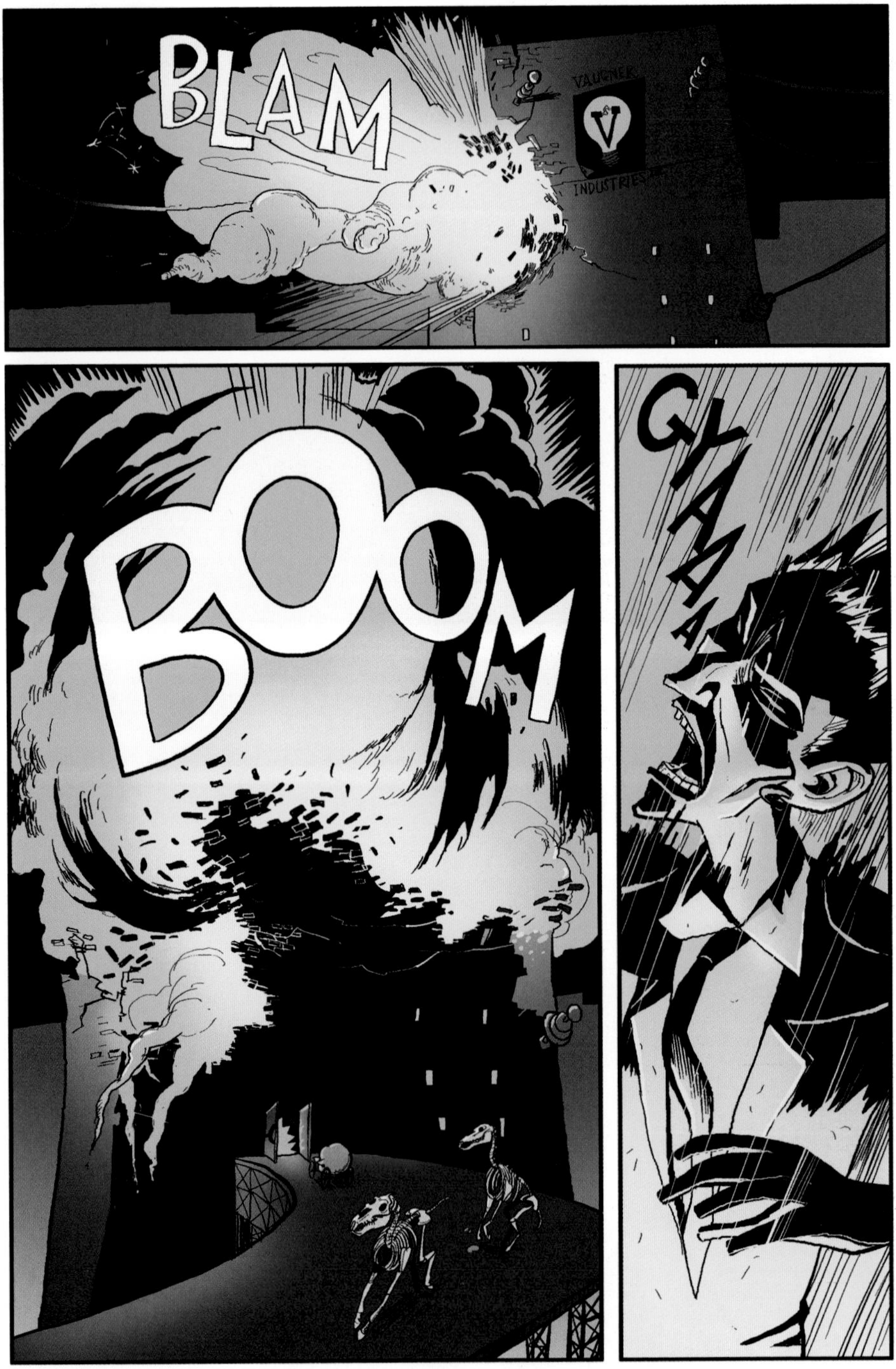
BLAM
VAUGHNER
V
INDUSTRIES
BOOOM
GYAAAA

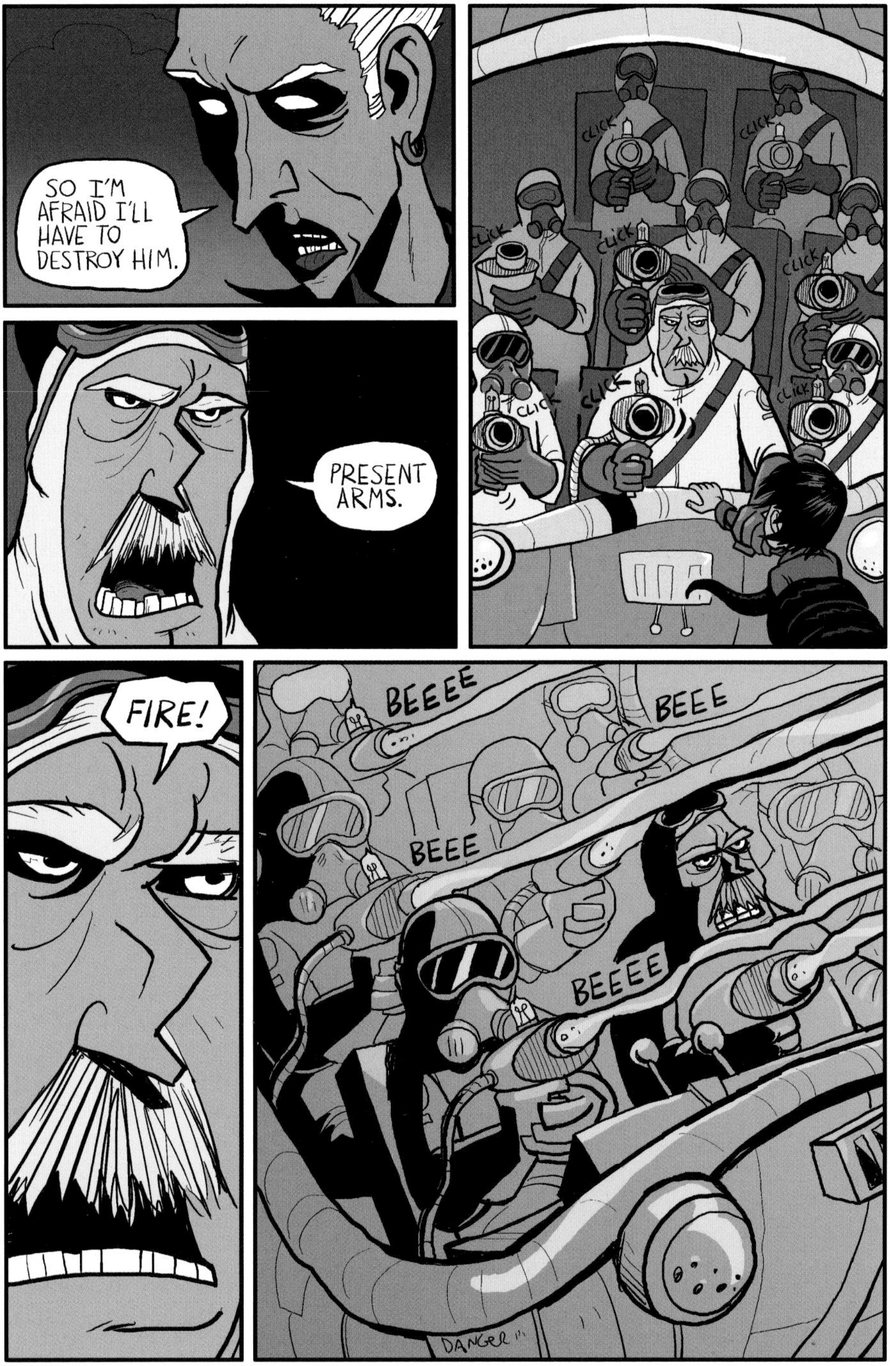
SO I'M AFRAID I'LL HAVE TO DESTROY HIM.
PRESENT ARMS.
CLICK
CLICK
CLICK
CLICK
CLICK
CLICK
CLICK
CLICK
FIRE!
BEEEE
BEEE
BEEE
BEEEE
DANGER

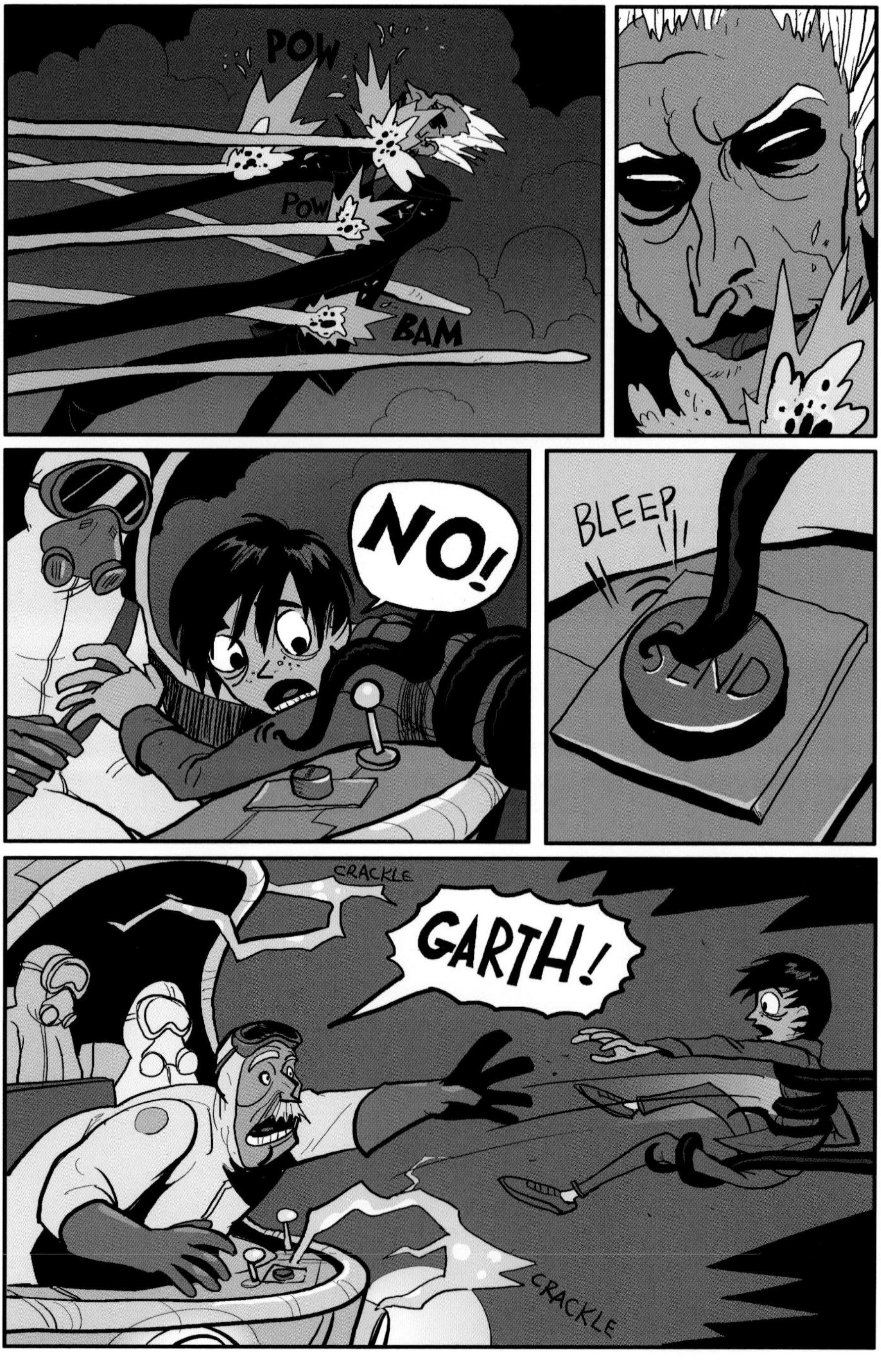
POW
POW
BAM
NO!
BLEEP
SEND
CRACKLE
GARTH!
CRACKLE

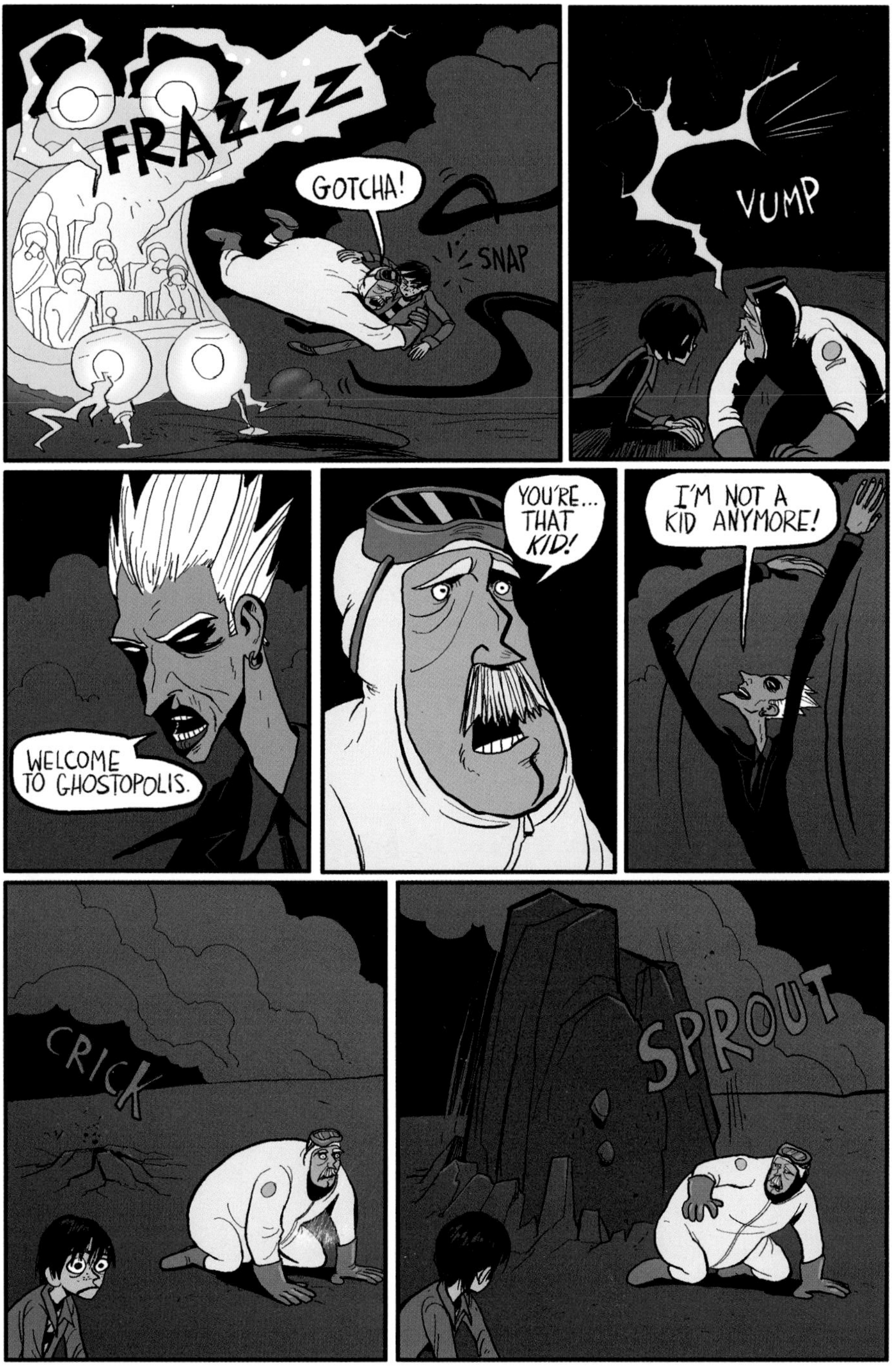
FRAZZZZ
GOTCHA!
SNAP
VUMP
WELCOME TO GHOSTOPOLIS.
YOU'RE... THAT KID!
I'M NOT A KID ANYMORE!
CRICK
SPROUT

218

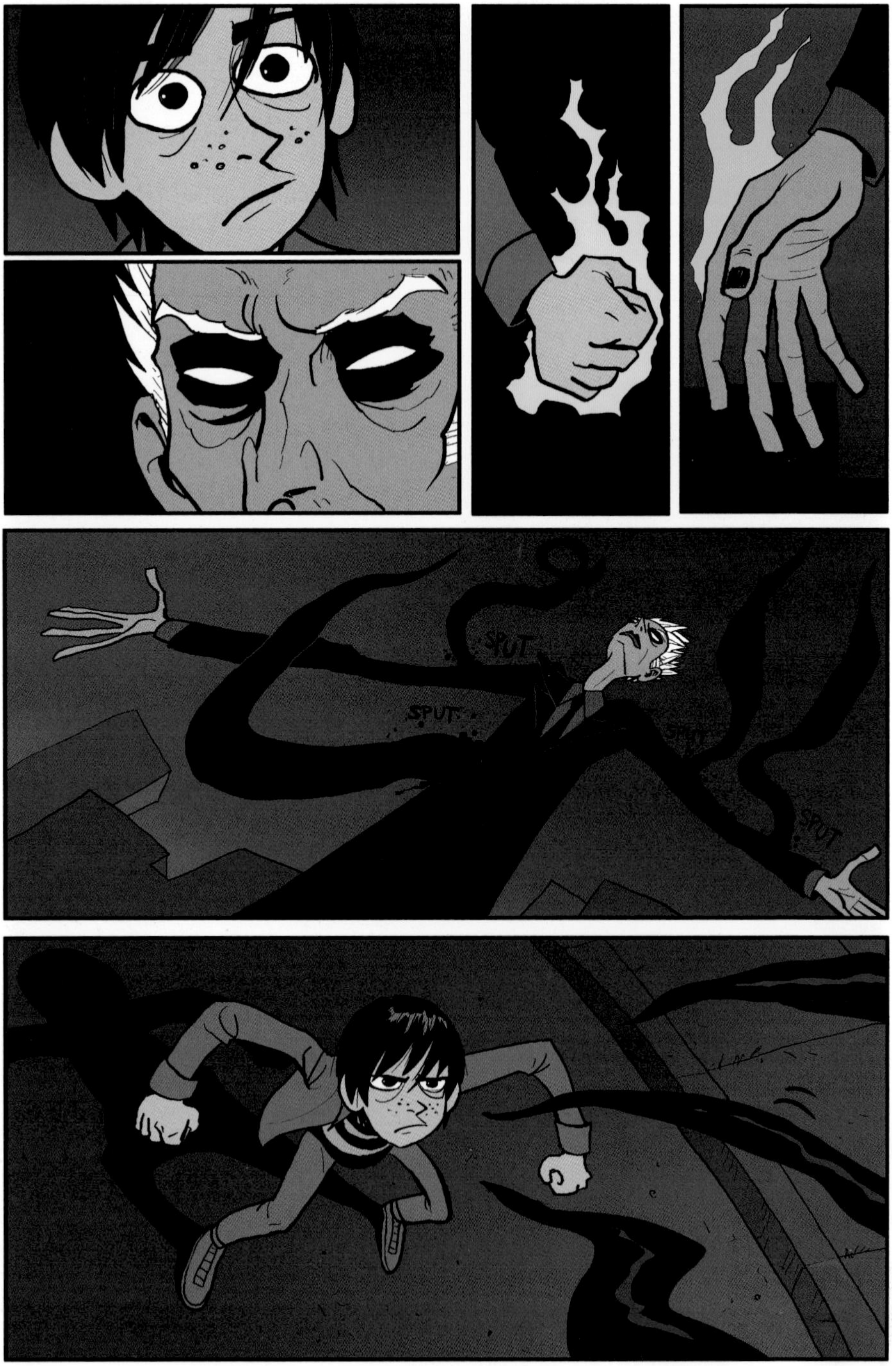
SPUT
SPUT
SPUT

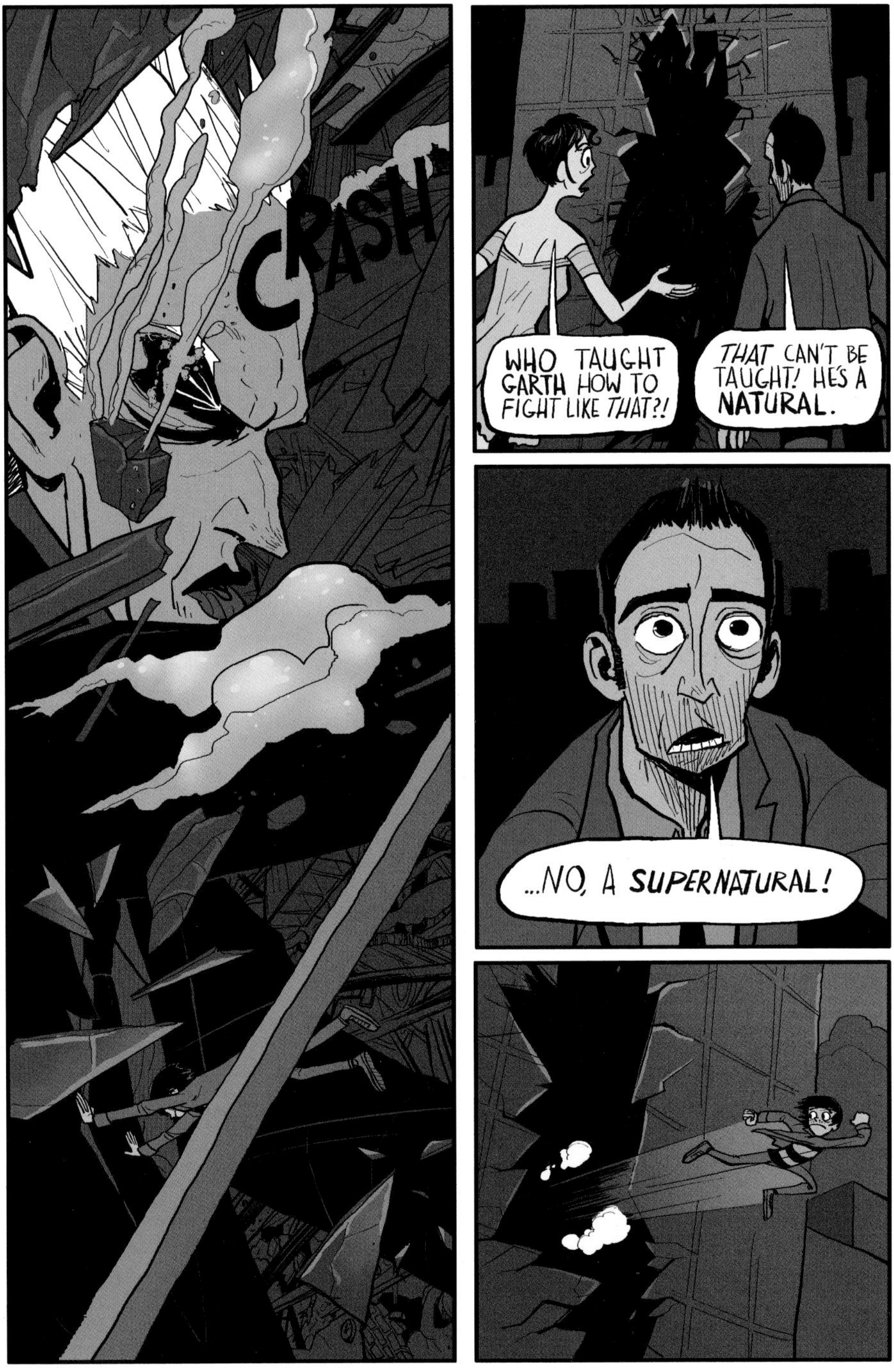
CRASH
WHO TAUGHT GARTH HOW TO FIGHT LIKE THAT?!
THAT CAN'T BE TAUGHT! HE'S A NATURAL.
...NO, A SUPERNATURAL!

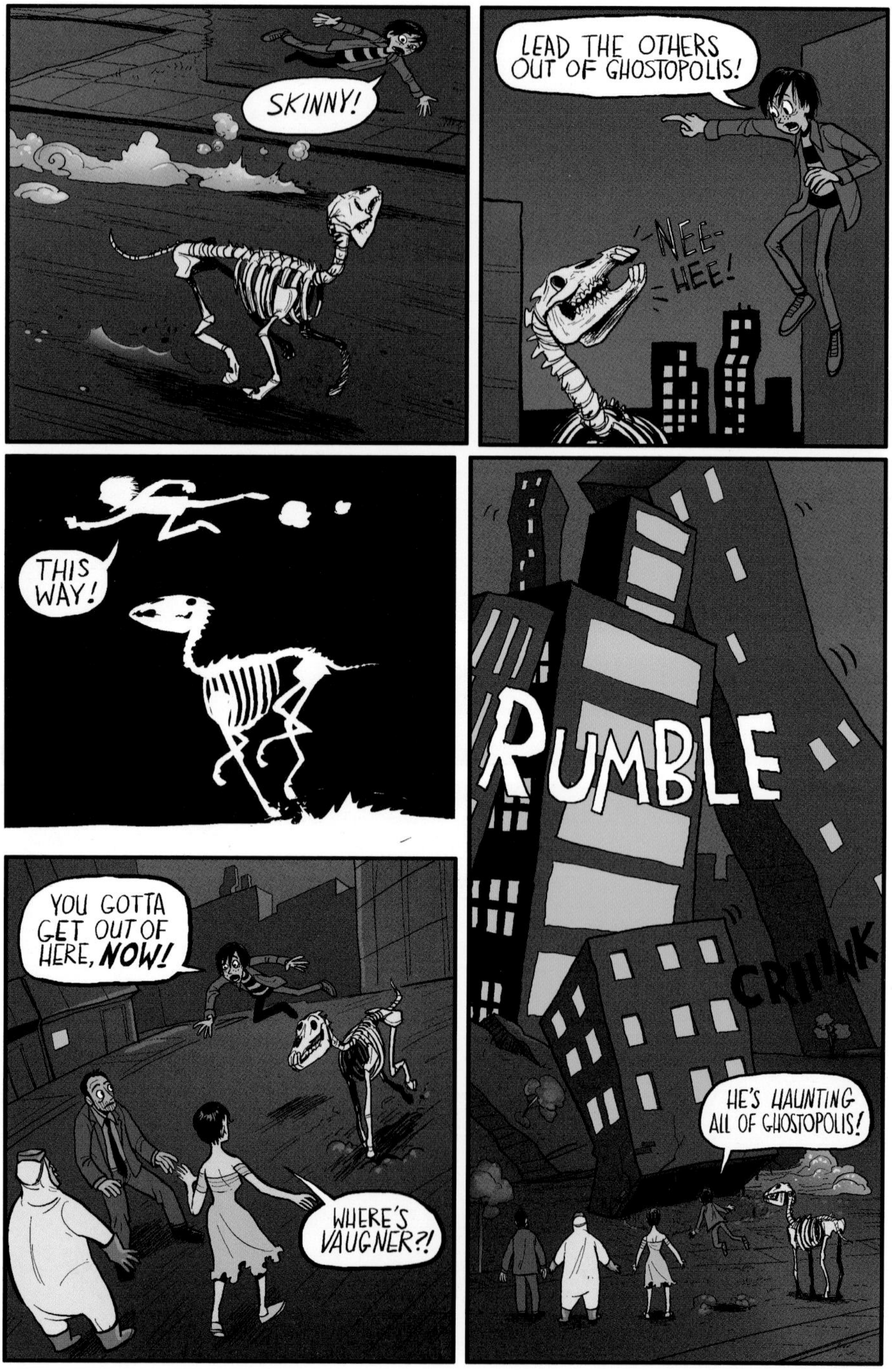
SKINNY!
LEAD THE OTHERS OUT OF GHOSTOPOLIS!
NEE-HEE!
THIS WAY!
RUMBLE
CRIIINK
YOU GOTTA GET OUT OF HERE, NOW!
WHERE'S VAUGNER?!
HE'S HAUNTING ALL OF GHOSTOPOLIS!

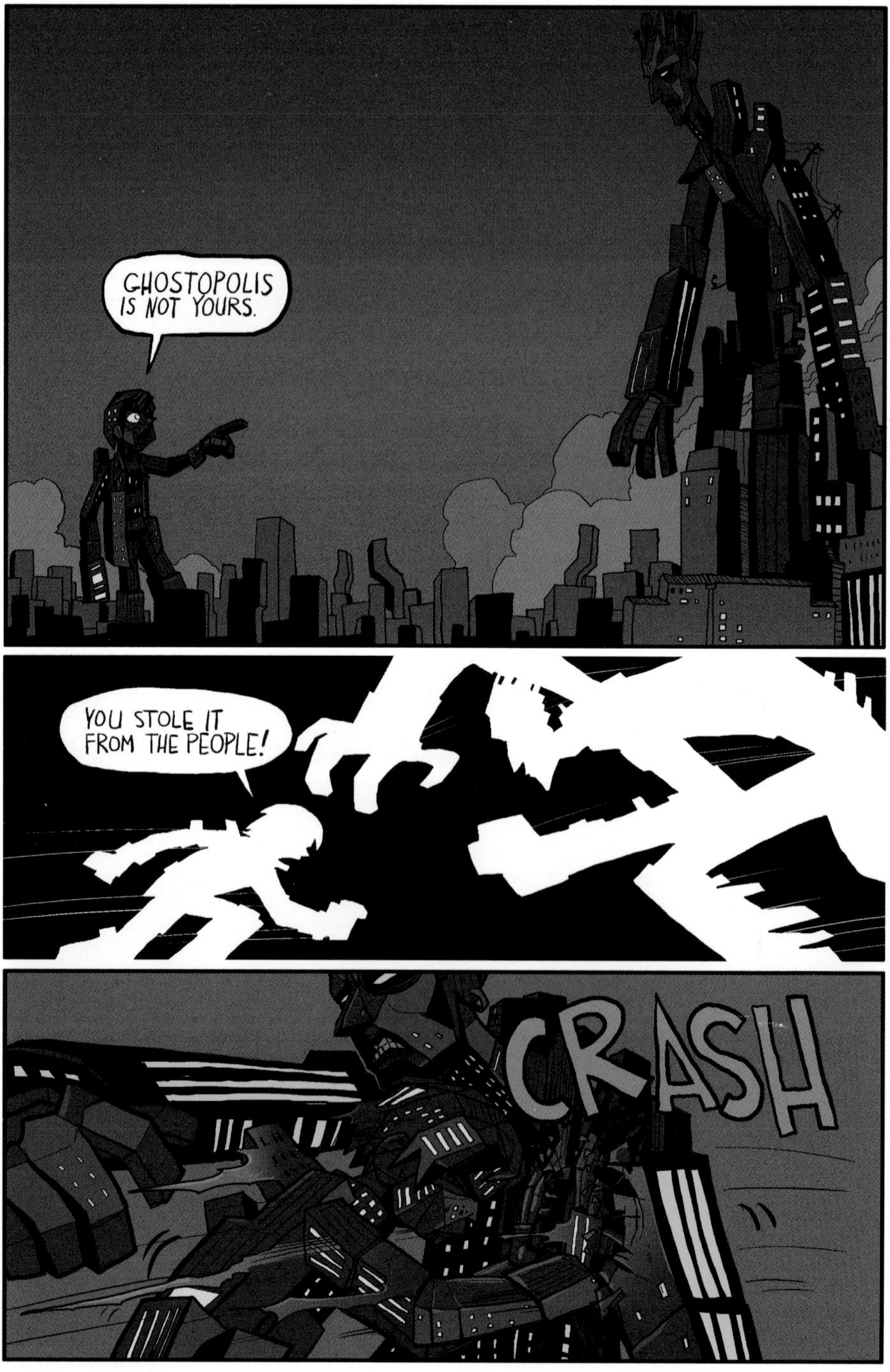
GHOSTOPOLIS IS NOT YOURS.
YOU STOLE IT FROM THE PEOPLE!
CRASH

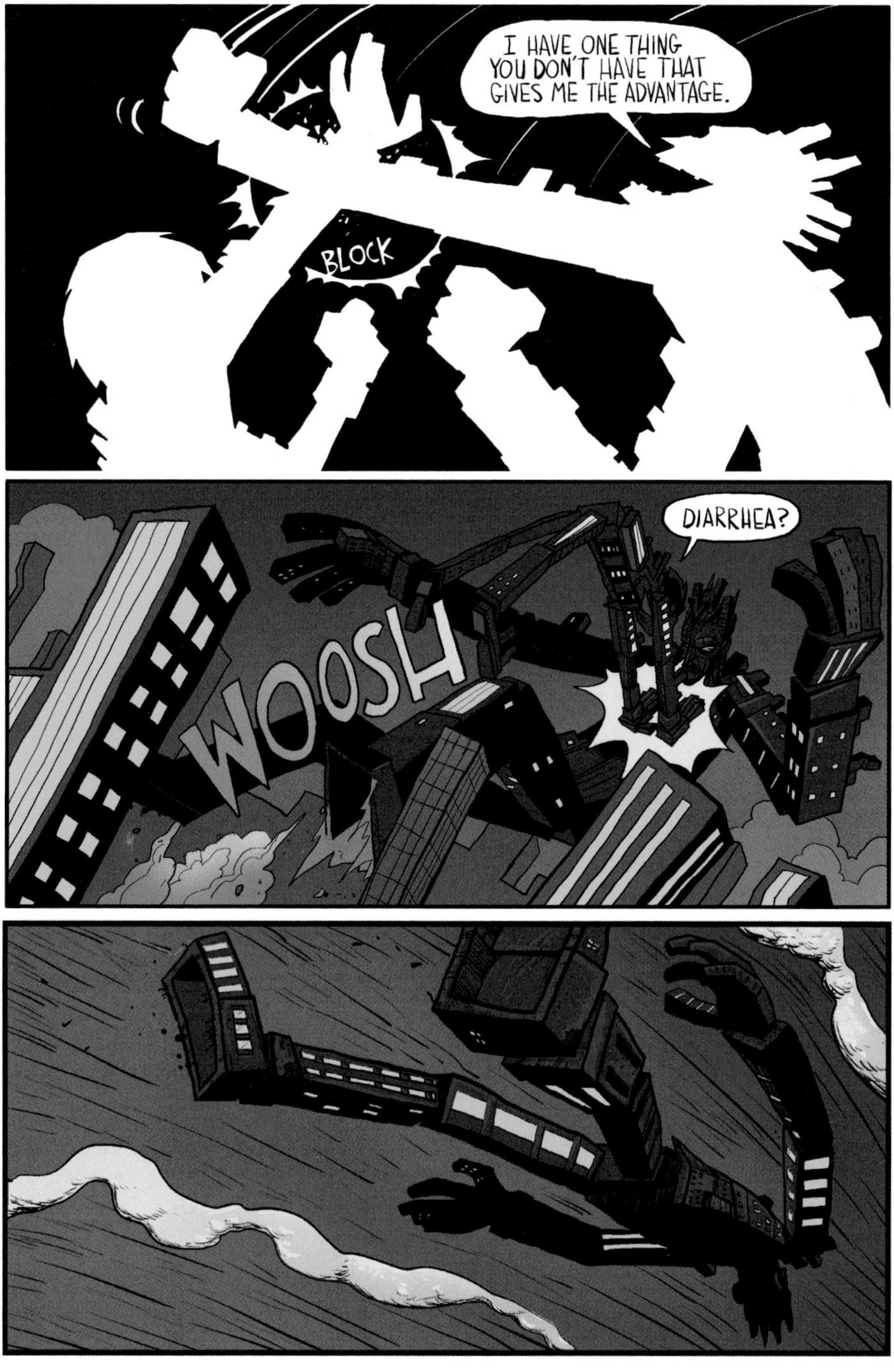
I HAVE ONE THING YOU DON'T HAVE THAT GIVES ME THE ADVANTAGE.
BLOCK
DIARRHEA?
WOOSH

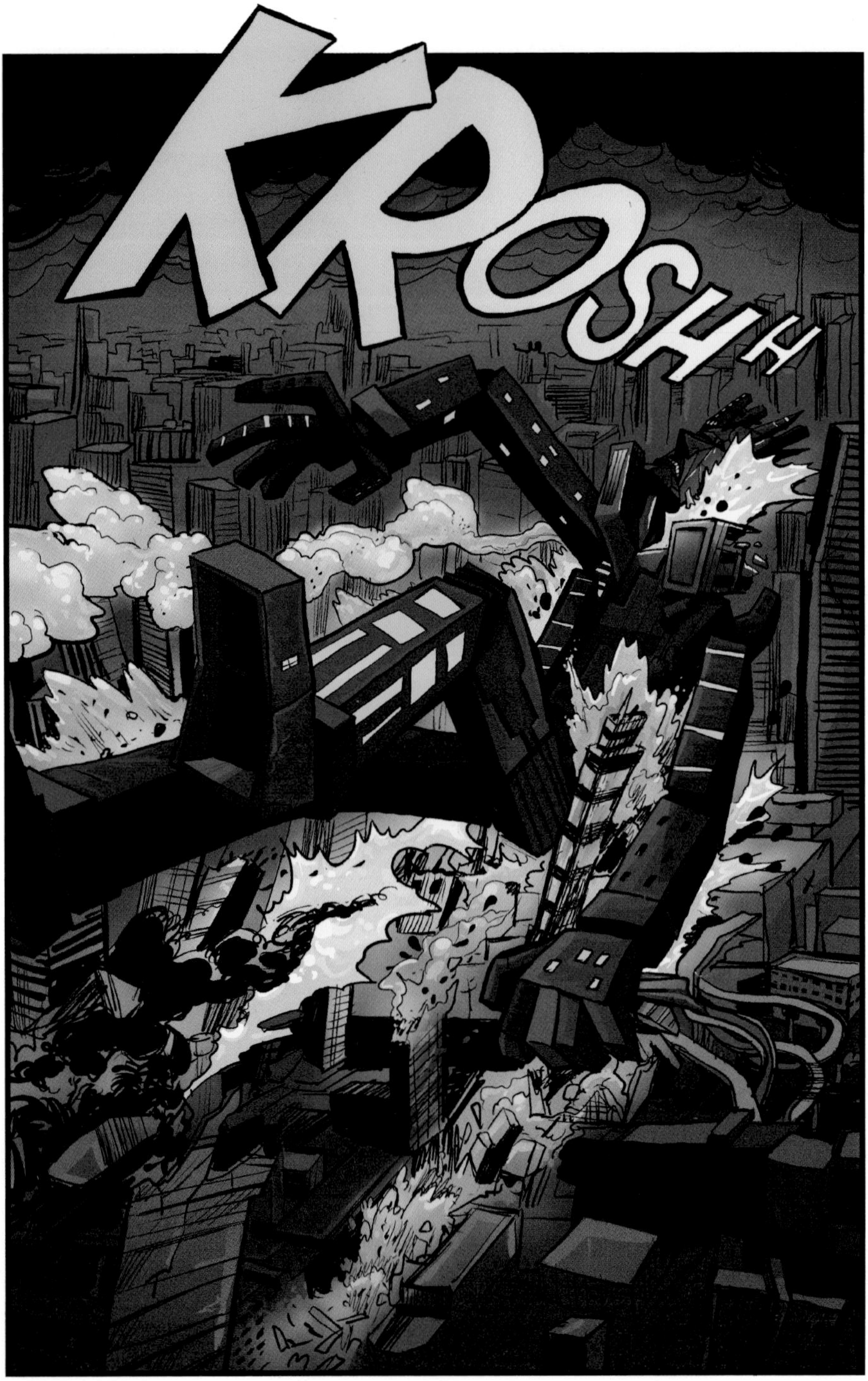
KROSHH

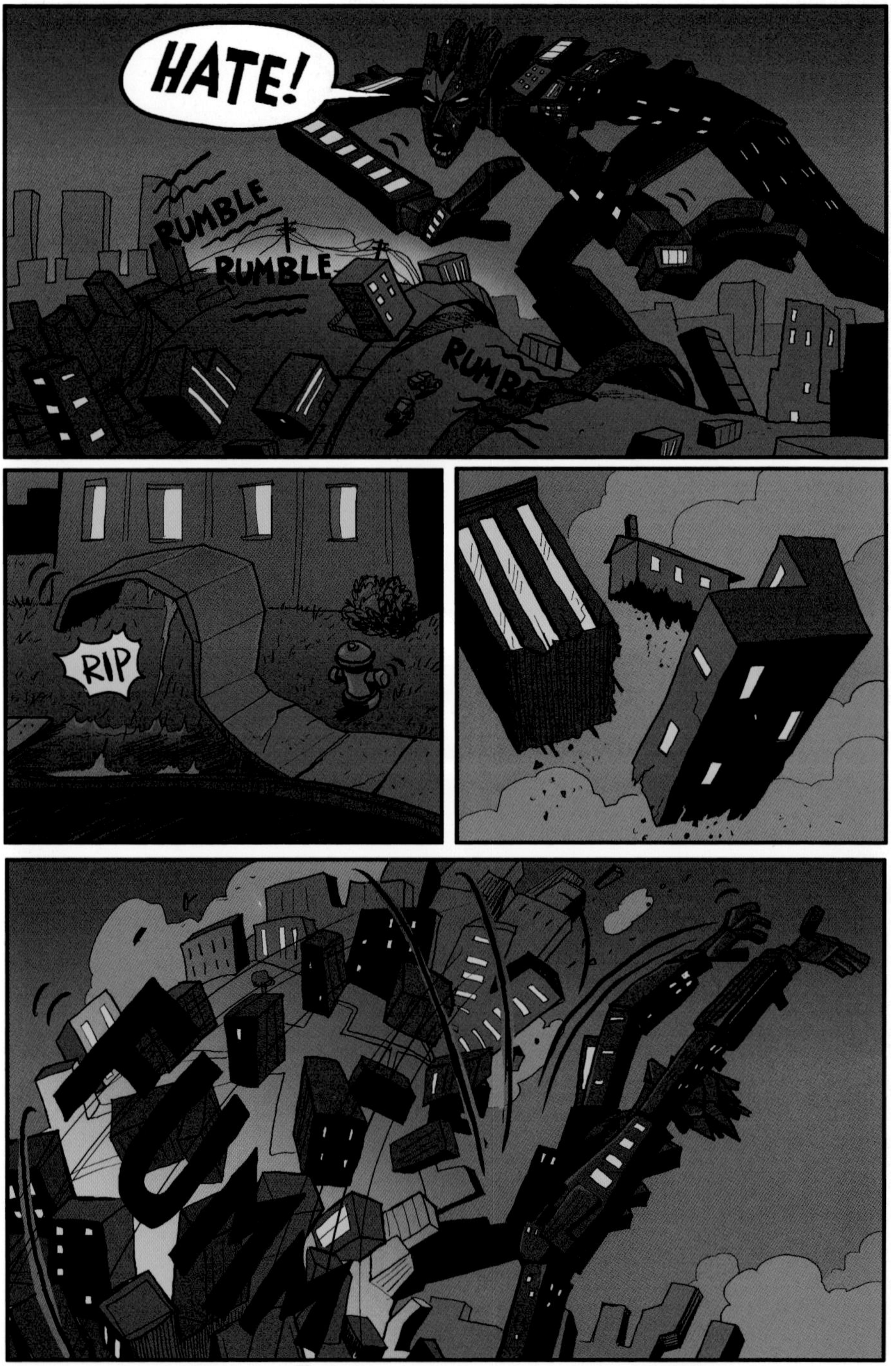
HATE!
RUMBLE
RUMBLE
RUMBLE
RIP

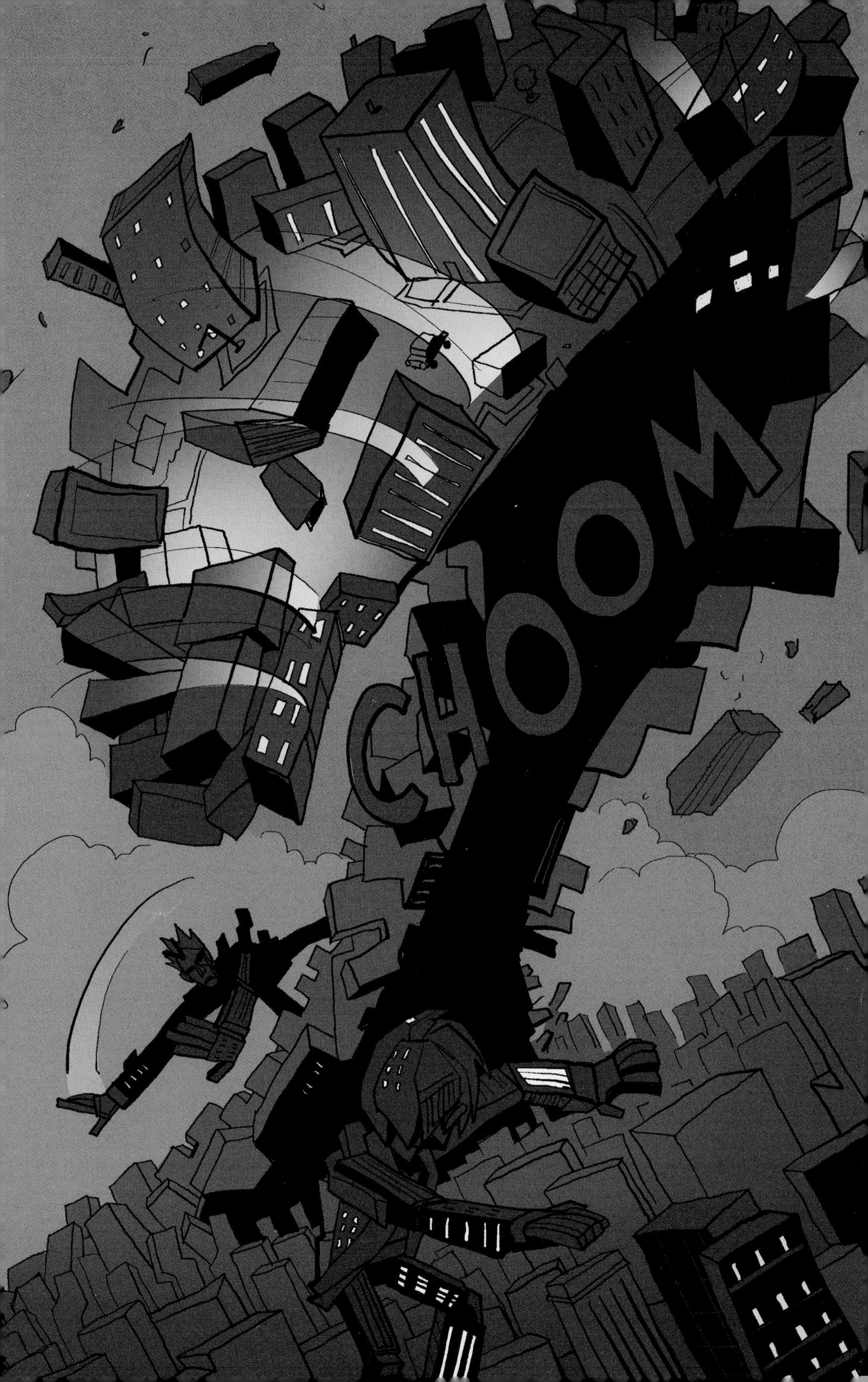
CHOOM

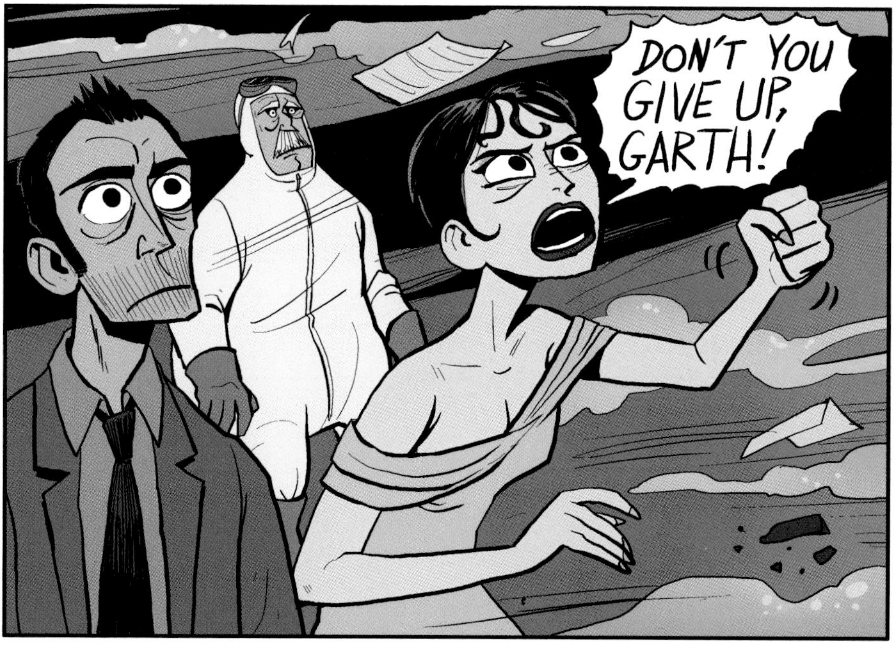
DON'T YOU GIVE UP, GARTH!

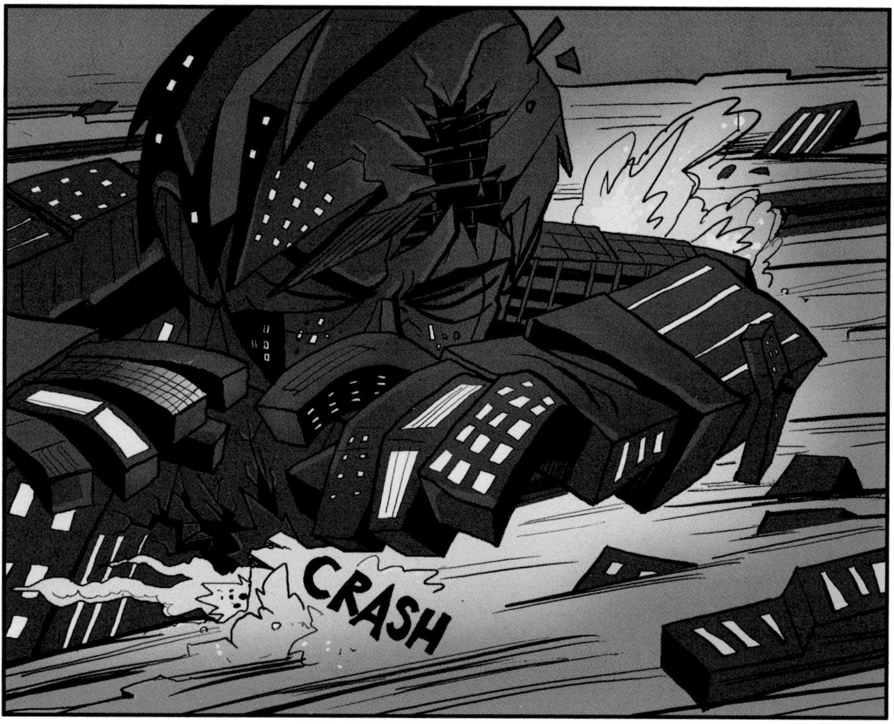
CRASH

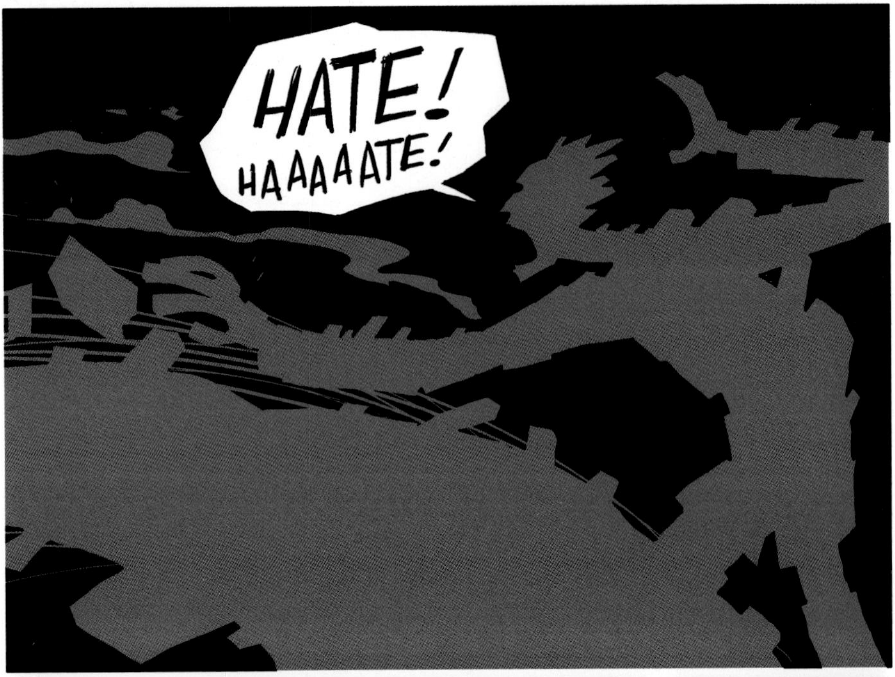
HATE! HAAAAATE!

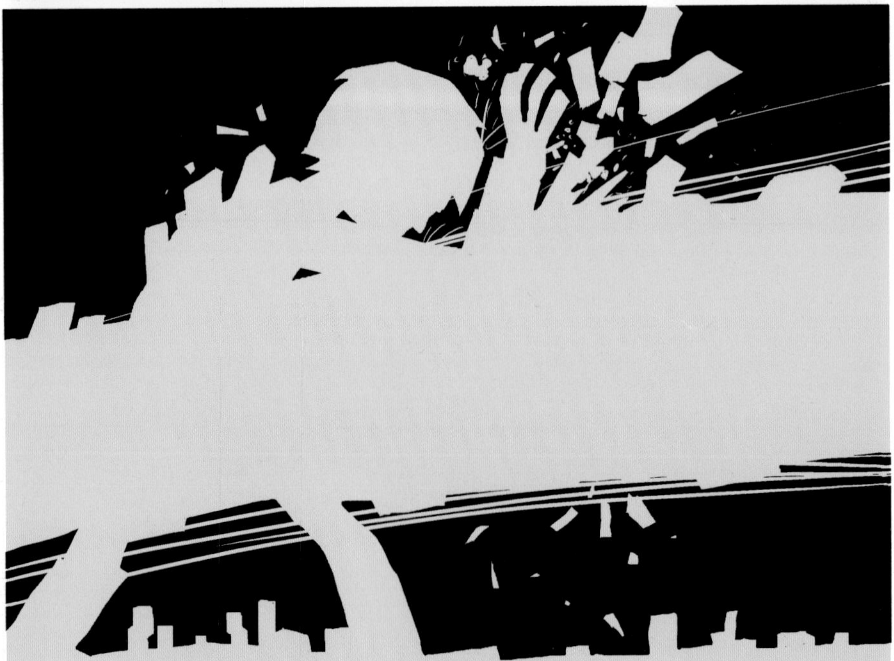

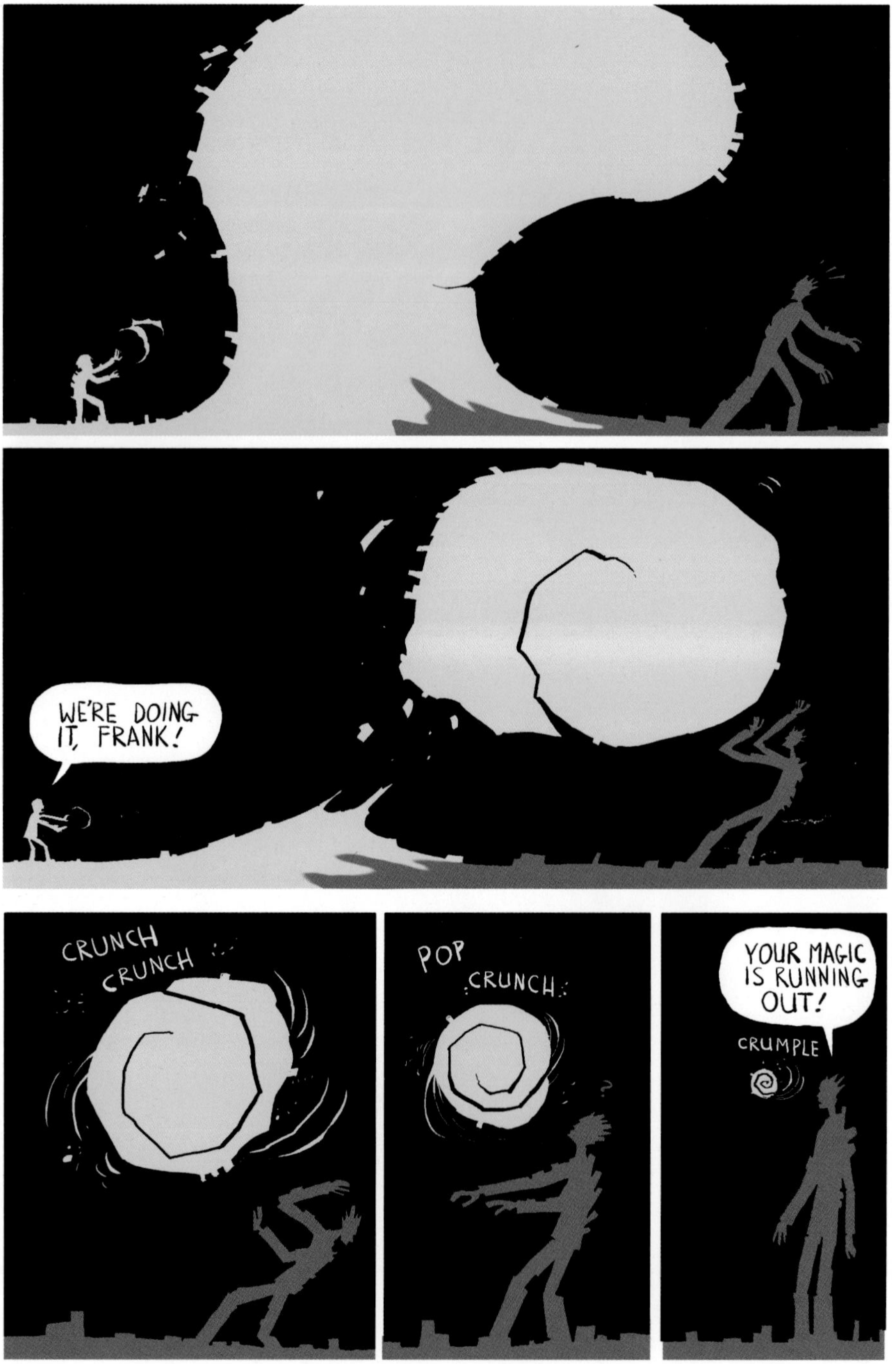
WE'RE DOING IT, FRANK!
CRUNCH
CRUNCH
POP
CRUNCH
YOUR MAGIC IS RUNNING OUT!
CRUMPLE

243

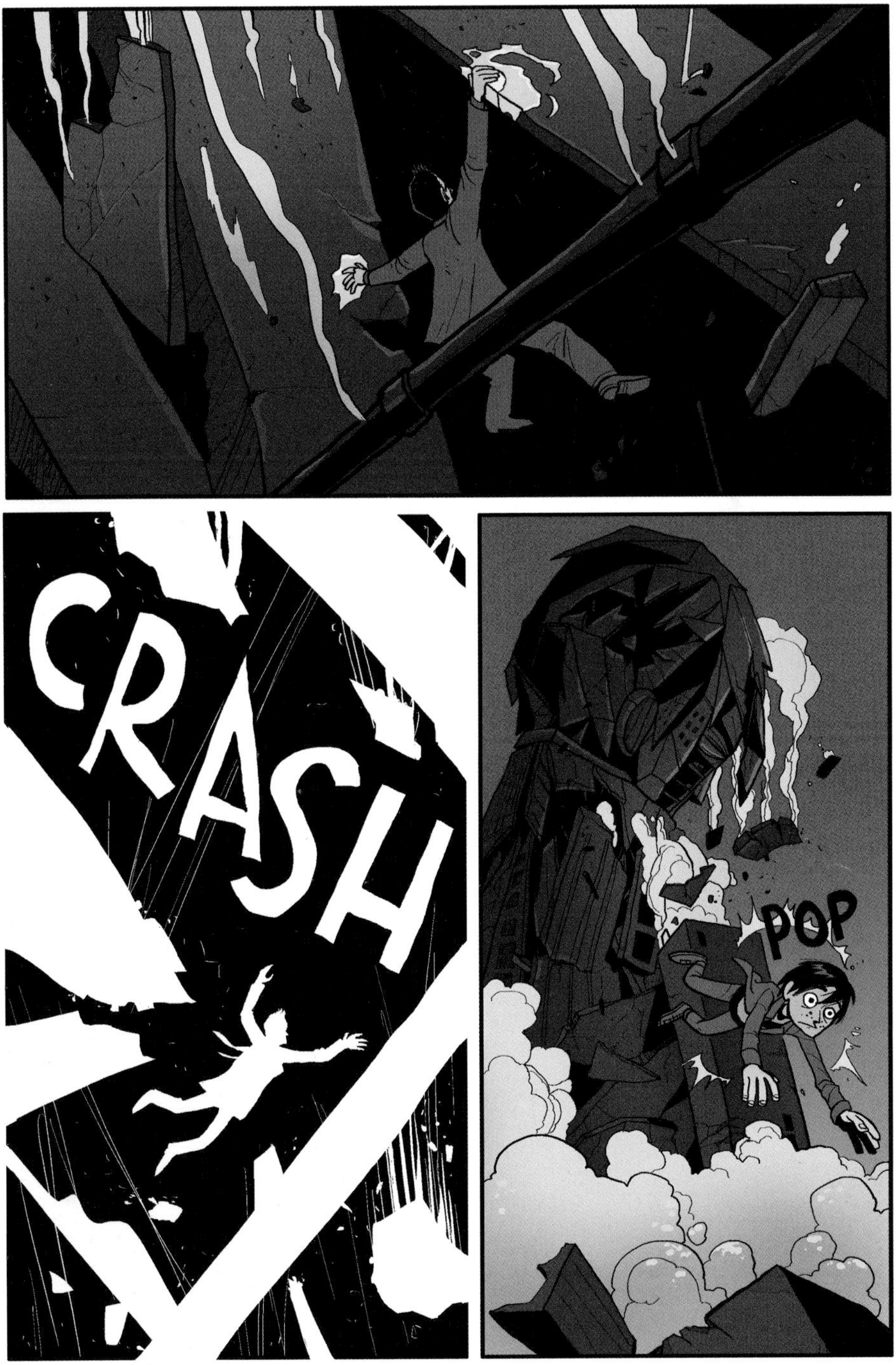
CRASH
POP

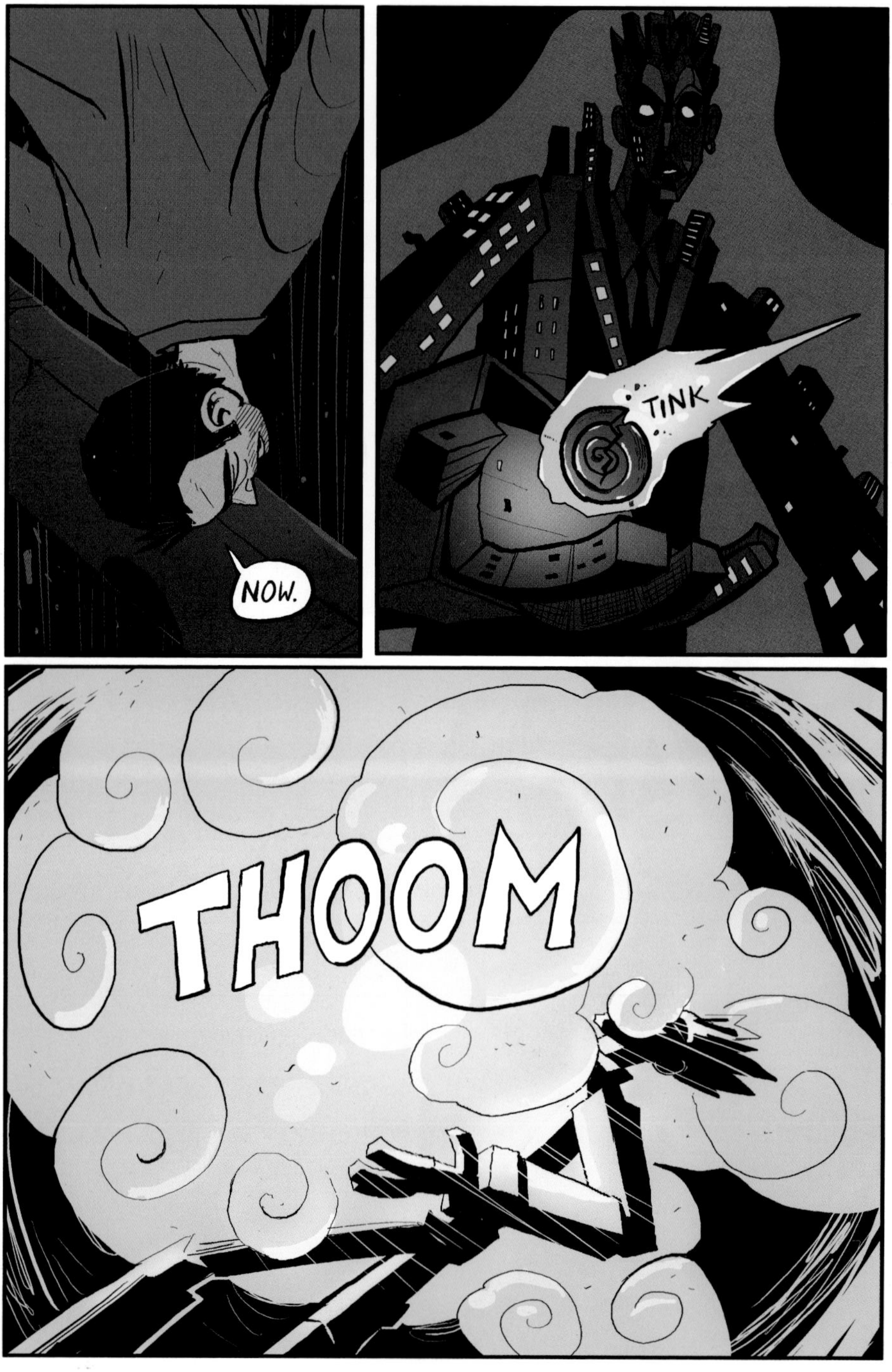
NOW.
TINK
THOOM

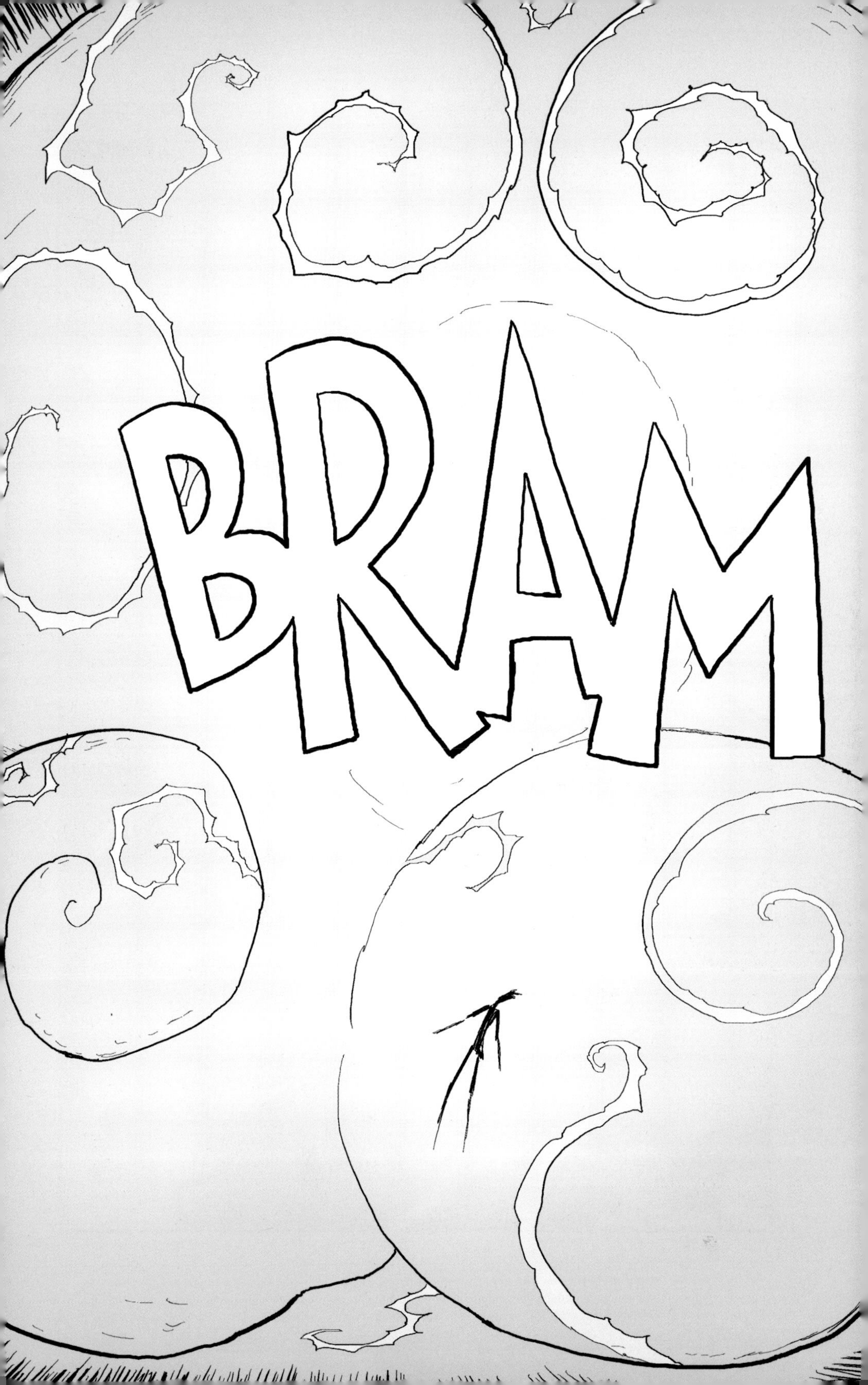
BRAM

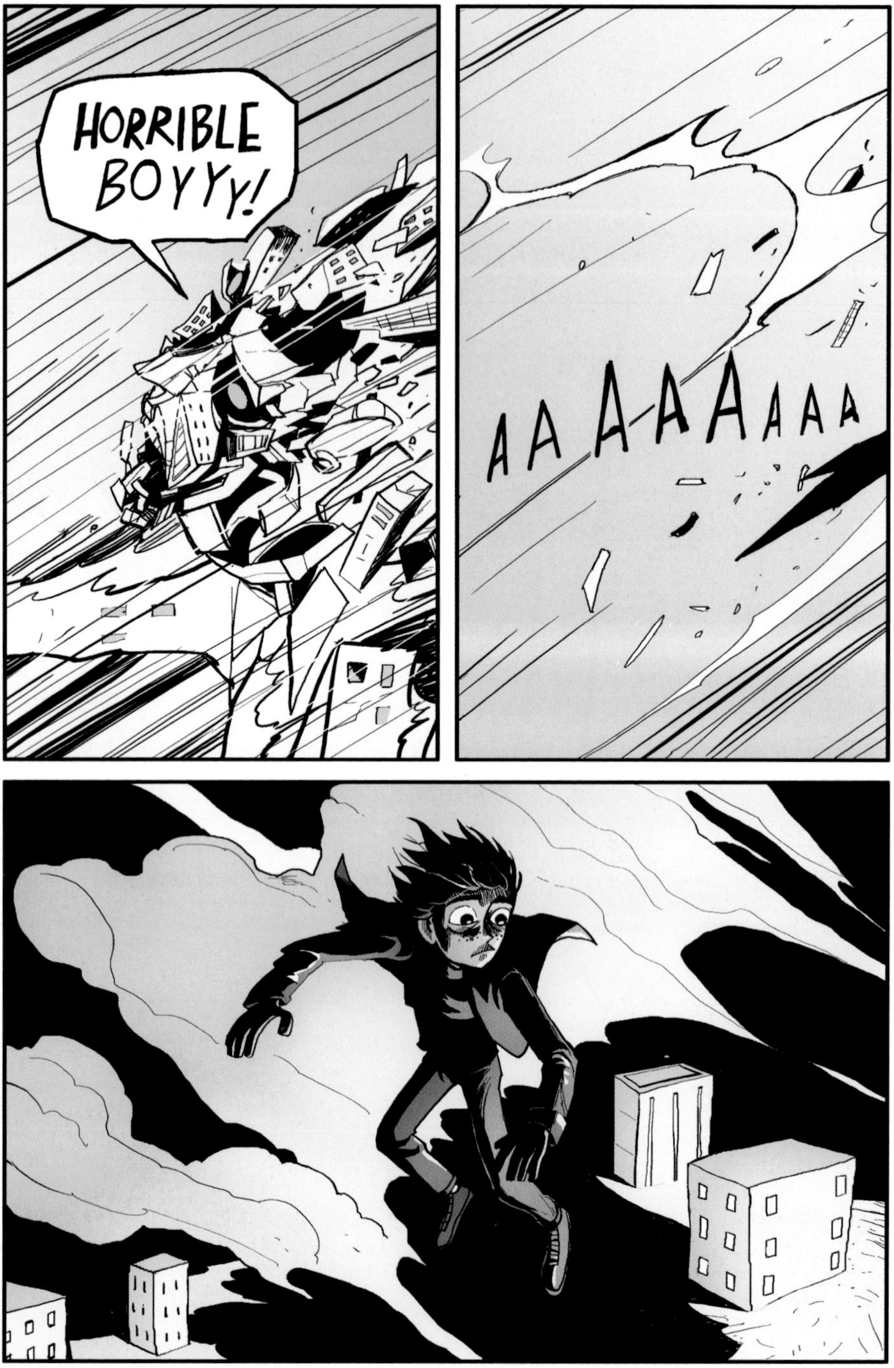
HORRIBLE BOYYYY!
AAAAAAAAA

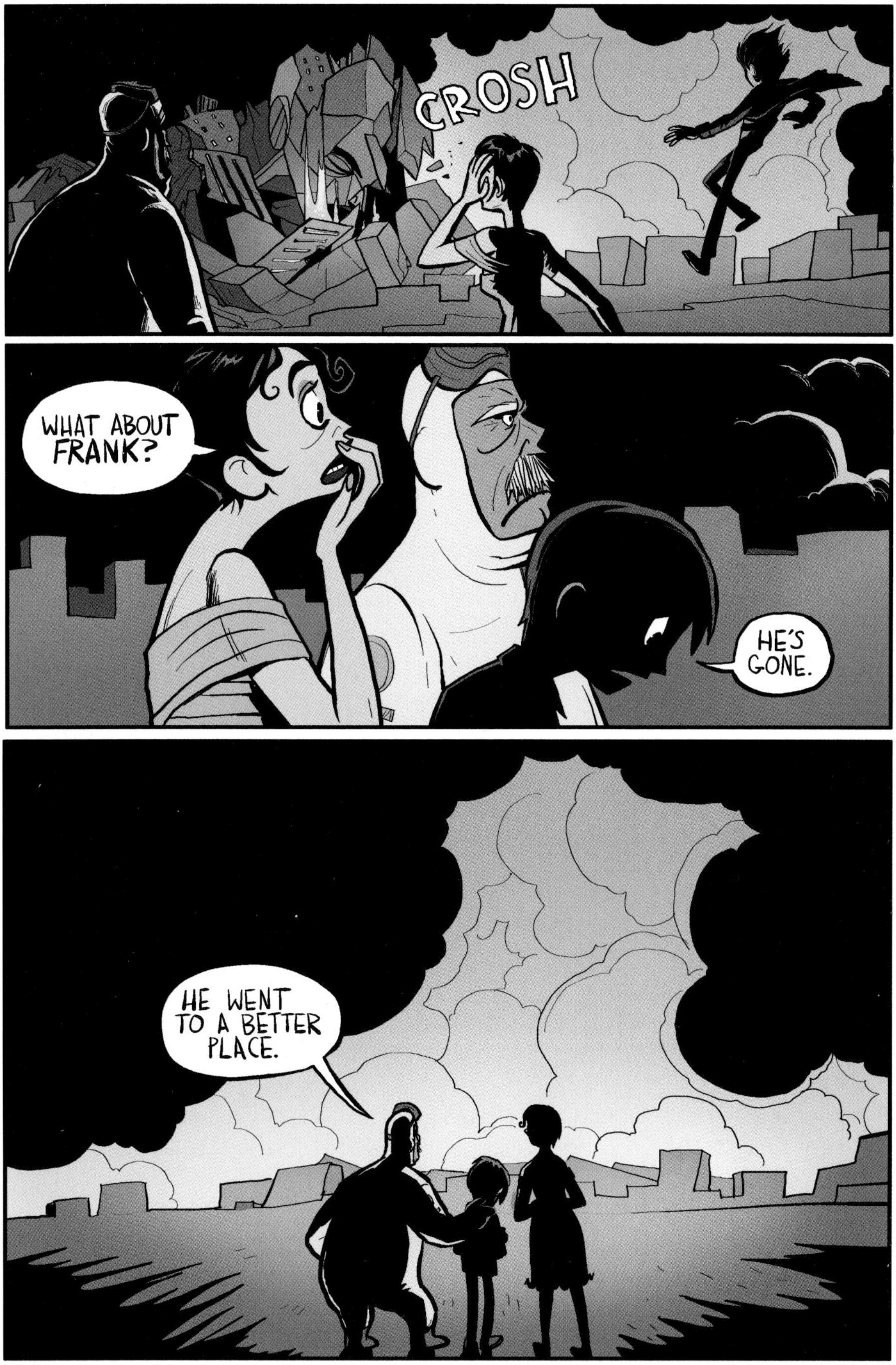
CROSH
WHAT ABOUT FRANK?
HE'S GONE.
HE WENT TO A BETTER PLACE.

253

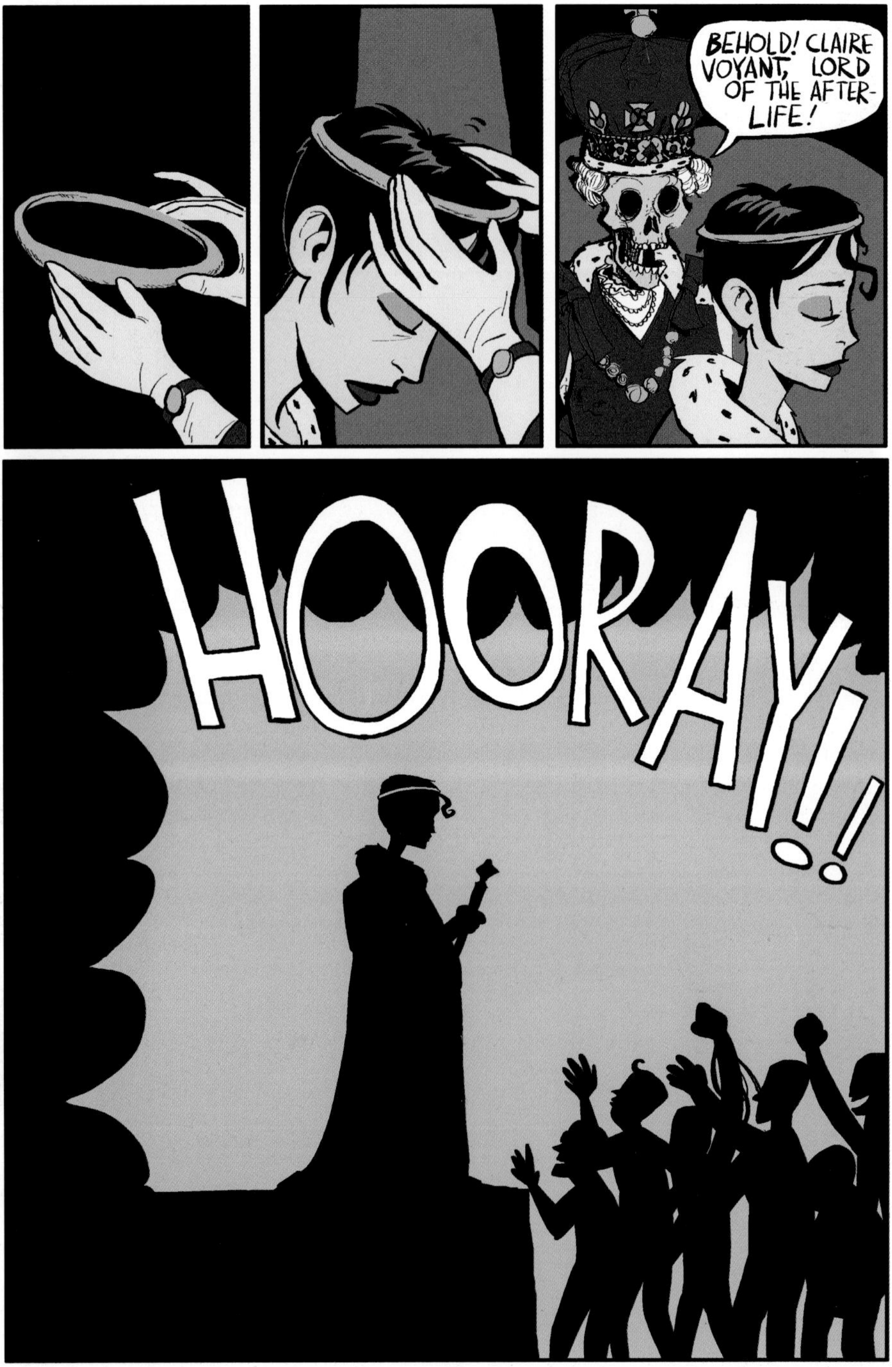
BEHOLD! CLAIRE VOYANT, LORD OF THE AFTER-LIFE!
HOORAY!!!

255

256

258

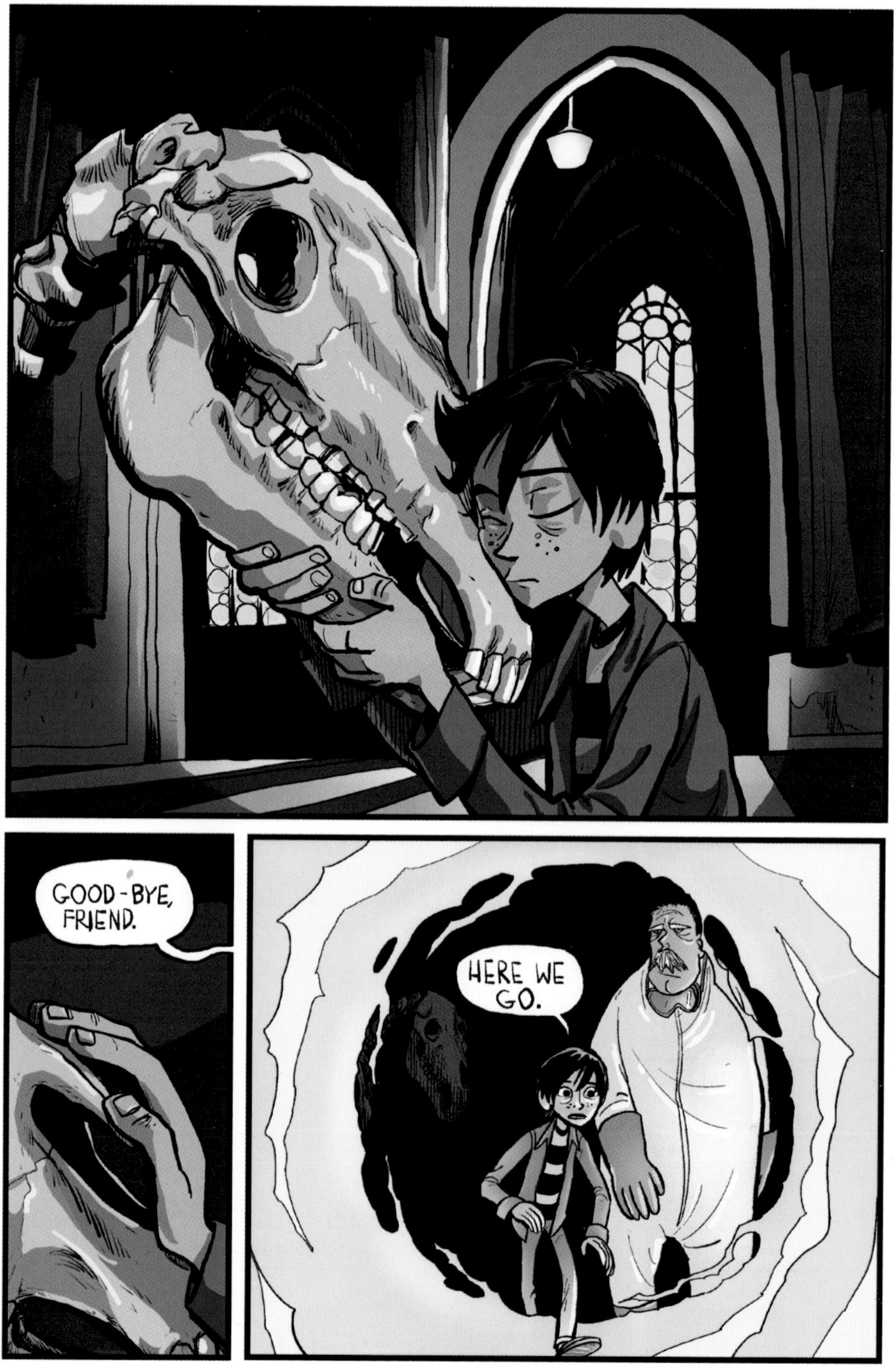
GOOD-BYE, FRIEND.
HERE WE GO.

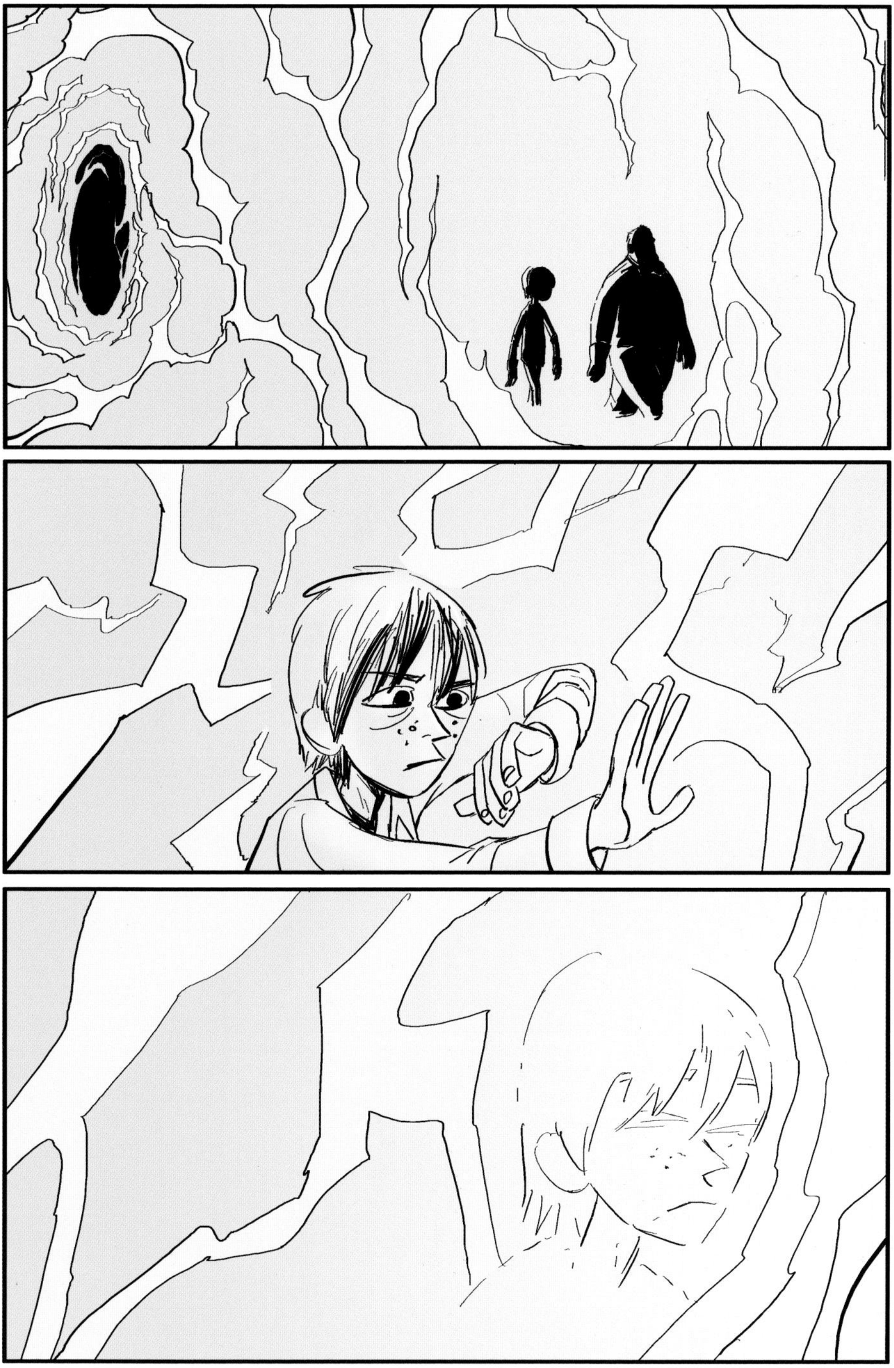

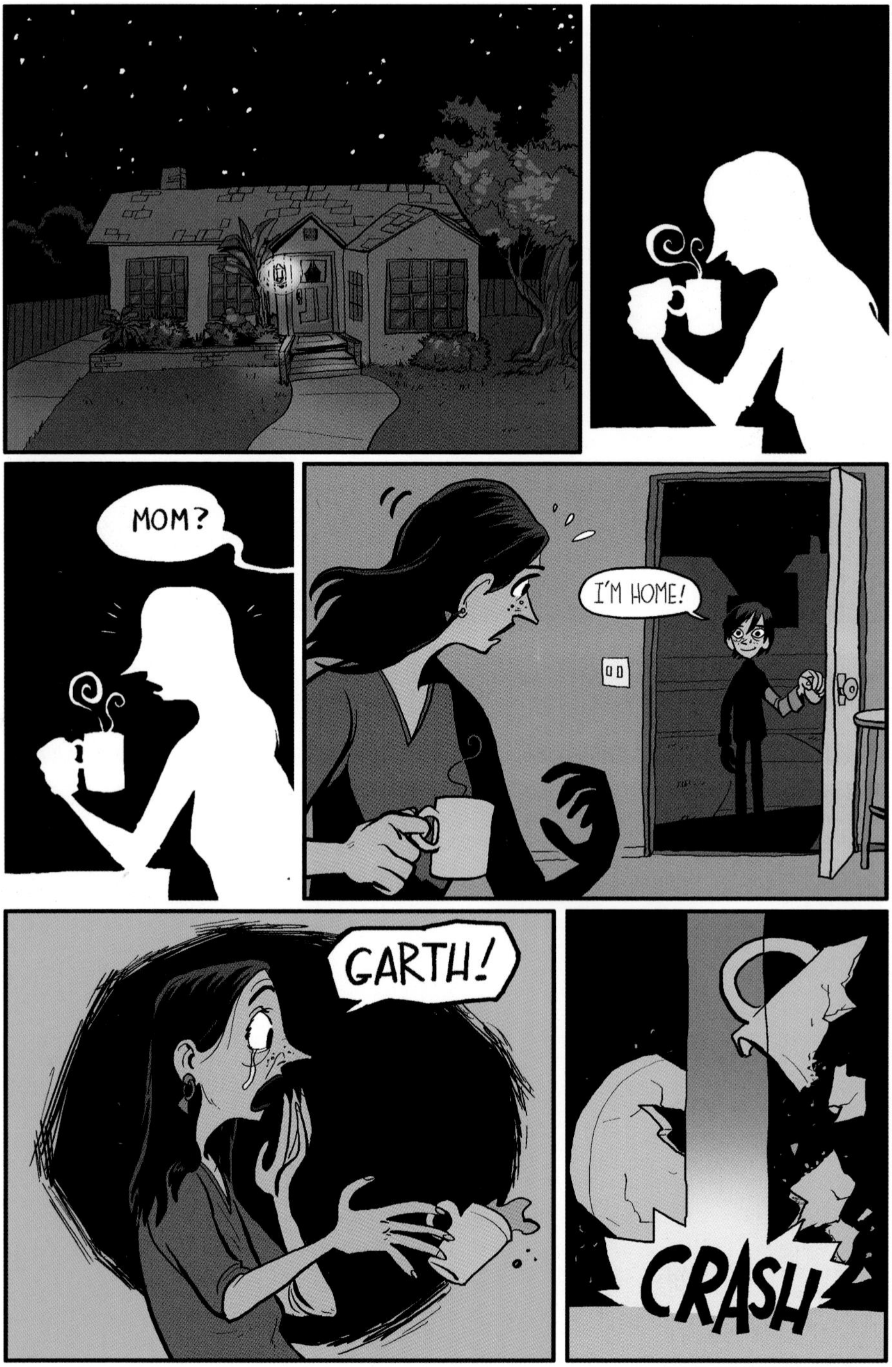
MOM?
I'M HOME!
GARTH!
CRASH

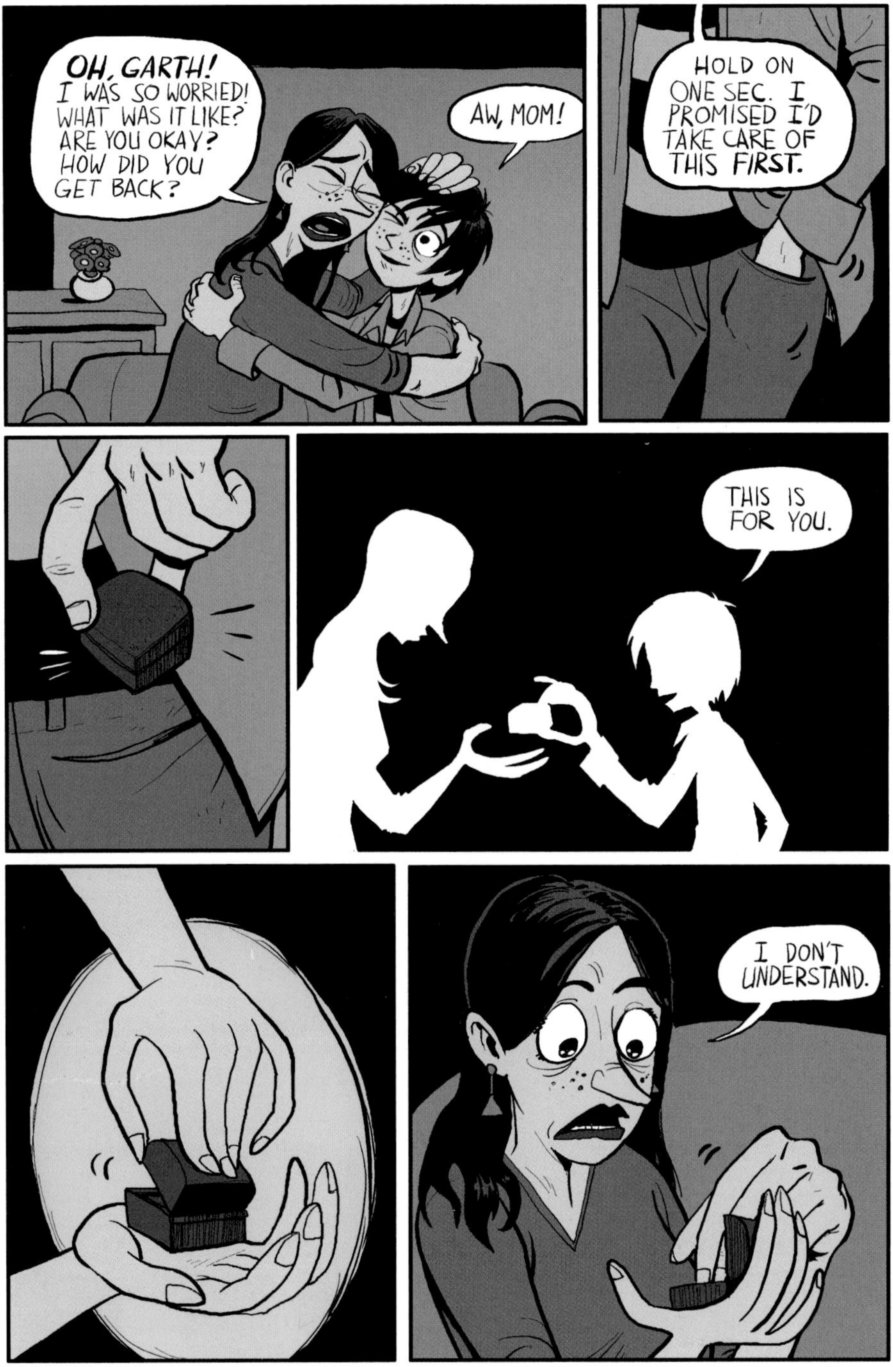
OH, GARTH! I WAS SO WORRIED! WHAT WAS IT LIKE? ARE YOU OKAY? HOW DID YOU GET BACK?
AW, MOM!
HOLD ON ONE SEC. I PROMISED I'D TAKE CARE OF THIS FIRST.
THIS IS FOR YOU.
I DON'T UNDERSTAND.

264

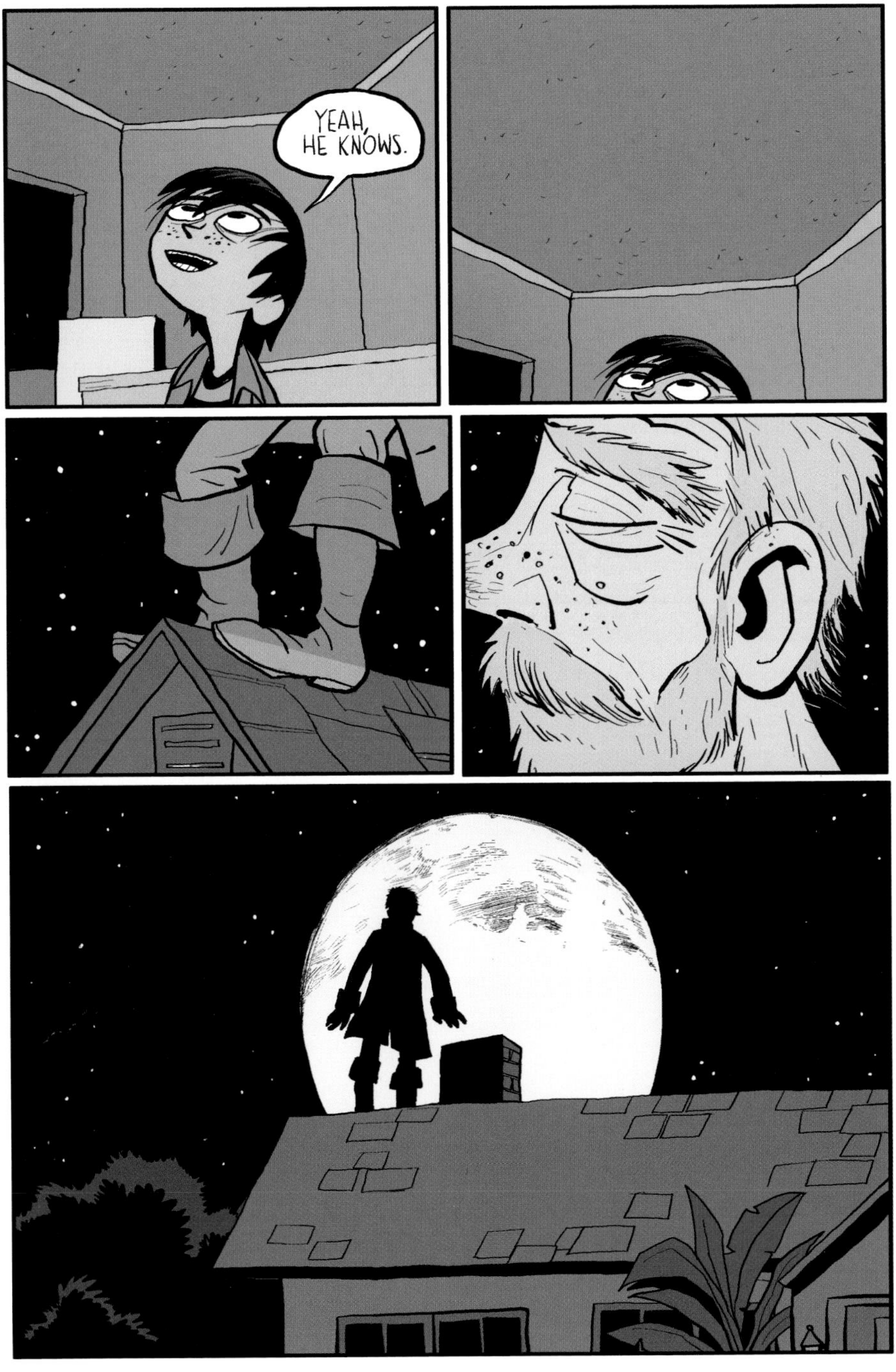
YEAH, HE KNOWS.

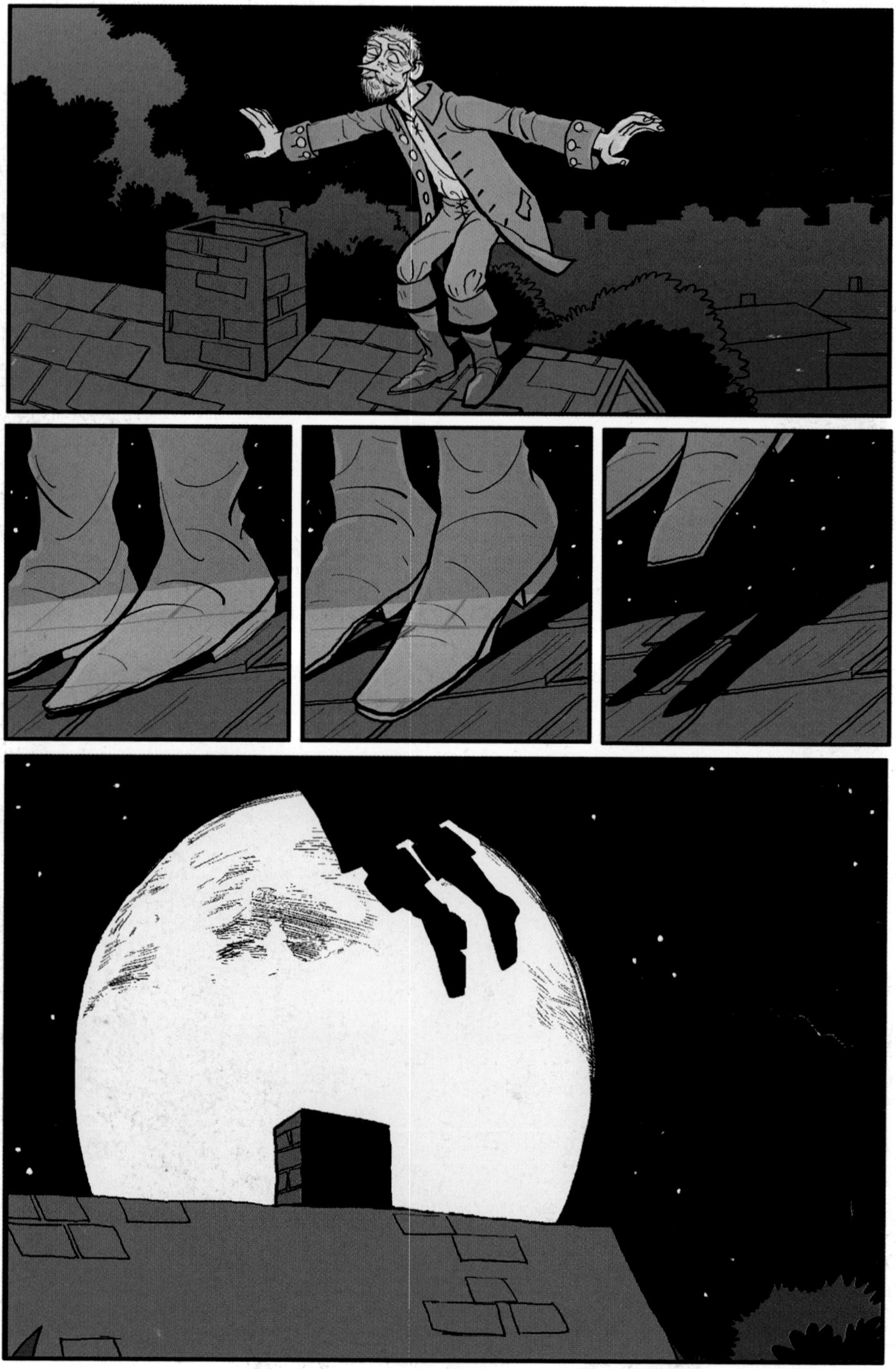

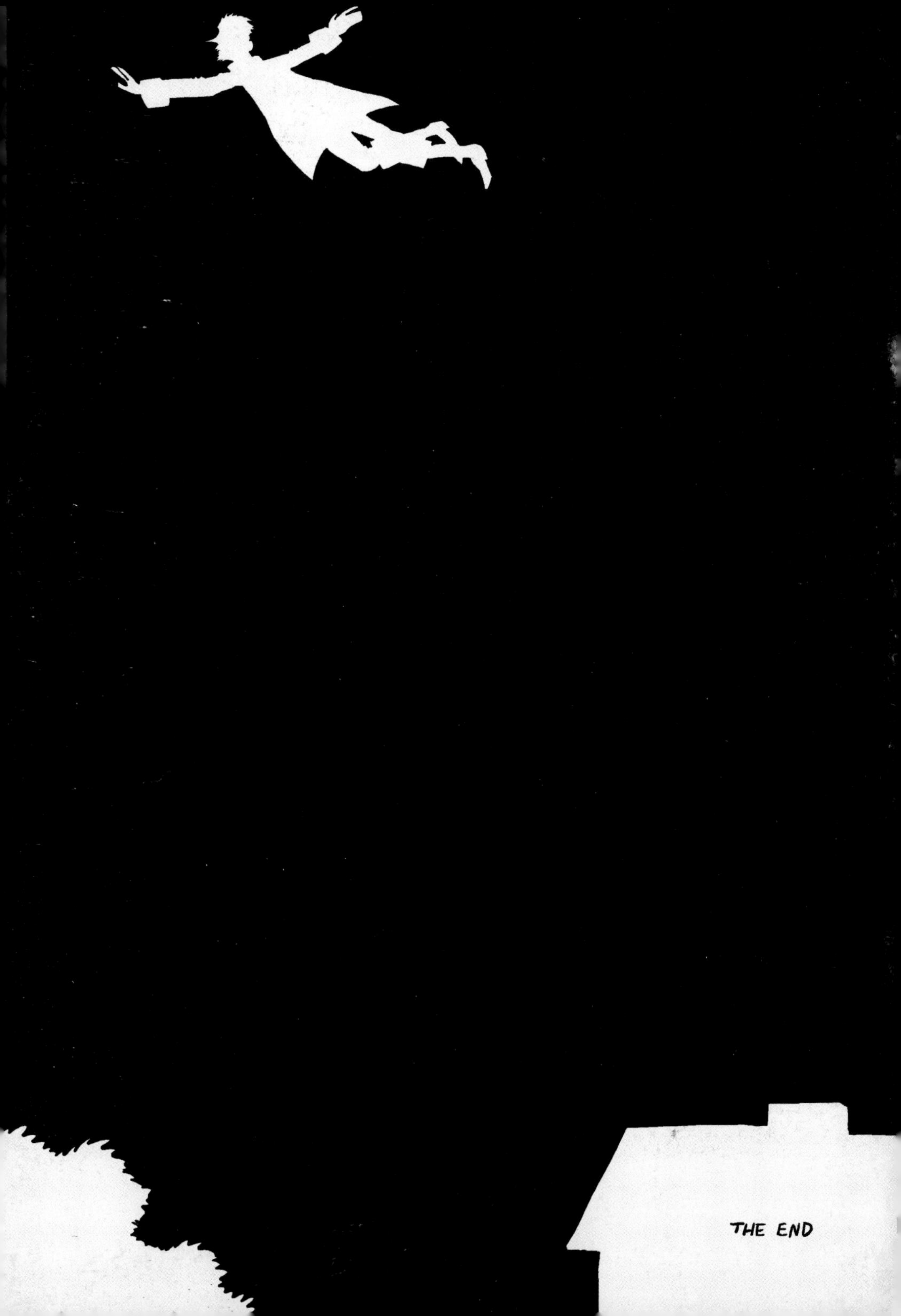

THE END

DOUG TENNAPEL

is the author and illustrator of such acclaimed graphic novels as *Tommysaurus Rex*, *Monster Zoo*, and *Creature Tech*, as well as the creator of the popular character Earthworm Jim. He lives in Glendale, California, with his wife and four children.

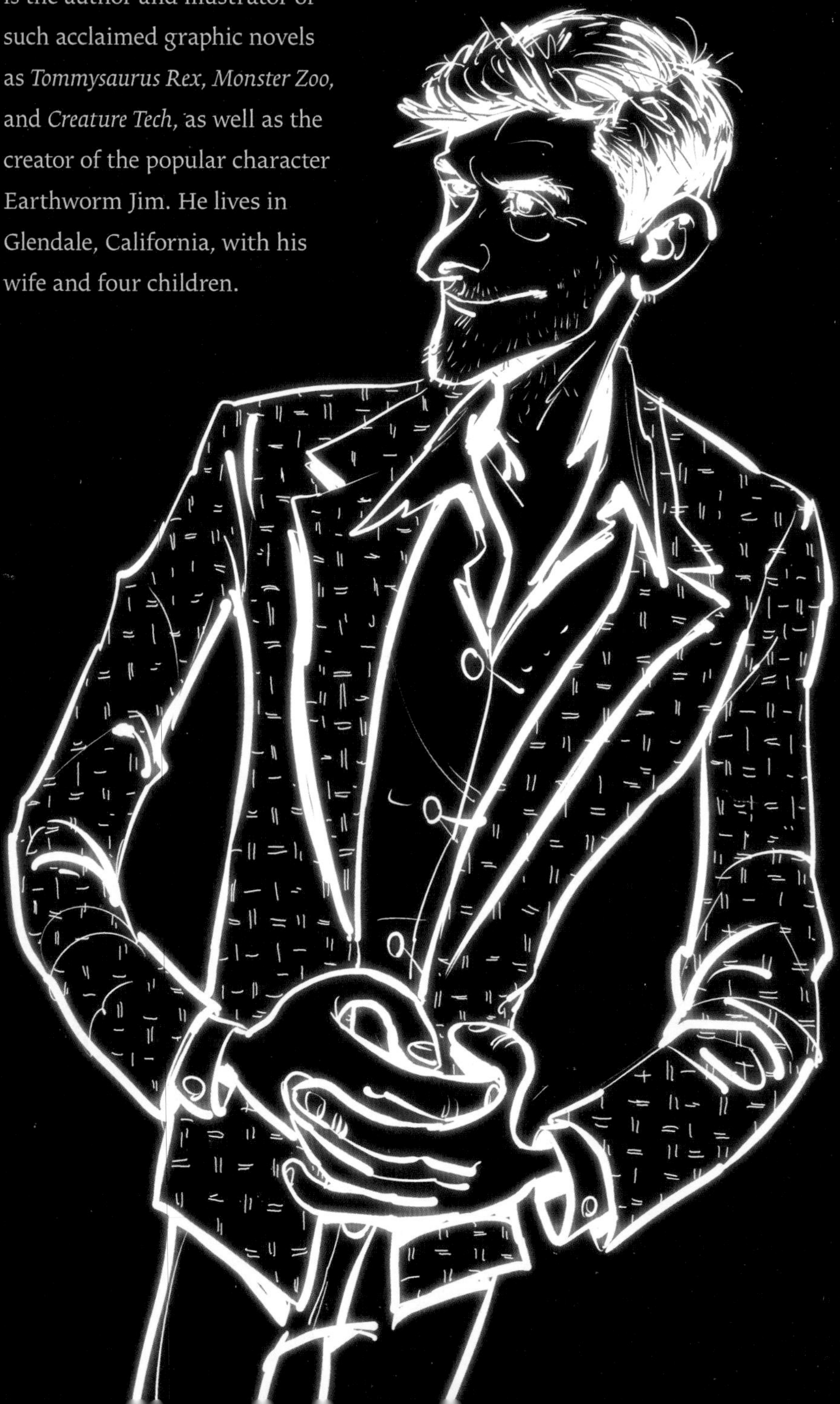